oing Straight

In the same series:

Porridge
Another Stretch of Porridge
A Further Stir of Porridge

Dick Clement
and Ian La Frenais

GOING STRAIGHT

adapted from the TV series
by Paul Victor

British Broadcasting Corporation

Published by the
British Broadcasting Corporation
35 Marylebone High Street
London W1M 4AA

ISBN 0 563 17487 0

First published 1978

Printed in England by
Love & Malcomson Ltd
Brighton Road, Redhill, Surrey

Going Home

All bad things come to an end. And yet, as he waited for the screw to find the small cardboard box containing the personal effects with which he had, more than three long years before, entered Slade Prison, Norman Stanley Fletcher still found it hard to believe. Could it really be over? Was he really going home? How many nights, after lights out, had he lain on his top bunk longing for this moment? And how impossible it had seemed that it would ever arrive. And now it had. In a very few minutes he would hear the gates clang behind him and see in front of him an ordinary street with free citizens walking up and down.

'Sign here,' said the screw.

Fletcher blinked. 'What?'

'The receipt,' and the officer pushed it closer to Fletcher. 'Sign it.'

Fletcher nodded ironically. 'Oh yes, just like that? Without so much as a cursory perusal?'

'What's to peruse?' asked the uniformed guard affably.

'These are my personal effects. What I came in with. And it may be that in the intervening years – well?'

And he emphasised the dark allegation with a meaningful gesture. It was wasted on the screw.

'Well what?'

'Just saying,' muttered Fletcher, who had made the protest more for form's sake than because he really suspected his possessions might have been tampered with.

'Just saying what?'

Fletcher began to regret he hadn't signed and got it over. Was there any point in holding things up at this late stage just to fire a final shot in the war between Them and Us?

'Are you implying,' continued the officer with mock incredulity, 'that there are people in this prison who would resort to stealing, Fletcher?'

'Yes. About eight hundred of them.'

'Steal this rubbish?' asked the screw, stirring the meagre contents of the little box.

'Rubbish?' snorted Fletcher. 'These is valuables.'

'All right then,' agreed the officer, who was not pushed for time on that particular morning. 'Let's check them off. And if anything's missing you'd better take it up with Lloyds.' He thereupon took up his list and began to call out the items. 'One penknife, tartan.'

Fletcher removed this possession from the box. 'Yes.'

'One belt, brown.'

'Yes.'

'One South African shilling.'

Fletcher fingered the coin ruefully. 'Yes.'

'One tin corn plasters. One –'

'Hold your horses,' protested Fletcher. He counted the little bandages. 'There's one missing.'

'Let's get on with it, Fletcher,' urged the screw, with a touch of asperity in his voice.

'And I don't see my billiard chalk – oh yes, here it is. Hey, someone's been using it – it's got a little hole in it.'

'Right, one billiard chalk – used,' and the item was duly ticked off. 'One key ring, Tottenham Hotspur, two keys.'

'Yes.'

'One receipt from the shoe repairers.'

'What?' Fletcher rummaged, found the ancient scrap of paper and contemplated it with interest. 'Oh yes, brown brogues, sole and heel. Wonder if they'll be ready yet?'

'One Ladbroke's pocket diary for 1974.'

'Hang about. Let's have shufty. Yeah, blank after 11 September. That day of infamy. Look what I've writ: "A tragic misdirection of a jury by a biassed judge," and then "Pound each way Laughing Boy, Haydock Park."

Fletcher held the little book out for the guard to see. The latter said drily: 'You spelt "biased" wrong.'

Fletcher smiled ruefully. 'I spelt Laughing Boy wrong and all. Should have been Red Rum. Here, look at this. "Fond farewells to wife and family. Remind our Ingrid to collect my shoe repairs." '

The guard asked wearily: 'Could we get on?'

'Not much of a sentimentalist, are you?' said Fletcher reproachfully.

'No.'

Fletcher shook his head sadly. 'You know, in all the time I've known you. You don't mind me saying this, do you?'

'Saying what?'

'What I'm about to say.'

'Don't know till you've said it.'

'I'm about to.'

'Go on then.'

'I will if you'll stop interrupting. Where was I?'

The officer cast martyred eyes at the roof. 'You were about to say.'

'Oh yes, I was about to say that in all the time I've known you, I have never seen you smile.'

He was rewarded with a very slight grin. 'What's there to smile about in here?'

'Not a lot, I admit, but even under the most adverse circumstances yer human spirit can find some spark to illuminate the gloom.'

'Like what?' asked the guard sceptically.

'The song of a thrush,' suggested Fletcher with a gentle smile. 'A kitten playing with a ball of thread in the mail-bag room. A cornflower blooming through a concrete crack in the prison yard. Mr Mackay slipping on the stairs and injuring his spine.'

But this elaborate joke was wasted on the screw. He merely looked thoughtful and said: 'I don't think I've smiled much since they abolished corporal punishment.'

'But what about when you puts work behind you? When you see your friends or family? When you're mellow down the pub with a few bevvies. I mean, you have a few laughs on the outside, don't you?'

The solemn screw leaned forwards. 'Fletcher, you haven't been outside for three and a half years, have you?'

'Three years, eight months, four days, sir, give or take a minute.'

'Well, let me promise you something: there's precious little to smile about out there.'

But Fletcher couldn't take this. Not with the whole wide world beckoning. 'Speak for yourself, my son. All the things you've took for granted are objects of insurpassable joy to me.'

'Like thrushes and kittens?' asked the screw sardonically.

'To hell with thrushes and kittens,' proclaimed Fletcher fervently. 'I'm talking about – clean sheets, a shirt what doesn't tickle, shaving in hot water, the right to sit on your own lavatory for as long as it takes to read *The Sun*. Privacy. No eyes at keyholes, no shuffling lines, no headcounts. No smell of disinfectant or waterlogged cabbage. Warmth. To sit of an evening by the flickering yellow flames of my artificial gas fire.'

This was a decided challenge. The screw shook his head and then gave his version. 'Gas bills. Hot water bills. All sorts of bills. Bigger bills than when you went in. That *Sun* you'll be reading in the bog will cost you 6p. Privacy? Warmth? In a dole queue?'

But Fletcher shook his head confidently. 'I'll be all right.'

'Oh, will you? You have the qualifications, have you, to leapfrog to the front of the queue? Leaving the nation's one and a half million unemployed behind you?'

Unperturbed, Fletcher said: 'You know, I think you're trying to spoil my day. But it won't work, this catalogue of gloom. If you lot never ground me down in here, they certainly won't out there. I'm leaving here today and I ain't coming back. Oh yes, I know you've heard it all before, but I'm serious. I'm going to play it on their terms and I'm going to make it on their terms. So this is not "au revoir". This is goodbye.'

With which, Norman Stanley Fletcher, ex-con, seized the ballpoint pen provided and, with a flourish, signed the receipt for his valuables. The guard thereupon pushed the box towards him and remarked:

'Well, if the worst comes to the worst you can always flog this lot. Best of luck, Fletcher.'

And, to the astonishment of the other, he actually smiled.

A little later, the convict McLaren, possessor of an accent from Glasgow and a complexion from Africa, heard a key grate in a lock. He looked up from his task – taking an inventory of boots – and saw a strange figure waddle in through the door. It took him a moment to perceive, beneath the curiously-creased suit, his old cobber, Fletcher. McLaren ceased his labours and goggled. Fletcher smiled uncertainly. McLaren sighed and shook his head enviously.

'Jammy Arab,' he remarked.

'How d'you mean?'

'Going out.'

'So?' Fletcher fiddled with the buttons of his jacket. Years of prison stodge had increased his girth and the old suit no longer fitted him very elegantly.

'Jammy Arab,' repeated McLaren.

Fletcher shook his head positively. 'No more than I deserve, my son. Done my porridge.'

McLaren shrugged. 'Aye, I reckon.'

'Your day will come.'

McLaren said thoughtfully, 'I'm the last of our little crowd.'

'Our sewing circle – yes.'

'Lennie's gone. Warren. Lukewarm. They've all embarked on their fresh starts in life.'

'Not so fresh for some,' corrected Fletcher. 'I had a letter from Lukewarm.'

'How's he doing?'

'Not so good. His case comes up Wednesday.'

McLaren shook his head sadly. 'Och no. He's only been out three months.'

'It's not easy for him,' Fletcher pointed out. 'Being a bit lilac.' Fletcher was referring to the fact that Lukewarm was one of those men who have never become totally reconciled to their gender.

'Who cares these days?' McLaren protested. 'Everyone's tolerant about things like that.'

'Not in Middlesbrough, Jock. Lukewarm lives in Middlesbrough. It's not easy being lilac there. Very hard inflexible breed of men in Middlesbrough. As demonstrated so ably by their football team.'

McLaren nodded. 'I see what you mean. The law up there will never give him a chance.'

'And the sad thing is, he don't flaunt it. He keeps a low profile.'

'What did they do him for?' asked Black Jock curiously.

'Lifting a lady's handbag. Of course, he claims it was all a mistake. Says he thought it was his own.'

McLaren scowled at the unfairness of both destiny and the fuzz. 'It's not easy, Fletch. We know that. We've both been in and out often enough.'

Fletcher said positively, 'This is it for me, though.'

McLaren grinned. 'Famous last – '

But Fletcher cut him off impatiently. 'Yes, yes, I know we've heard it all before. But at my age it's time to act like someone my age. Very few people in the nick over thirty-five, you know – ever noticed that? Only nutters and no-hopers. And I don't intend to become either of those. I worked it out. I'm forty-five now and, on average, I've spent seven out of every thirty days of my life inside. That's a week every month. Shocking waste.'

McLaren shrugged sourly. 'I'm doing worse than you. In and out since I was fourteen, and before that there was the orphanage which was another kind of prison.'

Fletcher said understandingly, 'Well, it's been harder for you, I admit. Lot of prejudice against your lot.'

McLaren nodded. 'Yeah, it's not easy being half black.'

'It's not that,' Fletcher corrected him. 'I meant, half Scots.'

'Dinna be daft. People are not prejudiced against the Scots.'

'I am,' affirmed Fletcher.

'All right, you are. That's because Mackay's a Scot. You blame the whole Scottish race on Mackay.'

'Your Scot,' explained Fletcher, as if stating a recent scientific discovery, 'is prone to violence.'

'Well, I'm curbing mine,' claimed McLaren and pointed proudly to a newly-acquired red armband. 'Trustee, see?'

Fletcher nodded, and urged: 'Do me a favour, old mate. Go on curbing it when you get out.'

A prison officer entered and said: 'Come on then, Fletcher. Have you finished your fond farewells?'

Fletcher shook his head. 'No. None of that for me, thank you. I've got no sentiment about this place. No nostalgic memories about all the good times we had.'

'But,' McLaren protested, 'we did have our moments, Fletch. Remember the time we –'

But he was again cut off. 'Save it,' said Fletcher. 'Save it for the Reunion Dinner.'

McLaren grinned enthusiastically. 'Where shall we have it? Should be London. How about the Savoy?'

Fletcher shook his head. 'No, I prefer Claridges for that sort of occasion. They do you very well there, Claridges.'

'Then on to a night club, eh?' asked the dusky crook eagerly.

'Certainly. Talk of the Town, ringside seat, Sacha Distel.'

'Or whoever it happens to be.'

'It's always Sacha Distel. Anyway, after that the wine will have mellowed us, made us a little devil-may-care, so we'll end the night doing what we do best, eh?'

McLaren chuckled lecherously. 'Oh ho – we will that.'

'Yeah,' nodded Fletcher, 'we'll rob a warehouse.'

McLaren's jaw dropped. Then he caught on and laughed. Fletcher nodded at the waiting screw and, with a final wink at McLaren, turned and moved off to freedom.

He followed the screw quietly. He did not look to right or left nor up nor down. When some con he knew called farewell, he acknowledged it with a slight wave of his hand. He was determined not to permit any sentiment for Slade Nick to enter his thoughts. And yet, when he finally stood outside the little door of the massive door that sealed off eight hundred men from the rest of England, he came to a surprising halt.

'On your way then,' urged the officer.

'A minute,' requested Fletcher humbly.

'Left something behind, have you?'

Fletcher nodded. 'Three and a half years of my life.'

'Well, on your way then.'

But Fletcher did not budge. 'I want to hear that door close behind me first,' he said.

The officer grumbled. 'I'm supposed to see you off the premises.'

'Well, do you think I'm going to try and get *back in*?' Fletcher exclaimed incredulously. 'I assure you, you'll never see me hammering on this door, crying "let me in".'

The screw gave him a suspicious look. But Fletcher's reasoning could hardly be faulted. 'All right then,' he said grudgingly, 'but after the door's shut you move off pretty sharpish.'

Fletcher turned his back on the prison and waited. The screw retreated into the grim precincts. A moment later there was a sharp slamming sound. Fletcher closed his eyes for a moment and then opened them and took a deep breath.

Now at last he really believed it. He was free! Free as other men. Free as the birds. He could step forwards and walk, or ride, anywhere in the world. And no one had the right to stop him. No one could question him. He was once again a law-abiding citizen. He squared his shoulders and stepped forwards. But the step was, curiously, never completed. He tried again. Something was holding him back. For a moment an icy fear rushed through his veins. Was it some mystic force? Had the prison claimed him for its own? Would it never let him go? He spun round and found, with a surge of relief, that it was no occult power restraining him but his coat which had got caught in the slamming door. He tried to tug it free, but was unable to. Should he abandon it? But he had few possessions and less money. He couldn't afford to write-off a perfectly good mac. Bitterly aware of the irony, he beat on the heavy door, crying:

'Let me in! Let me in!'

About an hour later, Fletcher, once again in possession of his raincoat, was speeding south at about seventy miles an hour. Opening a sliding door, he stepped into a small buffet bar on the southbound express that was carrying him to London. There were a few people at the tables but no one at the counter. Fletcher advanced on it and, resting his elbow on the bar, spoke to the steward, who was polishing glasses.

'A beer, please.'

'What sort?' asked the white-coated attendant.

'Fletcher shrugged. 'Don't matter. Make it a JC.'

Fletcher glanced at the board behind the bar which served as a menu. He continued: 'And – er – cheese and tomato sandwich.'

The steward shook his head mournfully. 'Haven't got any.'

Fletcher sighed. 'All right. Ham'll do.'

The steward, in a faintly apologetic tone, admitted: 'There's no sandwiches. Haven't had time to make them yet.'

'I see,' nodded Fletcher. 'Well, what have you got?'

'Scotch eggs,' offered the steward, a suggestion which caused Fletcher to bristle perceptibly.

'I'm not eating Scotch eggs, thank you. Not eating Scotch anything. I'll have a sausage roll, providing it's English.'

But again the steward wagged his head sadly. 'Just sold the last one.'

'Pork pie?'

'Sorry.'

Fletcher was not pleased by these tidings but he was still far too chuffed about his new freedom to get stroppy. He said calmly: 'Look. Let's start again. I'm famished. What have you got?'

'Kit Kat,' averred the steward.

Fletcher shook his head wearily. 'Just the beer, thank you.' He placed a 10p silver coin on the counter and turned to inspect his fellow diners.

The steward glanced at the offering in surprise. 'What's that?' he asked.

'Two bob – 10p,' said Fletcher evenly.

'Sixteen short,' observed the steward.

Fletcher was outraged. 'What? 26p for a beer?'

'Well, of course it is,' insisted the steward. 'Where have you been?'

Fletcher began to feel that he was being victimised. He scowled fiercely, leaned towards the tall, but somehow dainty, figure of the steward and snarled: 'Prison. For grievous bodily harm.'

'Oh?' exclaimed the man, drawing back sharply. 'Oh, I see. Well, I'll – um – I'll make you up a sandwich when I've got a minute. Cheese and tomato, was it?'

Fletcher smiled, but mirthlessly: 'That will do nicely, thank you.'

He took his beer and went in search of a seat. All the tables were either occupied or in such an unpleasant state from spilled beer and mangled paper cups, that Fletcher refrained from using them. One table held a couple on the outside seats. Fletcher addressed the man: 'Those inside seats being used, are they?'

The man, barely glancing at him, said: 'Yes.'

'I see.'

Fletcher poured out his beer and took a sip of it. He stood near the man who, after a moment, grunted: 'Warm.'

'I beg your pardon?' asked Fletcher.

'Beer's warm.'

Fletcher smiled wolfishly. 'Tastes good to me, though. First in three and a half years.'

'Been on the wagon?' asked the man interestedly.

'No. I've been in the nick.'

The man and woman looked at each other. The woman rose. 'I think we should check our cases, Geoffrey.'

'Er yes,' agreed the man. Then he indicated the seats to Fletcher as he rose. 'All yours.'

'Thank you,' said Fletcher politely, and seated himself with dignity.

Behind him, the sliding door of the buffet bar opened and a man entered. The new arrival went to the counter and, in a voice that was unmistakably Scottish, ordered:

'McEwans Tartan and a Johnny Walker on the side.'

At the first words, Fletcher went rigid. He closed his eyes. He felt giddy. Was his imagination playing tricks? The voice spoke again: 'I said a McEwans – '

But it was interrupted by the huffy one of the steward. 'I heard you. Can't you see I'm making a sandwich?'

'When you've got a minute.'

Fletcher nodded grimly. No mistake. He knew who was behind him. His first day, his first hour out of nick and this had to happen!

He heard the steward say to the man: 'Do you mind just handing this sandwich to that bloke over there?'

There was no reply but Fletcher waited expectantly. Sure enough, a few seconds later and the heavily-accented voice spoke from immediately behind him.

'I believe this is yours.'

Without turning, and in a voice that was as neutral as he could make it, Fletcher said: 'Thank you, Mr Mackay.'

It was the new arrival's turn to start. 'Good God, Fletcher!' exclaimed the Beast of Slade Prison, for it was he.

Fletcher turned and said accusingly: 'Don't pretend it's a surprise. You must have known I was going out today. What is this, surveillance?'

Mackay protested: 'It slipped my mind entirely. Otherwise I'd have got the earlier train.'

'Feeling's mutual.'

'Your drink, sir,' called the steward.

Mackay turned and went back to the bar. The steward, frowning, glanced from him to Fletcher. He asked:

'Are you with him, then?'

Mackay nodded. 'In a manner of speaking. We're from the same establishment.'

The steward swallowed. 'Well – er – here's your whisky and your beer, sir.'

Mackay reached into his pocket. 'How much is that?'

But the steward retreated hastily, warning off Mackay with a gesture.

'No mad rush. You may want another, you know.'

Mackay shrugged, took up his drinks, glanced about and then moved slowly back towards Fletcher's table. He grinned lopsidedly and asked: 'So?'

'So what?'

'First taste of freedom, is it?'

Fletcher nodded sourly. 'Expensive taste.'

'Cost of living,' shrugged Mackay.

There was silence for a moment, and then Fletcher grunted, 'Well, sit down then. You make the place untidy.' Mackay seated himself. Fletcher continued: 'Ironical twist of fate this. It was you that brung me up here on the train. You and Mr Barrowclough. Going down for some other poor nurk, are you?'

Mackay shook his head. 'No. Personal reasons.'

'Oh yes? Going to the smoke though, is it?'

'Yes.'

'Why?' asked Fletcher impertinently.

Mackay bridled. 'None of your business.'

Fletcher nodded knowingly. 'Oh, I see. It's that personal, is it? What's her name?'

Mackay half rose in an angry movement. 'Watch your lip, Fletcher.'

But Fletcher wasn't having any. He shook his head firmly. 'Here, here. Can't talk to me like that now. I'm a free man. You and me is equals now.'

The old, familiar sneer curled Mackay's upper lip. 'Never in a million years, man.'

'Nevertheless,' pointed out Fletcher calmly, 'no point coming the old sergeant-major. We're just two men. Strangers. On a train. Thrown together by a whim of fate and a British Rail timetable.'

Mackay subsided and they both pensively sipped their drinks. Fletcher had another go. 'Funeral, is it?'

'What?'

'Your trip to the great metrollopiss – if that's the right word.'

Mackay drew himself up like one who knows what it is to wield authority. 'Fletcher, I do not wish to discuss my private life with the likes of you.'

But, unabashed now by his old adversary, Fletcher rambled on. 'Well, if it ain't a woman – and it obviously isn't in that hat – let me see, let me see –'

'Save yourself the bother, Fletcher.'

'Oh, it's no bother, Mr Mackay,' Fletcher assured him cheerfully, 'I enjoy unravelling the tangled skein of truth from all the rumours that confuse it.'

'What rumours?' asked Mackay anxiously.

Fletcher grinned inwardly. He had breached the defences. He settled back to enjoy himself. 'Aha, we're nervy, are we?

On edge? That's a clue. Sensitive to rumours. Now, you ain't going on a course, because you done one last year down in Godalming. And you ain't going on leave, because you had two weeks at Easter. Went to Aberdeen, didn't you, and it peed down. And you ain't up for a Promotional Board because they passed you over last November.'

Surprised and disconcerted, Mackay asked: 'How do you know all this, Fletcher?'

The old lag grinned. 'No secrets inside, Mr Mackay. Now, on the other hand your birthday's coming up, 23 April, Taurus the Bull – very appropriate.'

Mackay asked, with a perceptible tremor in his voice: 'What's my birthday got to do with anything?'

Fletcher shook his head affably. 'Nothing, I shouldn't think. Unless, of course, you've reached the Compulsory Retirement Age.'

Strive as he would to conceal it, Mackay could not refrain from a nervous twist of his head and a faint, giveaway leer. Fletcher pounced.

'*That's* it, isn't it? Fifty-five. Twenty-five years of service and duty. Still fit. Still active. Still on top of the job. And it means naff all to the faceless men of Whitehall. Thank you very much for being such a good screw and goodbye. What do they give you, a golden truncheon?'

Mackay, aware that he'd been hopelessly outmanoeuvred, sighed and admitted: 'A digital clock.'

Fletcher smiled and then, to show that he could be generous in victory, turned and called to the steward: 'Oi – two Scotch – doubles.'

The steward nodded quickly. 'Yes, sir.'

Fletcher turned back to his former tormentor. 'Of course, you do have the option of going on until you're sixty, don't you? Even longer if you become a principal.'

Mackay looked at him narrowly. 'You seem very well versed in the facts, Fletcher.'

Fletcher nodded. 'Well, you could say I've studied the

prison service at close quarters for some time. Why are you leaving now?'

'If you must know, because I think I have a better chance of landing a job now than when I'm sixty.'

'A job,' exclaimed Fletcher, as this last piece of the jigsaw slid smoothly into place. 'That's it. You're wearing your interview suit.'

Mackay, although it was far too late for it, protested feebly: 'It's none of your business.'

Fletcher shook his head with a rueful smile. 'Ironical really. You and me. Went our very separate ways over the last twenty-five years and here we are in the same boat – jobless.'

'I beg your pardon!' Mackay reproached him. 'At least do me the courtesy of not putting me on the same footing as you.'

'But it's true, mate. Both shuffling along in the same dole queue.' Then he grinned, recalling what the other screw had said to him when handing back his personal effects. 'Or do you have the qualifications to leapfrog in front of the country's one and a quarter million unemployed?'

Mackay was beginning to acquire, whether as a consequence of emotion or of his native beverage, a somewhat ruddy appearance. 'You're not telling me,' he said bitterly, 'there's no room for an honest, diligent, industrious man who's willing to do a hard day's work for a fair day's pay?'

Fletcher looked at him in astonishment and shook his head in wonder. 'If that's true, you'll be such a unique case they won't know what to do with you.'

With a slight jerk, the train, which had been slowing down for some time, came to a halt at Stafford. Passengers left it and others boarded. Soon the percussion solo of slamming doors came to an end and the train jerked again and began to move out of the station. At this moment, two men, breathing hard, reached the platform and began to run after the long vehicle. They found a door and, without too much trouble, opened it and scrambled in before the train had picked up much speed. For a moment they rested.

Although together, the two were an ill-assorted pair. One of them was short and scruffy and had an ineradicably shifty expression. He was carrying a leather bag. The other was taller, better-dressed and might have been a solicitor or estate-agent. When they had recovered somewhat, they slid open a door and entered a second-class compartment. As they moved along it, the taller and more gentlemanly of the two took inconspicuous note of its occupants and their disposition. About halfway along, he turned and nodded briefly to the small, scruffy man. This one paused and then lifted his leather bag and placed it on the luggage rack. But, rather curiously, he did not sit down under the bag but continued a few seats further along the carriage. Then he turned and sat down on the other side of the aisle. From there, he could see the bag. Having watched this manoeuvre, the tall man gave a slight nod of approval and then moved on up the carriage and out of it. He was heading for the first-class section of the train.

Meanwhile, back in the buffet car, Fletcher was enjoying himself.

'I've just thought of a job you could do, Mr Mackay,' he said.

Mackay blinked and raised his head. There were now two more empties in front of each of them. Mackay seemed to be having slight trouble in focusing his eyes on the face of his old charge. He asked: 'Pardon?'

'Guard,' said Fletcher affably. 'Suit you that. Uniformed man. Trade in the truncheon for a flag and whistle.'

Mackay shook his head haughtily. The effect of the gesture was somewhat diminished by a tendency of his whole body to wobble. But he spoke firmly. 'Fletcher, I intend to seek a position which requires a little more dignity than railway guard.'

Fletcher looked impressed. 'Traffic warden? Commissionaire? Is that it? Of course, that's what you lot often end up as. Standing outside the Dorchester, with an umbrella, keeping the rain off some visiting sheikh.'

Mackay frowned. 'Why do you assume I need a uniform?'

'Because you've always had one. You've always had that mantle of security. Straight from school into the Army, weren't you? Boy soldier. It's all in your file. I've read it.'

Mackay, aware that it was important not to let the side down (but also aware that it was slipping a trifle) tried to say crisply: 'I became a boy soldier out of expediency, Fletcher.' But he was disturbed to find that the assertion sounded to him more like: I 'came boy sojer ev 'spediency, Fletcher. He tried harder. 'There were too many mouths to feed in my family. Lanarkshire coalfields. Unemployment. Hard times. I grant you the army did become a home. One I was grateful for and proud to serve.' Mackay gave himself a mental pat on the back. He was confident his words had emerged this time with dignity and pathos.

Fletcher nodded. 'Then the Prison Service. Never been out in the cold, have you?'

'Wrong!' exclaimed Mackay triumphantly. 'Between 1951 and 1953 Marie, my wife, and I ran a boarding house in Peebles. The Strathclyde.'

Fletcher sniffed disdainfully and retorted: 'It may interest you to know that at the same period I was in Kuala Lumpur at the height of the terror, fighting bandits, while you were serving bed and breakfast.'

Mackay smiled patronisingly, or could it be drunkenly? 'I've done my whack, Fletcher. I was a sergeant-major.'

'And that probably explains why the boarding-house went down the drain.'

Mackay started. 'Who told you that? That's not in my file.'

'It stands to reason. Sergeant-Major Mackay as a landlady. "Lights out, ten o'clock, stand by your beds – who left that kipper here?" '

But sad memories were flooding through Mackay's mind. He said heavily: 'You can laugh, Fletcher. But that place took most of my demob savings. I thought of re-enlisting and finally joined the prison service instead. Twenty-five years later, out to pasture like some retired pit-pony.'

He could feel tears of self-pity beginning to collect in the corners of his eyes and was glad when Fletcher embarked on a long speech. It gave him time to mop up the shameful moisture with his handkerchief.

'You uniformed men all make the same mistake,' pointed out Fletcher. 'Screws, cops, soldiers. You think your loyalty to the cause is eternally appreciated by them you serve. "The Regiment", "the Force" – they'll take care of us. You think there's some father-figure up there looks after his own. But there ain't. There's only a computer what works out when your time is up and gives you the chop. Or in your case the clock.'

Mackay said bitterly, 'It's criminal.'

'Of course it is, and that's why I speak with such authority. You're in a very precarious position, you know. Seen it happen. Bitterness leads to resentment. Think the world owes you a living. Probably end up in the dock.'

'The dock!' Mackay echoed in a shocked voice.

'On some pathetic charge. Stealing a tin of Duraglit in Tescos so you can polish up your medals and take them to the hock shop.'

This scenario did not appeal to Mackay and, moreover, he began to sense that it was humiliating to be subjected to this stuff by one of his old charges. 'If I were you, Fletcher,' he urged, 'I'd pay a little less heed to my future and a little more to your own. Not exactly a bright prospect, are you?'

Fletcher shook his head matter-of-factly. 'No. But I ain't got no illusions, see. I expect naff all from society. So the chances are I shan't be disappointed.'

Mackay wagged an unsteady finger at him. 'You'll be back in crime in five minutes. And back inside in five months.'

Fletcher shook his head firmly. 'No, I won't. Because I'm going straight.' Mackay chuckled cynically but Fletcher pressed on. 'I know – you've heard it all before. Well, I've said it all before and all. The difference is, in the past I never meant it. Said it for the benefit of the parole board. But in my heart of hearts I knew that going straight was going straight back into skullduggery. And when I said I ain't going back inside again, I meant I ain't going to get caught again. But this time I'm legit.'

Mackay frowned. 'But what will you do, man?'

'Same as you. Hope to hell I get a break.'

Mackay appeared to be considering this proposition. Then he shook his head slightly and struggled to his feet. Fletcher was taken aback.

'Was it something I said?' he asked.

His speech now decidedly slurred, Mackay explained: 'Just going to pay the water bill.'

And he reeled off towards the end of the carriage.

Fletcher sat brooding on the strange coincidence – Mackay and him in the same boat. There was a time, quite recently, when he'd have thought the *Queen Elizabeth* was too small for the pair of them. But life plays strange tricks. The steward appeared and busily tidied the table in front of him. Suddenly a voice, not that of the steward, exclaimed:

'Fletch!'

Fletcher glanced up and saw a small, scruffy-looking man gazing at him eagerly. It was, in fact, the late arrival at Stafford whom we last encountered eyeing a bag on the luggage rail. Since Fletcher did not immediately reply, the little man added, more tentatively:

'It is Fletch, isn't it?'

'Possibly,' admitted Fletcher, in a reserved tone.

The little man nodded with relief and smiled. 'I'm Oaksie, remember? We did time together. Maidstone.'

At the reminder, memories flowed back to Fletcher. 'Oh my Gawd, yes, so we did, Oaksie.'

'I heard you'd got sent up again,' said Oaksie sympathetically.

Fletcher nodded ruefully. 'Heard right then, didn't you?'

'How long you been out?'

Fletcher grinned. 'Oh, quite a while. Almost three hours now.'

'You mean – '

Fletcher confirmed it with a nod. 'On me way home.'

'Never.'

'True.'

Oaksie shook his head and grinned appreciatively. Then he looked thoughtful, glanced about with the villain's instinctive reflex, leaned a little closer and asked softly: 'Listen – er – what plans you got?'

'Very fluid at the moment,' quipped Fletcher. 'I'll have a scotch.'

Oaksie, whose wits were none of the sharpest, looked puzzled for a moment. 'What?' but then his expression cleared as he caught on. 'Oh yes, sure – you must be a bit short at the moment, are you?'

'Not exactly flush,' admitted Fletcher.

Oaksie looked at him thoughtfully. One could almost see the idea dawning in the space behind his eyes. He said: 'Wait here, Fletcher, I'll be back in a minute.'

And he was gone. The steward, who had been cleaning table-tops, sidled towards Fletcher.

'You – er – you seem to know a lot of people on this train?'

'So?' asked Fletcher lightly.

The steward smiled appreciatively but there was an anxious note in his voice when he asked: 'Not planning to knock it off, are you?'

Fletcher looked stern for a moment. Then he shook his head with a grin. 'Not till the beer's finished.'

Oaksie, meanwhile, hastened back to the first-class section of the train and scanned each compartment he passed until he came to the one that contained the unlikely companion with whom he had arrived. The distinguished-looking man was alone in a corner seat and, as the sliding doors grated open, he looked up and frowned.

'Mr Tanner,' began Oaksie eagerly.

'What?' returned Mr Tanner irritably.

'Listen – ' and he slid the door shut behind him.

Tanner, with a hint of menace in his voice, asked: 'Why aren't you watching the bag?'

'That's why I'm here, the bag,' Oaksie explained hastily. 'I mean, that's our worry, isn't it? If old Tom's tumbled us they're going to be waiting, isn't they? So I met someone.'

'Someone?' asked Tanner shortly.

Oaksie smiled ingratiatingly. 'Who could maybe take the bag off for us.'

Tanner frowned. 'Who is it?'

'Old mate of mine. Just come out of Slade Prison. Needs a penny. Very reliable. I mean, you know, solid.'

'How solid?' asked Tanner meaningfully.

'Oh, one of us,' Oaksie reassured him. 'Always has been. He's in the buffet. On his own. Judge for yourself. I'll introduce you.'

Tanner shook his head. 'No. You get back and keep an eye on that bag. I'll check out your old mate.' And he rose for the journey to the buffet car.

At that very moment, Mr Mackay re-seated himself next to Fletcher. He looked, with evident displeasure, at the bare table-top.

'Shouldn't we have got another couple in?' he asked.

'That depends,' said Fletcher judiciously. 'I mean, is your interview today?'

Mackay smiled confidently, the effect only slightly marred by a hiccough.

'I can handle it – don't you worry.'

Fletcher looked doubtful. 'Want to make a good impression, though.'

Mackay thereupon lost his cool enough to thump defiantly

on the table-top and roar: 'Twenty-five years, Fletcher! That's what I've got to offer. Twenty-five years unblemished service.'

'Well,' corrected Fletcher politely, 'not quite unblemished, is it? Don't forget I've seen the file. Couple of incidents of – what was it? – over-zealous methods of interrogation?'

Mackay sniffed bitterly. 'You don't mollycoddle riff-raff. And that's what I've been dealing with. You're referring to Hanrahan, aren't you? Well, I knew he was up to something. And so I leaned on him a little. What other language do the Hanrahans of this world understand?'

Fletcher said evenly: 'Knew enough to write to his MP, didn't he?'

Mackay snorted in disgust. 'That effeminate left-wing windbag.'

'Champion of the underdog,' corrected Fletcher.

'Champion of the underworld, you mean. Let him spend the time I've spent with them and he'd understand something about the criminal mentality. I could spot a wrong 'un ten miles away in a thick fog.'

'I'm sure you could,' conceded Fletcher. 'But if you're going to make it on the outside you'd be well advised to modify your rigid attitudes. Not all black and white you know. There's a lot of grey in the middle. You'd better start giving your fellow man the benefit of the doubt.'

At the conclusion of this speech, Fletcher stood up. It was Mackay's turn to be puzzled. Trying to keep his voice from wilting at the edges he asked: 'Have I offended you or something?'

Fletcher shook his head. 'Not me, no. Just going to take my first civilian slash.'

With which he departed the way Mr Mackay had recently returned. At the other end of the carriage, almost as if synchronised with Fletcher's departure, the door slid open and Tanner entered. He glanced swiftly about the compartment and noted that Mackay was the only customer. He thereupon ambled down the aisle at an easy pace and, when he reached Mackay, said cordially:

'Good morning.'

Mackay glanced up. He was not surprised at being addressed by a stranger. He was, in fact, past being surprised by anything. He nodded and returned the greeting: 'Good morning to you.'

Tanner glanced about in the old giveaway reflex and then seated himself in the chair Fletcher had just vacated.

'Someone just mentioned to me,' he began meaningfully, 'that you're on your way from Slade Prison.'

Mr Mackay's eyebrows lifted lethargically. 'Who might that be?'

Tanner tapped the side of his nose. 'A friend of mine.'

Mackay shook his head. 'If he recognised me the chances are he's no friend of mine.'

Tanner contradicted him politely. 'On the contrary, he spoke very highly of you.'

Mackay frowned, trying to get the drift of the conversation. 'Did he now?'

'Said you were a man of integrity – a man one could trust.'

Mackay confirmed this with an insecure nod. 'I like to think so.'

Tanner glanced at the bar and the steward. 'Drink?' he asked hospitably.

Mackay shook his head. 'Oh, I don't think I'd better.'

'Just as you like.'

Mackay said hastily: 'Well, perhaps just a wee dram.'

Tanner summoned the steward with a hooked forefinger. He nodded towards Mackay and ordered: 'Same again.' And then, when the steward had departed to fill the order, he leaned towards Mackay and asked simply, 'London?'

'Aye.'

'And then what?'

Mackay shrugged. 'Depends what I can get fixed up with.'

'Looking for a job, are you?'

Mackay nodded heavily. 'A position, yes.'

Tanner smiled. 'Perhaps I could help you there.'

This struck Mackay, even in his befuddled state, as odd. He blinked at his companion. 'Really? But I hardly – '

The other quickly thrust out his right hand. 'Tanner's my name.'

Mackay took the hand and shook it. He asked: 'And what – I mean, what sort – '

Tanner smiled meaningfully. 'Oh, I have my fingers in lots of pies.'

Mackay shook his head. 'But would I be qualified for – '

Tanner held up a restraining hand. 'Trust. Integrity. Those are the qualifications you can't put a price tag on.'

Mackay nodded fervent agreement. 'Absolutely. I was saying it only a little while ago. Nice to meet a man who endorses that opinion.'

At this point the steward appeared with a large Scotch which he placed in front of Mr Mackay. Tanner slipped a pound note smoothly from an expensive-looking wallet and held it out for the steward. When the attendant had taken it, Tanner made a gesture indicating that he expected no change.

'Thank you, sir,' said the steward gratefully, and returned once more to his bar.

Mackay, with slight wastage, poured his new drink.

'Argylls?' asked Tanner.

'What?' asked Mackay.

Tanner smiled and elaborated. 'Your tie. Argyll and Sutherland Highlanders, isn't it?'

Mackay's chest swelled with pride and pleasure. He glanced down at the beloved garment and spilled a little more whisky. 'You recognised it,' he exclaimed. 'Oh yes. Sixteen years, man and boy. Warrant officer, class two.'

Tanner nodded. 'I'd have guessed that, sergeant-major.'

Mackay blinked at his companion with new respect. 'Are you a military man yourself?' he asked.

Tanner edged the cuff of his coat back to reveal a cuff-link adorned with a regimental insignia. 'Green Howards,' he said crisply. 'Major.'

Mackay attempted to sit to attention as he exclaimed smartly: 'Sah!'

Tanner disclaimed the implied salute with a little shake of his head and a rueful smile. 'Long time ago,' he said modestly.

But Mackay realised that he'd found a kindred spirit. He mumbled fervently: 'But we know – you and I – comrades in arms – that sort of thing – I mean. No coincidence that this country's gone to the dogs since the abolition of National Service. Cheers.'

And Mackay downed his Scotch. Tanner a little taken aback by the emotion he had aroused, said deliberately: 'Look – I'd like to get straight to the point –'

'Sah!' exclaimed Mackay again, all bleary attention.

Tanner glanced about and then resumed. 'Now, I need to leave this train at Watford. But it's very important that I have something delivered in London. It's a bag,' and Tanner extended his hands to indicate that it was no very sizeable object. 'If you could deliver it for me, I'd be very grateful. And there'll be a suitable recompense.' Tanner withdrew a visiting card from his wallet and wrote something on the back of it. He handed the card to Mackay. 'This is the address to deliver it.'

Mackay, all smiles, said: 'Leave it to me, sir. Is this your head office?' He studied the card and a slightly surprised expression appeared on his face as he read: 'Ed's Paint and Body Shop, Mile End Road.'

Tanner rose to his feet and Mackay, with spontaneous deference, swayed upright after him.

'Just do this right,' urged Tanner, 'and we might see later about something more permanent.' He patted Mackay encouragingly on the shoulder and whispered, 'I'll get it to you by and by – the bag, that is.'

He turned on his heel and strode out of the buffet. Mackay frowned after him for a moment, then shrugged and re-seated himself. As he considered this unexpected development a smug expression spread across his features. Fletcher returned from the end of the carriage and noticed it.

'What are you so chuffed about?' he asked.

'Cold on the outside, is it, Fletcher?' Mackay chortled.

'What?' asked Fletcher, mystified.

Mackay leaned towards him. 'Let me tell you something. I have already had overtures made to me during the time it took you to have a Jimmy Riddle.'

'Overtures?' repeated Fletcher, glancing about the empty buffet. 'Where's he gone? Sailor, was it?'

Mackay beamed. 'I have been offered a job. Well, a position really.'

Fletcher looked round again. The only other occupant of the buffet was the steward. Fletcher nodded. 'Making sandwiches, is it? I'll have another cheese and tomato.'

But, when he glanced back, he found that Mackay was now impervious to his wit. The screw had fallen asleep.

Some time later, the train drew into Watford station. As it slowed, the door to the buffet opened and Oaksie, carrying the mysterious bag, slipped inside. The bar was, by this time, closed and the steward was nowhere to be seen. But Mackay and Fletcher were still in evidence, both of them asleep in their chairs. Having no spare time whatsoever, Oaksie hurried down the aisle to Fletcher and dumped the bag in his lap, waking him abruptly.

'What's this?' asked Fletcher in astonishment.

'You know – ' Oaksie made a 'shtum' sign with fingers over lips. 'Say no more.'

And the scruffy little man turned and bolted up the aisle like a rabbit. Fletcher called after him: ' 'ere!'

But the other had gone. The train came to a halt and, a moment later, Fletcher saw Oaksie and Tanner hurry past him towards the exit. What he did not see was that, at the barrier, both men were apprehended by plain-clothes policemen who had been waiting there for them. The train jerked and began to ease forwards again. Fletcher, with dark forebodings, opened the bag on his lap and peered inside. He made an involuntary exclamation and hastily closed it again.

'Bleeding hell, the crown jewels!' he announced to no one in particular.

Then he did some swift thinking, and this led him to the conclusion that it was imperative for the bag and he, Fletcher, to be parted immediately. He glanced at the sleeping Mackay and began to rise. Too late. The door of the buffet slid open once more and a gentleman dressed in civilian clothes, but immediately identifiable to any crook in the land as a plain-clothes policeman, entered briskly. As soon as their eyes met, Fletcher felt his heart sink. The bag was on his lap. There was no possible way he could jettison it. Worse still, the new arrival, on seeing him, stopped dead with a frown that was speedily replaced by a look of recognition as he exclaimed:

'Good heavens, Fletcher.'

'What?' asked Fletcher guiltily.

The man, grinning affably, advanced on him. 'Norman Stanley Fletcher,' he said firmly, as if demonstrating a phenomenal memory for names.

Fletcher cleared his throat. 'So?' he asked bravely, but despair filled his heart. The thing on his lap was not a bag. It was a passport straight back to Slade Prison.

The minion of the law shook his head. 'Don't be coy, Fletch, I collared you once.'

Fletcher peered at him. He'd already placed him as a cop but now he recognised the particular cop. 'Gawd,' he exclaimed, 'Scotcher – West End Central, isn't it?'

Scotcher shook his head. 'Flying squad now.'

'Flying squad?' echoed Fletcher, as if deeply impressed and interested. After all, as long as they talked he was safe.

Scotcher nodded. 'Yes. I had what you might call a meteoric rise.'

Fletcher smiled feebly. A hundred schemes of salvation formed in his mind, and were instantly dismissed. With sickening certainty he knew there was no way he could now divest himself of the fatal bag. The only glimmer of hope was that Scotcher, incredibly, had apparently not yet noticed its bulky presence.

'Well, yeah,' said Fletcher, glad to keep the conversational ball rolling, 'I expect there's a lot of vacancies in your upper echelons these days. With so many of them up on corruption charges.'

Scotcher shook his head with the sort of smile rat-catchers reserve for cornered rats. 'Your mouth always was your worst enemy, Fletch. What's in the bag?'

At the words, Fletcher's heart leapt out of his mouth and made a run for it. For two pins he'd have done likewise but Scotcher would have nabbed him before he'd taken a step. Still, he played the comedy to the end. He glanced around with a puzzled expression.

'What bag?' he asked.

Scotcher pointed to it. 'That bag.'

'This bag?' asked Fletcher, as if mystified.

Scotcher sighed. 'What's in it?'

'Why?' asked Fletcher boldly.

'I got a right to know.'

Fletcher shook his head fiercely. 'No, you ain't. You ain't got any right to get on this train and harass me.'

'Come on, Fletcher,' urged Scotcher wearily. 'A job has been done. The perpetrators are on this train and then I find you. Well, you don't have to be Colombo to put two and two together.'

Fletcher adopted an indignant air. 'Well, I don't want to cock up your hypothesis, Scotcher, but I just come out of Slade nick today. This morning. It's my first day of bleeding freedom.'

Scotcher raised an eyebrow. 'First day out?'

Fletcher nodded. 'Easily provable.' He pointed a finger at the inert figure of Mackay. '*He* can prove it.'

Scotcher surveyed the sleeping figure dubiously. 'Who's he?' he asked.

'Senior Prison Officer Mackay,' proclaimed Fletcher impressively.

Scotcher, unable to ignore the implications of this assertion, moved a step closer to Mackay and shook him slightly.

'What is it?' mumbled Mackay. He opened his eyes. 'What's going on?'

Scotcher extracted from his wallet an identification card. 'Excuse me,' he apologised, 'I'm Scotcher – Flying Squad. Is this man known to you?' He nodded contemptuously at Fletcher.

Mackay stared. Then turned to his drinking companion. 'My God, have you been at it already, Fletcher?' he asked disloyally.

Fletcher shook his head irritably. 'Come on, Mr Mackay. Just alibi me out of this lot, will you?'

Scotcher looked narrowly from one to the other. Then he addressed Mackay once more. 'Are you who he claims you are, sir?'

Mackay pulled out his wallet and began extracting his own ID card. 'I'm Senior Prison Officer Mackay.'

Scotcher took the card, inspected it and nodded. 'And this man left Slade Prison today?' he asked.

'Yes, he did,' confirmed Mackay. 'What's this all about?'

Scotcher explained. 'There was a jewellers done in Stafford. Get-away driver lost his bottle and the others whipped into the station.'

Mackay shook his head regretfully. 'This is not your man, I'm afraid. He got on with me at Carlisle.'

Looking foiled, Scotcher said: 'I see.'

'I suggest,' offered Fletcher helpfully, 'you now go and have a look for the real culprits.'

B

'Nabbed a couple,' said Scotcher, 'but they didn't have the gear on them. That's why I'm assuming its still on the train.'

'On your way then,' urged Fletcher haughtily.

Scotcher nodded. 'Right. I'll just take a look in the bag, Fletcher.'

But Fletcher hugged it protectively to his person. 'Hold on.'

Then salvation came from a totally unexpected quarter. Mackay announced: 'That's my bag.'

'Eh?' exclaimed Fletcher, incredulously.

Scotcher frowned at the prison officer. 'Yours?'

'Certainly,' insisted Mackay.

Scotcher sighed. 'Then why was Fletcher holding it?'

'I was minding it,' explained Fletcher. 'Lot of criminals use this line.'

'Exactly,' Mackay mercifully agreed.

Scotcher did not like being outmanoeuvred but he knew when he had been. He nodded genially but his eyes were narrow when he said: 'Right. Be seeing you, Fletch.'

'No, you won't,' corrected Fletcher. 'I'm going straight.'

Scotcher suppressed a laugh. 'Heard that one before, haven't we?'

And he departed to search the train for the missing loot.

Fletcher exhaled a deep sigh of relief. He placed the bag on the floor beside him. Mackay was studying him with an expression in which pity and contempt mingled.

'You're a marked man, Fletcher,' he commented.

Fletcher muttered: 'Just bleeding hard to keep on the straight and narrow, that's all.'

Mackay shook his head complacently. 'It's not when you've always been on the straight and narrow.'

'Listen,' asked Fletcher, still puzzling over the matter, 'why did you say it was your bag?'

'Simple,' explained Mackay. 'I knew it wasn't yours.'

'No, it isn't,' agreed Fletcher vengefully. 'Some bloke just dumped it on me.'

'As I suspected,' maintained Mackay. 'It's intended for me. The fellow who left it didn't want to wake me.'

'What do you mean – it's for you?'

Mackay smiled his twisted smile. 'The man I told you about. I'm going to deliver this for him and then we're going to discuss something more permanent.'

Fletcher glanced from Mackay to the bag and back again. The situation began to clarify in his mind and it was not, Fletcher decided, without its humorous aspect. He smiled.

'What's so amusing?' asked Mackay.

Fletcher shook his head sadly. 'Mr Mackay, if you was to deliver this bag, you *would* be discussing a more permanent position – with a judge.'

Mackay stared. Then he cocked his head and said: 'I don't follow you.'

The full irony of it struck Fletcher. He sighed deeply.

'Mr Mackay, you and I are old adversaries, and believe me I'm terribly tempted to drop you right in the clarts.' The thought brought a wistful smile to Fletcher's lips. But then he shook his head fiercely. 'But no – no, I can't. Day one – new life. Besides, you just done me a favour, even if you didn't know you was.'

Mackay was gazing at him in bewilderment. 'Fletcher, will you make some sense?'

Fletcher reached down, grasped the bag and lifted it on to the table in front of them. He said simply: 'Have a shufty.'

Mackay drew back indignantly. 'Certainly not. What, betray a confidence?'

Still in the same soft tone, Fletcher added: 'Think you should.'

Mackay frowned. There was something in Fletcher's voice. He looked hard at the bag and then curiosity got the better of him. He unzipped it and peered in.

'Good God!' he exclaimed.

Fletcher nodded soberly. 'Yes.'

Mackay sputtered: 'We must hand this to the authorities.

Where's that police officer?' He rose excitedly to his feet.

Fletcher put out a restraining hand. 'Just think a minute. If you get old Bill, you'll have to give evidence in a court of law, won't you? Have to admit they conned you into being the bagman.' Fletcher paused for this to sink in. 'Going to look a right nana. And you looking for a job.'

The force of this was not lost on Mackay. He swallowed and, in a small voice, asked: 'What are you suggesting?'

Fletcher shrugged. 'Not our bag, is it? Let the cleaners find it. The buffet's closed. I suggest we go back to our compartment.'

Mackay's neck seemed to go into spasm. Embarrassment, fear and resentment at having to concoct plots with one of his old charges fought for supremacy. But finally he nodded. 'I think that's an excellent idea, Fletcher.'

'Right.' But Fletcher could not resist drawing the moral. 'And let this be a lesson to you. The straight and narrow's none too easy.'

Leaving the bag where it was, the old lag and the superannuated screw moved off together. But when they reached the sliding door, Fletcher turned and looked back at the little Aladdin's Cave they were abandoning. He shook his head sadly.

'Shocking waste, though,' he murmured.

Going To Be All Right

Norman Stanley Fletcher took a deep breath, squared his shoulders and entered the swinging doors of the Magistrates' Court. As soon as he was inside his heart sank. This was it: the grim, familiar scene. It consisted of wooden benches, tiled walls, uniformed policemen lounging about in cheerful groups which were in marked contrast to the pathetic knots of felons and their dependents. This was it: the mill of justice which had ground him fine so many times in the past and which, when he had left Slade Prison only a few days before, he had vowed would never again be part of his life. But he had been unable to escape it.

Why was the probation office always in the same building as the court? Probably, he reflected, as he made his way past the courtroom, the authorities believed it would be salutary for ex-lags to be reminded at regular intervals of the majesty of the law. What they forgot was that it was just at such places that you were most likely to meet other villains and get drawn back into crime. Still, he, Norman Stanley Fletcher, was not going back to prison. He had made up his mind and once his mind was made up –

'Oh, Gawd!' he groaned.

He had just opened the door leading into Mrs Chapman's outer office and the first thing he had seen was: two thumping villains! There they sat, waiting their turn to see the probation officer. One was about thirty and the other was older. But both of them had stamped on his features, even in the hopeless slouch of his posture, the lineaments of crime.

Fletcher took his seat. At least they were strangers. Neither of them was going to edge towards him with the giveaway glance over his shoulder and the whispered ' 'ere, Fletch, I could put you on to something'. But why, Fletcher wondered, couldn't a probation office be different? Not a bleak crossroads of crime but an attractive way-station on the path back to society? He smiled, thinking about it. Of course, a probation office shouldn't be on the precincts of a court at all. It should be in some attractive, convenient neighbourhood, fitted out with soft carpets, concealed lighting, deep-sprung leather chairs, potted plants. Why not have a little bar, with a smiling barman to hand out free beers? That was the way to set about reforming people.

He sighed and, more to relieve his feelings than because he anticipated much in the way of conversation, said to the other two: 'Look at this place! Hasn't had a coat of paint since I was here last. Oppressive, isn't it?'

The two hard men contemplated him impassively. It seemed they were thickies as well as heavies. Fletcher had, at least, always steered clear of violence. He sighed and resumed: 'You feel guilty just walking in the door. Liable to admit to all sorts of things you never done. Know what I mean?'

But his overtures again went unacknowledged. Abandoning the attempt, he leaned forwards to inspect the grubby pile of magazines on the table in front of him.

'Same old magazines, I see,' he grunted. 'Yes, here's *The British Felon* and *The Safecracker.* Okay, just a little joke. I mean, you've got to, haven't you?'

No response. Their silence was beginning to irritate him. He asked: 'Someone in there, is there?'

The older man nodded sullenly.

Fletcher shook his head. 'And you two before me? Be eleven before I get in. Just like the dentist's, isn't it? Ten o'clock sharp they tell you. Four editions of the *Autocar* later you're still stuck there. Well, I can bide me time. We're used to that, aren't we?'

Blank stares. Fletcher began to feel decidedly miffed. A little more sharply, he said: 'Ironical, really. One of the main things they tells you on parole is don't mix with bad company. Then you sit out here for an hour with a couple of villains like you. This is the one place you're *guaranteed* bad company. Just think of the number of jobs that have been hatched out of the sheer frustration of waiting to see your probation officer. I knew two blokes once, in similar circumstances, got so bored they nipped next door and turned over the Borough Surveyor's. Straight up. Didn't net them much. I mean the Borough Surveyor's hardly Hatton Garden, is it? Mind you, since then they've never been short of carbon paper and tea-bags.'

Still no flicker of interest. Why wouldn't the nurks speak to him? They could hardly imagine he was beneath them. But then, to his surprise, the younger one asked: 'What makes you think we're bad company?'

Fletcher goggled for a moment. Right, he had tried to be friendly. But these two needed a few home truths and he was just the bloke to administer them.

'Well, come on, me old mate,' began Fletcher vehemently. 'You're in here for starters, aren't you? Besides which, I'm no stranger to the criminal mentality. Too many years spent in bad company. Certain signs are dead giveaways. I mean, take you two – hard lads, right? Taciturn. Years of inbred suspicion and mistrust is etched in the tight-lipped countenance which you assumed for all and sundry. The eyes are revealing. Grievous bodily harm. Assault with a deadly weapon – it's written all over you.'

The two men looked at each other. Their dead-pan countenances gave little away but that little, as far as Fletcher could see, was surprise. Then they looked back at him and the older one said quietly:

'We're here to give a quote for decorating.'

Fletcher's jaw dropped. He was trying to think of some way of compensating for his blunder when the inner door opened and the probation officer, a slim and attractive lady of some thirty years, looked out.

'Mr Fletcher?' she said.

Glad to be spared the necessity for apologising, Fletcher got smartly to his feet. 'Yes.'

She beckoned and he, with a lame smile at the two decorators, quickly followed her into the inner office. He knew the place, of course, and it was no more brimming with cheer now than it had been some years ago when he'd last visited it. There was the same small desk, filing cabinet, electric kettle, dossiers on unfortunate victims of biased judges.

'Sit down, please,' invited Mrs Chapman.

'Thank you,' said Fletcher, doing so.

She smiled at him, pleasantly but impersonally. She wasn't green. She knew the ropes. 'Mrs Chapman,' she said, extending her hand. 'Mrs Shirley Chapman.'

They shook hands. Fletcher then fumbled in his pocket, found a folded piece of paper, and thrust it towards her. 'You'll want this, will you?' he suggested. 'My dog licence.'

'Your *parole* licence,' corrected Mrs Chapman with a slight edge to her voice which suggested she had small liking for feeble witticisms.

Fletcher shrugged. 'Same thing, isn't it? Got me on a leash, haven't you?'

Mrs Chapman ignored this. 'There are certain conditions of parole you're expected to comply with and if you don't like it, you can go back and finish your porridge.'

'No, no,' protested Fletcher hastily. 'I'll go along with whatever you say.'

Mrs Chapman nodded. 'In your case, it's not too difficult. You report weekly to me. You stay out of the company that you previously mixed with, and as soon as possible you start the gainful employment which you guaranteed as part of your application for parole.'

Fletcher coughed discreetly. 'Ah, the job – yes. We may have a bit of a problem there.'

Mrs Chapman frowned. 'Problem?'

'Well, you see – Isobel, my wife – she fixed me up with that job.'

Mrs Chapman consulted the dossier in front of her. 'Yes. At the cardboard-box factory.'

'On the North Circular Road, right. You see, Isobel was very friendly with the works manager – a bloke called Jessop. So he was the one what guaranteed the gainful employment.'

Mrs Chapman nodded, a trifle impatiently. 'I know. I have his letter on the file.'

This was it. Fletcher took a deep breath. 'Well, what's happened is, in the intervening period, since the letter, the friendship between Jessop and my old lady has – blossomed.'

'Blossomed?' asked Mrs Chapman as if the word was new to her.

'Well, yeah – or put it another way, they now live together.'

'Live together?'

'Yeah, both at once,' Fletcher clarified earnestly. 'Cohabit, I suppose you'd call it. So you can see it would be intolerable for me to work for a bloke who's shacked up with my old lady.'

'But this is terrible!' exclaimed Mrs Chapman. Then her expression became hard and challenging. 'I had to submit your home circumstances report to endorse your application for parole.'

Fletcher nodded humbly. 'Yeah.'

'And I stated that those home circumstances were stable.'

Fletcher brightened, perceiving a witticism ahead. 'Oh, they're stable all right – but the horse has bolted. Or, in this case, the old mare. Still, give Isobel credit where credit's due. She wasn't going to let on, was she – and mess up my parole?'

'But,' protested Mrs Chapman, 'the two most important factors in obtaining a parole are A, marriage and B, employment. Here you are out of prison and I now find you have neither.'

Fletcher saw the force of this. 'If you put it that way, I suppose it's true – yeah.'

Mrs Chapman sighed irritably. 'This puts me in a most embarrassing position.'

'Little worse for me, isn't it, girl?' Fletcher suggested gently. 'My life in ruins around me.'

Mrs Chapman's tender heart failed to melt at this consideration. 'You don't seem particularly devastated,' she observed. 'But then I suppose you knew well in advance?'

'Me?' cried Fletcher, eyes widening in amazed innocence. 'No! A bombshell. Take me a while to get over it. If I ever do, that is. Think what I'm going to need is a period of readjustment – by the seaside, something like that.'

Mrs Chapman recovered her professional poise. 'Mr Fletcher, we have a practical problem here. Your wife supported your home and family while you were in prison.'

Fletcher nodded. 'Well yes – she had a good job.'

Mrs Chapman consulted the dossier. 'Manageress of a dry cleaner's, wasn't it?'

'Yeah, we were never short of coathangers. That was before he came along, Rollicking Reg Jessop, the cardboard king.'

'And am I right in supposing that, since him, your wife's income will no longer be coming into the house?'

Fletcher nodded agreement. 'No, it won't, no. She don't work no longer. Lives in the lap of luxury up near Chingford.'

'But you still have a family to support. And the mortgage payments to make.'

'That's all right, though,' Fletcher pointed out. 'My two daughters work. Ingrid and Marion.'

Mrs Chapman could not keep irony from her voice. 'So you're quite content, are you, to be supported by the female members of your family?'

Fletcher felt obliged to explain why this situation was inevitable. 'My son Raymond's still at school. But don't worry, it's his last term and then he can chip in with the rest of them.'

Mrs Chapman favoured him with a searching look and then said: 'I've had a thought.'

'Oh yes?'

'But perhaps you'll consider it outrageous.'

'Can't tell till I hear it.'

'*You* work. *You* assume some of the responsibility that others in your family have borne all the years you've been inside.'

Fletcher frowned in distress at her failure to understand him. 'I intend to work!' he averred. 'I just ain't going to work for my wife's cardboard lover.' He pointed to his dossier on the desk. 'Listen, you know all about me. It's all in there. But I'm going to write a new chapter to that file. I'm going straight. And I ain't going to no bleeding nick again.'

'The two,' said Mrs Chapman drily, 'don't always go together.'

Fletcher spoke with dignity. 'Now, look, Mrs Chapman, it's my second day out. Just give me the benefit of the doubt until I prove you wrong. And I won't. Okay?'

Mrs Chapman thought for a moment and then nodded. 'Okay. And you give *me* the benefit of the doubt. Let me decide what's best for you and how to go about it. I don't want to give you a bad time. My job's to help you. I'm not here just for the money.'

Fletcher couldn't let that pass. He smiled knowingly. 'Still, you must get a canny screw, don't you?'

'Not when I have to support a husband and two kids.'

Fletcher could hardly believe his ears. 'Oh, he sits at home, does he? Quite content to live off a woman?'

Mrs Chapman, realising she'd blundered, said grimly: 'He sits at home because he can't find a job.'

'Can't you find him one?'

'Not in his field.'

'Not in his *field*?' chuckled Fletcher. 'He's a farmer, is he?'

'He's an aero-space engineer,' said Mrs Chapman. 'And perhaps that tells you how tough it is out there.'

Fletcher, sounding distressed, commented: 'Oh well, little chance for me then, is there?'

'We'll find you something,' promised Mrs Chapman. 'And you'll take what you can get.'

Fletcher nodded sombrely and rose to his feet. 'Righty-oh, then. I'll check in next week and see what's turned up.'

'Unless,' said Mrs Chapman quickly, 'I get in touch with you before then.'

'No mad rush,' Fletcher assured her.

Mrs Chapman shook her head resignedly. 'Meanwhile, sign on. How are you fixed for cash?'

'Well, I did have all the money I'd earned inside, but I blew that right outside Euston Station.'

The hard look returned to Mrs Chapman's eyes. 'In a betting shop? Or a pub?'

Fletcher shook his head in mild reproof. 'Neither. I got two bars of fruit-and-nut from a slot machine. Tara.'

And, glad to have established a good working relationship with his new probation officer, Fletcher ambled out of the office.

When he entered his home a few hours later, Fletcher found his lovely, nubile daughter, Ingrid, curling her hair with electric tongs in the living-room.

'Hello, dad,' she greeted him cheerfully.

Seating himself in a chair and withdrawing the racing edition of the *Evening Standard* from his pocket, Fletcher returned: 'Hello, gel.'

'What sort of day have you had?'

Fletcher glanced about expectantly. 'Any tea, is there?'

Ingrid shook her head as far as the tongs would permit. 'No, but you can put the kettle on.'

Fletcher sniffed and turned to the results. Ingrid asked again: 'I said, what sort of day have you had?'

But Fletcher seemed disinclined to discuss the matter. 'What time do we eat around here?' he asked irritably.

'Well, I'm going out,' confessed Ingrid. 'And Raymond's eaten. But he can always pop down the road and fetch you something from the new take-away Kebab House.'

'Gawd, the Arabs have even encroached on Muswell Hill, have they?'

The little joke made Fletcher feel better. Ingrid said earnestly, 'Well, we need their money, don't we, dad?'

'Don't need their nosh though, do we?'

Ingrid shrugged. 'Suit yourself.'

Fletcher sighed. 'I thought we'd have a nice hot dinner in. The family.'

'Well, we've all made plans.' Ingrid wound another strand of her blonde hair into the hot irons and asked yet again: 'What sort of day d'you have then?'

'Not bad,' Fletcher finally admitted. 'Had a swift half at the White Hart. Pint and a pie at The Anchor. Signed on the Labour, of course. Had a swift half at The Magpie. Then I dropped by the Old Ship en route to the Rainbow Club.'

Ingrid was distressed by this recital. 'Why did you go down the Rainbow?' she asked reproachfully.

Fletcher shrugged. 'Well, Tuesday afternoon in Muswell Hill – where else are you going to get a drink?'

'But,' Ingrid protested, 'you're not supposed to mix with bad company.'

'I wasn't.'

'What, down there? You'd see all your old crowd.'

'No, no. The old crowd's all inside now.'

Ingrid decided not to press the point.

'Did you see the Probation Officer?'

'Course I did. Right little tartar she is.'

Ingrid nodded sagely. 'Yes. I thought when I met her, when she was compiling her home circumstances report, she's nobody's fool, I thought. Don't suppose she was taken in for one minute by your broken-hearted act. "How can I do a job of work with my life shattered?" '

Fletcher put down his paper and fixed his daughter with

a reproachful stare. 'My life *is* shattered. As I told her, bombshell.'

'Oh, leave it out, dad,' protested Ingrid irritably, 'you knew the situation months back.'

Fletcher nodded grimly. 'Yeah, but it's only hit me now. Getting home to a house without her.' Very pointedly, he continued, 'No kettle on. No dinner in the oven.'

But Ingrid turned the tables neatly. 'That's all mum was to you, a housekeeper.'

Fletcher shook his head. He said bitterly, 'Anyway, it's quite obvious absence don't make the heart grow fonder. Makes the heart forget.'

'Well, you gave her enough opportunity to forget, didn't you? All the years you've spent inside.'

'I'm not thinking of me,' said Fletcher with quiet dignity. 'But how could she abandon you kids?'

'Abandon?' echoed Ingrid incredulously. 'Abandon?'

'Well, scarper off with another bloke.'

Ingrid said firmly, 'Dad, I'm twenty-six. And it's been two years since Marion lived in this house on a regular basis.'

'What about Raymond?' said Fletcher quickly. 'He's a schoolboy.'

'Only just. And let me tell you Mum didn't scarper until Raymond had sat his last "A" level.'

Right on cue, Raymond wandered into the room, wearing his customary air of trying to remember something totally unimportant. He was a tall lad, with long hair and an improbable ear-ring in one ear. He was not much given to mirth or frivolity or, as far as Fletcher had been able to detect, anything else whatever.

'See my Led Zeppelin tape?' he asked.

'Don't ask me, Raymond,' fussed Ingrid. 'You leave things all over the place.'

Raymond accepted the rebuke without comment. He asked: 'What time is it?'

'Ten to,' Ingrid informed him.

Raymond glanced about vaguely. 'Seen my bicycle pump?'

'It's in the lavatory,' Ingrid snapped, 'though gawd knows why.'

From the moment of the boy's entrance, Fletcher had been studying him with faint incredulity. Now he swallowed and, with as bright a smile as he could summon, asked: 'Hello, son, how's it going then?'

Raymond murmured:

'I can't shake off this catarrh.' He turned to his sister again. 'Ingrid, you seen my extendable steel tape-measure?'

'Oh, Raymond,' protested Ingrid crossly, 'do you really need it this minute?'

'No,' confessed Raymond. He glanced about again. 'What time is it?'

'Ten to!' Ingrid repeated in exasperation.

Raymond nodded. 'I'm late then.' And, without any sign of haste, he wandered out of the room.

Fletcher shook his head and asked Ingrid, 'What did he take his "A" level in, lethargy?'

Ingrid rallied half-heartedly to her brother's defence. 'He's quite bright. Academically.'

Fletcher sighed. 'He seems to lack something. Charm for starters.'

Ingrid made a sound of assent. 'Mm, that's what his school report said. Bright but surly.'

'You know, since I got back, he's hardly exchanged two words with me,' Fletcher said sadly.

'Being the youngest he's seen the least of you over the years, Dad,' Ingrid pointed out.

'So?'

Ingrid smiled cheekily. 'Maybe he's not sure who you are and is afraid to ask.'

Fletcher was of a different opinion. 'He's withdrawn into a shell because his mum's left him.'

But Ingrid wasn't wearing it. She turned on him fiercely. 'Dad, Mum owes this family nothing. The reason this family's intact, the reason we've got what we have, is all down to Mum. We've all grown up now, and Mum's got the chance to snatch a few years' comfort and luxury. She didn't rush into it headlong, you know. There was nights of agonised heart-searching. And then we had this family conference. And me and Marion and Raymond all said: "Mum, you owe it to yourself – on your way." '

Fletcher nodded grimly. 'So it's comfort and luxury she wants, is it?'

'Don't we all?'

'Well, I'm here to tell you that I'm here to provide that.'

Ingrid snorted. 'Good, you can start with the garden. No one's touched it for a year. It's like the Matto Grosso out there.'

'The what?' asked Fletcher.

'The Matto Grosso. It's a deep, impenetrable jungle in Brazil. It was on *The World About Us* on BBC2.'

'Look,' urged Fletcher, 'I ain't come home to reclaim the bleeding jungle. I'm here to provide all the things this family apparently lacks.'

Ingrid sniffed. 'On what you draw from the labour?'

'Now, you just listen to me, Miss Nifty-Knickers – '

But Ingrid headed for the kitchen door. 'I've got to iron my dress.'

Fletcher said firmly, 'No, you sit down for a minute and listen to me.'

Ingrid sighed but, secretly glad that her dad was showing some spirit, did as he had ordered. Fletcher resumed:

'Now, whatever my faults, I've always instilled in you all the value of thrift and savings. When your Aunty Vi died and left you that bit of cash, I made you put it into Unit Trusts, didn't I?'

Ingrid nodded but also observed: 'A year later, you made me cash them in.'

Fletcher shook his head sadly. 'That was because their yield was so disappointing.'

But Ingrid disputed this. 'No it wasn't, Dad. It was because you wanted me to pay off Ladbrokes.'

Fletcher conceded the point. 'Well, yes, *their* yield was even more disappointing. Ingrid, the point I'm trying so painstakingly to make is that it pays to plan ahead. To put something aside for that rainy day.'

Ingrid, who had started manicuring her nails, exclaimed: 'Oh, blast! I've broken one.'

'Ingrid!' her father rebuked her.

'Sorry, Dad.'

Fletcher tried again to share his wisdom with his eldest daughter. 'I'm trying to tell you that way back, unbeknownst, I put aside a little nest egg. For the future. Which is now.'

Ingrid was impressed. She gazed at him, all attention at last. 'Did you really, Dad?'

'Yes. Which means that we're going to be all right, girl. All of us.'

'D'you mean like Post Office Savings, Building Society, something like that?' asked Ingrid with interest.

'No, not exactly. My little nest egg's buried in a turnip field in Essex.'

Ingrid looked surprised. 'Wouldn't it have been safer in a bank?'

Fletcher said firmly: 'No, it was a bank it came out of.'

'A bank!' exclaimed Ingrid, horrified. 'Stolen money?'

Fletcher pressed his fingers to his lips. 'Shhhh! Raymond.'

'Gawd forbid,' said Ingrid piously, 'I never thought you were in that league.'

Fletcher shook his head emphatically. 'I wasn't. I only drove. No one knows – never did. The blokes I did it with left the country with their share. Never been heard of since. So – long time ago. Past history.'

But Ingrid, not really her father's daughter, glared. 'So! This is the "going straight" we've heard nothing else about since you come home? This is the new leaf you're turning over!'

'I'm entitled,' grumbled Fletcher. 'I've paid my dues.'

But Ingrid, with inexorable logic, continued: 'Not for that job, you ain't.'

Fletcher was getting irritated. 'Look, no bother. Years have gone by. It's there! For us! Few thousand quid devaluating as we speak under a turnip field.'

Ingrid nodded grimly. 'So that's why you're so chipper since you come out. That's why you've had no anxieties about the realities of going straight and getting a job.'

'I *am* going straight,' protested Fletcher. 'That cash is for us. It's a cushion against the harsh realities which I don't want to impose on my family.'

Ingrid shook her head firmly. 'This family don't need it, Dad. This family's got by without it.'

'But I want to give you things,' pleaded Fletcher. 'All of you.' He sighed pathetically. 'And maybe your mum'll come back if she knows I've got more to offer than promises.'

'No, she won't,' said Ingrid positively. 'All she ever wanted – all any of us ever wanted – was an honest wage in this house – not a dishonest cushion.'

It seemed to Fletcher that Ingrid was wilfully misunderstanding him. He said irritably, 'I intend to *make* an honest wage. But it's not bleeding easy you know, with a record.'

But Ingrid was ready for that one. 'No, it's *not* easy. But I know someone who done it.'

'Who?' asked Fletcher moodily.

Ingrid did not answer at once and so he glanced up at her and repeated the question: 'Who?'

'Leonard,' said Ingrid in a small voice.

'Leonard?' repeated Fletcher with a puzzled expression.

'Lennie then,' clarified the blushing Ingrid.

'Young Godber!' exclaimed Fletcher fiercely. 'So, you're seeing him, are you?'

'We keep in touch,' admitted Ingrid. 'And he's doing all right. Even though he's got a job he don't like much, he's prepared to take the rough with the smooth.'

Fletcher chuckled. 'What is he, a French-polisher?'

Ingrid ignored the sally. 'He's driving. Heavy goods.'

Fletcher gave his handsome girl a narrow look. 'You can do better than him, you know.'

But Ingrid replied haughtily, 'I'm the judge of that.'

'How often do you see him?'

'When I can.'

Fletcher looked at the hair-grooming equipment and newly-lacquered fingernails. 'Well, who are you titivating yourself for tonight then?'

'Leonard,' she confessed.

Fletcher nodded ironically. His old cellmate. He should have guessed. 'So, he's in London, is he?'

Ingrid nodded. 'Yes, he is,' and then, as she headed for the kitchen to iron her dress, she added: 'He's upstairs having a shave.'

Fletcher looked incredulous. Then, nodding bitterly, as if to say: it figures, he rose to his feet with dignity and called out to Ingrid: 'Well, I don't want to get in the way of you two love-birds. I'm going down to the local.'

Half an hour later, as Fletcher sat forlornly at a table nursing a pint of bitter, the door of the pub opened and a very spruce Lennie Godber entered. He was dressed in a good suit and his face was newly-shaved. He glanced about and saw Fletcher. Their eyes met. Lennie smiled. Fletcher nodded coldly. Lennie sighed and went to the bar.

'Lager, please,' he said to the barmaid. Then he turned to Fletcher. 'Another beer, Fletch?'

'No,' growled Fletcher. 'A Scotch.'

Lennie transmitted this to the barmaid, and turned back to Fletcher. 'Took me a while to find you.'

Fletcher grunted. 'I told Ingrid I was going to the local.'

'But,' protested Lennie mildly, 'you've got about twenty locals.'

The barmaid placed the drinks on the counter. Lennie

settled the account, carried the drinks over to the table and sat down. He said cheerfully, 'Good to see you. Welcome home.'

Fletcher shrugged. 'Yuh well.' He studied him covertly. 'Shaved, have you?' he asked finally.

'Yeah,' nodded Lennie brightly.

'D'you use one of my blades?' asked Fletcher suspiciously.

'Oh, come on, Fletch,' urged Lennie. 'We're not inside now. Naffing heck.'

Fletcher nodded. 'You obviously did then.'

'I used one of Raymond's as a matter of fact.'

'Oh, he shaves, does he?' asked Fletcher with mild interest.

'Only just.'

'You'd know, of course,' said Fletcher nastily. 'Being esconsed.'

Lennie sighed and shook his head. 'Only twice a week. I still live in Brum.'

'Twice a week, is it? And I bet you pockets your bed and board allowance.'

Lennie nodded. 'I can do with every penny, Fletch,' he explained. There was a brief pause and then he said sadly, 'Ingrid's upset.'

Fletcher, sensing criticism, bridled. 'Upset? Why?'

'You know,' maintained Lennie.

'Do I?'

'Yeah.'

Fletcher looked irritable. 'Look, you've said she's upset – I'm asking you why?'

Lennie glanced around and said softly, 'Because of your nest egg.'

Fletcher stared at him aghast. 'She told you?' he exclaimed incredulously.

'I knew about it, anyway.'

'How?' challenged Fletcher.

'You told me once. One night inside.'

Fletcher shook his head positively. 'I never talk about that.'

Lennie grinned. 'You'd had one too many.'

'One too many what?'

'Prune vodkas.'

Fletcher frowned. 'I don't remember.'

Lennie pointed out sagely, 'Few people do after your prune vodka.'

'Anyhow,' grumbled Fletcher, 'it's none of your business.'

'Yes, it is,' maintained Lennie. 'Because you're my mate. And I don't like seeing Ingrid upset.'

Fletcher considered this for a moment. 'Upset is she?' he asked.

'Worried. Well, we both are.' His voice took on a reproving note. 'It's not the way, Fletch.'

'I'll be the judge of that,' Fletcher said positively.

Lennie changed his tack. 'Thought you were going straight.'

'I am going straight,' insisted Fletcher. 'Straight to that turnip field in Essex.'

Lennie looked disgusted. 'Oh, come on, Fletch!' he urged.

'Listen,' Fletcher attempted to provide a reasonable explanation that would appeal to any fair-minded person, 'that nest-egg is a legacy from way back. It's just something to put me on the right financial footing. I've paid my dues.'

Lennie shook his head. 'Not for this job you ain't.'

'Academic,' snapped Fletcher.

'Not to Lily Law,' maintained Lennie. 'Because when you was done, that wasn't one of the offences you asked to be taken into consideration, was it?'

'No, naturally. Because they didn't know about it.'

Lennie tried to keep the initiative. 'So supposing they find out? Be twice as bad. Throw the book at you. Ten years, I reckon.'

'How they going to find out?' asked Fletcher irritably. 'I'm not stupid.'

'Seems a bit stupid to me. You're on parole, Fletch. They watch your every move. I know. I've just finished mine.'

'They don't put a bleeding tail on you,' reasoned Fletcher. 'They got better things to do than keep tabs on Norman Stanley Fletcher.'

But Lennie knew where the fallacy lay. 'All right, so you pub. New washing machine. Down payment on a new dig it up. Got no job but suddenly it's doubles down the Cortina.'

'I wasn't born yesterday, sonny Jim,' Fletcher came back. 'I'm not going to put it around like Jack the lad.'

'Not much use to you then, is it?' Lennie clinched his point.

Fletcher saw that reasoned argument was getting him nowhere. 'Shove off, will you?' he requested.

'I'm in no hurry.'

'You will be if I kick you through that door.'

Lennie grinned. '"He who strikes the first blow admits that his arguments have run out." Chinese proverb.'

Fletcher scowled. ' "He who gets fist in mouth cannot no longer give lip." Muswell Hill proverb.'

Lennie reverted to heart-felt appeal. 'All I'm saying, Fletch, is it's not the way. How can you say you're going straight and then start life off on the proceeds of illicit gain? Your family don't want that.'

'It would appear,' said Fletcher mournfully, 'my family don't want me at all. My son ignores me. All he's interested in is his extendable tape-measure and his bicycle pump. Marion hasn't even been to see me yet. Called up to say hello and reversed the charges. And Ingrid's taken up with a long-distance lorry driver name of Leonard.' He stared hard at his young companion.

Lennie bore it very stoically and said gently, 'They love you, Fletch.'

But Fletcher was not to be distracted from his resentment. 'Yeah, like my old lady does. Her what lives in the lap of luxury up with Jessop the box-maker. She knew which side *her* cardboard was buttered.'

'They all care,' insisted Lennie. 'See, I know because – well, I know them all better than what you do now.'

The cheek of this deflated Fletcher. 'Oh, you think so, do you?'

'I know they love you,' Lennie reiterated.

Fletcher shook his head glumly. 'I'd like their respect. Funny thing is, I had respect in the nick. I knew where I stood and so did people round me. Precious little respect out here. Stuck at the end of a dole queue or working Paddington parcels. Money's respect, Len. Money's independence. Gives you the chance to say "I upped my income so up yours." '

Lennie gave him a reproachful look. 'Well, I always thought you had more bottle than that.'

'More bottle than what?'

'Than what you've apparently got. Look, Fletch, when I come out, *I* was scared. My bottle nearly went. Scared of "them", you know. Accepting their terms. I've had to learn to turn the other cheek and swallow me pride. But I've done so principally because of what you taught me inside. And because of the encouragement Ingrid's given me on the outside. So one way or t'other I'm beholden to you and your family. And I'm not going to let you ruin your life or theirs. So try it, will you? For a while. Promise me you'll try.'

There was no mistaking the lad's sincerity and it got through to Fletcher. He considered the advice, which he knew was sound, for a little while. Then he nodded. 'All right, Len. For a while, I'll try. I promise.'

But beneath the table, out of sight of Lennie's delighted eyes, Fletcher had tightly crossed the fingers of both hands.

Later that day, Fletcher called at the local shopping centre to make a minor, but bulky, purchase. He was disconcerted, on emerging from the shop, to find his daughter, Ingrid, waiting there for him.

'Hello, Dad,' she said grimly.

'What?' gulped Fletcher.

'What are you doing with that spade?'asked Ingrid.

Fletcher tried to conceal the implement behind his back. 'What spade?' he asked innocently.

Ingrid pointed. 'That one you just bought.'

'Oh, *that* spade.'

'Yes, that gleaming new spade,' went on Ingrid relentlessly. 'Which matches the gleam in your eye.'

Fletcher shrugged haughtily. 'I just bought it. What's wrong with that?'

'Spades dig things up,' observed Ingrid.

'I know,' agreed Fletcher, 'and I'm going to – start work on the garden, aren't I?'

Ingrid smiled. 'Oh, good,' she said.

Which explains why, still later in the day, Lennie stood at the living-room window of Fletcher's home contemplating the results of the earth-moving activity the master had been performing. Fletcher himself was not visible. Ingrid entered with a cup of tea.

'Here y'are, love,' she said tenderly.

Lennie accepted the fragrant brew. He nodded in the direction of the garden.

'He's done a heck of a job.'

Ingrid giggled. 'Yes, he's never stopped. Had to go through with his charade, didn't he? Much to our benefit.'

Lennie considered the new landscape judiciously. 'Now he's cleared that border you should put down some azaleas.'

'Are they nice?' asked Ingrid.

Lennie grinned. 'Need a lot of care.'

Ingrid caught on. 'Keep him occupied then, won't it?'

'Where is he now?' asked Lennie.

'Down the chemist's getting something for his blisters.'

Lennie frowned. 'Here, he might – '

'It's all right,' Ingrid reassured him. 'Raymond's tailing him.'

Lennie shook his head doubtfully. 'How long can we keep

this up, that's the thing? Watching him every minute?'

'D'you have to go back tonight?' Ingrid asked wistfully. She might have been thinking of the problem of maintaining surveillance on her father. Then again she might not have been.

'I should do,' Lennie said.

'Oh,' and the disappointment in the lovely girl's voice was plain.

Lennie put his arm round her hungrily. 'Unless I left first thing.'

Ingrid wriggled with delight. 'I think you should, don't you?' A thought struck her and she drew back for a moment. 'Here, you don't think he really bought that spade to do the garden, do you?'

'No,' said Lennie firmly.

Ingrid snuggled into his arms again. 'No, I don't neither,' she agreed.

Fletcher, with his impeccable sense of timing, entered at that moment. He stopped in exasperation at the sight of them embracing. 'Here, here, that's enough of that.'

Without relinquishing his delicious hold, Lennie said: 'Hello, Fletch.'

'Just unhand her, will you?' requested the affronted father.

Ingrid tactfully disengaged herself. 'Want a cup of tea?' she asked considerately.

Fletcher nodded. 'Yes, ta.'

Ingrid went off to fetch it. Fletcher turned to Lennie. 'Is that your lorry parked outside?'

'Yeah,' admitted Lennie.

'Best be on your way then, hadn't you? suggested Fletcher with small grace.

Lennie explained. 'I don't have to be back till eight in the morning.'

Fletcher's eyebrows rose. 'Meaning?'

The meaning was supplied by his daughter, calling from the kitchen. 'He's staying the night.'

Fletcher extended a severe forefinger in the direction of the living-room sofa. 'On that you are then.'

Lennie looked surprised. 'Where else?'

Raymond entered languidly. 'Seen my earphones?' he asked.

Lennie shook his head. 'Sorry, Raymond, I haven't.'

Raymond received the news without evidence of undue distress. 'What time is it?' he asked dully.

'Ten past,' Lennie informed him.

'Oh,' said Raymond, 'I've missed it then.'

Fletcher favoured his only son with a reproving glance. 'Then you shouldn't have accompanied me to the shops, should you?' he asked.

Raymond looked very mildly surprised. 'Did you notice?'

Fletcher grunted scornfully. 'Did I notice!'

'I thought,' maintained Raymond evenly, 'I'd took advantage of the natural cover.'

Fletcher glared about at those assembled, which included Ingrid since she returned with his cup of tea.

'I know what you're up to,' he said bitterly, 'all of you! It's pathetic.'

Ingrid placed the cup in his hand and said lightly. 'Not up to anything, Dad.'

'What you been doing today then, Fletch?' Lennie asked quickly.

'Oh, I had a very full and exciting day,' affirmed Fletcher, making no attempt to keep the ironic note from his voice. 'Did the garden, had a fishcake for me lunch and went down the shoe repairers. It's all in Madam's report.'

'Why did you go to the cobblers?' asked Ingrid. 'Your shoes is all right.'

Fletcher sighed. 'When I come out of nick they give me this box with my personal effects. In which there was a shoe repairer's ticket for one pair of brown brogues.'

Ingrid looked surprised. 'But that was nigh on three years ago. Did you think they'd still be there?'

Fletcher shrugged. 'Nothing to lose was there? I was passing.'

'What did they say?'

Fletcher smiled briefly. 'Said they'd be ready Thursday.'

Very early the following morning, at an hour when all decent citizens should still be abed, strange events occurred in the Fletcher household. Out of his bedroom, fully-dressed, stole the master of the house. Pausing at the head of the stairs, he listened carefully. Satisfied that sleep held sway, he then tiptoed down the stairs. On his feet were thick woollen socks and in his hands was a pair of Wellington boots. These he took to the front door and stationed them there. Then he returned to the cupboard under the stairs, opened it carefully and withdrew from it the very instrument that had tortured him all the previous day, the spade. He carried this too to the front door and placed it near the boots. Now for the hard part.

He went to the living-room door. Inside, he knew, young Godber was asleep on the sofa and Lennie's continued slumber was vital to the success of Fletcher's plan. With infinite caution he inched open the door. He paused. He peered. In the gloom he could just discern a human form beneath several blankets. He swallowed and set off across the floor. A couple of minutes later, so slow and canny was his progress, he reached the chair near the sofa on which hung Lennie's jacket. Keeping his eyes fixed on the motionless hump on the sofa, Fletcher reached carefully into one of the pockets and groped about until he had found what he sought. Then he withdrew his hand holding a bunch of keys. He gave a faint sigh of relief. But he was not in the clear yet. The figure on the bed had not moved, which was the way Fletcher wanted it. Holding the keys he inched back towards the door and, just before he reached it, stumbled over a cushion that had thoughtlessly been left there. As a result he crashed lightly into the table. Dishes on the table rattled. The noise, to Fletcher, seemed deafening. He froze and stared hard at the sofa. No sign of movement. He swallowed in relief and turned towards the door again. But then a curious thought struck him, and he turned back towards the sofa. He glanced from it to the ceiling above it, which was the floor of his daughter Ingrid's room. A suspicious frown appeared on his face. He crept to the sofa and leaned over it, listening for the sound of breathing. Then he reached down and gently plucked off the blankets. Beneath them was a row of cushions placed together to mimic a human form. With a muted oath, Fletcher shook his fist at the ceiling above his head. But what could he do? If he yielded to his impulse to storm upstairs and confront the guilty pair, he would blow his chance. And it was too good a chance to miss. Stifling his paternal rage, he left the living-room, went back along the passage, retrieved his boots and the spade and so left the house.

He glanced back. No lights showed. He looked up. A faint grey tinge in the sky indicated that it would soon be dawn. He pulled on his Wellingtons and then went down the garden path to Lennie's massive articulated lorry. Not the ideal vehicle for retrieving buried treasure but the only one at his disposal. With one of the keys, found by trial and error, Fletcher unlocked the cab and then heaved himself up into it. He found the ignition key by a similar technique and tried to start the engine. The starting motor whirred but the engine failed to ignite. He tried again. The same result. He glanced at the house. A light had come on! And he could see a figure outlined against it, obviously peering out. He tried the starter again. This time the engine coughed but did not quite make it. Now more lights came on. Fletcher could see that the staircase was illuminated. Any moment now the front door would open! He tried the starter again. It whirred, the engine coughed and finally the lorry's powerful motor sprang to life. He engaged the gear and released the clutch, nudging the great vehicle out from the kerb, just as the front door was flung open. As the lorry carried him up the street, he had time for a glimpse of his daughter Ingrid, becomingly attired in her best nightdress, waving frantically at him.

He grinned fiendishly.

In the house, Lennie charged down the stairs in the wake of Ingrid. She turned to him with a disgusted expression.

'He's gone,' she said.

Lennie gazed at the disappearing tail-light. 'And he's took my lorry,' he wailed.

Ingrid retreated into the house, pulling Lennie after her, and closed the door. 'What am I going to do, Leonard?' she asked wearily.

But Lennie had more immediate concerns. 'What am *I* going to do? I'm supposed to be back at the depot in Brum by eight o'clock.'

Ingrid said tartly, 'You shouldn't have left your jacket down here with those keys.'

Lennie nodded bitterly. 'Oh, I knew it would be my fault.'

Ingrid bit her lip and thought for a moment. 'I tell you what. Ring the police and report your lorry stolen. Chances are they'll apprehend him before he reaches Essex.'

Lennie nodded ironically. 'That would be a lot of help for a bloke what's on parole, wouldn't it?'

Ingrid shrugged gloomily. 'Better than them finding him when he's digging up buried loot.'

Raymond ambled into the room in his pyjamas and, more from habit than because of the strangeness of the hour for this unexpected family assembly, asked: 'What time is it?'

'Five o'clock,' snapped Ingrid. 'Go to bed.'

'What's going on?' asked Raymond listlessly.

'It's your dad. He's given us the slip.'

'He's took my lorry,' Lennie added.

With faint interest, Raymond asked, 'Oh, so he's gone to dig it up, has he?'

'Yes,' admitted Ingrid. 'It's everything we didn't want to happen. It's criminal. It's immoral. I'll never speak to him again. I want nothing more to do with him.'

But a faint gleam of something like animation had entered Raymond's cold eye. 'Still,' he mused, 'he might get away with it.'

'Even if he does,' said Ingrid disgustedly.

'No, but if he does – ' speculated the boy.

'What?'

'I want a motorbike,' proclaimed the practical lad.

In the rosy flush of dawn, a huge articulated lorry pulled off the road on to some rough ground that bordered a ploughed field in Essex. From it emerged Norman Stanley Fletcher carrying a spade and a grubby scrap of paper on which was drawn a crude map. He placed the spade against the side of the lorry and took from his pocket a small compass. He consulted this, nodded, grasped his spade and set off across the field.

Soon the excitement of the hunt gripped him. Counting under his breath he pursued a straight course until he reached a tree. There he changed direction. Still counting he breasted a small rise. Beyond it, he was disconcerted to see, were several new houses. But treasure fever had him in its grip. He stormed on, counting: 208–209–210. A fence barred his way. He was over it in a trice. His foot crashed through a cucumber frame. He ignored the trifling mishap. His Wellingtons now encrusted with mud he approached a new brick house still counting: 396, 397, 398, 399 – triumphantly, he cried: '400.' Then a look of horror appeared on his face. There was no longer soft earth beneath his feet. He looked down. He was on the concrete apron surrounding the house. His treasure had been sealed in for ever!

A woebegone Norman Stanley Fletcher pushed open his front door some time later to face the music. And loud and ringing it was too. Fletcher bore it all patiently. When the first onslaught had subsided somewhat the lethargic voice of his son was heard saying:

'So – no motorbike.'

'Well, all I can say,' interposed Ingrid, 'is "thank heavens".' She rounded on her father again. 'We wasn't going to speak to you no more. And you got Len into trouble.'

Fletcher sighed. 'Didn't expect to be away so long, did I?' and he looked apologetically at Lennie. 'Won't get the sack or anything, will you, son?'

'I rang them up,' said Lennie. 'Said I'd broken down. They said, get it fixed and bring a load up tonight.'

The bitterness of the situation struck Fletcher anew. 'It's right there!' he cried. 'Can't be more than a few feet under. Here, I know, we could sell this house and buy theirs.'

'What and have you digging up the floors of each room one by one?' cried the scandalised Ingrid.

'Save hoovering, wouldn't it?'

'Yeah,' Lennie interposed. 'You could grow a lawn instead of carpet. You wouldn't hoover it, you could mow it. Anyway, it's probably been found by now.'

'How?'

'When they built that estate. Probably a couple of Irish drain layers living in the lap of luxury in Palma by now.'

Fletcher granted him a baleful look. 'Well, if they are,' said Ingrid philosophically, 'it's probably ruined their lives. Too much too soon – spend, spend, spend.' She looked hard at her father as she delivered this homily. But Lennie gave her a look which said: 'go easy on him'. Ingrid nodded and, more gently, said: 'Anyhow, nuff said, Dad. One bit of good news today.'

'What?' asked Fletcher without much enthusiasm.

'Mrs Chapman rang.'

'Oh?' said Fletcher dully.

Ingrid tried to sound as if she was announcing some unprecedented windfall. 'Got you a job. Already – fancy that.'

Fletcher was silent for a moment. Then he grunted: 'What kind of job?'

'With the Council – Local Government,' enthused Ingrid.

But Fletcher did not consider this a satisfactory answer. He repeated the question more emphatically. 'What kind of job?'

'Down Wilmslow Road,' explained Ingrid.

Fletcher frowned. 'What,' he asked, 'are the council doing down Wilmslow Road?'

Ingrid opened her mouth to explain but seemed to have difficulty in finding sufficiently joyous words to break the glad tidings. She looked appealingly at Lennie. He nodded faintly, turned to Fletcher with a somewhat strained smile of enthusiasm and said:

'Digging it up.'

Going Sour

Norman Stanley Fletcher hammered nails into wood. He was making a bookcase. As he worked, he thought happily of how pleased and surprised his family would be when they found that the unsightly alcove above the fireplace had at last been usefully filled. Suddenly a sharp voice from the direction of the door reached his ears.

'Dad!'

With his hammer raised, Fletcher turned to behold his daughter Ingrid, unmade-up and wearing a dressing gown, glaring at him.

'What?' he asked innocently.

'What's all this bang-bang-bang first thing in the morning? It's only seven o'clock.'

'Just making myself useful,' Fletcher returned.

'But why do you have to start so early?'

Fletcher sighed. 'Because I wake up early. Three years in the nick, you do. And I don't sleep.'

'Well, Lennie does,' his daughter retorted, 'and you'll wake him up with all that racket.'

Fletcher said glumly, 'Oh, *he's* here again, is he?' He turned towards the sofa. 'He's supposed to be on the sofa. Where's he sleeping?'

'In Raymond's room,' Ingrid replied.

'Where's Raymond then?' asked Fletcher grimly.

'He's in my room,' his daughter offered.

'Where are you then?' he persisted.

'Well, I was down here but I went back up.'

Fletcher thought he was on to something. 'Where to?' he asked.

'Raymond's room.'

But he had lost direction. 'You've lost me,' he said. Turning towards the window he observed that it revealed only the side of an enormous articulated lorry. 'I thought it was a bit gloomy in here. Tell him not to park that thing right outside the window. We get precious little sun in here to begin with.'

'He only got in at two,' Ingrid explained. 'On his way back from Dover.'

'Well – '

'And it's better he stops here than some doss-house off the North Circular. He gives me what they give him for bed and board.'

'I know what he gives you,' said Fletcher, who could never resist an opening.

Ingrid sniffed. 'Don't be crude, Dad.'

'That's why I never get to sleep at night.'

'Well, nor can we with your bang bang bang first thing in the morning.'

Fletcher tried another indelicate sally. 'Makes up for your bang bang bang last thing at night.'

Ingrid shook her head reprovingly. 'Don't be crude, Dad.'

Fletcher put down his hammer and stood up. 'Look, I ain't got a job so I'm channelling my energies into fixing up this house.' Then, with eager but justifiable pride, he asked, 'Seen my new pelmets in the front room?'

'They fell down, Dad,' Ingrid informed him.

It was Fletcher's turn to sniff. 'Small wonder. That ceiling's right under your bed.'

Ingrid, ignoring this latest example of her father's incorrigible crudity, gazed about at the mess that high-class carpentry inevitably produces. 'I wish,' she said feelingly, 'you'd put your things away after you. Yesterday I found a three-inch nail in the marge.'

Fletcher sighed. He had read somewhere that a prophet was never appreciated in his own country but he hadn't realised that the same thing applied to handymen. 'You obviously ain't noticed that the flush now works, have you?'

'It always did,' Ingrid affirmed.

'Only if you knew the right tune. Now it works every time.'

Ingrid spied a tray containing a teapot and a bottle of milk. She went over to it and lifted the teapot lid. 'Is this tea warm?' she asked.

But Fletcher's mind was full of his good works. 'And the sink don't clog up no more,' he boasted.

Ingrid noted approvingly the steam that issued from the teapot. 'Might as well have a cup now I'm up,' she murmured, and went into the kitchen to fetch a mug. Fletcher bawled after her.

'And Raymond's bedroom door, what never shut properly because it got warped with the damp last winter. It shuts now! Because I took it off its hinges, shaved the bottom and rehung it.'

'Has the paper come?' asked Ingrid, returning with a mug.

'You didn't hear a word I said,' Fletcher reproached her.

Ingrid contemplated the assembly of short planks that Fletcher had produced and said discouragingly, 'I don't know why we need bookshelves. No one reads in this house.'

'*I* intend to,' proclaimed the master, 'I ain't got nothing else to do.'

'Shall I top you up?' asked Ingrid, as she poured herself a nice cuppa.

Fletcher did not appear to hear. He was studying the walls of the room. 'When was this room last papered?' he asked.

'Nineteen sixty-nine,' said Ingrid promptly, 'when you robbed that do-it-yourself shop.'

Fletcher nodded. 'Oh yeah –'

Acidly, Ingrid continued, 'And then you never done it yourself. Mum done it.'

Fletcher pointed to an irregularity in the design. 'That panel's the wrong way round.'

'Is it?' asked Ingrid with scant interest.

'Of course it is. Look, the wine glasses, or whatever they is, is all upside down.'

Ingrid now perceived the irregularity and was struck by it. 'Oh yeah. Funny, how you can live with a thing all that time and never notice.'

'You'd notice if you had as much time on your hands as what I've got.'

'D'you want some toast?' asked Ingrid affably.

Fletcher realised that his labour had produced a certain empty feeling in the abdominal region. 'Yeah,' he said enthusiastically, 'and maybe a boiled egg.'

But Ingrid shook her head. 'No, we've only got two eggs and I'm saving those for Len. You can have toast and Marmite.'

Fletcher looked outraged. 'Even in the nick I got an egg of a morning,' he exclaimed. 'Godber'll have to make do with one.'

'One egg's no good,' Ingrid affirmed. 'You don't know you've had it.'

'Oh, I see,' said Fletcher, and he made no attempt to keep the sarcasm from his voice. 'Well, if I won't know I've had it, I might as well not have it. Let *him* have it. Then I shall *know* I haven't had it. And he'll have definitely had it. Twice. At least.' He nodded emphatically. He wasn't absolutely certain what he'd said but he was quite sure that he'd meant it.

At this poignant juncture, young Raymond, following the Fletcher family tradition of casual early-morning wear, entered clad in pyjama trousers, a vest and an old sweater.

'Morning, Raymond,' his sister greeted him.

'My head hurts,' announced Raymond, without fervour.

'Why?' asked his anxious father.

'Bedroom door fell on it,' announced the youth.

Fletcher gulped. Out of the corner of his eye, he noted that Ingrid, on her way back to the kitchen, had paused to listen. He smiled paternally and asked: 'How's the rest of you then, son?'

'What time is it?' asked Raymond predictably.

'Ten past.' Fletcher strove to keep his voice cordial in spite of an impulse to empty the teapot over his dismal son's head. 'Sleep well?'

As was his invariable custom, Raymond ignored his father's question and asked: 'Has the paper come?'

'Not yet. Where you off to today then?'

But Raymond, apparently under the impression that filial respect had been fully exercised, turned towards the kitchen door and called: 'Ingrid, have you seen my bicycle pump?'

The urgent but muted tones of his sister came back. 'Keep your voice down. Leonard's trying to sleep.'

Fletcher made one last attempt to engage Raymond's interest. 'Cycling, is it?' he asked cheerfully. 'Going to the country, are you? Breath of fresh air? Good for you.'

Raymond frowned slightly and murmured, 'I had some pliers here yesterday.'

As the boy languidly raised a cushion on the sofa to peer under it, Ingrid re-entered to collect the tray.

Fletcher shook his head and said bitterly, 'Extraordinary thing in this house. There is a lack of conversational rapport. I say one thing. Someone says another. I ask a question – no one gives me an answer. Have either of you noticed that? Are you aware of it?'

'Brown bread or white?' asked Ingrid, as she hastened back into the kitchen.

Fletcher shook his head incredulously. He turned to Raymond. 'See what I mean, son? She's proved me point exactly, hasn't she?'

'Why,' asked Raymond, 'are you making bookshelves? No one reads in this house?'

Ingrid poked her head round the kitchen door and said peevishly, 'I asked a simple question, brown or white?'

'Brown!' thundered Fletcher.

'Shhhh!' exclaimed Ingrid, pointing meaningfully at the ceiling.

But Fletcher had had enough. 'Don't you shush me. I'm on

the brink of a breakthrough here. That is the first direct question my son Raymond has asked me since the day I come out of the nick, when he said: 'Who are *you*?' Fletcher turned patiently to his son. 'Now then, what was the question again?'

But Raymond was now shaking his head faintly as he contemplated the new shelves. 'They don't look too secure to me,' he commented.

'Of course they are,' protested Fletcher. 'I took up carpentry inside.'

Raymond thumped his fist on the top shelf and, to Fletcher's gratification, the assemblage remained intact.

'There we are,' he said proudly.

But Raymond was still reluctant to bestow credit where credit was obviously due. 'Don't think they go in this room,' he said glumly.

'They will do,' Fletcher assured him, 'when they're personalised. A family photograph, an ornament, a piece of bric-à-brac.'

He glanced about and saw a suitable piece of bric-à-brac. He took up the small china dog from the mantelpiece and placed it on the top shelf. The bookcase promptly collapsed. Wonderful to tell, Raymond, for the first time since his dad's reappearance in the family home, smiled.

'Get out!' roared Fletcher.

Raymond stopped smiling. 'I didn't do nothing.'

'Of course you did,' insisted Fletcher. 'You weakened it. They weren't designed to be banged on. Any shelf will collapse if you go round banging it. Shouldn't go round banging things – and that goes for you too, Godber,' he shouted upstairs.

With which, he turned on his heel and stamped into the kitchen for his morning nosh. Ingrid provided it and then went upstairs to dress for work. Fletcher lingered over his coffee, engrossed in the sports page of *The Sun.* Ingrid in due course reappeared, dressed and made up for work.

'Well, I'm off then,' she announced. She cleared her throat

diplomatically. 'Er, Dad, if you've got a moment – '

Fletcher chuckled ironically. 'If *I've* got a moment – '

'Well, could you nip down to Cochrans and get a few things in?' The efficient girl thereupon handed him a shopping list and a five-pound note.

Fletcher nodded with mock eagerness. 'Oh, this has added a bit of excitement to my day. I can nip down to Cochrans and converse with that asthmatic twit.'

Ingrid, ignoring the irony, read the list over his shoulder. 'Tea bags. Golden Shred. Brussels sprouts. Mandarin oranges. Bananas. Scouring pads – oh, and I forgot – ' She reached over his shoulder and scribbled something at the bottom of the list. Fletcher peered at it.

'Is that shredded wheat?'

'Yeah.'

Fletcher shook his head. 'I don't like shredded wheat.'

Ingrid said brightly, 'Ah, but they got a special offer this month. Genuine Folk Art Watering Can Kits.'

'Oh, good,' enthused Fletcher, 'give me something to do this afternoon. I can come home and erect a watering can.'

Ingrid looked at him questioningly. 'You got to see your Probation Officer today, don't you?'

'Tomorrow,' grunted Fletcher.

Ingrid turned to leave and then turned back. She knew how her father was feeling. 'Dad,' she said encouragingly.

'What?'

Ingrid took hold of Fletcher's raised newspaper and gently eased it down so that she could talk to him without impediment, 'Dad, I know it's hard. I know what you're going through. But you knew it wasn't going to be easy. You mustn't let things get on top of you. You never have.'

Fletcher was touched by her concern. He sighed deeply. 'I never thought it was going to be this hard, gel. If I had a job – if I could feel useful – but with my record – '

But Ingrid cut him off in a no-nonsense tone of voice. 'Now, that's not true, dad. There's over a million unemployed in this country. There's boys what left Raymond's school two years ago who don't know anything else but a dole queue.'

Fletcher nodded sadly. 'It's just,' he pointed out, 'that I keep coming up against cynicism and mistrust everywhere, which in turn makes me more cynical, which is something I've always resisted. I goes in the park Tuesday. There's two youngsters five or six. I was helping them fix their model aeroplane. Mother comes racing up – if looks could kill I'd be dead and buried. Goes down the post office to get a postal order for me pools. They've got a fourpenny biro, *chained* to the wall.'

That's normal these days,' Ingrid insisted. 'They didn't do i because they saw you coming.'

'I'm not so sure,' returned Fletcher darkly. 'As soon as old Cochran at the corner shop saw me coming yesterday he whipped out that notice.'

'What notice?'

he one that says: "Do not ask for Credit as a Refusal often Offends". I only went in for a box of matches.'

'It's the mood of the country, dad, you got to get used to it. Been like that for a while. Of course, we had a brief respite for the Jubilee Celebrations, but that's behind us now.'

Fletcher shook his head despondently. 'Well, whatever it is, it's getting me down, I can tell you.'

Ingrid studied him. He looked downtrodden, nothing like the man she had known, with long gaps admittedly, all her life. Where was the energy, the cockiness, the ready jest which had always made her father the life and soul of any gathering? Ingrid's heart was touched.

'How's your sex drive, Dad?' she asked.

Fletcher looked affronted. 'What sort of question is that for a daughter to ask her father?'

'Perfectly healthy one. I don't think these things should be swept under the carpet no more.'

Fletcher shrugged wearily. 'Anyway, what's my sex drive got to do with anything?'

'Could be a great deal,' maintained Ingrid sagely, 'because I think your lack of it is symptomatic of your general malaise. You were always a man with a man's appetite.'

'Speaking of which,' said Fletcher, making a dispirited attempt at a jest, 'what happened to my boiled egg?'

But Ingrid would not be deflected. 'You know what I mean, dad. Here you are, with Mum gone, out of prison, and you ain't so much as looked at a woman.'

Fletcher snorted indignantly. 'You think I'd bring another woman into this house? I have some standards of decorum and decency, my gel! And I would not embarrass members of my family by consorting in this house with a member of the opposite sex.'

Ingrid shrugged indifferently. 'Don't know why you shouldn't. All the rest of us do.'

'Not Raymond, surely,' protested Fletcher. 'He hasn't got the energy – or the charm.'

'You'd be surprised,' insisted Ingrid. 'Girls like Raymond.'

Fletcher frowned incredulously. 'You can't be serious. What do they like about him – his National Health acne?'

'Still waters run deep,' said Ingrid, somewhat obscurely.

'Nothing very deep about a drip.'

But Ingrid said firmly, 'You can take it from me that Raymond has no problems in that direction. It's you I'm worried about. I think you're going through your mid-life crisis. Like what this article in *Cosmopolitan* said last week: "The Male Menopause: Cause and Effect".'

This seemed to Fletcher much too intimate a subject to discuss with his daughter. 'We'll have none of that language in this house,' he rebuked her sternly. 'You shock me, you do.'

But Ingrid remained unabashed. 'I'm not being rude. That's medical.'

'Medical matters *are* rude,' returned Fletcher.

Ingrid shook her head. 'You're so set in your ways.'

'I know! And I don't want any of this permissive liberated talk in my house. I'll tell you what my mid-life crisis is – do you want me to spell it out for you? I'm a forty-six year-old ex-lag, with no money, no prospects and as of now no wife. For the sake of my family I'm going straight. Which at my age, with my qualifications, means my future offers as much excitement as a wet Sunday afternoon in Merthyr Tydfil.'

The reference escaped Ingrid. 'Why Merthyr Tydfil?' she asked, puzzled.

'Why?' said Fletcher heartedly. 'They got more pubs than anywhere else in Britain! And they're all shut on Sundays!'

And to show that, as far as he was concerned, the discussion was concluded, he raised his paper once more and studied it fiercely. But Ingrid did not depart. She contemplated him for a moment, biting her lip. Then she opened her handbag, reached into it and withdrew another fiver.

'Dad – '

'What?' asked Fletcher, without raising his eyes.

Ingrid held out the note. 'Here, take this.'

Fletcher glanced up and then returned his attention to *The Sun*. 'You give me the money for the groceries already.'

But Ingrid shook her head and said tenderly, 'This is for you. Just to have something in your pocket, you know.'

Fletcher shook his head with haughty mien. 'I don't need a handout from my family, thank you, Ingrid.'

'You always took it from Mum,' the wise girl pointed out. 'I get plenty of tips, you see. That's one of the perks of being a manicurist. That and free nail varnish.'

Fletcher laid his paper aside once more. 'I appreciate the gesture, love, but – I ain't down to that yet – know what I mean?'

'All right then,' said Ingrid brightly, 'I'll leave it here – under our Jubilee tea caddy. In case you change your mind.' She slipped the fiver carefully under the tea caddy.

Fletcher shrugged. 'Suit yourself.'

Ingrid smiled and turned to leave. Then she glanced about.

None of the windows was open. Why had she shivered so fiercely? 'Dad,' she asked, 'have you done some of your "do-it-yourself" to that kitchen door?'

Fletcher brightened perceptibly. 'I have, as a matter of fact,' he admitted, 'I've fitted one of them draught excluders.'

'Thought you'd done something,' nodded Ingrid, 'because it's freezing in here.'

She turned and tripped off to work.

When he had done the shopping, Fletcher found that his craving for adventure had still not been fully satisfied. What could he do? A walk in the park? It was a bit cold for that. There was only one other alternative – at least until the boozers opened. He headed for Dante's 'caff'.

A few minutes later he pushed open the swing doors and entered. He glanced about. No, the company today would not consist of cabinet ministers and famous authors. No film stars or top executives met his gaze. There were, in fact, only two other people in the place at that moment. One was Perce, a milkman known casually to Fletcher, and the other was a young girl sitting near him.

Perce was engaged in counting his loot. His leather shoulder bag, full of loose change, lay on the table next to him and, in front of him, were little piles of pennies and halfpennies.

The unknown girl, clad in tatty jeans, an old sweater and an ex-army combat jacket, was warming her hands round a cup of Dante's tea. She looked as if, properly groomed, she might be quite pretty but her youthful face was set in an expression of mistrust and cunning. She made Fletcher think of a stray dog that you might consider petting but that would probably take your finger off if you tried it.

Dante, the Cockney Italian, greeted him. 'Hi, Fletch.'

'Less of the Italian bonhomie, Dante,' Fletcher reproved him jovially. 'Cup of tea, quick. And a Kit Kat.' He turned from the counter and surveyed the frowning milkman. 'Morning, Perce.'

'Shut up,' returned the purveyor of pintas without looking up, 'I'm doing me additions.'

Fletcher took the reproof in good part. 'You finished your round early,' he observed. 'Been giving your horse benzedrine, have you?'

'Haven't had a horse since you went in,' observed Perce.

Fletcher frowned in sympathy. 'Must be a hard life pulling that cart on your tod.'

'Don't be daft,' urged Perce. 'It's all electric now.'

'My word, an electric horse. Whatever next!'

Dante turned from his hissing boiler and said cheerfully, in stage Italian: 'One-a cuppa tea-a.'

'Thank you-a,' said Fletcher ironically.

'Help yourself to sugar,' said Dante in his normal cockney.

Fletcher turned to do so and, to his profound disgust, found the sugar spoon secured to a piece of string. 'Oh, look at this – sign of the times. Afraid I'm going to knock off your plastic spoon, are you, Dante?'

Dante frowned. 'What's wrong with you? You get out the bed the wrong end?'

'No,' sighed Fletcher, 'just wondering why I got out of bed in the first place.' He thoughtfully put five spoons of sugar in his tea. 'Here, you're about my age or thereabouts, ain't you?'

'I'm thirty-nine,' said Dante.

'You lying git,' protested Fletcher. 'You got a son of twenty-six.'

Dante shrugged modestly. 'In Sicily we come to manhood early.'

'Agreed, yes,' said Fletcher. 'But you're from Stoke Newington.'

Dante turned away haughtily. 'Listen, I'm a busy man.'

'Oh, really?' asked Fletcher, gazing pointedly about the almost empty room.

'All right,' said Dante. 'What do you want to ask me?'

'Not ask. Just want to try something.'

Fletcher opened his copy of *The Sun* and held it up for Dante to see. He held it open at page three which was adorned with a large picture of a girl who was exceptionally well endowed but grievously unprotected from the elements.

'Santa Madre!' exclaimed Dante, clutching his chest. *'Che culo! Dio mi perdoni!'*

Fletcher nodded. 'Yeah. I don't understand that, of course, but I get the gist. I used to react much the same way meself, especially in the nick. But today – I just skipped straight past her to the sports section. I was actually more interested in Orient's crippling injury list.'

Dante shook his head in disbelief. In the stage Italian which he could never resist for long, he asked: 'What are you saying me? I doan get it.'

'Precisely,' agreed Fletcher. 'I don't get it either. The point I'm trying to make is, I'm not sure I want it. Very worrying, I can tell you. Maybe my system's been ruined by that stuff they put in the prison tea. It's just beginning to work.'

He sighed deeply and turned from the counter. He was just in time to see the girl seated next to Perce swiftly insert her hand into the milkman's leather change bag. Dante, who had started smearing margarine on sliced bread, had not noticed. Fletcher moved swiftly across the floor and seated himself opposite the girl. Seeing him from the corner of her eye, she withdrew her hand as swiftly as she had inserted it. Fletcher could tell that she had failed to nick anything. He said to her calmly: 'Mind if I sit here, love?'

She gave him a look that was not brimful of human kindness but remained silent. Fletcher picked up Perce's bag and handed it to the calculating milkman. 'Here you are, Perce. Don't tempt me.'

Perce shook his head desperately and wailed: 'Come on, Fletch, now you've made me forget the total. I've got to start that whole column over.' But he took the bag and dropped it at his feet.

'There's gratitude for you,' Fletcher said breezily to the girl, but no reply was forthcoming. He tried again. 'It's freezing out. Want a fresh cup of tea or a bit of Kit Kat?'

At last she spoke. 'You sod.'

'Pardon?' asked Fletcher, genuinely surprised.

'You heard.'

Fletcher shook his head in disgust. 'I was hoping I heard wrong.'

'Well, you didn't.'

Fletcher contemplated her. She was a little alley cat, a runaway probably, and she didn't look much more than sixteen. 'How old are you,' he asked, 'to talk to me like that?'

'How old do I have to be to talk to you like that? Didn't ask you to sit here.'

'I sat here to save you from yourself,' he said solemnly.

She favoured him with a contemptuous smile.

'I can look after meself, thanks very much.'

Fletcher pushed his own cup of tea across the table towards her. 'Here,' he offered.

'What?'

'Get something hot inside you. Reckon you need it.'

The girl eyed the tea with obvious interest but then shook her head. 'No, I don't.'

Fletcher jerked his head towards Dante behind the counter. 'What you here for then – his Italian cuisine?'

The girl shrugged. 'I just come here, don't I?'

Fletcher leaned towards her and said softly, 'Look, if you're desperate enough to stick your hand in Percy's purse in broad daylight, you're in dire need of a cup of tea, so drink it.' He turned and called to the flamboyant proprietor. 'Two more cups of tea, Dante.'

'Ah,' exclaimed Dante, 'the last of the beeg spenders.'

Perce gave a sigh of satisfaction. 'All tallies,' he said proudly. 'That's me finished.'

'Back home to the wife, is it then, Perce?' asked Fletcher cheerfully. Out of the corner of his eye, he noticed that the girl was sipping the tea. 'Or you going round to that little number on Sycamore Crescent?'

'What little number?' asked Perce, looking mystified.

'The one whose old man's on a North Sea oil rig.'

Perce shook his head firmly. 'I'm not your common or garden randy milkman, thank you.'

Fletcher for some reason felt quite cheerful. He essayed a little pleasantry. 'I'm not talking about in the garden, or on the common. I'm talking about round the corner in Sycamore Crescent.

'I'm not that sort, either,' protested Perce, with mock indignation.

'You ain't?' asked Fletcher incredulously.

'No, I ain't.'

Fletcher shook his head wonderingly. 'You must have got what I've got then.'

Perce called to Dante. 'I'm round the betting shop, then,' and he rose, carefully shouldering his bag, and went to the counter where Dante handed him a pound note and a slip. The gambling milkman turned back to Fletcher. 'You want anything on, Fletch? I'd try Arctic Lady in the fourth at Kempton.'

Fletcher shook his head piously. 'No, thank you. "Gambling is the child of avarice and the father of sin." George Washington said that – or was it Eric Catchpole?'

'Who's Eric Catchpole?' asked Perce.

'Philosopher and wit,' explained Fletcher. 'Used to play left back for Brentford. He was also the man who said: "Show me a milkman in high heels and I'll show you a dairy queen".'

Fletcher was gratified to find that this little sally succeeded in extracting appreciative sniggers from both Perce and Dante. Then Perce moved towards the exit. Fletcher called after him.

'Mind how you go, Perce. Tara.'

Dante arrived with the two fresh cups of tea. 'Is sugared,' he promised.

Fletcher accepted the cups suspiciously. '*Just* sugar, I trust. I wouldn't put it past that probation officer to be keeping up the treatment.' He turned his attention back to the hard-eyed girl. 'Good one that – did you get it? Milkman in high heels – dairy queen – ' but no glimmer of appreciation showed on her face. 'Oh well – never mind.'

'Life and soul of the party, aren't you,' she said bitterly.

Fletcher sighed. 'I'm not anything.'

'Like a rabbit though, don't you?'

Fletcher nodded. 'I do have a more highly-developed conversational sense than what yourself does, obviously.'

'I can't pay for this tea,' she announced.

'I didn't think you could,' returned Fletcher. He looked her up and down. Her canvas sneakers were worn and there was mud on the cuffs of her jeans. 'Sleeping rough, are you?'

'What if I am?'

'Runaway, are you?'

'What if I am?'

'Not from round here?'

'What if I'm not?' she said, breaking the run.

Fletcher sighed in exasperation. 'Oh blimey! Look, I ain't the law. I ain't the probation service. I ain't health and welfare and I ain't the vicar.'

'So?'

'So you can relax, girl, is all I'm saying. Look at you. You're as taut as a fiddle-string. On drugs, are you? Uppers, is it?'

The girl said grimly, 'Bleeding wish I was.'

Fletcher nodded in satisfaction. 'Ah, we have found a point of contact.'

A little speculative gleam appeared in the girl's eyes. 'Why?' she asked. 'You got some?'

Fletcher smiled. 'No.'

'Well, what's your game then?' she asked irritably. 'I mean, you come over, you sit down. I didn't ask. Tell me what you're not – well, what are you, a dirty old man? Buy me a chocolate bar, get a quick touch-up?'

Fletcher shook his head regretfully. 'You are a dirty little girl,' he observed, 'and in more ways than one.'

'You don't know me,' protested the girl.

'I know you need a bath. What's your name?'

'Margaret Thatcher!' she returned sarcastically.

Fletcher took it lightly. 'Nice to meet you, Margaret. Norman Fletcher, commonly known as Fletch.'

The girl, uncertain as to Fletcher's degree of political sophistication, confessed, 'I was joking.'

'Oh?' said Fletcher, as if with genuine interest.

The girl burst out scornfully, 'Don't you know who Margaret Thatcher is? You stupid or something?'

Fletcher cocked his head thoughtfully. 'Who is she then?'

The girl, in spite of herself, leaned forward eagerly. It was not often she found herself in a position to teach another. 'She's the government, isn't she? One of that lot. Ain't you seen her on the telly with her hair-dos?'

Fletcher shook his head positively. The time had come to initiate a true conversation. 'She's not the government,' he explained. 'She is, in fact, the leader of Her Majesty's opposition.'

The girl drew back and pondered this. Then she said: 'Same thing, isn't it? MPs.' She paused and then added reproachfully, 'You said you didn't know her.'

'That was to stimulate a political debate.'

In spite of herself the girl smiled a twisted little smile. 'You don't half talk funny.'

'How old are you?' asked Fletcher aimiably.

'Thirty-six,' she said mockingly.

'You look older,' returned Fletcher.

Before the girl could think up a smart-alecky reply, the café door swung open and a blue uniform entered. There was a man inside it but it was the menacing costume that caused the girl to shrink quickly to one side, trying to conceal herself from view. Fletcher guessed at the reason without needing to see the new arrival.

'You are a runaway, right?' he said quietly. 'Look, I'm not going to turn you in. But I reckon you can do with a hot bath and some fresh clothes. I only live round the corner and I've got two daughters with a wardrobe that's permanently obsolescent. Now that's an offer you're in no state to refuse.'

Fletcher watched the girl's eyes as they tracked the policeman, who had entered simply to buy cigarettes, moving from the counter back to the door and then out. When the limb of the law was no longer visible, she looked back at Fletcher, shrugged wearily and said: 'Okay, then.'

Fletcher grinned, rose and went to the counter to pay Dante. He found the Italian leering knowingly at him. 'Eh, Fletcher – it din take you long!'

'What didn't?' asked Fletcher innocently.

Dante chuckled evilly. 'To get your urges back – '

Fletcher swung at him playfully. Then he and the girl left together and walked, in almost unbroken silence, back to his house. Once they had reached it, he ran her a bath and left her with some of Ingrid's cast-offs in the bathroom. He went down to the kitchen and made soup. The bath did not occupy the girl long. The soup had only just begun to boil when, with wet hair, she wandered in, almost invisible in Ingrid's bathrobe.

'Here we are then,' said Fletcher, pouring the soup and setting it in front of her.

'Water wasn't very hot,' she complained.

But Fletcher was determined to remain affable. 'Well, the soup is,' he promised. 'Get it down you.'

She took an experimental sip and exclaimed crossly: 'Gawd, it is an' all. I've burnt my bleeding tongue.'

Fletcher ignored this. 'Find yourself some clothes up there, did you?'

She shrugged. 'Don't really fit me.'

'They weren't bought for you, were they?'

She cautiously took another sip of soup. 'What's your name again?' she asked.

'Fletch.'

'My name's Penny,' she informed him at long last.

He was pleased. The barriers were beginning to fall. 'Good. So where you from then, Penny?'

'I used to live in Camberwell. It's all right there. I mean, I always lived there. That's where all me mates are. Then me mum and Arthur moved to Portsmouth.'

Fletcher eased the bread towards her. 'Who's Arthur?' he asked.

'Bloke what she lives with. He's all right. Just that he works in Portsmouth. There's nothing to do there.'

Fletcher shrugged. 'Handy for the Isle of Wight though.'

'I just left,' explained Penny. 'I was going to stay with this friend of mine – Terry. He's great, Terry. Well – he's a bit mad like, but he's all right. He don't give a monkey's, Terry, about anything. You'd like him.'

'I doubt it,' said Fletcher feelingly. 'One of these "punks", is he?'

'He is not!' declared Penny. 'He hates the punks.'

Fletcher nodded. 'Oh, we have something in common then.'

'That's why they sent him away, because he duffed three of them up behind Peckham Odeon.'

'Charming,' commented Fletcher. 'So what are your plans now then?'

Penny looked glum. 'Well, I can't hang around Camberwell. The cops know me there. And I'm on probation.'

It was Fletcher's turn to look glum. The word 'probation' always had that effect on him. 'Oh yes?'

'But I had this other friend who lives round here called Pauline Slocum. Do you know her?'

Fletcher shook his head.

'She may have moved,' said Penny vaguely. 'Don't know what I'll do next.'

'Well, I suggest after you've had something to eat you get some kip.'

A knowing light sprang into the waif's eyes. 'What, with you?' she asked.

'Pardon?' asked Fletcher incredulously. Penny smiled her twisted smile. 'Well, don't you fancy me? It's all right. I don't mind.'

Fletcher closed his eyes for a moment. But no – anger would undo everything he'd achieved so far. He shook his head and tried to explain. 'Now listen, there seems to be a prevalent attitude in this country which is to view everything I do in the worst possible light. I didn't ask you back for that! But I'll tell you why I did, shall I? I saw in you someone who was bound on the same course I took.'

'How do you mean?' asked Penny, puzzled.

'You're on probation, aren't you? Well, I'm on parole. On top of which I've spent eleven years of my life in the nick. Even if I hadn't seen you with your hand in Percy's purse, I'd have still known what you was all about. And I know that all the social workers and the magistrates of this world can't tell you nothing. But maybe you'll listen to the words of an old lag like me.'

Penny looked disgruntled. 'All right, keep your shirt on.'

'I certainly will with you around, young lady,' Fletcher returned feelingly.

Penny shook her head wearily and explained. 'I only said what I did because I can't pay for the food and the clothes and that.'

'Finish your soup,' ordered Fletcher.

But Penny pushed it away. 'Don't like tomato.'

Outraged, Fletcher exclaimed: 'Gawd, I can see why people get discouraged trying to help people. Think I'll leave it off after you.'

Penny shrugged. 'I just don't like tomato.'

It was Fletcher's turn to be sarcastic. 'I'm very sorry. I shall order a case of mock turtle from Fortnums for your dinner.'

But his brand of sarcasm was beyond the girl. 'Oxtail,' she said. 'I quite like oxtail.'

'Just get some sleep, will you? Use my room, upstairs, second on the left.'

Penny rose and moved to the door. Then she paused. Fletcher observed her, wondering what new objection she was about to make. For a long moment, she did not move. Then she turned slowly and obviously with a great effort said: 'Thanks.' Then she turned again and slouched out of the kitchen.

That evening, Ingrid returned from work to find Fletcher seated at the kitchen table, frowning in perplexity at the back of a cereal packet. On the table in front of him were some oddly-shaped bits of coloured plastic.

'Hello, Dad,' she carolled cheerfully.

'I can't do this,' said Fletcher in mournful reply.

'Do what?' asked Ingrid, removing her coat.

'I'm trying to make a racing car.'

Ingrid looked distressed. She hurried to the table and seized the packet.

'Oh, you haven't gone and done Raymond's racing car, have you? That's the only reason we get that cereal. He's collecting the set. He'll be ever so cross.'

Fletcher shrugged irritably. Ingrid, shaking her head, switched on the radio which promptly began to belt out a chart-topping favourite. Matching her voice to the competition, she asked: 'So? What have you done today?'

His fingers in his ears, Fletcher urged: 'Turn that racket off.'

'What?' bawled Ingrid.

Fletcher tried harder. 'Turn that racket off!' he roared.

'Why? I like it,' thundered Ingrid.

Fletcher rose and switched off the wireless. To assuage Ingrid's wrath, he explained: 'There's someone asleep upstairs.'

Her look of anger was replaced by one of surprise. She glanced at the ceiling. 'Who?' she asked.

'Girl I met,' explained Fletcher.

'What?' exclaimed Ingrid incredulously.

'Girl I met. Down Dante's caff. Name's Penny. She's – '

But Ingrid was no longer listening. 'Now, look here, Dad,' she began, 'when I said what I said this morning, I didn't think you'd take it so literal, so quick.'

'Leave it off, Ingrid,' Fletcher urged wearily. 'She's only sixteen. She's in trouble. She needs a place. I brought her home and gave her a bath and a bed.'

Ingrid's eyes widened. In a horrified tone she exclaimed: 'You give her a bath!'

'I didn't *give* her a bath,' Fletcher clarified irritably. 'I loaned her the facilities. I was trying to help someone. God knows I've got nothing better to do. More worthwhile than making plastic racing cars and watering cans, isn't it?'

Ingrid considered this explanation for a moment in silence. Then she asked: 'What's she like?'

Fletcher shrugged. 'Waif and stray, that's what she is. Little alley cat.'

'Did anyone see you bring her here?'

'I dunno – why?'

'Well – ' said Ingrid uneasily, 'what might they have thought?'

Fletcher shook his head disdainfully. 'Same as what you thought. I don't give a rat's.'

'You've got to be very careful in your position though, Dad,' she pointed out, accurately enough.

While this conversation proceeded, a figure entered the living-room next door. It was Penny, now clad in a pair of Ingrid's jeans and a sweater under her old army combat jacket. She moved towards the kitchen and then paused to listen. She heard Ingrid say: 'What do you intend to do about her?'

'I'd like to think I could make her see sense,' Fletcher proclaimed. 'I'd like to think that she'll go back to her mum voluntary.'

There was a moment's silence. Penny glanced about the living-room. Her eyes focused on Ingrid's handbag laying on the table. She did not move. Ingrid's voice resumed: 'Shouldn't you just hand her over to the authorities?'

'Worst thing you could do,' protested Fletcher. 'I'd be betraying her trust. If you don't show people trust, how are they ever going to learn it?'

Penny moved silently to the table. She picked up Ingrid's handbag, turned and left the room.

At about the hour of noon, a week after these melancholy events, Fletcher, casually dressed in pyjama jacket and out-door trousers, sat at the kitchen table putting the finishing touches to a nice plastic watering can. Ingrid, flouting the family tradition of casual dress about the house, entered wearing a very smart street outfit. She paused on seeing her father and shook her head irritably.

'Dad, come on,' she urged. 'It's twelve o'clock and you're still not dressed.'

Fletcher glanced at her moodily. 'I'm not going anywhere, am I?'

'It's Saturday,' urged Ingrid.

But the news seemed to have little effect on Fletcher's spirits. 'Is it?' he asked dully.

'It's a lovely sunny day,' she pursued. 'Why don't you go to the match?'

'They'll lose,' grunted Fletcher.

Ingrid stamped her foot slightly. 'Dad, I'm not having this! For a week now you've sat around the house, morose and depressed. It was me what lost my handbag, not you.'

Fletcher smiled mournfully. 'I lost more than that, Ingrid.

I lost my fundamental belief in mankind. And that certainly ain't going to be restored by seeing Orient play Mansfield Town.'

'Dad,' said Ingrid sternly, 'you got to start doing something with your life.'

'Why?' asked Fletcher. 'It'll only go wrong. Always has, always will.'

'That's not true,' proclaimed Ingrid stoutly. She glanced about for something to support the claim and her eyes fell on the watering can. She picked it up lovingly. 'You made this, didn't you? I mean, it's not easy putting one of these together. Lovely job you done. I'm going to christen it now. I'm going to water the geraniums.'

Fletcher watched with dull interest as she took the watering can to the sink and began to fill it. But, alas, the experiment was not a one hundred per cent success. As fast as water fell into the can it jetted out again in various directions. The result was attractive but not functional. Ingrid stared at it in dismay. To her relief, the doorbell rang.

'Oh?' she asked brightly, 'is that the door?'

'No,' said Fletcher, 'it's the window.'

Ingrid favoured him with a withering look before hurrying out of the kitchen in the direction of the front door. Fletcher rose, crossed to the sink, picked up the now-empty watering can, turned, crossed to the waste bin and, with an expression of distaste, dropped it in. Ingrid, looking flustered, returned.

'Dad, it's – er – come through – ' the last words were spoken to someone who was clearly behind her. And that someone took the advice.

A man in his late thirties, looking embarrassed and clad in a cheap but quite smart suit, entered. He looked at Fletcher awkwardly and said: 'Er – my name's Arthur Boyle,' and then, in his turn, he turned and spoke to someone behind him. 'Come in here.'

And lo! there entered from the corridor the girl, Penny,

looking as scruffy as ever. She was still clad in Ingrid's cast-offs but she looked as if, for the past week, she had employed them for sliding down council rubbish tips. She gave Fletcher a quick glance and then turned her attention to the décor of the kitchen. The man stammered:

'I'm Penny's – well, not her dad, like, but next best thing.'

Fletcher, who had by now come to grips with the situation, nodded. 'Oh, right. Arthur – that's what she said.'

Arthur swallowed and looked even more uncomfortable. 'Could I have a word in private, like?'

Fletcher shrugged. 'I suppose so.'

Arthur turned to his step-daughter. 'You wait here,' he instructed her. She gave a barely-perceptible shrug.

Fletcher led the way into the living-room. Arthur and Ingrid followed him, the latter closing the door after her, to secure privacy. Arthur held something up and offered it to Fletcher. 'Believe this is yours,' he suggested.

Fletcher recognised it as Ingrid's handbag. Something inside him gave a little jump. But he shook his head. 'Not mine, mate. Belongs to my daughter.'

He took the bag and handed it to Ingrid who opened it and began to check the contents. Arthur went on: 'I got the address from your driving licence. I expect there's some cash missing. Let me know how much and I'll make it up to you.'

Fletcher asked cautiously: 'Did the law nab her?'

Arthur shook his head. 'No. She rang us up. Reversed the charges, of course. So I drove up and fetched her.' He swallowed awkwardly and then resumed, 'Listen, I know what you did –'

Fletcher was instantly on the defensive. 'What does she say I did?' he asked challengingly.

Arthur looked puzzled. 'What? She said you tried to help. So I just wanted to say thanks.'

'Oh,' said Fletcher. To his surprise, he felt himself flushing. To his still greater surprise, he found that he was enjoying it.

'I mean,' Arthur struggled with his message, 'if there was a few more people like you – well – who knows what?'

Fletcher gulped. 'Yuh, well – '

'She's a bit of a tearaway, I'm afraid,' Arthur apologised. 'Still, she did make the phone call – thanks to you.'

Fletcher could think of no better response than to repeat: 'Yuh – well – '

Arthur smiled nervously. 'I suppose it's down to her mum and me now.'

Ingrid asked politely, 'Would you like a cup of tea?'

And Fletcher added hastily, 'Yeah – or a beer?'

Arthur shook his head. 'No, I'd best be off. The traffic and that.' He was not a man used to expressing his emotions and the effort had exhausted him. He walked towards the door, calling to Penny, 'Come on.'

The girl, looking as enigmatic as ever, slouched into the room, as Ingrid followed him out, saying, 'I'll see you to the door.'

'All right, girl?' asked Fletcher. 'I'm glad you thought better of it. So it's back to Portsmouth, is it?'

'Yes – suppose so,' said Penny vaguely.

'Nice down there,' opined Fletcher. 'Healthy. Keep away from the sailors.'

'I can look after myself.'

'So you said.' He paused. 'Any rate, thanks for bringing Ingrid's bag back.'

'I can't help pinching things,' she said. 'When I see 'em I take 'em. First thing I've ever given back.'

'Well, that's a good start. No harm done. You took it, you returned it. Just think of it as a library book.'

'I pinch them as well.'

'Oh dear, do you? I could do with a few of them to put on my new shelves over the sideboard – only they're under the sideboard at the moment.' The girl looked at him, puzzled. 'Well, off you go then.'

Fletcher watched her out of the room. It was silly, the

way he felt. She was just a little tearaway. There was no point in concerning himself with her. But somehow when he turned and went back into the kitchen, he found that he was whistling. A moment later, Ingrid joined him.

'Well!' she exclaimed.

'Well what?' asked Fletcher, trying to sound indifferent.

But Ingrid's face was wreathed in smiles. 'Wasn't in vain then, was it? All that "If I can help somebody stuff"? Worked, didn't it?'

Fletcher said modestly, 'I must admit it's done something to restore my faith in human nature. Maybe I will go to the match. After this, who knows, they could just scrape a point.'

Ingrid smiled at him warmly. 'Bucked you up, hasn't it?'

Fletcher smiled. 'I have to admit it has, gel. It's a good feeling. Missionaries must feel like this. I mean, they must sometimes feel like jacking it in. All them years in the jungle with the heat and the tsetse flies. Then one day a bunch of young headhunters walk in, chuck down their spears and say, "We want to learn the catechism".'

Ingrid nodded wisely. 'Makes it all worthwhile.'

'Then they eat them. No – I'm only joking.' He glanced down at his shabby attire. 'I'm going to take a bath, have a shave, clean shirt – and I think this calls for a little celebration.'

Ingrid nodded approvingly. 'Do you good.'

Fletcher said ponderously: 'I will now accept your offer of a free handout, and I shall take you and your young man and Raymond and whoever down the White Hart tonight. Where did you put that fiver last week?'

'Under the tea caddy,' said Ingrid.

Fletcher marched over to it and lifted it. 'Naffing hell!' he exclaimed.

'What?' asked Ingrid surprised.

'She took the bleeding fiver!'

Going To Work

Norman Stanley Fletcher stood in a grey London street and contemplated the grey building that housed the offices of the Inner London Probation and After-Care Service. He sighed deeply, flicked his fag-end into the gutter and strode forwards through the swinging doors. He made his way past the court and along to the office of Mrs Chapman, his personal probation officer. He was just about to knock on the door when it opened and a pale, shifty-eyed man emerged. Fletcher stood back to let him pass and then, with a brief tap, pressed forwards into the office. Mrs Chapman rose to her feet as he entered. Fletcher noticed that she frowned slightly as if she might have relished a slightly longer gap between clients. But she rallied and said pleasantly: 'Norman, come in. Cup of tea?'

Fletcher did not appear to have heard her. He nodded towards the door through which he had just entered and remarked: 'You got your work cut out with him.'

'Who?' Mrs Chapman poured two cups of tea.

'Ackroyd.'

'Oh? Do you know him?'

Fletcher smiled bitterly. 'Course I do.' He seated himself before the desk. 'We was sat out there for an hour last week. He's not right in the head, he isn't.'

Mrs Chapman frowned again. She did not approve of her customers commenting on each other. 'How do you mean?' she asked tightly.

Fletcher shook his head in disgust. 'He told me – put it on the nose. Four o'clock, Sedgefield. Lady of the Lake. Bleeding horse fell at the water jump.'

Mrs Chapman was quick to seize the opportunity for a

professional reproach. 'So you have enough money to fritter on horses, do you?'

Fletcher realised that he'd blundered. But he was expert at wriggling out of official traps. He protested indignantly. 'I didn't say I had bet on the horse.' He raised his eyes piously towards the ceiling. 'Heaven forbid! I was just saying his advice was idiotic. What's he done?'

'None of your business,' snapped Mrs Chapman.

Fletcher nodded ironically. 'I thought you and I were supposed to have a relationship of trust and confidence.'

'Not when it comes to breaking the confidence of one of my other clients.'

Fletcher shrugged haughtily. 'Oh, I see. Right you are. Please yourself. Don't matter because I'll find out soon enough down the Black Lion.'

Again Mrs Chapman pounced. 'So you have enough money to fritter on drink, do you?'

But Fletcher went on smoothly. 'I only pop into the Black Lion because they sell my favourite brand of potato crisp. Smoky Bacon flavour. Seven pee a packet. I admit it *is* wildly extravagant but then you only live once.'

Mrs Chapman said pointedly, 'There's one thing I can say for our departed friend. He's managed to hold down a job for eleven weeks now.'

Fletcher sighed. He knew probation officers. Certainly he knew them. It sometimes seemed to him that he'd spent as much time in their dreary offices as he had in prison cells. But he could never accustom himself to their single-minded obsession with work. Still, he couldn't afford to antagonise Mrs Chapman. He asked, with an air of keen interest: 'What job then?'

'It doesn't matter what job –'

'Yes, it does. What job's he doing?'

Trying to make it sound like an impressive appointment, Mrs Chapman said enthusiastically: 'He's an assistant park keeper.'

Fletcher smiled knowingly. 'Well, yes, that is a feather in his cap. And he's obviously got the right qualifications. He's probably got a university degree. I mean, it takes a keen mind to oil swings and check the radius of the holes on the putting green once a week!

'No, not a keen mind, Norman! Just the willingness and the guts to stick at what you're offered.'

She was a smart one all right. She had the indispensable probation officer's knack of turning everything into either a reproach or an exhortation. But Fletcher was no novice at these encounters either. He sipped his tea and frowned critically.

'Not sugared, is it?'

'It's not stirred.'

'Oh?' He reached forwards for her ball-point pen, aware that it was a provocative act but also confident that it would distract her mind from the Holy Topic for a moment or two. He stirred his tea with the pen and glanced about inquiringly. 'Got any of those Lincoln Creams left?'

Mrs Chapman was a veteran of these fencing matches with idle old lags. Realising she'd been outmanoeuvred, she nodded, reached down and withdrew a packet from the lower drawer of her desk. But the packet contained a less succulent type of biscuit than the ones Fletcher had specified. As she placed them in front of him, she said earnestly: 'Can I say something to you, Norman?'

Swiftly he deflected her. 'These aren't Lincoln Creams. They're Osbornes.' But he took one and dipped it in his tea.

'You have a very low opinion of other people,' Mrs Chapman suggested.

'No, I don't. I just have a low opinion of Osbornes.'

Mrs Chapman shook her head irritably but maintained the earnest, sincere note in her voice. It came from Chapter Three in the Probation Officers' Handbook. 'You don't really believe in me. You don't think I *really* care about your problem.'

Sensing that the tide had turned in his favour, Fletcher said breezily: 'Not down to you, love. Down to me. I mean with all the best intentions in the world, you're a very overworked young lady. You got – what is it? – forty clients? And that means I occupy a fortieth of your time. Even less when you think some of them take more than their share. Like that bloke last week, who climbed up Centre Point and threatened to plummet into Charing Cross Road.'

Mrs Chapman, aware that she'd lost the initiative, said firmly: 'I do not give priority to anyone.'

But Fletcher, confident now in his handling of the situation, pretended not to hear. Gazing earnestly out of the window, as if seeking guidance, he mused: 'How did he get up there? That's what puzzles me. With all that security and that. Course, we know how he come down.' Fletcher shook his head mournfully. 'Tragic.'

Mrs Chapman, realising that she'd lost the round on points, reached for her cigarette packet. Fletcher gave a disapproving 'tisk'.

'You smoke too much,' he said critically.

Mrs Chapman lit her gasper and blew out a comforting plume of toxic blue smoke. She had the good grace to admit: 'I know.'

Fletcher leaned towards her. Good move that, if you picked your moment. It reversed the roles. 'Your old man got a job yet?' he asked.

Mrs Chapman shook her head. 'Not yet.'

Fletcher nodded in satisfaction and said earnestly: 'Now that *is* tragic, because he's qualified – got degrees and that. You'd be better off trying to place him than me.'

Mrs Chapman said primly, 'I'm not paid to handle his problem.'

Here Fletcher made a tactical error. Having diverted the conversation from himself with great success, he now allowed his real feelings to get the better of him. He tapped his right temple and said earnestly: 'My problems are all up here.

You say I've got a low opinion of people? Well, I just don't believe they're going to do you any favours. And why should they?'

Mrs Chapman was quick to exploit the opening. 'Would you rather still be doing porridge?'

Fletcher sighed, aware that he had blundered. 'No, but – at least when you were doing porridge you had a goal. It was called "getting out". Kept you going, that did. Sufficient unto itself. But when you're out it's a bit of a letdown, you see.'

Mrs Chapman (Chapter Five of the Handbook) said encouragingly: 'You've coped with it before – it's not the first time you've come out.'

Fletcher said, with feeling: 'Yeah, but this is the first time I've gone straight, isn't it? Previous, I'd always been planning my next bit of skullduggery. I had a purpose in life then. Not to get caught. Even if you didn't do nothing for a while, there was the thought of that jackpot round the corner.' He smiled wistfully as nostalgic memories flooded through his mind. He continued reverently: 'Those cosy evenings round the kitchen table. Me and the lads, a few bottles of pale ale, fish and chips and dinky toys.'

Mrs Chapman was surprised. She had heard many bizarre confessions from many hard men. But dinky toys? Knowing that it was tactically undesirable, she still couldn't prevent herself from asking: 'What were the dinky toys for?'

Fletcher smiled patronisingly. 'Well, you know – one for the getaway car, one for the wages van –'

'Oh, come on,' chided Mrs Chapman, who knew her customers' form, 'you were never in that league.'

'True, but – the planning, see? Pipe dreams, maybe, but they kept you going.'

Mrs Chapman, conscious that time was passing and the purpose of the interview remained unfulfilled, made a determined effort to regain control. She said firmly: 'Look, you have more resilience than most and I'm sure you can hold down a job if I can find one. Now, I've already been in touch with some of our Voluntary Associates – '

Alarmed, Fletcher tried to ward off the obsessive subject. 'Oh, don't bother. I know they mean well. But you know what these philanthropop – philanthropip – these do-gooders are like. They all live in Hampstead, read the *Guardian* and support abortion law reform.'

But Mrs Chapman was not to be deterred. 'That's a very sweeping and stupid generalisation about a group of people who want to help – and *do* help – people like you to help yourself.'

Fletcher nodded ironically. 'Oh, yeah. They helped old Nosher Kelly to help himself. He helped himself to two of their office typewriters. I bet they'd have liked to call him a few names after that. They couldn't, though, because he'd pinched the swear-box and all.'

'All right, Fletcher, what's your alternative? Would you rather sit on your backside round the kitchen table, playing with dinky toys?'

Fletcher shook his head sombrely. 'No, don't want that. I'm nothing if not realistic. Even when I had me pipe dreams, there was a point where I'd say to meself – come on, Fletch.'

Mrs Chapman pursued her advantage. 'I understand your problems. You've decided to take a certain route in life and you've come up against a No Entry sign. You feel impotent.'

Purely for form, Fletcher grunted: 'Leave my sex life out of this.'

'As you know, I'm not talking about sex. I'm talking about work. But the two things *are* comparable. You feel impotent because you're not functioning as a man. And the best thing I can do for you is to fix you up with a good solid job.'

Fletcher, reasonably confident that she hadn't one to offer him on the spot, smiled wryly and rose. He spoke his parting shot over his shoulder. 'If the choice is mine, I'd sooner have a bit of the other.'

But he'd underestimated his fairy godmother. Before he reached the door, a firm voice said: 'Fletcher, don't you want to know what it is?'

Thus it came about that, a couple of hours later, Norman Stanley Fletcher stood disconsolately in a grey London street peering across it at a very different kind of building from the one that housed the probation office. It was, in fact, a small hotel and it was situated in a street of once-attractive family houses which had by now been mostly converted into similar hotels. It was the kind of place patronised by commercial travellers and low-budget tourists. But Norman Stanley Fletcher was certainly not there for a holiday. He sighed very deeply, crossed the street, and entered the lobby.

He glanced about. He saw a reception desk and behind it a small room containing a desk, typewriter and a little switchboard. Opposite the desk was a recess holding a tiny bar and a few chairs and tables. On the walls were theatre playbills and also a map of London equipped with buttons and lights to indicate museums, underground stations and so forth. There was a small, automatic lift beyond the reception desk. But the thing that captured most of Fletcher's attention was a young woman, who was installed behind the reception desk and who was eyeing him with a critical, even – Fletcher could not help feeling – a disapproving air.

As he approached her humbly, she said firmly: 'Sorry, we have no rooms.'

Fletcher stopped and gulped. 'Pardon?'

In a distant, professional tone of voice she continued: 'I suggest you try the Ilfracombe two doors down, or failing that, the Sussex in Praed Street.'

Fletcher edged right up to the desk. 'I'm not looking for accommodation, young lady,' he explained. 'I'm looking for Mr McEwan, the owner.'

'Why?' asked the receptionist crisply.

Fletcher gathered his dignity about him. 'I think that's between him and me.'

'D'you have an appointment, like?'

That 'like' went some way towards humanising her. Feeling a little more confident, Fletcher nodded. 'Yeah. Name's Fletcher. It's about a position.'

Her eyebrows shot up. 'Oh, the night porter's job.'

'The term used was Night Security Officer,' Fletcher countered firmly.

She nodded. 'That's right – porter. Just a minute.'

There was a new claim on her attention. Into the small lobby from the stairs had come two young people equipped with rucksacks and cameras and instantly recognisable as foreign tourists. The young man's accent established him as North American.

'Excuse me,' he said to the receptionist 'How would we get to Covent Garden?'

Fletcher spotted a chance to show his mettle. He instantly replied: 'Paddington. Bakerloo line to Piccadilly Circus. Change to Piccadilly Line – Covent Garden.'

The young man echoed uncertainly: 'Oh . . . change at Picadilly Circus – ?'

Fletcher nodded. 'To the Piccadilly Line. That's it. Leicester Square, Covent Garden.'

The young woman smiled and, also with a transatlantic accent, said: 'Thank you.'

'Americans, are you?' asked Fletcher politely, while the receptionist watched narrowly.

The young man corrected him. 'Canadian.'

And his wife, or girl friend, amplified. 'Toronto.'

'Must be wonderful,' enthused Fletcher. 'All that scenic grandeur. The great plains, the Rockies at dawn, ice hockey in the evening.'

The young man looked uncertain but contented himself with also saying: 'Thank you.'

'Goodbye,' said the girl, and they started to leave.

But Fletcher was enjoying himself. Maybe there was something to be said for the hotel world after all. You got to meet people. He called after them expansively. 'You'll enjoy Covent Garden. Fresh fruit and veg. Best in the world.'

They did not respond but the receptionist, with a disdinct edge to her voice, affirmed: 'The market isn't in Covent Garden any more.'

Startled, Fletcher exclaimed: 'What?'

'It's in Nine Elms – Battersea. Where have you been the last few years?'

'Canada,' muttered Fletcher.

At that moment a thin, nervous-looking man arrived in the lobby. The receptionist immediately spoke to him. 'Mr McEwan, this man says he's got an appointment with you.'

The proprietor of the Studleigh Hotel looked at Fletcher with interest and Fletcher looked back, reassured by what he saw. This McEwan seemed a mild-natured fellow.

'Mr – ah – Fletcher, is it?' McEwan asked.

'Yes.'

'Please, come through.'

And McEwan led the way past the reception desk into his little office. When they were both inside, he closed the door to secure privacy. He shivered. 'Brrr. It's bitter out.'

In spite of the Scottish name, McEwan did not, Fletcher noted with approval, have even a hint of that barbaric accent. 'Mind you, it's pretty parky in here, ain't it?' he said with scant grace.

McEwan glanced about helplessly. He said: 'I suppose I could put that gas fire on, but you see I'm in and out all morning. I've got a cardigan in here somewhere.'

Fletcher shook his head dismissively. 'Don't bother, I'm used to the cold. Probably wouldn't fit me anyhow.'

McEwan looked taken aback. 'I meant for me. I feel the cold more than most. I spent my early years in Africa – Nyasaland as we called it in those days. Of course, it's now Malawi.'

Fletcher grunted.

'It's all change, isn't it? Covent Garden's in Battersea now.'

McEwan, who had been rummaging fitfully at his desk, now produced from it a piece of paper. He studied it briefly. 'Yes. Now, I've spoken to Mrs Chapman and, as she probably told you, I help out the Probation Service – when I can – on a voluntary basis.'

Fletcher nodded encouragingly. 'Oh yes. Where would we be without you lot?' And he concluded, with some effort, 'Sir?'

McEwan confided: 'A lot of people, you know, think I'm asking for trouble, quite frankly. But I've never had cause to regret – except on two unfortunate occasions.'

'Oh dear,' sympathised Fletcher. Then he said earnestly, 'Well, don't worry sir, I won't let you down. Should you see fit.'

McEwan eyed Fletcher cautiously. 'I may be old-fashioned in this day and age, but I like to give my fellow man the benefit of the doubt. Call it instinct, call it experience, but I'm generally able to assess a man. It was the same in Africa. I had to hire natives, fresh from the bush. And basically I had to judge at a glance whether these chappies were the sort who would do an honest day's work or run off with your livestock. Well, I never had cause to regret – except on two unfortunate occasions.'

Fletcher said blandly, 'I can assure you, sir, if you give me the break I so badly need, I shall not run off with your livestock.'

For a moment, McEwan looked doubtful but then the twinkle in Fletcher's eye reassured him. He smiled and even ran to a little chuckle that collided with a sniff and petered out a trifle dismally. Unexpectedly, he swung round and extended a finger towards the far wall.

'See that?' he asked.

Fletcher gazed along the finger. 'What?'

'That. A wall safe.'

Fletcher perceived the implications of what McEwan was saying and was not specially chuffed by them. He sighed. 'Oh, so it is, yeah.'

McEwan pointed in a different direction. 'The keys for it are in that drawer there.'

'Are they?' asked Fletcher without much feeling.

'In that very drawer. And they'll be there every night when you're here. On your own. Not that a man with your experience would probably need keys. Clickety click, open sesame, what?'

Fletcher sighed again and nodded. 'I get the drift, Mr McEwan. You're demonstrating your trust. On the other hand, I'd be a bit of a nana to turn *you* over. I mean, it wouldn't need no Hercules Piorrhea to finger the Prime Suspect, would it?'

McEwan nodded approvingly. 'Exactly. You have more to lose than most.'

Fletcher assured him solemnly: 'I won't blow it, sir. I quite fancy this job. I mean, it could lead somewhere, you know. Hotel management. And its warmer than night watchman on a building site – ' he shivered and glanced at the cold gas-fire, ' – just.'

McEwan gazed at him hard for a moment. Then he nodded. 'Very well. Start tonight. Hours are eleven till seven. In a minute, I'll show you where everything is. We keep the front door locked after midnight, so anyone later than that will have to ring. Anyone registering after that will have to pay a night's board in advance. So you'll be handling cash.'

Fletcher nodded owlishly. 'Cash? Right you are, sir.'

McEwan turned and moved briskly towards the door 'Come along then – time and tide, etc.'

He opened the door and led the way back out into the reception area. He addressed the aloof young woman.

'Pamela, this is Mr Fletcher. Fletcher, this is Pamela.'

She nodded at him, without excessive warmth, and he

nodded back. Somehow he felt doubtful as to whether much in the way of friendship would spring up between them. McEwan sniffed and resumed: 'One thing I forgot – have you got a dark suit? Black or navy blue?'

Fletcher assumed an expression of surprise.

'Oh, it's not provided, then?' he asked.

McEwan looked doubtful. 'We *do* have one but your predecessor – ' his glance wandered to Fletcher's ample girth, 'didn't have your stature.'

Pamela contributed, 'Anyway, when he left he took it with him – that and my digital clock.'

McEwan bravely tried to mollify the girl. 'Now, now, Pamela. You know my philosophy. It's not going to change because of one – or two – regrettable incidents.'

And Fletcher said diplomatically: 'I have a suitable suit, sir.' With which he turned to Pamela and, with muted defiance, continued, 'It's the one I always wear in court. Or used to. You may as well know, Miss, that I was recently released from one of Her Majesty's Prisons.'

'I'm really amazed,' said Pamela calmly.

McEwan sighed and said, 'Pamela knows the score. She knows my policy. Judge not lest ye be judged.'

Pamela nodded. McEwan turned to his new employee. 'Wait here a tick, would you, Fletcher? I just need to check over a couple of things. Pamela – can you come through, dear?'

The girl followed him into the inner office. Fletcher positioned himself obediently by the desk and tried to look every inch a night security officer. But the effect was a trifle spoiled by Pamela suddenly dashing out of the office again and, with a suspicious look at Fletcher, snatching up her handbag from the desk. Fletcher sighed philosophically.

That evening, Fletcher's nubile daughter Ingrid was busy in the kitchen preparing a packet of sandwiches and a thermos of soup when the door behind her slowly and silently swung open. All unsuspecting the lovely girl pursued her task as a sinister shape stole towards her from the open door. She was actually humming a little air (number three on the charts that week) when two strong hands grasped her from behind.

Immediately the girl cried out: 'Oh, Geoffrey, stop it!'

'Who's Geoffrey?' asked Lennie Godber indignantly, removing his hands from her eyes.

Making no attempt to turn and verify the identity of her assailant, Ingrid asked in a puzzled voice: 'Oh, isn't it Geoffrey? Alastair then? Or Brian?'

'Here!' exclaimed Lennie, sounding shocked, 'I've only been gone a week.'

At this, Ingrid whirled and clasped him about the neck. Her eyes twinkled. 'I knew it was you, you daft thing! I heard you parking your lorry.'

Mollified, Lennie grinned and said, 'Give us a kiss then,' and was rewarded by a peck on the tip of his nose. He wrinkled it and protested: 'That's not very romantic.'

Ingrid unclasped her hands from about his neck. She admitted: 'I'm not feeling very romantic.'

'No? A pity that because I've got a night stopover.'

The words seemed to have a distinctly cheering effect on Ingrid. 'Have you?' she asked eagerly.

'Don't have to leave till tomorrow afternoon. Lie-in and everything.'

And he reached for her avidly. But Ingrid, after a moment of hesitation, pushed him away firmly. 'Not now. I'm fixing me Dad's thermos.'

'Thermos?' asked Lennie, as surprised as if she'd said she was polishing his cornet. 'What's he want with a thermos?'

Ingrid gulped faintly and then, as if the news were slightly shameful, whispered: 'He's got a job.'

Lennie gaped and gasped. 'Fletch has got a job?'

Ingrid nodded soberly. 'In a hotel. Night security officer.'

Lennie whistled. He brooded on these amazing tidings

for a moment or two, then asked: 'Porter, like?'

Ingrid shook her head. 'Don't call it that. He's a bit prickly about his status. Because you know it's not the most dignified job in the world. Bit lonely too, I should think. Not much to do but read magazines and clean shoes.'

'It's a start, though,' said Lennie with growing enthusiasm. 'I hope he sticks at it. This could be the turning point in his life. Ours too, come to that.'

'How do you mean?' asked Ingrid.

Her devoted paramour reached for her with a lecherous grin. 'Get the place to ourselves at night, won't we?'

Ingrid smacked his hands away. She pretended to be cross. 'Len! Always thinking of yourself – ' but then a soft look filled her eyes and she murmured, 'Not wrong though, are you?'

This time, she allowed his arms to encircle her and his eager hands to stray about her person. As their lips met, Fletcher, carrying his shoes and elegantly clad in a faded navy-blue double-breasted suit, waddled into the kitchen. He stopped with a sigh and exclaimed:

'Godber! Would you mind removing your hand from my daughter's left buttock?'

Without undue haste, the young lovers separated. Ingrid, gazing at Lennie still but addressing her father, said: 'Oh, hello, dad.' And then, a trifle superfluously, she added, 'Len's here.'

'When is he not?' grumbled Fletcher. 'Every time I enter a room he has some portion of you in his hand.'

Lennie smiled shyly and asked: 'How are you, Fletch?'

But the affronted father pointedly ignored this civil query. Handing his shoes to his daughter, he requested: 'Could you give these shoes a polish, Ingrid?'

The girl frowned. 'I don't see why I should. I mean, isn't that what you're going to do all night at work?'

Fletcher shook his head in mild exasperation. 'That's precisely why I don't intend to do my own. I have my pride.'

Interrupting this fond exchange, Lennie coughed hesitantly and repeated his earlier question. 'I said, how are you, Fletch?'

Fletcher favoured him with a cynical glance. 'I heard you, Godber. Another night stop-over, is it? Which reminds me. Ingrid, the sofa's collapsed. Leg broke off.'

'Oh, that's Lennie's fault,' admitted Ingrid, 'staying the night.'

'Don't blame *him*!' protested Fletcher. 'Three cushions bunched up under a blanket won't break any sofa.'

Ingrid swallowed and had the good grace to blush faintly. 'I don't know *what* you mean, dad.'

'Yes, you do,' said her implacable father. 'We all saw the repeats of Colditz. Anyhow, all I'm saying is keep off it, the sofa that is. I'll mend the bad leg in the morning – either that or saw the others off. Is there any tea?'

Lennie cleared his throat meaningfully and ventured: 'This job, then – '

'What about it?' growled Fletcher, ready to fend off any mockery.

But such was far from Lennie's intention. The lad said eagerly, 'Milestone, isn't it?'

Fletcher looked wary but prepared to be mollified. 'How do you mean?'

'Well, it must be your first legitimate job in – er – how long is it?'

Fletcher laughed shortly. 'Ever.'

'Straight up?' marvelled Lennie. 'You have never before been gainfully employed?'

'Never. Unless you count the army.'

Here Ingrid disloyally chipped in. 'Which we don't, because you was on the fiddle then. When I was a nipper, all my party dresses was made out of parachute silk.'

Fletcher smiled faintly. 'You wouldn't have complained if you'd ever fallen out of a window.'

But Lennie couldn't get over it. 'I never realised you'd

never worked. Never known someone of your age who'd *never* worked.'

Fletcher nodded. 'There you are then. Perhaps you'll realise how difficult it is to change the habits of a lifetime.'

Ingrid felt that a word of encouragement might be in order. She was basically a loving daughter and was anxious that her father should make the most of the opportunity. 'I was saying to Len,' she assured Fletcher, 'that you deserve a lot of credit.'

Fletcher smiled ruefully. 'Well, it's not much of a job. But then, what else can I expect? When I decided that I was going to – ' the word seemed to stick in his throat, 'work, I sat meself down and assessed all the qualifications I had to offer. Chronologically. Know what they boiled down to?'

'What?' asked Lennie.

Fletcher sighed. 'One G.L.C. driving licence. The sum total of forty-six years existence on this earth is a driving licence.'

Ingrid, struck by the pathos of this observation, added: 'And even that's got two endorsements.'

But Lennie tried to lighten the mood. 'A licence is all I've got, too,' he pointed out.

But Fletcher, of course, knew this wasn't the whole truth. 'What about your two O levels you're so proud of?'

Lennie shook his head. 'Ain't done me as much good as me driving licence. Here, Fletch, why don't you get a driving job?'

'Out of the question, with my back.'

'I like the job, meself.'

'You're lucky then, ain't you?'

'I suppose I am. I love the open road. No gaffers breathing down your neck, telling you what to do. I'm trying to get on to juggernauts. Y'know, in Europe. Lots of money there.'

But Ingrid bridled. 'You can forget that idea.'

Lennie, however, had a touch of the diplomat about him. He explained: 'Lots of money there – to put away! For us.'

'You can see what she's worried about,' commented Fletcher. ' "Sur le continong"? All them Frauleines and Signorinas. All waiting to ease the loneliness of the long-distance lorry driver.'

'Oh, come on, Fletch,' Lennie protested. 'Ingrid trusts me.'

Ingrid nodded grimly. 'Yeah – about as much as I trust me dad.'

Fletcher turned to her with a wounded expression. 'What's that supposed to mean?'

'Oh,' she corrected herself, 'I didn't mean it that way, dad.'

'I think it's just what you meant,' pursued Fletcher huffily.

'No, I didn't. It just come out.'

Fletcher smiled ruefully. 'Yeah, well, I just come out and all. And that's the kind of attitude I've been coming up against everywhere. I thought at least me own home would be a refuge from the mistrust and animosity I've been facing. Apparently I was wrong.'

'Now, don't get on your high horse, dad,' suggested Ingrid with a touch of asperity. 'You can't blame this family for being a bit sceptical. Over the years every time that doorbell rang we never knew if it was a neighbour to borrow tea or the law come to borrow you.'

'Well, that's behind me. I'm talking about now.'

'Oh yes? Only two weeks ago you was off to the wilds of Essex with a shovel in your hand.'

Lennie began to feel uncomfortable as the family tension mounted. He took a step towards the door. 'I think I've left me gauntlets in the lorry.'

But Fletcher waved dismissively. 'Don't leave on my account. I'm the one that's going.'

'No point in leaving yet,' Ingrid pointed out. 'You don't start the job till eleven.'

Fletcher went and gazed moodily out of the window at Lennie's articulated lorry. Then he turned back. 'I ain't so sure I'm going to show up,' he said sullenly. 'You think it's the greatest job in the world, do you? Cleaning the shoes of commercial travellers. I only took it to prove a point to my family. But obviously that point's gone for nothing. And so what's the point?'

With quiet dignity, he crossed the room and departed. Lennie looked after him, shaking his head. 'Shouldn't have spoken like that to your dad,' he said to Ingrid. She gave him a reproachful look.

'Don't tell me what I should or shouldn't say in me own house. None of your business.'

Lennie countered mildly, 'I should have thought whatever happened to this family *was* my business.'

'Not yet, it ain't.'

As if punctuating her words, the front door slammed. Fletcher had left. Lennie rose to his feet.

'O.K. then. Until the time when you think it is, I shall go elsewhere.' He looked at her, hoping she'd protest. But Ingrid, who had the mettle of her father, merely shrugged.

'Suit yourself.'

'That's it then – I shall have to find bed and breakfast for the night.'

Once again his eyes signalled that his determination was not as hard as granite. But Ingrid contented herself with observing coldly. 'You won't have any trouble, I'm sure.'

Without moving, Lennie said: 'Right. I'll say goodnight then.'

'Goodnight then,' echoed Ingrid.

Lennie sighed and turned heavily towards the door. Then he turned back. 'You know where to find me.'

Ingrid thawed very slightly. 'No, I don't, do I?'

'No, what I meant was – I know where to find you.'

'Should do by now. All the free nights you've had here.'

'Oh, if it's the money you're worrying about – '

'It isn't,' said Ingrid quickly.

Lennie tried a different tack. 'Something's worrying you, that's obvious.'

'Well, don't you think I've got things to worry about round this house?'

'Certainly, and I'm trying to help.'

'Well, you're not.'

This seemed to close the door firmly on a possible reconciliation. But Lennie was reluctant to abandon Ingrid on one of his few precious nights in London. He said feebly. 'May as well be off then – ' He waited a second or two for the protest which never came. 'I said I'll be going now.'

Ingrid jumped up, seized the bread and margarine and began stowing them away in fridge and cupboard. Over her shoulder, she snapped: 'Suit yourself.'

But the sight of the food had given Lennie a final stratagem. He patted his tummy and said feelingly: 'I haven't eaten, you know. Not since Coventry.'

'Well, you can get a meat pie down the Black Lion.'

Crestfallen, and with his hopes finally dashed, Lennie made for the door. As he slouched through it, he muttered: 'Lost me appetite.' He picked up his cap without even the semblance of jauntiness and headed out into the night.

Meanwhile, down at the Black Lion, Fletcher was just receiving a brimming Scotch from Alfie, the barman. He raised the amber glass appreciatively to the light.

'What I need, that. Thanks, Alfie.'

Alfie was studiously clocking Fletcher's grand appearance. He said, with unfeigned admiration: 'Like the whistle, Fletch.'

'What?'

'Very smart. Been in court, have you?'

Fletcher felt that so many straws had been loaded on his back recently that one more wouldn't break it. So he contented himself with glaring at Alfie, and then pointedly taking up his drink and carrying it to a side table. There he sat for a while savouring the rich spirit. A few minutes later, the swing door opened and, to Fletcher's surprise, Lennie entered carrying his overnight grip. Lennie, without glancing round, made straight for the bar. He gazed moodily at the stacked bottles behind it until he had secured Alfie's attention. Then he ordered.

'Pint of lager, please. And do you do sandwiches?'

Alfie shook his head resolutely. It was years now since customers had been pampered. 'Not at night. Peanuts?'

'No.'

Alfie drew his lager and handed it over. Lennie paid. Then he took the frothy glass, turned and saw Fletcher. He was not surprised. He ambled over to his prospective father-in-law who asked: 'What are you doing here?'

'Felt like a drink,' Lennie muttered, seating himself.

'Come off it. I know what you two gets up to the moment I'm out of the house.'

'Normally, yes – but we had a tiff.'

'Oh yes?'

'About you. At least I think it was about you. Not sure what it was about really.'

Fletcher adopted his worldly-wise expression. 'Arguments,' he said, 'are seldom about what they seem to be about. Arguments is two people in search of an exit line.'

Lennie nodded glumly. 'You certainly made a hasty exit.'

'Felt like it, didn't I?'

Lennie reached down, opened his grip and produced from it a pair of unsparkling shoes. 'Thought you'd better have these.'

Fletcher glanced stealthily at his feet and found that he was still wearing his slippers. He was annoyed but unwilling to admit his slip. 'You needn't have bothered.'

Lennie smiled faintly. 'You can hardly go to work in your carpet slippers. Not a very good impression, first night.'

'Who said I'm going to work?'

Lennie shook his head wearily. 'Don't be daft.'

'You heard what I said in the house. I was making the effort for my family – '

'What was said in the house was said in the heat of the moment. Same with Ingrid. She didn't mean what she said.'

Fletcher stuck out his lower lip, which made him look like a sullen baby. 'Yes, she did.'

'No, she didn't.'

'Yes, she did.'

'No, she didn't.'

'Yes, she did.'

'I'm just saying – '

'Don't change the subject. Did she or didn't she?' And he grinned contentedly at his witticism. But Lennie was in no mood for humour.

'The point I'm trying to make – '

'Oh, there's a point to this, is there?'

'The reason Ingrid got upset with me was because she was really upset with herself because of how she'd upset you.'

Fletcher blinked. 'You sound like the prison shrink.'

'Then let me put it another way – '

But Fletcher waved him silent. 'Look, what Ingrid said, what Ingrid thinks, is just what everyone else thinks.' And to curtail further discussion he raised his glass, drained it and turned towards the bar. He called: 'Alf!'

'Yeah?'

'Same again.'

'Not for me,' demurred Lennie.

'I didn't mean you,' declared Fletcher haughtily.

Lennie shook his head sadly. 'You know your trouble, Fletch? You have a very low opinion of other people.'

This rang a bell. Fletcher frowned and then remembered Mrs Chapman. 'You're the second person today who's told me that,' he said quietly.

Lennie leaned forward. 'And you know the person you have the lowest opinion of?'

Fletcher looked evenly at his old cell-mate. But Lennie shook his head firmly and declared: 'No, not me. You. If you don't approve of me, it's only because you don't trust me with Ingrid. And do you know why? Because in me you see *you*. And you don't trust yourself.'

Fletcher contented himself with sighing and mumbling: 'Don't trust no one.'

Lennie said, more gently, 'I know what you mean, Fletch. But we've got to lick that, us ex-cons. Got to stop being on our guard all the time.'

'Let your guard down for one minute, my son, and they'll have you.'

'Nine times out of ten, yes. But if you keep your guard up all the time, you'll never recognise the one genuine act of trust when it comes along.'

Alfie appeared at the table and planted another large Scotch in front of Fletcher. 'There you are, Fletch.'

'Thanks, Alfie.'

Fletcher started rummaging in the pocket of his suit for money. Alfie eyed him critically. Lennie continued: 'Bloke who gave you this job trusts you. Trusts you to turn up on time – sober.'

Fletcher turned his attention to another pocket, remarking: 'Stuff the job!'

Lennie pointed to the beverage. 'I reckon you need a job if your taste has turned to double scotches.'

'Am I asking you to buy them?' There was a pause while Fletcher rapidly explored his remaining pockets. Then, keeping his gaze lowered, he asked casually: 'Got a quid on you, Len?'

Lennie shook his head, not in refusal but in ironic comment, reached into his pocket and withdrew a note. He plonked it down in front of Alfie who promptly scooped it up. Lennie knew that now, at the very least, he'd bought a spot of attention. He said earnestly: 'I'm not taken in, you know. By you walking out of the house in your carpet slippers because Ingrid upset you. I know what's up with you. You've lost your bottle.'

'My what!' exclaimed Fletcher, outraged.

'First honest job in your life and you can't face it.'

'What do you know about it?'

'I come out of prison, same as you. Had to swallow all the snide remarks. Take what was offered.'

Fletcher took a deep breath. 'You are twenty whatever it is years of age. You've got bleeding years to recover from the setback of your delinquent youth. D'you think at my age any job I get is going to lead somewhere? Jobs I get offered, mate, are a dead end.' He paused and took a sip of his whisky. 'Besides, I'm allergic to work. Can't help it. Other people have allergies, don't they? Some people are allergic to cats, or carpet fluff, or camel hair. With me, it's work. I know that by tomorrow morning, if I went through with this job, I would have a terrible migraine and my body would be covered in red blotches.'

'Cobblers,' said Lennie.

'Them as well. Doubtless, medical science will in time come up with a cure. But until it does, it's best to play it safe.'

Lennie shrugged. 'You can believe that if you want to. Wouldn't fool anyone else, but if you fool yourself, so be it.'

Fletcher shook his head irritably. 'Look, Len, I'm sick of sermons. Sick of words of advice and encouragement. Why don't you just go home, make it up with Ingrid, and leave me here to get quietly Brahms and Liszt? And lend me another fiver while you're about it.'

At precisely five minutes to eleven that night, Ingrid entered the lobby of the Studleigh Hotel. She carried a thermos and a packet of sandwiches and her lack of any other luggage was immediately noted with displeasure by the worried-looking man at the reception desk. Approaching him deferentially, Ingrid began: 'Excuse me – '

But, raising his hand in a warning gesture, McEwan interrupted her. 'I'm sorry, Miss, we have no vacancies. I suggest you try the Ilfracombe two doors down.'

Ingrid shook her head vigorously. 'No, I don't want a room. I'm looking for – erm – a Mr Fletcher.'

McEwan sighed deeply. 'Oh. Well, we all are, aren't we?'

Ingrid smiled winningly. 'I'm his daughter, Ingrid. He's my Dad.'

McEwan, more in sorrow than anger, declared: 'I must say, young lady, I thought your dad would have showed up a little early on his first night.'

With as much conviction as she could muster, Ingrid maintained: 'Oh, he will.'

'But,' insisted McEwan, eyeing the lobby clock, 'he hasn't.'

Ingrid became flustered. 'Well, he was going to – that is – if he – if he – '

'If he what?'

Ingrid had her father's talent for drawing inspiration from her surroundings. She held up the thermos and sandwiches triumphantly. 'If he hadn't forgot these. He left home in ever such good time, see. But what obviously must have happened was, he was on the bus and he says to himself "Oh dear, I must have forgot my supper". So obviously he's nipped back home, not knowing that meantime I brung them here – obviously.'

McEwan, a tolerant but not imbecilic man, contemplated her shrewdly and, without much conviction, said: 'I see.'

Ingrid pursued her advantage. 'He's ever so keen about the job, Mr er – '

'McEwan.'

'Mr McEwan. He's got his best suit on and everything. He was saying to me, you know, what a nice man you was. Giving him a chance and that.'

McEwan confessed: 'I was about to ring his probation officer – what's her name – yes, Mrs Chapman.'

Ingrid implored: 'Oh, don't do that.'

McEwan shook his head firmly. 'I've given him a chance. I told everyone – benefit of the doubt and so on. But when I say start at eleven, I mean at eleven. You understand my point of view – cuts both ways, doesn't it?'

Ingrid gulped and looked hopefully at the clock. 'But it's – it's not quite eleven – '

'As I said, I thought he'd be early. First night. So I let her go. I let my girl go. I said "I'll hold the fort." Now I'm late for *my* supper.'

Ingrid nodded sympathetically, biting her lower lip. Then she had an inspiration. She unscrewed the top of the thermos, thrust it towards him and said hospitably: 'Why don't you have a cup of oxtail?'

At precisely that moment, Fletcher, somewhat indebted to Lennie for support, lurched round the corner into sight of the Studleigh Hotel. Lennie breathed a sigh of relief.

'There it is. And we're right on time.'

As if offended by the notion, Fletcher immediately halted and tried to shake off Lennie's sustaining arm. 'Len, you are hurting me. I am not drunk. I'm not going to fall down, Godber.'

Without relinquishing his grip, Lennie agreed soothingly. 'I know you're not, Fletch. This is more moral support. I'm just afraid if I let go, you'll scarper.'

Fletcher grunted. At least the sound began as a grunt but ended as a belch. Then he mumbled: 'Norman Stanley Fletcher is on his way to work. Goes against the grain, that does. I feel like a nun about to take a sauna bath.'

Lennie laughed and maintained the merry mood by saying: 'Well, Fletcher, the *habits* of a lifetime, eh? Gerrit? Gerrit?'

But Fletcher seemed to have lost his taste for jesting. Freeing himself with a quick movement, he turned to Lennie. 'Godber, this is no laughing matter. How's my breath?' With which he expelled a proud exhalation full in Lennie's face. The younger man gasped audibly and stepped back a pace.

'You'd better have another polo. Here, take the packet.' He handed them to Fletcher who was now busy patting his formal jacket.

'How do I look?'

'Immaculate.'

'Don't feel it,' grumbled Fletcher.

But a brooding look had come into Lennie's eyes. 'Know what this reminds me of? Did you ever see that film "On the Waterfront"?'

'I did, but has this any relevance?'

'Don't you remember the ending? When the priest picked Marlon Brando up and said: "You can do it. You can walk to work on your own." While Eva Marie Sainte watched with tears in her eyes?'

'And all I've got,' commented Fletcher with poor grace, 'is Godber with a smirk on his face.'

'Brando did all right,' pointed out Lennie cheerfully. 'Since then he's gone from strength to strength.'

Fletcher nodded. He gave the threatening hotel a determined look, squared his shoulders, waved away Lennie's attempt at assistance, and strode forward – for two full paces. Then he stumbled, nearly fell, reeled upright again and, lurching and staggering, completed his crossing of the street. He mounted the steps and, just as the lobby clock struck the final notes of eleven, entered his place of gainful employ. Ingrid and McEwan, hearing the door open, looked in his direction whereupon Ingrid exclaimed joyously: 'Dad!'

Fletcher stopped and gazed at her in bewilderment. For a moment he wondered if he was really in the Studleigh Hotel or if, by some wizardry, he'd been transported home.

'Ingrid? What are you doing here?'

'Brought your sandwiches, dad, which you went back for, which is why you cut it so fine, isn't that it?'

Fletcher began to shake his head but, catching Ingrid's imploring look, he changed in mid-shake to a nod. He stammered: 'Oh yes, that's what happened. I'm sorry about that, Mr McEwan.'

McEwan nodded tolerantly. 'It's all right. I admit I was

getting a little worried. But all's well and so on. Now are you sure you know where – '

Making a strenuous effort to retain control of his faculties, Fletcher offered what he hoped was a confident smile. 'Quite sure, sir. You showed me the ropes this afternoon, didn't you? So you can toddle off now.'

McEwan eyed him for a moment. 'Oh well, if you're sure, I'll get upstairs and heat up my casserole.' He turned politely to Ingrid. 'Nice to meet you, miss.'

Ingrid turned on the charm. 'Mutual.'

'Right, then – ' but McEwan still seemed slightly reluctant to go for his dinner. He looked Fletcher up and down. 'Very suitable the suit.'

Fletcher fought down an urgent hiccough. 'Thank you, sir.'

'Well then, don't forget – any late registrations –'

'Cash up front, sir.'

'Oh, and I probably should have mentioned – ' here he paused and gave Ingrid an embarrassed glance. But it had to be said. 'The thing is we – sometimes get ladies of the night – '

Fletcher began to tut-tut but, as the belch rose, thought better of it and simply frowned disapprovingly. McEwan continued: 'Yes, you'd be surprised.'

Feeling that comment was unavoidable, Fletcher ventured carefully: 'I expect they work round Paddington Station, do they?'

McEwan nodded. 'That's right. They seem mostly to solicit Welshmen.'

His confidence rising, Fletcher permitted himself a longer speech. 'It's the direct line from Cardiff, isn't it? And I mean they don't get much of it down there, do they? Never could see what they've got to sing about.'

'Quite. Anyway, as I was saying, none of that here, obviously.'

'Say no more, sir. I won't bring any in if you won't.'

McEwan once more eyed Fletcher closely. Then, apparently finally convinced of his Security Officer's readiness for the long night's toil ahead, he turned and departed to the stairs. Fletcher exhaled a sigh of relief and stretched out a hand to steady himself on the counter.

Ingrid looked at him reproachfully and said: 'Didn't think you was going to make it.'

'I'm sure you didn't.'

He carefully made his way round to the back of his desk and began straightening things. Ingrid, in a friendlier tone of voice, said: 'Made you some nice sandwiches. Cheese and chutney. Tongue with a little piccalilli.'

Fletcher accepted them haughtily. 'Thank you.'

He began, unneccessarily, checking the keys in the key-rack. Ingrid got the message. She said winningly: 'Dad?'

'Mm?'

'I'm sorry.'

'What?'

'About what I said. Uncalled for.'

Fletcher shrugged. But he stopped fiddling with the keys. 'You had every right.'

'No, I didn't.'

'Water under the bridge.'

'I only wanted to say – '

'Ingrid – do you mind? I have a job to do.'

Ingrid beamed at him. 'I never thought I'd hear you say those words.'

Fletcher gazed at her but then a smile involuntarily surfaced.

'No, nor did I – ' At this point the lobby of the hotel decided that it might really be a pinwheel and began to revolve slowly. Fletcher put his hand to his head. 'I think I feel a little faint.'

Ingrid was with him in a moment and in another moment she was embracing him fondly. 'You'll be all right, dad. I love you, and I'm proud of you, you know?'

Fletcher patted her fondly on the head. He was about to murmur some suitable paternal endearment when the customer's bell on the counter gave its unmistakable 'ping'. Realising that the best present he could give Ingrid would be a demonstration of zeal, Fletcher instantly disengaged himself from the embrace, straightened himself up and said, in a winning tone of voice: 'Good evening, sir. What can I – oh, it's you.'

His sudden descent into informality had been caused by seeing at the counter the familiar figure of Lennie Godber.

With a cool glance at Ingrid, Lennie said: 'I'd like a room, please.'

'You what?' asked Fletcher, mystified.

Lennie shrugged. 'Got to sleep somewhere. Good a place as any.'

Ingrid swallowed and said in a small voice: 'Hello, Len.'

Rather stiffly, Lennie replied, 'Good evening, Ingrid. And how are you keeping?'

By now, Fletcher had resumed his professional role. He held out his hand, palm upwards, towards Godber. 'Cash in advance for late registrations.'

'Don't be daft,' remonstrated Lennie. 'You know me.'

'I do indeed. That's why I want cash on the nail.'

Lennie exclaimed bitterly, 'Is there no flaming trust between you and me?'

But Ingrid was staring at her father in amazement. 'They let *you* handle cash?' she asked weakly.

'Now watch it, my girl,' cautioned Fletcher.

This provided Lennie with an opening. 'No worse than what you just said to me.'

'Got you there, dad,' added Ingrid.

Fletcher looked sternly from one to the other. Then he sighed and a smile appeared on his face. 'I didn't think you seriously wanted a room for the night, Len,' he explained to his future son-in-law.

'Nowhere else to go.'

This time Lennie's haughty, but pained, glance at Ingrid achieved results. She burst out: 'Yes, you have. As you well know, Lennie Godber.'

'Do I?' asked Lennie, striving to keep the elation from sounding.

'Of course!'

Lennie grinned cheerfully. 'Oh well, if you say so.'

'Well, I do, don't I?'

During this exchange, some mysterious natural force had pushed them closer and closer together until, by now, there were several points of contact between their young forms. Then Ingrid sniffed critically and said: 'You've been drinking.'

Lennie nodded. 'Just enough.'

'Enough for what?'

'You know what.'

'Do I?'

Fletcher had been watching this moving scene impassively. But now he frowned, as if at the realisation of some drawback or obstacle to the happiness of the young pair. 'Excuse me for interrupting you,' he said soberly, or at least trying to sound it, 'but I think there's something you have overlooked. He can't stay at our house. The sofa's broken.' He glanced from one to the other meaningfully. 'And there's nowhere else in the house, is there?'

But Ingrid did not seem at all perturbed. She said lightly: 'It's all right, Dad, no bother. You're on night work now. He can have *your* bed.'

Fletcher's jaw dropped. But he rallied and proved he was a good sport by grinning and patting them both on the back. After this, Ingrid took Lennie's arm and, with a pleasant 'Cheerio, dad', marched her swain out of the lobby. Fletcher looked after them fondly. Then he turned and surveyed his new little kingdom and, as he did so, he absently unscrewed the lid of his thermos flask. He felt at home already.

Going Going Gone

Norman Stanley Fletcher had just arrived at work. He found his boss, Mr McEwan, at the wall safe in his little office behind the reception desk.

'Good evening,' said Fletcher respectfully.

McEwan glanced round. 'Oh, Fletcher,' he returned, 'come in, will you?'

Thereupon the Night Security Officer, carrying a thermos in one hand and a packet of sandwiches in the other, entered. McEwan glanced at his watch. 'You're a little early.'

Fletcher nodded wryly. 'I know. My son's got some friends round at home. Sort of party.'

Mr McEwan replaced an envelope in the safe. 'That sounds nice,' he said.

'Not really,' sighed Fletcher. 'And some of the things they get up to – well, I thought it best to absent myself, being on parole.'

'I'm not going to complain, Fletcher. Means I can hand over the reins a bit earlier. I might pop round to the "Anchor" for a quick one.'

Fletcher shook his head sombrely. 'I wouldn't advise it.'

'Why?'

'Bunch of Scotsmen in there tonight. I think they're down for some union confab. or something.'

'Are they causing trouble?'

'Oh no. Quite merry as a matter of fact. But you know your Scotsmen. They can turn ugly in the twinkling of a sporran. And at times like that they tend to be seized by an insatiable desire to pummel the head of an Englishman.'

McEwan, without any trace of a Scottish accent, confided, 'I'm Scots. At least my forebears were.'

Fletcher brightened. 'Oh, you had *four*, did you? One more than Goldilocks.'

McEwan frowned and said: 'Pardon?'

Fletcher permitted himself a little chuckle. 'You said you had four bears – forebears, get it?' McEwan still looked baffled. A trifle anxiously, Fletcher continued, 'Godlilocks only had three – Goldilocks and the three Bears? Oh, never mind, it was only a joke.'

McEwan nodded. 'Oh, I see, yes.'

Fletcher pointed at the open safe. 'I don't think you should leave that open, do you, sir?'

'No, of course not. I'm thinking of getting a better safe, you know, but they're not cheap.'

It was too tempting. 'On the other hand, sir, better safe than sorry, eh?'

This sally, at least, was not wasted. But McEwan's response was not as hearty as Fletcher could have wished. He nodded thoughtfully and said: 'That's very witty, Fletcher.'

Stifling a sigh, Fletcher said humbly: 'Thank you, sir. Well, you can only do your best. Not much to laugh at these days. Even Mastermind's not on at the moment.'

McEwan did not appear to catch the reference. 'Well, Fletcher,' he said expansively, 'tonight marks the end of your first week here. I'd like you to know I'm well pleased and I'd like to give you this.'

He took up from his desk a brown envelope. He held it out to Fletcher, clearly expecting some response. Fletcher, however, merely asked wonderingly as he took it: 'What is it, sir?'

'Your pay packet. Surely you've seen one before?'

'Hm? Oh, not for a very long time, sir. My money normally goes straight into a bank – or comes straight out of one.' He gazed interestedly at the column of figures on the envelope. 'What does all this mean?' he asked.

'The top figure is gross and the bottom figure is net.'

'But what has happened in between?'

'Deductions. National Insurance. PAYE and so on.'

Fletcher shook his head disconsolately. 'And all that explains why most of the gross has slipped through the net, does it?'

Neither of them thought fit to smile at this effort. McEwan explained: 'That's your welfare state, isn't it? Now that you're on the right side of the law it's one of the things you'll have to get used to.'

'Yes, there do seem to be a number.'

'It's a question of adjustment. I understand what you're going through because I had to adapt myself when I came back from Nyasaland. Did I mention that?'

McEwan had, in fact, mentioned his colonial past several times. But Fletcher showed no sign of impatience. 'You did, sir. Malawi as it now is. Africa.'

'That's right. We lived such a different life style out there. You had the wonderful climate and servants and wildlife. Magnificent scenery. Not altogether unlike Scotland.'

Fletcher was interested. 'Really? And after a jar did the natives get just as surly and belligerent?'

McEwan shook his head. 'Not until the spread of Pan-African Nationalism. Which is one of the things which forced us out, of course. And suddenly after all that luxury there I was working as a clerk at twenty pounds a week in the Rates Office. Having to get used to queues and rain and stuck in the wife's sister's maisonette in Ruislip.'

'Not much wildlife in Ruislip, is there?' Fletcher asked sympathetically.

'Not much of anything. I was a farm manager in Africa. Enormous spread. Far as the eye could see. We grew tobacco, and some coffee. And a local crop called "betel-wok". The natives used the fibre to make rope. Or soup – depending on their needs at the time.'

At this point, something behind Fletcher caught McEwan's eye. He made a discreet gesture. Fletcher glanced round, nodded, then rose and made his way out to the desk.

There, Sharleen, a big, bustling Australian girl, was waiting for her key. This was perfectly in order but what was less in accordance with the house rules was the young man with her. The poor chap was really *very* young and obviously embarrassed. Sharleen gave Fletcher a big, open smile. The young man attempted to do likewise but Fletcher noticed that the corners of his mouth quivered faintly.

'Number fourteen, please,' requested Sharleen.

'Certainly, miss.'

However, instead of turning and unhooking the key, Fletcher gazed with raised eyebrows at the nervous young man. Sharleen, who had a genuine, if minor, talent for acting, promptly addressed him.

'Why don't you wait here, Tony, and I'll go up and get the book for you?'

'Oh, if you like,' gulped the wretched Tony.

Fletcher turned and unhooked the key. He handed it to Sharleen who rewarded him with another juicy smile. Then she took Tony's hand.

'On second thoughts, why don't you come up and I'll give you the book? Save me coming down again, won't it?'

'Oh, if you like,' gulped Tony once more.

Whereupon the ill-suited pair made their way to the stairs. Fletcher nodded and muttered under his breath: 'Ten to one he stays up there to read it and all.'

Mr McEwan emerged from his inner office. 'Did you say something, Fletcher?'

'I was just thinking, sir, that we'll be charging double occupancy in fourteen.'

McEwan nodded approvingly. 'Well spotted, Fletcher. Keep your eyes open, that's the ticket.'

Fletcher nodded with assurance. 'Not much gets past me, sir. I caught twenty-three this morning. Checking out with two dozen wire coat-hangers in his rucksack. He'd bent them square to fit.'

McEwan said appreciatively, 'You've earned your keep,

no question. I shall give your parole officer a tinkle. Tell her I'm well pleased and so on.'

'Very grateful, sir,' said Fletcher modestly.

'Well, I'm off. Just catch "The Ship" before closing time.'

Fletcher drew himself up, like a man entrusted with a great office. 'I shall be here, sir, never fear.'

McEwan nodded and left by the lobby door. On his way out he passed another man entering. The new arrival was familiar to Fletcher, being a guest in the hotel. He was about thirty-five and sported a noble paunch. His unsteady gait, and the flush on his cheeks, suggested that he had been augmenting it quite recently. On his arm hung a young lady. When he reached the desk, he said:

'Robbins. Eleven.'

Fletcher turned to get the key. The man asked: 'Any calls for me? From Wakefield Textiles? I was expecting a call from my Sales Manager.'

Fletcher shook his head as he handed over the key. 'Nothing from your Sales Manager, I'm afraid, sir.'

Robbins nodded, accepted the key and, with a wink at his companion, set off with her towards the stairs. He had not gone far before Fletcher, reading from the slip of paper he had withdrawn from Robbins' pigeonhole but concealed until this point, shouted after him: 'But there was one call, sir. At ten past eight. Your wife rang.'

Robbins froze in his stride and then turned and favoured Fletcher with a reproachful glare. Fletcher smiled amiably and said: 'There was no message.'

And thus, with long periods of tedium but also with moments of diversion such as this one, the night slowly passed for the doughty security officer.

Early the next morning, while the streets were still unfrenzied, Fletcher emerged from the Studleigh Hotel and glanced about at the cold world. In his right hand, he held a shopping bag weighed down by his now empty thermos and sandwich tin. He felt at peace with the world. Like everyone else, he was now an honest, hard-working citizen. With an easy conscience, he set off towards his underground station. He was chuckling inwardly at the memory of Robbins' discomfiture when, from somewhere quite close by, he heard a voice call: 'Oi!'

Frowning, he glanced in the appropriate direction. He saw two men gazing at him from the opposite side of the street. Next to them was the Ford Granada from which they had just emerged. There was nothing of an official nature about either the car or the men's clothing but Fletcher knew them immediately for plain-clothes detectives. He sighed and stopped walking. Without unseemly haste, the camouflaged cops approached him. Fletcher recognised one of them.

'Fletcher, isn't it? Fletcher – Norman Stanley?' asked the one Fletcher had encountered in the past.

Fletcher did not deign to confirm the identification but merely stated, in the same neutral tone: 'Crowther. Thomas Clifford. West End Central.'

Crowther shook his head. 'Flying squad now.'

Fletcher nodded. 'Yes, I heard the Sweeney was pushed for personnel.'

Det. Sgt. Crowther turned easily to his junior colleague, Det. Const. Nulty, and confided: 'Cheeky this one, Nulty. Lot of lip.' He turned back to Fletcher. 'When d'you come out then?'

'Two months back.'

'Where've you been?'

'Work.'

Crowther permitted incredulity to register on his face. 'Pull the other one,' he suggested.

Fletcher's eyebrows lifted delicately. 'I heard you hadn't got another one.'

With an evil smile, Crowther glanced at Nulty again. 'Told you. Lip.' Then, with a sudden change of mood, he snarled at Fletcher, 'What you got in the bag?'

Instinctively, Fletcher clasped his innocent shopping bag to his middle. 'Listen, you got no cause – '

But Crowther cut him off rudely. 'No cause? What you doing at seven o'clock in the morning so far from your turf?' He nodded at Nulty who promptly reached forwards and grabbed Fletcher's shopping bag.

Fletcher sighed and explained. 'I got a job, see. Hotel in Sussex Gardens. Look!' and he produced his pay packet which Crowther promptly seized.

Meanwhile Nulty had been rummaging in the shopping bag. He was soon forced to admit: 'Nothing in here, Tom. Except half a tongue sandwich.'

'Despicable, this is,' said Fletcher feelingly.

Crowther handed back the pay envelope with a disappointed shrug. 'They don't overpay you, do they?' he sneered.

'Have to accept it, don't I?' said Fletcher bitterly. 'Just as I have to accept this.'

'What else do you expect?' asked Crowther, a little more reasonably. 'This is a high crime-rate area.'

At that moment, Fletcher saw something that gave his spirits a lift. For some time, while exchanging pleasantries with the law, he had been idly watching a kid of fourteen or fifteen who had been closely inspecting the officers' Ford Granada across the street. Now, to Fletcher's delight, the kid glanced about swiftly and then slipped in behind the wheel.

'Oh, is it?' asked Fletcher, determined to hold Crowther's and Nulty's attention. 'High crime area? Must require a sharp eye and constant vigilance.'

'It does,' grunted Crowther.

With which, the detective sergeant turned to leave. But Fletcher wasn't having that. He asked, trying to sound deeply concerned, 'What do you, personally, attribute the rise in crime to? Is it unemployment? The dissatisfaction of youth, frustrated by blocked opportunities?'

'Well – ' began Crowther, but Fletcher had more to say.

'Or is it part of a greater sickness? One which permeates our entire society?'

Fletcher permitted himself a swift glance in the direction of the Granada. The kid wasn't too skilled at nicking cars. Would he make it?

'Look, I haven't time – ' said Crowther roughly.

At that moment, the Granada's engine roared.

'Or is it,' cried Fletcher triumphantly, 'that you can't afford to turn your back for a bleeding second?'

Alerted, Crowther roared: 'What?'

And he sprang round, as did Nulty, just in time to see the car disappearing up the road, 'Hey!'

As he watched the two cops belting after their purloined car, Fletcher chuckled quietly. His day was off to an excellent start.

In another part of London, a young long-distance lorry driver was contentedly finishing his breakfast. With enthusiasm, if not elegance, he mopped up the ketchup from his breakfast plate with the remains of a slice of white bread. Meanwhile, Fletcher's nubile daughter, Ingrid, attired in little more than a housecoat, was at the range making toast. She glanced round at her beloved and cooed:

'Don't mop your grease up with your bread. That's the trouble with your job. Spend all your time in transport caffs picking up manners like that.'

Lennie said lightly, 'I've always had manners like that.'

'Well, I don't like it. I don't like the way you eat with your elbows on the table. And everything I cook for you put into a sandwich.'

'I'm used to eating on the run,' Lennie explained.

'It's not nice.'

'Oh dear, someone got out of bed the wrong side.'

'I have a lot to do of a morning,' grumbled Ingrid. 'Get you off, then make dad something when he comes in. Then

I've got to get meself to work. And Raymond's no help.' She looked crossly at the kitchen door and then stormed over to it and shouted up the stairs: 'Raymond! Get out of that bathroom.'

Lennie said soothingly, 'When we're married, beloved, you'll only have me to worry about.'

But Ingrid was not so easily mollified. 'Well, you won't come down to breakfast in a vest when we're married. You're the same as Dad in that respect.'

Lennie grinned. 'Got a lot in common with your Dad, haven't I?'

Ingrid snorted. 'Unfortunately, yes. It's always going to embarrass me, that is. When we live somewhere nice. People will say: "How did you meet your husband?" And I'll say: "Oh, he shared a cell with my Dad".'

Lennie could think of little soothing in response to this. So he just gulped down his last bit of red bread, stood up and started putting on his shirt and donkey jacket.

'I must be off – hit the road.'

Ingrid eyed him thoughtfully. 'Incidentally, while on the subject, have you mentioned it yet?'

'Mentioned what?'

'Us. To Dad. Our intentions.'

Lennie shook his head. 'Haven't had a chance, have I?'

Ingrid said accusingly, 'You've been putting it off since he come out of prison.'

'I haven't,' Lennie protested. 'But I'm on the road all the time. And now he's working nights.'

'You're just prevaricating.'

Lennie sighed. 'What do you expect me to do? Go down on one knee and ask for his daughter's hand? If he refuses it won't make naff all difference.'

Ingrid sniffed. 'I do think you should make our intentions formally clear.'

'I will, I will,' Lennie promised. 'Now, give us a kiss.'

Ingrid put up a token struggle, chiding him with: 'You're

just like dad – put off, put off, put off –'

But before long she was nestled in his arms and Lennie's capacious palms were cupping an easily-cupped part of her. At this point, inevitably, Fletcher plodded in.

'I don't believe it,' he remarked.

Reluctantly, Ingrid and Lennie broke usunder.

'Morning, Fletch,' said Lennie cheerfully.

'Hello, dad,' contributed Ingrid.

Shaking his head mournfully, Fletcher commented: 'First thing in the morning. Even before the breakfast things are cleared away. I couldn't be like that.'

'How's the job going?' asked Lennie.

'Let's talk about *your* job,' suggested Fletcher feelingly. 'Do you ever drive that thing outside anywhere?'

Lennie nodded. 'Driving it now. Just off. West Bromwich. Then Walsall, Sutton Coldfield and back here.'

'I see,' Fletcher granted the lorry, which blocked out most of the light from the room, a reproachful glance. 'Just wondered because I've never actually seen you drive it. Come to that, I've never known you not here. In this house. Molesting Ingrid.'

'How many sausages, dad?' asked the molested one.

'Two. 'Ere, want to show you something.'

'What?' asked Ingrid irritably. 'I haven't got time.'

But Fletcher, with quiet paternal authority, insisted. 'Ingrid, please.' Being essentially a dutiful daughter, she sighed, left the stove and moved to her old man. He, with studied nonchalance, confided: 'This is a matter of some moment to me. How about this then?'

With which, he tossed his pay packet on to the table and stood back modestly.

For a moment Ingrid was puzzled, then her eyes lit up. 'Oh, Dad! Your first-ever pay packet!'

'Yuh well –'

'Congratulations, Fletch,' offered Lennie with a grin.

'Yuh, well –'

'You don't mind,' suggested Lennie, reaching for the envelope, 'if I take the six quid you owe me?'

'What six quid?' bristled Fletcher.

'From the pub last week.'

Fletcher sighed. 'Oh, *that* six quid.'

But Ingrid felt keen proprietory rights in the brown envelope. She snatched it from Lennie, exclaiming: 'Here, give me that.'

She tore it open.

'What are you doing?' asked Fletcher in alarm.

'You owe me a fiver from the previous week,' began Ingrid in a rush. 'And we can pay the insurance man now. It's a month behind but it's worth it, because if anything happened to you, we'd be quids in. Here's your six, Len.' And she handed her paramour his cut.

'Here, listen,' protested Fletcher. 'What about him paying board and lodging? He gets an allowance – they all do.'

'He gives me his allowance,' Ingrid assured him.

'Well, where is it?' asked Fletcher, peering about. 'Let's share *that* out.'

Lennie shook his head positively. 'No, Ingrid puts it away towards our – ' here he swallowed and backtracked, 'well, towards our – you know – our fund like – '

'What fund?' asked Fletcher.

But Lennie suddenly realised that he was late for the road. He slipped hastily out of the door, calling: 'I must be off.' And, blowing a kiss to Ingrid, he departed.

'What was he talking about?' Fletcher demanded.

But, before she could reply, and to her considerable relief, Raymond entered. Raymond looked, as usual, as if he was ready for nothing. He was simply clad in vest and pyjama bottoms and he asked his customary question:

'What time is it?'

Making his customary effort, Fletcher assumed a hearty tone and said: 'Morning, son.'

The greeting was apparently lost on Raymond who gazed

vaguely about the kitchen and asked: 'Anyone seen my earphones?'

Ingrid addressed her younger brother. 'Look what your dad's brought home, Raymond.'

At the sight of the plundered pay envelope, Raymond's expression brightened perceptibly. 'Oh, good, because he owes me money.'

'What for?' asked Fletcher indignantly.

His son offered him a cool glance. 'You broke the stylus on my stereo. Said you'd replace it.'

Fletcher snorted. 'You're like vultures, the lot of you. Give me that back!' And with the kind of lightning grab with which he'd snaffled up many a snout in the nick he regained his now-limp pay packet. 'Have you left me anything?' He turned it over and shook vigorously. A small coin fell out.

'Five pence!' he exclaimed in incredulous disgust.

Ingrid snatched it from the table. 'Oh good, we need that for the gas meter.'

Fletcher was still brooding on the swift evaporation of his first-ever well-gotten gains that evening as he polished a pair of shoes behind his desk in the Studleigh Hotel. From time to time he muttered resentfully. On one of these occasions he suddenly became aware that he was not alone. Pretending that he'd merely been clearing his throat, he glanced up and saw a neatly-dressed man in his mid-thirties. The man smiled faintly and asked:

'Can I have my key, please? I'm Mr Wellings – room twenty-six.'

'Certainly, sir,' said Fletcher briskly. 'Check in today, did you, sir?'

'Yeah, this afternoon. Haven't been to London for a bit. Ain't half changed.'

Fletcher nodded agreement. 'Lots of changes. I noticed that when I come out – er – back. That is, back out. You know, when I come *back* to live *out* here.'

'Arabs,' said Mr Wellings laconically.

'Everywhere,' agreed Fletcher. 'Oxford Street's like the Casbah now. Can't get down it for flying carpets.'

'They're the ones with the money though.'

'Indisputably.'

'And this country needs it.'

Fletcher said wryly: 'Yeah, but I wish a few of 'em stayed here instead of the Dorchester.'

Wellings smiled and rubbed fingers and thumb together meaningfully. 'You mean for the – er –'

'Absolutely. Do you know, there's a bloke I know, out St John's Wood way. He's a window cleaner. He does this Arab lady's windows. She says: how much. He says: two-fifty, love. So she gives him two hundred and fifty knicker.'

'Never!'

'Straight up.'

Wellings shook his head in wonder. 'Did he give it to her back?'

'No, but he left her the ladder.'

As he moved off towards the staircase, Wellings remarked: 'We're in the wrong game.'

But Fletcher was frowning after him. A tiny chord of memory had been struck. He called: 'Excuse me asking – you're not from North London originally? Round that way?'

Mr Wellings turned back towards the Night Security Officer. 'No.'

'Oh, sorry,' said Fletcher apologetically, 'I thought you seemed familiar.'

Wellings smiled amiably. 'Anyway, nice talking to you.'

'Nice talking to *you*, sir.'

Wellings turned again and departed. For a moment or two, Fletcher gazed after him, a slight frown on his face. Then he shook his head. He couldn't *quite* bring the memory to mind. He was prevented from further brooding on the matter by the entrance of two people. One was a man of about forty-five, with a ruddy countenance, and the other was a pretty girl of about twenty-eight. Fletcher was by now quite good at summing up new arrivals and their possibilities. This pair, he felt, had definite possibilities.

'Good evening, sir – madam – ' he said cordially, but not too cordially.

Yes, he was right. He could tell by the way the man's eyes darted nervously about the lobby as if fearing the absurd mischance of seeing an acquaintance. But the chap rallied, smiled and said, in a rather too-friendly tone, 'Good evening. Um – the thing is, I don't suppose you have any rooms?'

Willing but not too willing – that was the Fletcher strategy on these occasions. He said non-committally: 'Don't you, sir?'

'I – ' The man turned to the girl. 'I said they probably wouldn't.'

Fletcher swiftly added: 'We *might* have, sir.'

He first glanced meaningfully down at the man's hand where a fiver was making crinkling noises. Then he turned and studied his key-board anxiously like a physicist contemplating a mal-functioning computer.

'I *could* take a chance, sir,' he observed finally. 'There *is* one room. It's permanently reserved for an Arab potentate. However, should he turn up in the middle of the night off of his private Concorde, that's his tough luck, isn't it?'

With which he slid a key across to the man and, in the same movement, plucked the fiver out of his hand. The man started and then stammered:

'That's awfully decent of you.' And, with heavy jubilation, he enthused to the girl, 'We're in luck, darling.'

She smiled and blushed faintly.

'Shall I send someone to help with the luggage, sir?' asked Fletcher, glancing about for it.

The man looked flustered. 'Erm – there is no luggage.'

A faint smile crossed Fletcher's face. 'Just as well – we've got no one to help with it.' He gave the man an expectant look which produced no result. 'I'm afraid it's cash up front, sir, this time of night.'

'Oh, of course.'

'It's twelve for the double, sir.'

The man gave him three fivers and Fletcher rummaged about for change. Revealing his overwrought state, the man embarked on an unnecessary, and unconvincing, explanation. 'You see, my – erm – my wife and I – have been to a do, and we were driving back to Reading – that is, Redhill – and the car broke down – just round the corner. I think it's the big end. And I said to you – ' He smiled hopefully at the girl who was by now wishing she'd never met him at the party. 'Didn't I, darling, why don't we stop over in town for the night and let the AA deal with it in the morning?'

'Best thing, sir,' agreed Fletcher smoothly.

At this point, unobserved by any of the three at the desk, someone else arrived. But instead of crossing the lobby the new arrival, a young man, paused and watched the scene with interest. It was Lennie Godber.

'Well, I'll say – erm – goodnight then,' the man stammered.

'Do you want a call in the morning, sir, or shall we let nature take its course?'

'Oh, I think we'll just – erm – don't you, darling?' And they departed hastily towards the lift.

Fletcher called after him apologetically: 'Sorry, the lift's not working, sir, but it's only five floors up.'

He chuckled as he watched them disappear up the stairs.

Lennie approached and remarked: 'That should take the wind out of his sails.'

'What are you doing here?' asked Fletcher in surprise.

'Just dropped by, you know.'

'Had a row with my Ingrid?'

Lennie shrugged affably and repeated: 'Just dropped by.'

'Why? You in trouble?'

Lennie shook his head reprovingly. 'Fletch, you always think the worst, you do.'

'I do not.'

'I just dropped by because these days I never get a chance to talk to you. With you working nights and me days and vice versa. And you and me is mates. And I value that and – and tonight, I wasn't sleepy and I thought to myself, what a good chance to go round and while away the hours with me old mate, Fletch.'

Fletcher exclaimed: 'Ingrid's pregnant!'

'She is not!' protested Lennie.

But Fletcher was not to be deflected that easily from his dark forebodings. 'You have ruined my daughter's life. I saw it coming. I tried to tell her but she wouldn't listen.'

'Will you shut up a minute? Ingrid is *not* pregnant. Do you think we're daft or something?'

Fletcher eyed him narrowly.

'You're here about something. You didn't just "drop by".'

Lennie perceived that he was trapped. 'All right. I am here because of Ingrid. But not that. She wanted me to come here to tell you something which I should have told you way back.'

Fletcher cocked his head suspiciously. 'Oh yes?'

'Well – to come straight to the point – '

But he was thwarted in the attempt by the entrance of a lady. And, at a glance, a real lady who looked incongruous in that shabby little hotel. She was an elderly lady, very smart and gracious in appearance, and she was wearing a fur coat and jewellery.

'Good evening,' she addressed Fletcher in pleasant tones. 'I'm Mrs Appleby.'

'Oh, good evening, madam,' returned Fletcher in his best professional manner.

'I haven't had the pleasure before, have I?' asked Mrs Appleby.

'Haven't you, Madam?' Fletcher unwisely tried a pleasantry. Mrs Appleby looked uncomprehending and he went on hastily. 'Oh dear, never mind. My name's Fletcher, madam.'

She smiled. 'How do you do, Fletcher. I'm in room two.'

Fletcher unhooked the appropriate key for her. Mrs Appleby took it and then reached up and fumbled at the clasp of her necklace. She had difficulty and, turning her back towards Lennie, asked him politely: 'Could you help me with this, young man?'

'Oh, certainly,' said Lennie.

He swiftly removed the ornament. Then Mrs Appleby unclipped her glittering bracelet. She handed both items to Fletcher. 'I'm going to have to give these to you, Fletcher. For your safe keeping.'

'I see, Madam,' said Fletcher and took the precious things.

'It's my custom,' explained Mrs Appleby. 'I'll sleep easier in my mind.'

Fletcher disappeared into the inner office to place the valuables in the safe. Mrs Appleby addressed Lennie.

'Do you work here?'

'No, mum.'

She smiled agreeably. 'I have a son your age. He's in the theatre.'

'Is he?'

'He's an actor. Very good too. But they don't seem to give him very big parts.'

Lennie said encouragingly: 'Oh well, one day – who knows?'

Fletcher returned with a receipt book. He made out a receipt for the jewellery and handed it to Mrs Appleby. 'There you are, Madam.'

Placing the receipt in her handbag, Mrs Appleby said: 'I should like some tea in the morning at nine-thirty. And a *Daily Telegraph*.'

'I'll make a note of that, Madam.'

Mrs Appleby smiled at both men and turned to depart, saying: 'Goodnight.' And she moved with dignity towards the stairs.

Fletcher gazed after her with an intent expression. When she was out of earshot, Lennie said: 'Nice old soul. Anyway, where was I? Oh yes, Ingrid thought that it was about time – '

At which point Fletcher slammed his palm on the counter and exclaimed: 'Got it! Got it!'

'What?' asked Lennie, mildly alarmed.

'I've just twigged, ain't I?'

Lennie, misconstruing this remark, gave a sigh of relief and said: 'Oh, well in that case I may as well be off.'

But, with a sneer in his voice, Fletcher went on: 'Nice old soul? Butter wouldn't melt? She's a bleeding con artist.'

Lennie frowned in astonishment. 'Who? The old dear?'

'Yeah.'

'Don't be daft, Fletch. That's typical of you, seeing the worst in people.'

But Fletcher shook his head firmly. 'No, no, it's all clicked, my son. Listen, before you arrived, bloke come in here and I was sure I knew him from somewhere, see. Well, it's all come back. It's *Wellings*, aka Foster, aka Stansfield.'

Lennie was mystified. 'Aka?'

'A.K.A. equals "also known as". I was in Maidstone nick with that bloke. "Worm" Wellings.'

'So? What's the connection between this bloke and that nice old lady.'

'I'll tell you – '

'I'd rather talk about me and Ingrid.'

But Fletcher waved him silent irritably. 'Oh, leave it off about you and Ingrid. Now Worm Wellings used to do this con with a lady who some said was his mother. Used to work the South Coast, places like Bournemouth, Torquay. Small hotels, with safes like this one, you know? You could pick it with a paper clip.'

'What was the con?'

'They would insure jewellery. Declare a value of say ten thousand quid. Right. They check in separately. Different days even. No connection. She leaves her tomfoolery in the night safe. Then, middle of the night, she'll get the porter out of the way. Headache, you know, bring me a Beechams. Beggerlegs comes down and does the safe.'

Lennie nodded at the ingenuity of it. 'Oh, I see – then they collect the insurance, is it?'

'Yeah. And probably a backhander from the hotel to keep shtum. Course, the jewellery's fake. Look, I'll show you.' Beckoning Lennie to follow he retreated into the inner office.

Lennie thought of an objection. 'Even if it's fake, they'd have to pay a big insurance premium.'

'Only till they pull the job off. Then it's new name, new town, new policy.'

He opened the safe and withdrew the jewellery. He examined it closely. 'Just as I thought – rubbish!'

'Let's have a shufty,' asked Lennie eagerly. He took the glittering pieces from Fletcher and inspected them. Fletcher murmured knowingly:

'Well, well, Worm Wellings –'

Lennie said: 'Looks real enough to me.'

'Oh, it would do to *you.* It's paste, you nurk.'

But another, and much more sinister, aspect of the situation suddenly struck Lennie. He exclaimed: 'Here, Fletch –'

'What?'

'Not good this. You and me. Ex-cons. Open safe.'

Fletcher nodded soberly. 'You're not wrong, Len.'

He swiftly replaced the sparklers in the safe and locked the door. At that moment, the buzzer on the switchboard sounded and both of them started guiltily. Then Fletcher pulled himself together and went to the switchboard. He picked up the phone.

'Hello? Oh, Mrs Appleby, is it?' Over the top of the instrument he gave Lennie a meaningful wink. 'Cup of hot milk? In a jiffy, Madam.' He replaced the phone and addressed Lennie sadly. 'What did I tell you? What did I tell you?'

Lennie, his brow furrowed in thought, exclaimed: 'This could be a golden opportunity for you, Fletch.'

'How?'

'Call the law, right? They hide somewhere. You take up the milk. Wellings comes down, does the safe and they collar him. Who's the hero? You are – think how that would go down with your parole board. Not to mention the owner of this hotel. Flaming golden opportunity.'

He smiled proudly. But the smile was wiped off his face by Fletcher growling: 'That's despicable.'

'Pardon?'

Fletcher shook his head in disgust. 'And to think you're taking up with my daughter.'

'I don't follow.'

'Look, sonny Jim, you and I have had the strength to go straight, right? This bloke obviously hasn't. But would you want to see him inside and what's more live with the knowledge that you were party to it?'

Lennie looked crestfallen. He shook his head sadly. 'No – wouldn't wish that on anyone.'

'Call the law!' echoed Fletcher contemptuously.

Lennie said humbly, 'Sorry. I didn't think it through.'

'No, you never do, do you?'

It was strange. As soon as the subject of crime had come up, Fletcher and Lennie had resumed their old prison relationship. Fletcher was again the experienced pro and Lennie the apprentice.

'All the same, Fletch,' said Lennie hesitantly, 'you can't risk anything untoward on your turf.'

Fletcher nodded. 'That's true. That *is* true.'

'Not in your position.'

'No.'

Fletcher was thinking hard. 'So – er – what are you going to do then?' asked Lennie.

Later that night, Fletcher knocked loudly on the door of the small, upper room of the hotel. The occupant, Mr Wellings, was a sound sleeper and so, while registering the tumult dimly, he did not respond. Hard on the heels of the knock, however, there came the grating sound of a key turning in a lock. The door flew open. The light in the room came on and Mr Wellings sat up in bed, asking crossly: 'What's going on?'

Fletcher smiled reassuringly. 'Sorry to disturb you, sir, but I had no choice. This is Sergeant Godber of the Yard.'

'The Yard!' said Wellings, in dismay.

At this point Lennie, trying to remember the right procedure, flashed his union card quickly enough for it to be mistaken for a detective's I.D. card, and announced: 'Fraud Squad.'

'Fraud Squad?' echoed Wellings.

Lennie assumed a hard, accusing expression. 'We know your game, chummy. We know the number you've been running.'

Fletcher, looking anxious and flustered, addressed Lennie. 'I hope we'll be able to keep this quiet, Sergeant? Don't want the hotel getting a bad name.'

Wellings looked from one to the other and said, in a tired voice: 'I don't know what you're on about.'

Lennie smiled faintly. 'Do you deny that you're Worm Wellings, also known as Foster, also known as Stansfield?'

A bitter expression played about Worm Wellings's thin lips. 'They never let you forget, do they? It was years ago.'

Lennie nodded. 'Got away with it down the South Coast, did you? Well, you'll find we're a little more alert in the smoke, sonny Jim.'

Fletcher, fussing like an old maid, pleaded: 'Listen, sergeant, if there's going to be an arrest, could we do it surreptitious, like down the fire escape with a hood over his head?'

Wellings climbed wearily out of bed. He was wearing Marks and Spencer pyjamas with (prophetically?) stripes. He said to Lennie, 'Listen, I'm going straight.'

At this point Fletcher made an abrupt switch of character.

The old maid disappeared and Fletch, the three-time loser, addressed the other old con, Worm Wellings. 'You are now, if you've got any sense, my son.'

Wellings, astonished by the transformation, stared at him. 'Pardon?'

Fletcher smiled mirthlessly. 'You don't remember me, do you? Fletcher. We was in Maidstone many moons ago.'

Wellings glanced from Fletcher to Lennie and then back at Fletcher. 'Did you shop me?'

Fletcher jerked his head sideways at Lennie. 'Only to him.'

'What do you mean, only to him?' cried Wellings indignantly. 'He's only the Yard.'

Fletcher shook his head. 'He's a truck driver. Only yard he knows is the one he backs his lorry into.'

Wellings looked perplexed. 'Is this supposed to be a joke then?'

'No,' said Fletcher sternly. 'It's a warning. If you've got anything up here, you'll take heed of it. Here, take this lot.' Whereupon he produced Mrs Appleby's glittering ornaments from his pocket and threw them on to the bed. He continued: 'There's your Christmas cracker jewellery. Take it and then you and the old lady clear out of here in the morning.'

Wellings looked from the jewellery to Fletcher and back. He seemed dazed by having been caught out.

Lennie said encouragingly: 'Listen, I've done time and all. And now I'm going straight. Fletcher and I both are. And you can do it too. I know it take patience and bottle but if you –'

At this point, he broke off with a faint 'whoof' because Fletcher had dug him in the ribs. 'That's enough, Billy Graham! No one's taking up a collection.'

And they left Worm Wellings to his conscience.

Nothing else of note occurred that night. The next morning,

the usual delivery of papers for the guests occurred and Fletcher began laying the journals out in neat piles. As he was doing so, the couple whose car had conveniently broken down just round the corner crept down the stairs. Fletcher noticed that they didn't look particularly refreshed by their night's sleep. But he said cheerfully:

'My word, you're early risers.'

The man nodded and tried to smile. 'Yes – well, the thing is, I called the AA and they said they'd already fixed the car.'

'Really?' said Fletcher interestedly. 'Must have taken a bit of doing that, since there isn't a phone in your room.'

'I – ' said the man helplessly. Then he gave it up, turned to the girl and urged: 'Come along, let's be off, Beryl.'

'Cheryl,' said the girl sourly.

As they left, they passed Mr McEwan who was just entering.

'Good morning, Fletcher,' said McEwan, looking approvingly at the orderly newspapers.

'Morning, Mr McEwan,' returned Fletcher.

The boss flicked his thumb towards the now-departed couple and asked: 'Late arrivals, were they?'

Fletcher nodded. 'Yes, sir. But don't worry, sir. It was cash up front.'

McEwan smiled briefly. 'That's the ticket.'

He took up the receipt book for the night-safe and read the carbons. He nodded with satisfaction.

'And I see you put Mrs Appleby's jewellery in the night safe.'

Smiling complacently, Fletcher nodded: 'Yes, it's quite secure, sir.'

McEwan put down the book. A reminiscent light came into his eyes.

'Delightful old soul, Mrs Appleby. She's been coming here for years.'

There was a sudden flutter in Fletcher's chest. 'Did you

say – for years, sir?' he asked, and he could hear himself how his voice quavered.

McEwan nodded. 'Last Friday of every month. She always stays here even though she could afford Claridges if she wanted. Always leaves her jewellery in the safe.'

'Worth a bit, is it, sir?' Fletcher managed to force out.

'About twelve thousand pounds, so I understand. Her husband – that is, her late husband – was Appleby's toffees.' He noticed that Fletcher had become rather pale and was gripping the edge of the counter for support. He asked anxiously: 'Fletcher, is anything wrong?'

Fletcher nodded. 'Feeling slightly queasy, sir. I think I'll just pop upstairs and see if I can get something for it.'

There was, however, nothing suggestive of weakness in the way Fletcher shot across the lobby and bounded up the stairs like a baboon. A moment later, using his pass-key, Fletcher unlocked and flung open the door of the room that had, but a short time before, been occupied by Worm Wellings. The worm, however, had flown. Nothing, as far as Fletcher could see, remained to suggest that Wellings had ever occupied the room. Fletcher knew that Mr Wellings could not have departed by the front door. He would have seen him. Fletcher saw the curtains stir slightly. He hurried to the window and gazed out. A fire escape led very conveniently to the street below.

'Oh, my Gawd!' wailed the Night Security Officer.

Later that morning, Fletcher sat slumped on a chair beside the kitchen table in his own home. Ingrid and Lennie glanced at each other and then back at Fletcher with concern. They had already spent a long time trying to console the stricken parolee.

'Would a cup of tea help, dad?' asked Ingrid.

'No,' sighed Fletcher. 'I might as well pack me little bag and get the train up to Slade Prison. Save the tax payer the expense of an arrest.'

Ingrid tried to sound encouraging. 'They might well believe you, dad.'

'Don't be daft, Ingrid,' said Fletcher, without heat. 'I'm an ex-con.'

'Never know though,' Lennie said judiciously. 'I mean, the story's so ludicrous it does have a ring of authenticity.'

'That's right,' said Ingrid. 'And you're a witness, Len.'

But Godber protested at once. 'Leave me out of it. I'm an ex-con too, remember?'

'Oh, thank you,' exclaimed Fletcher sardonically. 'That's nice, ain't it?'

'Well, there's no point in us both being falsely arrested,' maintained Lennie.

'Look, dad,' urged Ingrid, 'you got till tonight. And you got a lot of contacts. You know all the bent people around. Put the word about and maybe someone will nail Worm Wellings for you.'

Fletcher shook his head bitterly. 'By now, Worm Wellings is probably in Amsterdam or wherever they fence priceless jewellery.'

'I always thought it was the real McCoy,' said Lennie, unintentionally rubbing salt into his old mate's wounds. 'I mean, I could tell at a glance they weren't paste.'

'Oh, you knew they weren't paste?' returned Fletcher ironically. 'You know they weren't fish-paste – that's about all you knew.'

'It's not surprising they were genuine, though,' Ingrid pointed out. 'Not if you say her husband was Appleby's toffees. I mean it's a famous brand that.'

Fletcher nodded. 'Yeah. And to think I used to be very fond of their weekend assortment and all. This has put me off toffee for life. I'm obviously being punished for things I got away with in days gone by. It's not fair but then when was life ever fair? My only hope is I get sent to a different nick. Because the thought of Mackay's face when he sees me coming through that door is more than I can bear.'

Fletcher gave a hoarse sob and buried his face in his hands. Ingrid and Lennie shook their heads sadly. Then Ingrid attracted Lennie's attention with a hooked forefinger and, when she had obtained it, mouthed the words to him silently.

'Did you tell him last night?'

Lennie looked puzzled but mouthed back:

'What?'

'Did you tell him last night about you and me?'

'No.'

'Put off, put off, put off.'

'How could I with all that going on?'

'Better tell him now.'

'Can't now,'

'Before its too late!'

Perhaps, in their excitement, their mouthings had turned into whisperings. Because at this point Fletcher uncovered his face, looked up at them and asked pointedly: 'Before what's too late?'

Lennie gulped uneasily. 'Well, er – it's probably not the best time to tell you, Fletch, what with you having so much on your mind and that – but – er – Ingrid felt that we should probably let you know that – er – we're getting married.'

Having actually brought it out, Lennie made a nervous gesture and edged towards Ingrid, as if for protection. She also moved a little towards him. They looked as if they were ready to fly into each other's arms to escape a father's wrath. Fletcher, looking from one to the other, rose slowly to his feet. He spoke:

'Congratulations. I'm sorry I won't be there to see it. I hope you'll both be very happy.'

And he ambled sadly from the kitchen. Lennie and Ingrid looked at each other in astonishment. Then Lennie called after the retreating form: 'There's no need to take it like that, Fletch!'

At about 7 o'clock that evening, Mr McEwan was surprised to see Fletcher plod slowly into the lobby of his hotel. The Night Security Officer was not due for hours. Nor was he clad in his working suit.

'Hello, Fletcher,' he exclaimed. 'What are you doing here at this time of the evening?'

Fletcher sighed heavily and said: 'I just wanted to have a word with you, sir. Has Mrs Appleby been down yet?'

McEwan shook his head. 'No. She'll be down any minute now. In time for the theatre.'

'Yeah. Well, I wanted to have a word with you before she did. I'm afraid there's something I have to tell you – '

But McEwan glanced towards the stairs and forestalled him with: 'Can it wait just a tick, Fletcher? I'm in the middle of something. I've got a plumber in fourteen.'

'No mad rush,' Fletcher admitted. 'All the time in the world, in fact.'

McEwan nodded gratefully and headed for the stairs. Fletcher glanced about the lobby. A few weeks ago, when he'd first entered it, it had seemed pretty dreary. Now he gazed upon it with the fondness of a reluctant emigrant taking his last look at his native shore. He sighed and went round to the back of the reception desk. He opened a drawer and slowly removed from it his meagre possessions. A voice spoke his name. He looked up and was amazed.

'Wellings!'

The Worm nodded soberly. 'I hoped you'd be here. Brought you these.'

He withdrew from his pocket a manilla envelope and handed it to Fletcher. Incredulously, Fletcher peered inside. He saw Mrs Appleby's jewels! Wellings took out his wallet. 'And I want to pay for my room too.'

Fletcher, with a strenuous effort, pulled himself together. He gave Worm Wellings a questioning look. 'I have to ask, Worm – why?'

Wellings sighed faintly. 'I really have been going straight

– for six years now. I didn't know what the hell was going on last night. But what you did was, you handed me temptation. And suddenly all my intentions, all my promises to myself and family, just went out the window.'

Fletcher could not suppress a smile. 'Much as you did – down the fire escape.'

'Right. It ain't been easy, the straight and narrow. Making do, getting by – just.'

'Don't have to tell me, son,' Fletcher said feelingly.

'I got a fairly decent job now. I sell bathroom tiles. Car goes with it, expenses. It's not much but it's honest. And you sleep at night.'

'Good evening, Fletcher,' said a musical voice from the direction of the stairs.

They both turned and beheld Mrs Appleby, radiant in evening attire, bearing down on them. Fletcher instantly assumed his porter's dignity.

'Oh, good evening, Mrs Appleby.'

Wellings nodded politely at the glamorous arrival. Mrs Appleby favoured him with a gracious smile before turning to Fletcher.

'I'll be needing my jewellery.'

Fletcher nodded briskly. 'Certainly, mum. I've got it right here.' And he slid the trinkets from their envelope.

Mrs Appleby frowned slightly. 'Wasn't it locked up?'

Fletcher nodded. 'I just got it out, ma'am. Knowing you'd be coming down, like.'

'I see,' and she took the necklace and held it to her neck. Then she turned to Wellings. 'Could you help me with this, young man?'

Behind her back, Wellings and Fletcher exchanged a wry glance as the Worm, a dab hand with jewels, did as he had been asked.

Fletcher said: 'Where is it tonight, Ma'am?'

'I'm going to see a new play,' she said with enthusiasm. 'I'm told it's rather sordid and sexually explicit.'

'Oh dear,' commiserated Fletcher.

'I do hope so. It's three-fifty a ticket.'

'D'you need a cab, ma'am?'

Mrs Appleby shook her head. 'Mr McEwan's already taken care of that. By the way, Fletcher, last night I never got my hot milk.'

'Sorry, ma'am,' apologised Fletcher earnestly. 'Emergency come up. Won't happen again.'

Mrs Appleby forgave him with a gracious smile.

'Goodnight then.'

'Goodnight,' said Fletcher.

'Goodnight,' echoed Worm Wellings.

Mrs Appleby swept out of the lobby. Wellings looked after her. Then he nodded. 'I get it. You thought me and her was working the old game together.'

Fletcher nodded. 'You can see my point of view, Worm. Afraid people like us just see the worst in others.'

'You weren't far wrong. At ten o'clock this morning I was round at the fence's. Ernie Fish – d'you know him?'

Fletcher was surprised. 'Is Ernie Fish still alive? I thought he'd snuffed it years ago.'

'He's still there. Off the Caledonian Road. And so was I with the gear. Scares me that. How easy I succumbed. Thought I'd kicked the habit. But I was like an ex-alcoholic who suddenly finds a case of scotch on his bed.'

Fletcher drew himself up. 'Now, my son,' he began, 'don't sell yourself so short. Sure you was tempted. But you licked it. As your presence here indicates, you brought the stuff back. You'll be all right, mate. Why you're an example to us all.'

But Worm Wellings seemed far from convinced. Shaking his head mournfully, he said: 'Am I? What worries me is, would I have brought it back if Ernie Fish had said it was genuine?'

Going Off The Rails

At a sign from the inspector, the sergeant opened the door leading into the yard. From it issued a file of men who shuffled uncomfortably forwards until halted by a word from the sergeant. The men were then asked to face the front. Their expressions varied from resigned to indignant and none looked more indignant than Norman Stanley Fletcher.

The inspector spoke in a low voice to the middle-aged, middle-class lady with the flustered expression standing beside him.

'Now, Mrs Gilchrist, I want you just to walk along the line and if you recognise the man in question, point to him. No need to speak. Just point him out – right?'

Mrs Gilchrist swallowed nervously and nodded. She thereupon set out to inspect her guard of dishonour. Now it is an astonishing fact that any man alive, placed in a police line-up, immediately acquires the look of a hardened felon. If the police assembled a line-up of saints, mystics and dedicated philanthropists the uninformed observer would doubtless find in each and every one of them the appearance of a ruthless enemy of society.

Mrs Gilchrist, shuddering slightly, passed down the line. Evil they may have all looked but she had a clear impression in her mind of the man she sought. And she did not see him there. After she had passed Fletcher and his neighbour, the former whispered:

'You look relieved.'

'I beg your pardon,' remonstrated the neighbour, who happened to be a very ethical accountant, 'I do not.'

'Yes, you do. I heard your knees knocking.'

'Quiet!' called the inspector.

Mrs Gilchrist paused at the end of the line and looked hard at a dapper little man in his late thirties sporting flashy cuff-links. But then she sighed and shook her head.

'I'm afraid not,' she admitted.

The inspector looked disappointed. 'Are you sure, madam? Take your time.'

But Mrs Gilchrist was not of a hysterical nature. She shook her head firmly. 'I'm positive, inspector. As I told you he had ginger hair. Curly ginger hair.'

'Could have been a wig,' suggested the inspector hopefully.

Fletcher looked outraged. He hissed: 'Clutching at straws. He wants an arrest – don't matter who.'

'Quiet!' roared the sergeant.

The inspector, with a vengeful look at the line-up, escorted the lady back into the station. The sergeant said: 'Thank you for your co-operation, gentlemen.'

Fletcher grunted. 'Little choice, some of us.'

'Don't moan, Fletcher,' the sergeant advised. 'Got a free cup of tea, didn't you?'

'I wasn't looking for a handout. Why do you harass us old lags?'

'It's not harassment, Fletch,' the sergeant pointed out. 'It's just that you've got a villainous face. Gives our line-up the right tone.'

The little man with the glittering cuff-links asked the sergeant: 'What did she allege he done then? The bloke you're looking for?'

The sergeant returned grimly: 'Oh, we've been after him for a while. Been annoying a lot of people in this area.'

'Doing what?'

'Flashing.'

Fletcher pricked up his ears and grinned. 'Why did she look at our faces then?' he asked.

The sergeant disdained to reply and the little band of helpful citizens was dismissed. As they left the prison yard,

Fletcher became aware that the dapper little man was walking at his side. He gave him a questioning look and the other asked: 'You don't recognise me, do you?'

'Should I?'

'Dave Pybus. Used to use your local in the old days. The Hand and Flower. When Alf Tonks was there.'

That rang a bell. Fletcher nodded. 'Oh, Alf, yeah.' He considered his companion more closely but then shook his head. 'I'm sorry though – I just don't – '

'You know my brother. Eric "Clapper" Pybus.'

'Oh, Clapper, yes. Yes, I remember him.'

It counted as a reunion. A few minutes later, Pybus and Fletcher were stationed in the saloon bar of the nearest boozer and the barmaid was handing them their drinks.

'Thank you, love,' cooed Pybus, 'and have one yourself.'

'Oh ta,' exclaimed the barmaid. 'I'll have a tonic.'

'Look no further,' said Pybus roguishly.

Then Pybus took his large scotch, and Fletcher his foaming pint, to a table and they both seated themselves. Pybus remarked: 'Over the teeth, behind the gums, look out stomach, here she comes!'

And they both sampled their tipples enthusiastically. Then Fletcher asked: 'So how is Clapper, then?'

Pybus grinned. 'Going like them, isn't he?'

'Like what?'

'The clappers. He does very nicely, does Eric. Got a big house up Mill Hill. Georgian style with a full-size billiard table, sauna bath, the works. He does very nicely. And he's never done, you know. Got no form.'

Fletcher nodded non-committally. 'How about yourself?' he asked.

'Oh, I had a bit of a setback – couple of years ago.'

Fletcher grunted. 'Yes, well, we've all had a few of those.'

'Not been out long, have you?' asked Pybus sympathetically.

'Not long, no.'

'How's it going?'

'Very well indeed,' maintained Fletcher.

Pybus looked at him doubtfully. 'Oh?'

'I made provision, didn't I?' elaborated Fletcher. 'I got a house and all. Muswell Hill. Also Georgian. In my case, George the Fifth. Ain't got a sauna bath, but we've got a little shed in the back what houses two bicycles and a wringer.'

'What about readies?' queried Pybus. 'Got anything going?'

'Quite a few things,' Fletcher assured him. 'I've been thinking, in fact, of transferring most of my assets to an off-shore tax shelter haven in Bermuda.'

'Oh?' asked Pybus, a trifle out of his depth.

'On the other hand, what with all the political unrest in the Caribbean, it may be wiser, in the long run, to leave them where they are, in the Piggy Bank on the mantelpiece.'

Pybus laughed pleasantly. 'Almost had me going there, Fletch.'

'Oh, don't worry about me. I got a lot of irons in the fire. Trouble is, I can't afford to light the fire.'

Pybus nodded sympathetically. 'I know what it's like, me old mate.'

'Do you?' Fletcher gave Pybus's flashy gear a significant look. 'I must say, Dave, you don't look as if you're on your uppers. The whistle, you know, and the car we drove here in. Automatic, two-tone, real leather upholstery, wing mirrors.'

Pybus shrugged modestly. 'Thinking of changing it. It's coming up to twenty thousand and my bloke, you know – what puts the spanners to it – he says, best do it now, Dave, before something big goes like the gearbox.'

Fletcher nodded approval. 'I got the same problem with my bike. Might have to trade it in before the chain drops off.'

Pybus smiled understandingly. Then he turned and called to the barmaid. 'Same again, love.'

Fletcher, moving his hand experimentally to his pocket, said, 'I'll get these. My round, pay my whack.'

Pybus shook his head firmly. 'No, you're all right.'

'Suit yourself,' agreed Fletcher, thankfully withdrawing his hand again.

Pybus glanced about and then pulled his chair a little closer to the table. He lowered his voice. 'Here, listen, Fletch. It might be quite fortuitous, bumping into you like this – '

A guarded look immediately appeared on Fletcher's face. 'Oh yes?'

'It might be that I'm in a position to help you.'

'Oh yes?'

'It might be that I could put something your way.'

Fletcher considered this for a moment in silence. Then he asked: 'Put what my way?'

Pybus smiled knowingly. 'Something – you know – '

His hand flickered slightly and so did an eyebrow. Fletcher looked askance. Pybus tapped the side of his nose. Fletcher frowned. Pybus did a little tap-dance on his temple with a forefinger and winked. Finally he gave utterance: 'Enough said.'

'You ain't said nothing yet,' Fletcher pointed out.

'I think we understand each other,' Pybus maintained.

Fletcher sighed and asked: 'Why should you do me any favours?'

'Not a question of favours, is it? You're a gen bloke, you are, Fletch. Hard to come by these days. Solid reputation. I know people who value integrity.'

'Before you go any further, me old son,' Fletcher cautioned, 'I should make it clear that I'm going straight.'

Pybus nodded. 'Course you are. That's understood.'

'So it should be clearly understood that anything you put my way would only be considered if it is strictly within the letter of the law.'

With a show of indignation, Pybus asked shrilly: 'What sort of person do you think I am?'

'A crooked person,' said Fletcher calmly. 'The sort of person my parole officer is most anxious for me to avoid.'

Pybus shook his head sadly. 'Depends how you define crooked, mate. I mean, there's crooked and crooked. I got a legitimate business now. We manufacture party novelties, paper hats, jokes. Amuse your friends, and so on.'

'Anyway,' said Fletcher, 'I appreciate your offer and the drinks, Dave, but I have to keep me nose clean. Not just for me – it's the family. My eldest daughter's getting married in a couple of weeks.'

The barmaid placed the new order on the table, accepted the money from Pybus and withdrew.

'Really?' asked Pybus. 'Here, I can let you have some cut-rate confetti.'

Meanwhile, back at the Fletcher spread, wedding preparations were proceeding. In the living-room Ingrid was cutting out patterns for a lovely new dress with which to delight the eyes of her betrothed, Leonard Godber. This same Leonard Godber, rubbing the sleep from his eyes, presently entered the room. The fact that he was newly-awakened was also indicated by the fact that his shirt was unbuttoned and was being worn over his trousers. Hearing him, Ingrid looked up and said fondly: 'Hello, love. You *did* have a sleep.'

'Should have woke me,' said Lennie.

'Couldn't bring meself to. You look ever so sweet when you're asleep. About six years old.'

The knight of the motorways grinned lecherously. 'Yeah, but when I wake up I feel a bit older than that.'

He advanced upon his beloved and allowed his feelings to spill over into action. Ingrid, wriggling happily, said: 'Yes, I know what you feel like when you've just woken up.'

'I feel like *you*,' declared the Lone Trucker. 'But when I reached out for the firm contours of your nubile young body, you weren't there.'

Ingrid tried to disengage herself. 'Don't. You'll mess up

me pattern. I'm halfway through the bodice.'

'Nice word that, bodice,' said Lennie appreciatively. ' "He drew her to him, and then with his teeth loosened the strap of her pink bodice".'

His teeth were chewing gently but amorously on Ingrid's quivering shoulder when, right on cue, Fletcher made his entrance.

'Oh my Gawd!' he exclaimed, more from habit than outrage.

'Hello, Fletch,' Godber greeted him.

'Hello, dad,' echoed Ingrid.

Fletcher said wryly, 'I suppose my presence gives your courtship a bit of spice. A hint of the illicit. Because you never know when I'm going to walk in. When you're married and it's all above board, your sex life will probably fizzle out.'

'Nothing will change,' Lennie reassured him. 'Because we'll still be living here until we find a decent place.'

'And you'll be just as irritable when you come in the door,' Ingrid added.

'Some people,' began Fletcher with slight sarcasm, 'put something aside before they rush headlong into marriage. So they won't be a burden to their in-laws.'

'Come on, dad,' remonstrated Ingrid. 'You'd hate it if I left. Who'd look after you then? Not Raymond, that's for sure.'

'Nothing will change,' Lennie amplified. 'I'll still be away a lot of the time, on the road. So for half the week you can still treat this house as if it were your own.'

Fletcher said humbly, 'You're too good to me, you are, Len.'

He went to seat himself but Ingrid said sharply, 'Don't sit there, dad. There's pins all over the place.'

Fletcher made his way to a safer chair, saying, 'Wedding dress, is it?'

'Going away outfit,' Ingrid corrected him.

'Oh, going away? Must be nice to be able to afford going away. Where is it you're going?'

'Oh, I can never pronounce it,' grumbled Ingrid. 'What's it called, Len?'

'Lanzarote,' supplied Lenny.

'That's it, Lanzarote,' agreed Ingrid.

'Len's a rotter, you mean, don't you? We all know that. Where is it,' asked Fletcher.

'We're not quite sure,' confessed Ingrid. 'Can't find it on the map. But it's out the ordinary. Not too touristy.'

'It's volcanic,' Lennie said.

'Oh, nice that,' enthused Fletcher. 'Should get you out of bed in the morning.'

'Oh, don't be silly, dad,' protested Ingrid. 'The volcanoes are dormant.'

'All volcanoes is dormant, gel,' insisted her father, 'until that terrible night when they erupt and cover everyone in molten rocks and flying sherbert.'

Ingrid shivered faintly at this graphic disaster scenario. 'He could be right, Len,' she said. 'Never know with those things.'

'Don't listen to him,' advised Lennie. 'If there was any danger, would it be described as a "fast-growing holiday centre" in the brochure?'

Genuinely puzzled, Fletcher asked: 'How come you choose a place you can't pronounce, can't find on the map and it's got volcanoes?'

'Because,' said Lennie, with crushing logic, 'it's cheap. Because we're watching every penny. We got this special deal from Marion's boyfriend.'

'Him what's got the travel agency,' Ingrid amplified.

'He's not still in business, is he?' asked Fletcher incredulously. 'Haven't they tumbled him yet? Every time you see one of them headlines "Holidaymakers in Uproar at London Airport" – that's him.'

'He's always been very good to us,' maintained Ingrid

stoutly. 'It was him who got us to Rimini last year.'

'The miracle is he got you back,' grunted Fletcher.

Lennie nodded. 'Eventually,' he said reminiscently.

But Ingrid, loyal to her sister's tycoon boyfriend, rounded on him. 'Now don't you start.'

Fletcher asked: 'Isn't he the bloke what left a plane-load of Welshmen stranded in Morocco? None of whom have been heard from since. Still, I suppose they must be there somewhere, singing away, keeping a welcome in the Wadis.'

'Now leave it off, dad,' said Ingrid crossly. 'No need to put the mockers on this wedding.'

'Just concerned about your finances, girl. Who's paying for everything – that's what I'd like to know.'

'I'll tell you, shall I?' offered Ingrid. 'Honeymoon's courtesy of Marion, indirectly. My wedding outfit's courtesy of the girls at the salon who had a whip round. Len's Mum's brother, his Uncle Bertram, he's donating the cake because he's a master baker.'

'He's a *what*?' asked Fletcher.

'Master baker,' repeated Lennie. 'One of the best in Droitwich.'

Fletcher shrugged. 'Not much else to do up there, is there?'

And Ingrid concluded: 'And we're doing it in the Registry Office to save the expense of a church.'

'Oh yes?' asked Fletcher cynically. 'And what about this reception you want? You need a hall, caterers, and loads of booze, knowing our family. Not to mention the hordes of Godbers who'll come creeping out of the woodwork. Who's paying for all that?'

Neither Ingrid nor Lennie seemed to have ingenious solutions to this important problem. They exchanged a quick glance and then Ingrid asked: 'Have you seen my thimble, Len?'

But Fletcher was tenacious. 'I said, who's paying for that then?'

Ingrid glanced about on the floor. 'Have I dropped it somewhere?'

And Lennie, also apparently keenly interested in the thimble hunt, asked: 'Could it be on the floor, love?'

'Never mind hunt the bleeding thimble,' urged Fletcher irritably. 'Let's discuss this. You both know my – situation. But you are my daughter and I am the father of the bride, so naturally I shall do my best. I'm not saying I can run to the Dorchester but I had a word with Ernie Lax, him what's got the Lamb and Flag, and he don't mind if we use that room round the back. He says he'll unboard the windows, air it out a bit. We could get a few chairs in and maybe put a big cloth over the old billiard table.'

Lennie and Ingrid exchanged another glance. But neither of them could think of any more evasive action. Ingrid said: 'Dad, that's very sweet of you but – '

'Well, we can't have it here, girl,' Fletcher rightly pointed out. 'There's just not the room.' A thought struck him. 'Tell you what – we could use Dave Greener's garage.'

Ingrid swallowed and then said quietly, 'It's all been taken care of, dad.'

But Fletcher did not catch the remark. He did a little dancing whirl, as if with a partner, and said with a chuckle, 'Room for dancing there.'

'I said,' affirmed Ingrid with a little more lung, 'it's all been taken care of.'

Fletcher stopped twirling and gazed at her hard. Lennie cleared his throat and then said: 'I'll see if that thimble's in the kitchen, Ingrid.'

But she quickly ordered: 'You stay here, you!'

Fletcher asked curiously, 'You've made arrangements?'

Ingrid nodded. Then she said, 'You know the old manor house? Up near Edgware?'

'Yeah.'

'Well, it's going to be there, in their Gilbert and Sullivan room.'

Fletcher said wearily, 'I can't afford *that!*'

'It's booked and paid for,' Ingrid said firmly.

There was a pause. Fletcher looked from Ingrid to his prospective son-in-law. Then he asked quietly, 'Who by?'

Ingrid swallowed hard. 'Well – mum was over Tuesday, see. You know, discussing this and that. She was sorry to miss you, but I think you was down the Probation Office.'

'Yes,' said Fletcher impatiently. 'Yes? Yes?'

'And she suddenly told me that this was a present from her and – Reg.'

Fletcher's voice became hard. 'What? What right have you got to accept anything from Reg Jessop? He is not family. He is merely the bloke what lives with your mother.'

Lennie attempted to be diplomatic. 'Well, that sort of makes him – '

'Shut up, you! It doesn't make him anything. Apart from exhausted.'

Ingrid, with steel in her voice, said, 'I have known Reg for years. He's almost like an uncle. Besides, it's Mum's present. It's just that it's him who's got the – '

'The money!' exploded Fletcher. 'Go on, say it – money, money, money.'

'Well, he's not short, Fletch,' Lennie tried again. 'He could buy the Manor House and not even notice the difference.'

Fletcher had passed beyond the first flush of rage. He said bitterly, 'You only think of yourselves, don't you?'

'Well, it *is* our wedding,' Lennie pointed out with some justice.

'You don't see how humiliating this is for me. Everyone's down there, nibbling chicken and sipping champagne, no doubt. Know what they'll be saying, don't you? "Know who paid for this? Her fella!" '

'He's not going to advertise the fact, dad,' Ingrid protested.

'Oh? He ain't the most modest of men, Reg Jessop. He'll

make sure they all know. "Drink up," he'll say, "I can afford it." '

'Fletch,' said Lennie, adopting a low and winning tone of voice. 'You're wrong when you say that we don't think of you. Isn't he, Ingrid?'

'Course he is,' she loyally agreed.

'It's just that,' Lennie continued in his most tactful manner, 'we know your circumstances. We know that at this point in time you haven't got the wherewithal. But believe me, if you had anything at all, Ingrid and me would be only too glad to take it!'

With an outraged snort, Fletcher stormed out of the room, slamming the door behind him. Conscious that somehow his diplomacy had fallen short of Whitehall standards, Lennie said to Ingrid: 'I didn't mean it that way.'

His future wife glared at him.

Late that night Fletcher sat in the lobby of the Studleigh Hotel polishing a pair of shoes when the swinging doors opened and Dave Pybus strolled in. With a quick movement, designed to prevent the affluent felon from observing him engaged on so menial a task, Fletcher swept the shoes out of sight.

'Hello, Fletch,' said Pybus, approaching the desk.

'Oh – hello, Dave.'

'Sorry I'm late but I only got your message an hour ago. I was at the White City.'

Fletcher looked puzzled. 'And who was that I spoke to at your home?'

'That would have been the wife.'

Fletcher shook his head. 'Not unless you married a fellow.'

'A fellow?' repeated Pybus, his jaw showing a tendency to sag. 'Round my house?'

'Yeah.'

'Answering my telephone?'

'Yeah.'

A look of understanding, that failed to be totally convincing, appeared on Pybus's face. 'Must have been her brother. Did he have a West country accent?'

Unyielding, Fletcher shook his head. 'More your West Indian.'

Agitation once more possessed Dave Pybus.

'What, round my house?'

'Oh, dear me,' clucked Fletcher, 'I've obviously opened a whole tin of mangoes here. There's doubtless a perfectly simple explanation why a West Indian is round your house with your wife at nine o'clock of an evening.'

'Like what?' asked Pybus hopefully.

'I don't know, do I? I don't know your wife. Didn't even know you *had* a wife until I rang up and spoke to her lover – I mean, the bloke what was round there, doing whatever he was doing,' Fletcher hastily corrected himself.

Pybus looked grim. 'I'll sort this out later.'

'Good – yes – I would do, Dave, because it's not the reason I asked you to come round –'

'No, I'm sure it isn't.'

'But I am sure,' pursued Fletcher in a meaningful tone of voice, 'you can work out why I *did* ask you to come round.'

Pybus nodded. 'Put two and two together, yes.'

'Good, good. Much as your wife was doing with that West Indian. All right, all right! You'll sort him out later.'

Pybus devoted a searching look to the surroundings. 'All right to talk here, is it?'

'Oh yes, safe as houses.'

Pybus nodded. 'Seems quiet enough.'

Fletcher nodded at the door. 'Anyone comes in now they'll be drunk – or randy.'

'This is what you do, is it?' asked Pybus. 'Night porter?'

Fletcher nodded sourly. 'Pro tem, yes.'

'I can see why you had second thoughts. Can't be making much at this.'

Anxious to keep the record straight, Fletcher cautioned:

'I haven't had second thoughts yet. Not until I know a bit more.'

Pybus shrugged. 'There's a limit to what I can tell you, of course. If you want in, you'd have to meet the blokes.'

Fletcher nodded. 'Naturally.'

'I can tell you one thing. You know a couple of them and they know you, so there'd be no problem.'

'What would be my function?' asked Fletcher calmly.

'Just peripheral – is that the word?'

'It's *a* word, certainly. What does it mean?'

'On the fringe. You know, lookout, like.'

Fletcher declared his principles. 'I won't have no truck with violence. Never have and not about to start. So if they're going in armed, or about to break heads, count me out.'

Pybus was affronted. 'You make a lot of demands, you do. For a night porter.'

'Yeah, well I'm not that desperate. I just need a few readies for – for something.'

Pybus smiled reassuringly. 'You can put your mind at rest, my son. There'll be none of that. These blokes, I tell you, they're a twenty-four carat bunch.'

Fletcher could never resist an opening. 'That's a big bunch of carats.'

But it was wasted on Pybus who continued: 'None of *them* is desperate either. It's been planned meticulous. It is the ace job.'

Fletcher sighed deeply. 'Every job I've ever done was the ace job.'

'Well, this certainly is. And for doing next to naff all there's five hundred quid in it for you.'

Fletcher could not suppress a faint gasp. 'Five hundred – when is it?'

'Saturday week.'

'Saturday week?' echoed Fletcher. 'Oh well, that's it then. Can't be done. Out of the question.'

'Why?'

'My daughter's getting married that day.'

The force of this one was not lost on Pybus. 'Oh dear! What time?'

'Two o'clock.'

Pybus's expression lightened. 'Oh, you're all right then. We'll be through by noon.'

'Noon?' repeated Fletcher doubtfully.

'Guaranteed.'

Fletcher shook his head. 'Too dodgy.'

'No honest. Has to be.' From long habit, Pybus glanced again about the empty lobby and lowered his voice. 'Some of the kids have planes to catch.'

'Planes?'

Pybus nodded smugly. 'I told you, this is big, Fletch. Not talking about you and me. But for the top echelon, like, these lads is off away. To sunnier climes. They're going to be tax exiles. Like Rod Stewart and the Rolling Stones.'

'Yeah?' Fletcher grinned. 'Funny, *they* made their money through daylight robbery and all.'

After a little more chit-chat the deal was concluded. And once it had been concluded, Fletcher gave it no more thought. He was, after all, a pro. He had tried to go straight but was it his fault that his daughter needed a wedding reception? He would never have resumed a life of crime on his own behalf but there was such a thing as paternal responsibility. He would do this one job, give Lennie and Ingrid the reception of a lifetime, and then resume the straight and narrow. It was settled.

So clear was his conscience that, the following morning, nothing impeded him from dropping off to sleep in his living-room when he got home from work. But although his conscience allowed him to sleep his future son-in-law did not. Lennie tiptoed into the room bearing a steaming mug of tea. He contemplated the sleeping porter with affection. He was sorry to have to shatter his well-earned slumber but there were matters to discuss. He moved to Fletcher's side and prodded him gently.

'Fletch?' he said softly.

Perhaps the mind of an old lag can never be entirely at peace. Fletcher started and said, 'Yes, Mr Mackay. What?'

'Sorry,' apologised Lennie.

Fletcher blinked away the sleep, recognised his assailant and shook his head sadly. 'Sorry for what?'

'For waking you.'

'You woke me,' exclaimed Fletcher indignantly, 'to tell me that you're sorry for waking me?'

'I had to wake you. I have to go to work.'

Fletcher glanced at the window and saw that, as usual, Lennie's massive lorry was obscuring most of the daylight. 'You're actually going to drive that thing that's been stuck outside my front window depriving me of warmth and sunlight?'

'Driving it to Wallasey,' explained Lennie proudly. 'Wallasey to Brum. Bristol, Swansea. Then up to Hull.'

Fletcher shook his head irritably. 'I don't want to know your bleeding itinerary.'

'Cracking the overtime, see.'

'You woke me up to tell me you were off to Wallasey?'

Lennie tactfully held out the steaming mug. 'Made you some tea.'

A suspicious look immediately sprang into Fletcher's eyes. 'If your battery's flat and you want a shove, forget it. I haven't got my elephant with me.'

'Wanted a word with you, Fletch,' said Lennie humbly. 'And with all this overtime I'll be doing I won't get much of a chance before the wedding.'

'Word about what?'

'The wedding.'

A mischievous sparkle replaced the suspicion in Fletcher's orbs. 'Cold feet? Calling it off?'

Lennie was hurt by the suggestion. 'You'd like that, you would. You don't think I'm good enough for Ingrid, you don't. Never have done.'

'Well, you're not,' maintained Fletcher with brutal candour.

'I am,' insisted Lennie stoutly. 'I'll make her happy.'

Fletcher grunted. 'Happy? What is happy? Happiness is a warm truck-driver, is that it?'

'I suppose,' said Lennie resentfully, 'you saw Ingrid marrying someone with a nice accent who wears a hacking jacket and a cravat. Bit like Dirk Bogarde when he was a Doctor in the House.'

'Don't get all chippy with me,' Fletcher rebuked him. 'You know what I'm like when I've just woken up.' A delicate tendril of steam from the mug reached his nostrils. He reached forwards and took the bevvy. 'Is this sugared?' he asked.

'Course it's sugared. Two and a half. I should know how to make your tea. The cups of tea I've made for you in the nick. Waiting on you, hand and foot.'

'Oh, listen to her,' chortled Fletcher. 'What are you so grumpy about all of a sudden?'

Lennie shook his head dispiritedly. 'Because you get up my goat, you do.'

'Wrong,' said Fletcher firmly.

'Pardon?'

'I *get* your goat,' Fletcher corrected the lad. 'I don't get *up* your goat. I get up your *nose*. Or on your wick.'

Lennie favoured him with a reproachful look, turned and headed for the door, calling back: 'You do all three. I'm off.'

'Hoy, you haven't told me –'

'Not going to now,' snapped Lennie.

'Hang on. It must have been important to wake me up.'

'It was,' confirmed Lennie, pausing. 'It was something nice I was going to say, but I'm not in the mood now.'

'Look, Len,' began Fletcher in a more conciliatory tone

of voice, 'your tea is wonderful. Finest cup you ever made. Fact is, you usually stew it.'

'Never again!' said Lennie with feeling. 'Never again will I make you a cup of tea, or fry you an egg or anything.'

Fletcher's expression brightened. 'Have you fried me an egg and all?'

'No.'

'Pity. I fancy an egg.'

Lennie sighed in exasperation. 'You just – I mean – I don't know. You make it almost impossible to be nice to you, you do.'

'Sit down,' urged Fletcher calmly, 'and cool down. Now what is it? Get it off your chest.'

Lennie tried. 'I may not be the most desirable of son-in-laws –'

'True,' said Fletcher promptly.

Lennie glared at him but continued: 'The fact remains, on Saturday I am marrying your daughter, Ingrid.'

Fletcher nodded. 'I have accepted that fact – just.'

'Fletch,' suggested Lennie desperately, 'it might be best if you let me say what I have to say, without any interruption.'

'Very well,' agreed Fletcher. 'My lips are sealed.'

'Okay then.' Lennie took a deep breath. 'Ingrid and I have been at loggerheads about your role at the wedding.' This inevitably provoked an indignant gesture from Fletcher, but Lennie hastily continued: 'Let me go on. You see, as Ingrid's dad, you should be giving her away.'

'Who else?' asked Fletcher, eyes narrowed dangerously.

'No, no,' protested Lennie. 'No one else. But there's a bit of a problem. How can you be in two places at once?'

Immediately a shifty look appeared on Fletcher's face. 'What are you on about? Who you been talking to?'

'No one. Only Ingrid.'

Fletcher tried to make sense of this. What did Lennie know? 'Then what,' he finally asked, 'are you trying to say?'

'Only that – I want you to be my best man as well.'

This declaration came as a complete surprise. 'Best man?' Fletcher echoed.

'You see, Fletch, I haven't got a lot of friends me own age. I used to have but prison changed all that. Half of them didn't want to know me, while the other half are still inside themselves. Besides, I thought it over and I said to meself, "Len, who's been closest to you over the past year or so?" Truth is, it's you, Fletch. Got me through stir, didn't you? You've been my cellie, my mate, my mentor. Father figure in some ways. Father-in-law, soon to be. But most of all – friend. More than that really. You've always been – an example to me. I respected you in nick. But nothing like the way I respect you on the outside. Not been easy for you, going straight. Tougher for you than for me. Because I'm younger and I've got Ingrid's love to sustain me. But doing what you're doing – that takes a lot of bottle.'

At this point Lennie noticed that, although obviously pleased by the torrent of praise, Fletcher was wriggling with embarrassment. But he continued: 'So anyhow, what we decided – with your say-so – was that you would accompany Ingrid on your arm, as the father of the bride. Then at the appropriate moment switch over to my side with the ring in your pocket. Okay?'

Fletcher felt unaccustomed emotion fill his breast. Then a thought struck him. 'Are you sure,' he asked, 'you haven't come up with this as an economy measure?'

'Oh now look, Fletch, I know you're hung up about not paying your whack – '

'Well, it's important to a father!' maintained Fletcher with fervour. 'If you hadn't rushed into things I'd have taken care of everything – in about five years.'

Lennie nodded. 'We know that. But let me tell you something, Fletch. If you agree to what we've asked, your contribution to this wedding will be a ruddy sight more than paying some catering bill.'

Fletcher was silent for a moment, reviewing certain things

and commitments in his mind. Then he nodded slightly. 'I see.'

'So is it on, then?'

'Can't see why not,' said Fletcher with little grace.

But Lennie was too delighted to notice his apparent lack of enthusiasm. He sprang forwards and clapped his father-in-law-to-be on the back. 'Great!' Then he turned towards the door again. 'I'll be off then.'

But Fletcher halted him with a quiet but somehow urgent word: 'Len?'

'Yeah?' asked Lennie, turning.

Fletcher sighed. 'I ain't the bleeding saint you think I am.'

Lennie smiled. 'None of us are, is we?'

Fletcher closed his eyes for an instant. Then he opened them again and, with an immense effort, mumbled something.

'Pardon?' asked Lennie.

'I said: I'm glad you're – ' and again his voice trailed off into incomprehensible mumbling.

'Sorry, Fletch, I still didn't catch it.'

'Okay. I said – ' and this time he practically bellowed it, 'I'm glad you're marrying my daughter! And now – piddle off to Wallasey!'

The wedding day arrived. From the four corners of the earth – well anyway from as far away as Birmingham – the wedding guests converged on the feast. The bride, assisted by her bridesmaids, groomed and cosseted herself and fan-dried her hair. The groom gulped Dutch courage with a couple of lorry driving mates. The mother of the bride, and her new paramour, inspected the catering arrangements in the luxurious chambers appointed for the reception. And the father of the bride sat in a van labelled 'Jeffcock and Sons: Woodworm Control' keeping a sharp eye out for the rozzers.

Had the rozzer happened along, he might have been surprised to discover that your modern Woodworm Controller apparently goes about his pesticidal business wearing his best suit with a black tie and a carnation in the buttonhole. Mercifully no rozzer showed up but Dave Pybus did, giving Fletcher a nasty moment as he swung open the van's door and slipped into the next seat.

'How's it going, Fletcher?' asked the dapper felon.

'You tell me, Dave,' said Fletcher reproachfully. 'You told me it would be over by twelve. Its quarter-to now.'

Pybus shrugged. 'Took them a bit longer to get through than they reckoned.'

'Through from where?' asked Fletcher, gazing at the street scene which included a nearby bank.

'The shop next door. Apparently there was a problem with the alarm circuit and all.'

'I've had to feed the meter twice,' grumbled Fletcher.

'Well, what do you want – expenses?'

'I'm just saying it wouldn't do to get towed away at this point, would it?'

This pleasant exchange was interrupted by an electronic bleep from somewhere in Fletcher's lap. He glanced down, picked up the walkie-talkie and, after pulling out the tiny aerial, spoke into it: 'Alpha Tango, over.'

From the handy little instrument came a voice:

'Alpha Tango, this is Casablanca. We would estimate revised point of departure to be fourteen hundred hours.'

Aghast, Fletcher turned to Pybus. 'Fourteen hundred? That's two o'clock!'

The voice from the little black box continued: 'Relay this message to transport, please. Over.'

Fletcher spoke wearily into the instrument. 'Message received and understood. Over and out.'

He pushed the aerial home and complained bitterly to Pybus, 'I thought you said they had planes to catch.'

Pybus shrugged again. 'No point getting on a plane without the spondulicks, is there?"

'Meticulous!' sneered Fletcher.

'You better go and ring transport, hadn't you?' suggested Pybus.

With a martyred air, Fletcher descended from the van and made his way to a telephone box several streets away. He entered it, made the important phone call, hung up and emerged once more. But he had taken no more than a couple of steps back towards the van when the blood froze in his veins.

'Morning, Fletch.'

Fletcher spun round. His worst fears were confirmed. A rozzer! A uniformed rozzer! In fact, the very same police sergeant that had recently harassed him on the identification parade.

'Morning,' he grunted back.

'Looking very spruce,' said the sergeant with a grin.

'Oh – yeah, well – I'm going to my daughter's wedding.'

'Nice day for it. Where's she getting married?'

'Muswell Hill. Registry Office like.'

'What you doing down these parts then?'

Alarm bells rang furiously in Fletcher's brain. He'd known old lags – plenty of them! – who'd ended up doing ten years of porridge because they couldn't think up a plausible answer when suddenly faced by a question of this kind. Doing in these parts? What the hell *could* he be doing in these parts? And then he became aware that his glance was, at that moment, being held by a cluster of leaping puppies. The dogs were in the window of a pet shop just behind the sergeant. Fletcher said: 'I just come about the present, see?'

'What present?'

'The puppy, of course.'

The sergeant turned and contemplated the endearing creatures. He shrugged. 'Funny sort of present.'

Fletcher shook his head firmly. 'She's always wanted one. And – er – I have to pick it up at the last minute, see? You can't hide a dog like you can a tea service, can you?'

'Which one is it?' asked the sergeant.

'It's in the back.' Fletcher grinned, sure of himself now. 'They're gift-wrapping him.'

The sergeant smiled at the pleasantry. 'I see. Well, don't let me stop you.'

'No – no.'

Fletcher marched confidently into the pet shop and the sergeant resumed his patrol. A little later, Fletcher emerged from the pet shop again. He was carrying something but it was not a puppy. He hurried to the Woodworm Control Van, pulled open the door and said: 'Look, Dave, count me out, right?'

'What?' asked Pybus in amazement.

'I'm off.'

'You can't do that!'

'I ain't letting anybody down. Job's almost done. I'm fairly superfluous really.'

Pybus said nastily, 'You quit now, you don't get paid!'

Fletcher smiled wistfully. 'Don't want to be. You can have my share. Don't want a penny. I'm off to my eldest's wedding.'

And with no further ado he closed the van door again and set off up the street towards the bus stop. Pybus was astonished to see, dangling from Fletcher's hand, a small cage with a canary in it.

'Who,' asked the registrar formally, 'gives this woman to be married to this man?'

'I do,' Fletcher said clearly.

Behind the bridal group were clustered eight or nine wedding guests. Ingrid looked lovely.

'Do you, Leonard Arthur Godber,' intoned the registrar, 'take this woman to be your lawful wedded wife?'

'I do,' said Lennie reverently.

'And do you, Ingrid Susan Fletcher, take this man to be your lawful wedded husband?'

'I do,' gasped Ingrid.

The registrar fixed his gaze on the vacant space at Lennie's side where the best man should have been stationed. He frowned slightly.

'Who has the ring?'

'Oh!' exclaimed Fletcher, emerging from a brown study. 'I do.' He hurried to the best man's position and produced the ring. Lennie took it from him and placed it on Ingrid's finger.

'I now pronounce you man and wife,' said the registrar.

Lennie, an expression of devotion on his manly features, leaned towards Ingrid. Just as their lips were about to meet, a faint but sharp voice announced: 'Casablanca calling all points. Mission accomplished.'

This cryptic announcement was followed by a medley of rascally voices chanting: 'We're in the money! We're in the money! We're in the money!'

As everyone, including the registrar and the bride and bridegroom, gazed about for the source of the unseemly interruption, Fletcher very surreptitiously fiddled with something in his pocket – and the voices stopped.

That evening, Fletcher, having fulfilled to perfection his duties as father of the bride, sat alone in his local having a pint. He still wore his best clothes but the carnation was a trifle wilted. He was idly running his eyes over the sports page when he was surprised by a slight 'clink' from the table in front of him. He shifted his paper and saw that someone had placed down two whiskies. He glanced up. Lennie!

'What are you doing here?' he asked anxiously. 'You're supposed to be off on your honeymoon.'

Lennie grinned reassuringly. 'The plane's delayed.'

Fletcher sighed. 'I warned you. didn't I?'

'Probably just fog.'

'Probably because the bleeding engine fell off. Where's Ingrid? Left her at home already?'

'She's in the ladies. We'll be away soon enough,' insisted Lennie confidently. 'I've found out where Lanzarote is.'

'Oh yes? Where?'

'Canary Islands.'

'And where would they be?'

Lennie looked surprised. 'I forgot to ask that.'

Fletcher contemplated Lennie's happy face. He said gently: 'Won't make much difference to you two where you are, will it?'

Lennie shook his head fervently. 'No.' But then the beatific expression left his face and a puzzled one replaced it. 'Speaking of canaries – why did you bring one to the wedding?'

Fletcher took a sip of his whisky. He looked thoughtful for a moment. Then he gave the faint snort of a man who has decided to come clean. 'If I tell you,' he said solemnly, 'you're not ever to mention this to our Ingrid. Or anyone else for that matter.'

'O.K. Cross me heart.'

'Well, you know I was very surly about this wedding. It wasn't anything to do with you. It was because I was the only one who seemed to be making no contribution. Anyhow, I got this proposition put to me.'

'At your age!' exclaimed Lennie roguishly, but Fletcher waved him silent.

'I mean, skullduggery.'

Lennie looked genuinely stricken. 'Oh, Fletch!'

'Let me finish. I didn't go the distance. Know why? I come to me senses when I was in this pet shop. I saw all those little animals: birds, hamsters, guinea pigs, puppies – all caged up behind bars. Just like we was, Len. Like we swore we'd never be again.'

'So you didn't do it?'

Fletcher shook his head. 'No. I'm clean. Just. I think they got away with it, funnily enough. Nothing in the stop press about it.'

'Ironical that,' mused Lennie. 'The perfect job is the one you opted out of.'

'Don't give a rats,' said Fletcher in a quiet but convincing tone. 'Well out of it, my son. I'm just getting a taste for freedom. Living without guilt – lot to be said for that. Of course, on my wages I'm also living without a lot of other things, but there you are.'

'We're winning, Fletch,' said Lennie, also with quiet confidence. 'We're winning.'

'They raised their glasses and drank a silent toast.

'Noses in front,' murmured Fletcher.

'What are you going to do with the bird?' asked Lennie curiously.

'Oh, he's gone. That's why I bought him. So I could set him free, in the garden.'

'Oh, that's nice,' said Lennie appreciatively. 'A symbolic act. You saw you and me in that bird. And you opened the cage and gave it that most precious of gifts – freedom.'

Fletcher took a solemn sip from his glass. Then he said sadly : 'But don't get too carried away, sonny Jim. Two minutes later that big cat from next door ate it!'

The Third Bumper Book of Ghost Stories

Also available in this series
The Bumper Book of Ghost Stories Vols 1 and 2

edited by James Hale

The Third Bumper Book of Ghost Stories

Pan Books London and Sydney

First published 1978 by Barrie and Jenkins Ltd
as *The Midnight Ghost Book*
This edition published 1979 by Pan Books Ltd,
Cavaye Place, London SW10 9PG

ISBN 0 330 25909 1
Printed in Great Britain by
Richard Clay (The Chaucer Press) Ltd, Bungay, Suffolk

Contents

Introduction

The one time I thought I had encountered a ghost I woke up from a complicated dream, in the middle of the night, and heard the sound of rasping, stertorious breathing, which seemed to come from the other side of the room. I knew it wasn't a burglar because I was in a police station at the time. And it took me a good five minutes to realize that it was my own breathing. But when my heart stopped bouncing around my rib-cage I realized that I was not so much relieved as disappointed. No ghost! I *still* hadn't seen a ghost.

Many people have a ghost story of their own to tell, and most of them are very ready to tell it. Those of us who have had no ghostly experiences at all are desperately envious; it makes us feel we lack sensitivity and imagination. It is also unfashionable to have no psychic powers of any kind. For the hundreds who had their cutlery bent by Uri Geller over the television waves there were thousands who were mortified to see theirs stay straight. We sat stolidly in front of our sets, poker-faced and white-knuckled, heaving silently and uselessly away at our spoons, and nothing happened. We want to receive messages from the ether, we want to see ghosts; we want to be the kind of people who do. And we'd probably be terrified if we were.

That's where *The Bumper Books of Ghost Stories* come in. Forget the ruined castles, the lonely graveyards, the haunted catacombs and vaults; here, at no personal inconvenience, you can relax in bed at night and meet a whole phalanx of ghosts. It may seem a vicarious way of going about things, but it will also seem much safer.

Curiously enough, it's not always so safe for those who *write* ghost stories. One lady who had agreed to contribute to this third collection admitted defeat after several weeks' application; every time she began to put pen to paper something dreadful happened to her and her family. And another writer wrote to the accompaniment of crashing china:

plates flew from wall to floor and all about her, pianos moved, and the front door, while perfectly constructed, would not stay shut.

The stories in *The Third Bumper Book of Ghost Stories* are, I think, remarkable for their variety. They are all original, and they come from the grave, from the beach, from mid-ocean, from New York, from the opera, from Suez, from Austria, from Germany, from seventeenth-century Hampshire, from India, from war-time Suffolk, from real life and from the imagination, by authors pseudonymous, well-known and previously unpublished. They frighten me, and I hope – without malice – that they will frighten the reader.

James Hale

Fay Weldon
Breakages

We blossom and flourish
Like leaves on a tree
And wither and perish
But naught changeth the-e-e –

sang David's congregation in its laggardly, quavery voice. Some trick of acoustics made much of what happened in the church audible in the vicarage kitchen, where tonight, as so often, Deidre sat and darned socks and waited for Evensong to end.

The vicarage, added as a late Victorian afterthought, leaned up against the solidity of the Norman church. The house was large, ramshackle, dark and draughty, prey to wet rot, dry rot, woodworm and beetle. Here David and Deidre lived. He was a vicar of the established church; she was his wife. He attended to the spiritual welfare of his parishioners; she presided over the mothers' union, the Women's Institute and ran the amateur dramatic society. They had been married for twenty-one years. They had no children, which was a source of acute disappointment to them, and to Deidre's mother, and of mild disappointment to the parish. It is always pleasant, in a small, stable and increasingly elderly community, to watch other people's children grow up, and sad to be deprived of that pleasure.

'Oh no, please,' said Deidre, now, to the Coronation mug on the dresser. It was a rare piece, produced in anticipation of an event which had never occurred, the Coronation of the Duke of Windsor. It was, so far, uncracked and unchipped, and worth some £300, but had just moved to the very edge of its shelf, not smoothly and purposively, but with an uneven rocking motion which made Deidre hope that entreaty might yet calm it, and save it. And indeed, after she spoke, the mug was quiet, and lapsed into the ordinary stillness she had once always associated with inanimate objects.

Immortal, invisible,
God only wise –
In light inaccessible –

Deidre joined in the hymn, singing gently and soothingly, and trying to feel happy, for the happier she felt the fewer breakages there would be and perhaps one day they would stop altogether, and David would never, ever find out; that, one by one, the ornaments and possessions he most loved and valued were leaping off shelves and shattering, to be secretly mended by Deidre, with such skills as she remembered from the early days, before marriage had interrupted her training in china restoration, and her possible future in the Victoria and Albert Museum.

Long ago and far away. Now Deidre darned. David's feet were sensitive to anything other than pure, fine wool. Not for him the tough nylon mixtures that other men wore.

Deidre darned.

The Coronation mug rocked violently.

'Stop it,' said Deidre, warningly. Sometimes to be stern worked better than to plead. The mug stayed where it was. But a fraction further and it would have fallen.

Deidre unpicked the last few stitches. She was in danger of cobbling the darn, and there is nothing more uncomfortable to sensitive skin than a cobbled darn.

'You do it on purpose,' David would complain, not without reason. Deidre's faults were the ones he found most difficult to bear. She was careless, untidy and extravagant. She broke dishes, lost socks, left lids unscrewed, taps running, doors open, saucepans burning: she bought fresh bread when yesterday's at half-price would do. It was her nature, she maintained, and grieved bitterly when her husband implied that it was wilful and that she was doing it to annoy.

The Coronation mug leapt off its shelf, arced through the air and fell and broke in two pieces at Deidre's feet. She put the pieces at the very back of the drawer beneath the sink. There was no time for mending them now. Tomorrow morning would have to do, when David was out parish visiting, in houses freshly dusted and brightened for his arrival. Fortunately, he seldom inspected the sink drawer, as he did the others in the house, looking for dirt and disorder. It smelt, when opened, of dry rot, and reminded him too forcibly of the large sums of money which ought to be spent on the repair of the house. 'We could sell something,' she would sometimes venture, but the prospect upset him. His mother had died when he was four, his father had gone bankrupt when he was eight: relatives had reared him and sent him off to boarding school where he had been sexually and emotionally abused. Possessions were his security.

She understood him, forgave him, loved him and tried not to argue. She had her own problems, with her mother.

She darned his socks. It was a larger pile than usual. Socks kept disappearing, not by the pair, but singly. They always had. David had lately discovered a pillowslip stuffed full of them pushed to the back of the wardrobe. It was his wife's deceit which worried him most, or so he said. Hiding socks! That and the sheer careless waste of it all. Losing socks! So Deidre tried tying the socks together for the wash, and thus, in pairs, the night before, spun and dried, they had neatly lain in the laundry basket. In the morning she had found them in one ugly, monstrous knot, and each sock oddly long, as if stretched and stretched by a hand too angry to know what it was doing. Rinsing had restored them, fortunately, to a proper shape, and now she darned where the ordeal had worn the wool thin.

It was always like this. David's things were attacked, as if the monstrous hand were on her side, yet it was she, Deidre, who had to repair the damage, follow its source as it moved about the house, mending what it broke, wiping tomato purée from the ceiling, toothpaste from the lavatory bowl, replanting David's seedlings, rescrewing lids, closing doors, refolding linen, turning off taps. She scarcely dared leave the house for fear of what might happen in her absence, and this David interpreted as lack of interest in his parish. Disloyalty, to God and husband. Times were bad between them.

Deidre's finger was bleeding. She must have cut it on the sharp edge of the broken Coronation mug. She opened the table drawer, and took out the first piece of cloth which came to hand, and wrapped the finger. The cold tap started to run, but she ignored it. Blood spread out over the cloth but presently stopped.

The invisible hand swept the dresser shelf, knocking all sorts of treasures sideways but breaking nothing. It had never touched the dresser before, as if awed, as Deidre was, by the ever increasing value of its contents – rare blue and white pieces, frog mugs, barbers' bowls, lustre cups, a debatedly Ming bowl.

It was getting bolder.

David did not give Deidre a housekeeping allowance. She asked for money when she needed it, but David seldom recognized that it was in fact needed. He could not see the necessity of things like washing-up liquid, sugar, toilet rolls, new scourers. Sometimes she stole money from his pocket: once she took a coin out of the offertory on Sunday morning instead of putting a coin in it.

Deceitful, dishonest; Deidre knew the sort of person she was and despised herself for it. A bad wife, a barren wife, and a poor sort of person.

David came home. The house fell quiet, as always, at his approach. Taps stopped running and china rattling. David kissed her on her forehead.

'Deidre,' said David, 'what have you wrapped around your finger?'

Deidre unwrapped her binding and found that it was a fine lace and cotton handkerchief, put in the drawer for mending, which once had belonged to David's grandmother. It was now sodden and bright, bright red.

'I cut my finger,' said Deidre, inadequately and indeed foolishly, for what if he demanded to know what had caused the wound? But he was too busy rinsing and squeezing the handkerchief under the tap to enquire. Deidre put her finger in her mouth and put up with the salt, exciting taste of her own blood.

'It's hopelessly stained,' he mourned. 'Couldn't you just for once have used something you wouldn't spoil? A tissue?'

David did not allow the purchase of tissues. There had been none in his youth: why should they be needed now, in his middle age? 'I'm sorry,' said Deidre. She was always saying she was sorry, and always providing cause for her own remorse.

He took the handkerchief upstairs to the bathroom, in search of soap and a nailbrush. 'What kind of wife are you, Deidre?' he asked as he went, desperate.

What kind, indeed? Married in a registry office in the days before David had taken to Holy Orders and a Heavenly Father more reliable than his earthly one. Deidre had suggested that they re-marry in church, as could be and had been done by others, but David did not want to. Hardly a wife at all.

A barren wife. A fig tree, struck by God's ill-temper. David's God. In the beginning they had shared a God, who was bleak, plain, sensible and kind. But now, increasingly, David had his own jealous and punitive God, whom he wooed with ritual and richness, incense and images, dragging a surprised congregation with him. He changed his vestments three times during services, rang little bells to announce the presence of the Lord, swept up and down aisles, and in general seemed not averse, in church as at home, to being mistaken for God.

The water pipes shrieked and groaned as David turned on the tap in the bathroom, but that was due to bad plumbing rather than unnatural causes. She surely could not be held responsible for that, too.

When the phenomena – as she thought of it – first started, or rather leapt from the scale of ordinary domestic carelessness to something less explicable and more sinister, she went to the doctor.

'Doctor,' she said, 'do mumps in adolesence make men infertile?' 'It depends,' he said, proving nothing. 'If the gonads are affected it well might. Why?'

No reason had been found for Deidre's infertility. It lay, presumably, like so much else, in her mind. She had had her tubes blown, painfully and unforgettably, to facilitate conception, but it had made no difference. For fifteen years she endured the monthly cycle of hope followed by disappointment, and bore the weight of David's sorrow, as she, his wife, deprived him of his earthly immortality, his children. 'Of course,' he said sadly, 'you are an only child. Only children are often infertile. The sins of the fathers—' David regarded fecundity as a blessing; the sign of a woman in tune with God's universe. He had married Deidre, he vaguely and hurtfully let it be known, on the rebound from a young woman who had gone on to have seven children.

David's fertility remained unquestioned and unexamined. A sperm count would surely have proved nothing. His sperm was plentiful and he had no sexual problems that he was aware of. To ejaculate into a test-tube to prove a point smacked uncomfortably of Onanism.

The matter of the mumps came up during the time of Deidre's menopause, a month or so after her, presumably, last period. David had been in the school sanatorium with mumps: she had heard him saying so to a distraught mother, adding 'Oh, mumps! Nothing in a boy under fourteen. Be thankful he has them now, not later.'

So, he was aware that mumps were dangerous. And Deidre knew well enough that David had lived in the world of school sanatoria after the age of fourteen, not before. Why had he never mentioned it to her? And while she wondered, and pondered, and hesitated to ask, toothpaste began to ooze from the tubes, and rose trees were uprooted in the garden, and his seedlings trampled by unseen boots, and his clothes in the wardrobe tumbled in a pile to the ground, and Deidre stole money to buy mending glue, and finally went to the doctor.

'Most men,' said the doctor, 'confuse impotence with infertility and believe that mumps cause the former, not the latter.'

Back to square one. Perhaps he didn't know. 'Why have you *really* come?' asked the doctor, recently back from a course in patient-doctor relations.

Deidre offered him an account of her domestic phenomena, as she had not meant to do. He prescribed valium and asked her to come back in a week. She did.

'Any better? Does the valium help?'

'At least when I see things falling, I don't mind so much.'

'But you still see them falling?'

'Yes.'

'Does your husband see them too?'

'He's never there when they do.'

Now what was any thinking doctor to make of that?

'We could try hormone replacement therapy,' he said.

'No,' said Deidre.

'Then what do you want me to do?'

'If I could only feel angry with my husband,' said Deidre, 'instead of forever understanding and forgiving him, I might get it to stop. As it is; I am releasing too much kinetic energy.'

There were patients waiting. They had migraines, eczema and boils. He gave her more valium, which she did not take.

Deidre, or some expression of Deidre, went home and churned up the lawn and tore the gate off its hinges. The other Deidre raked and smoothed, resuscitated and blamed a perfectly innocent child for the gate. A child. It would have taken a forty-stone giant to twist the hinges so, but no one stopped, fortunately, to think about that. The child went to bed without supper for swinging on the vicar's gate.

The wound on Deidre's finger gaped open in an unpleasant way. She thought she could see the white bone within the bloodless flesh.

Deidre went upstairs to the bathroom, where David washed his wife's blood from his grandmother's hankie. 'David,' said Deidre, 'perhaps I should have a stitch in my finger?'

David had the toothmug in his hand. His jaw was open, his eyes wide with shock. He had somehow smeared toothpaste on his black lapel. 'This mug has been broken and mended. Why was I not told? Did you do it?'

The toothmug dated from the late eighteenth century and was worn, cracked and chipped, but David loved it. It had been one of the first things to go, and Deidre had not mended it with her usual care, thinking, mistakenly, that one more crack among so many would scarcely be noticed.

'I am horrified,' said David.

'Sorry,' said Deidre.

'You always break my things, never your own.'

'I thought that when you got married,' said Deidre, with the carelessness of desperation, for surely now David would start on an inspection of his belongings and all would be discovered, 'things stopped being yours and mine and became ours.'

'Married! You and I have never been married, not in the sight of God, and I thank Him for it.'

There. He had said what had been unsaid for years, but there was no relief in it, for either of them. There came a crash of breaking china from downstairs. David ran down to the kitchen, where the noise came from, but could see no sign of damage. He moved into the living room. Deidre followed dutifully. 'You've shattered my life,' said David. 'We have nothing in common. You have been a burden since the beginning. I wanted a happy, warm, loving house. I wanted children.'

'I suppose,' said Deidre, 'you'll be saying next that my not having children is God's punishment?'

'Yes,' said David.

'Nothing to do with your mumps?'

David was silent, taken aback. Out of the corner of her eye Deidre saw the Ming vase move.

'You are a sadistic person,' said David, eventually. 'Even the pains and humiliations of long ago are not safe from you. You revive them.'

'You knew all the time,' said Deidre. 'You were infertile, not me. You made me take the blame. And it's too late for me now.'

The Ming vase rocked to the edge of the shelf: Deidre moved to push it back, but not quickly enough. It fell and broke.

David cried out in pain and rage. It was as if he himself had broken.

'You did it on purpose,' he wept. 'You hate me.'

Deidre went upstairs and packed her clothes. She would stay with her mother while she planned some kind of new life for herself. She would be happier anywhere in the world but here, sharing a house with a ghost.

David moved through the house, weeping, but for his treasures, not for his wife. He took a wicker basket and in it laid tenderly – as if they were the bodies of children – the many broken and mended vases and bowls and dishes which he found. Sometimes the joins were skilful and barely detectable to his moving forefinger: sometimes careless. But everything was spoilt. What had been perfect was now second-rate and without value. The finds in junkshops, the gifts from old ladies, the few small nicknacks which had come to him from his dead mother – his whole past destroyed by his wife's single-minded malice and cunning.

He carried the basket to the kitchen, and sat with his head in his hands.

Deidre left without saying another word. Out of the door, through the broken gate, into the night, through the churchyard, for the powers of the dead disturbed her less than the powers of the living, and to the bus station.

David sat. The smell of rot from the sink drawer was powerful enough, presently, to make him lift his head.

The cold tap started to run. A faulty washer, he concluded. He moved to turn it off, but the valve was already closed. 'Deidre!' he called, 'what have you done with the kitchen tap?' He did not know why he spoke, for Deidre was gone.

The whole top of the dresser fell forward on to the ground. Porcelain shattered and earthenware powdered. He could hear the little pings of the Eucharist bell in the church next door announcing the presence of God.

He thought perhaps there was an earthquake, but the central light hung still and quiet. Upstairs heavy feet bumped to and fro, dragging, wrenching and banging. Outside the window the black trees rocked so fiercely that he thought he would be safer in than out. The gas taps of the cooker were on and he could smell gas, mixed with fumes from the coal fire where Deidre's darning had been piled up and was now smouldering. He closed his eyes.

He was not frightened. He knew that he saw and heard these things, but that they had no substance in the real world. They were a distortion of the facts, as water becomes wine in the Communion service, and bread becomes the flesh of the Saviour.

When next he opened his eyes the dresser was restored, the socks still lay in the mending basket, the air was quiet.

Sensory delusions, that was all, brought about by shock. But unpleasant, all the same. Deidre's fault. David went upstairs to sleep but could not open the bedroom door. He thought perhaps Deidre had locked it behind her, out of spite. He was tired. He slept in the spare room, peacefully, without the irritant of Deidre's warmth beside him.

In the morning the window cleaner arrived to do the windows which Deidre could not reach. He could not get into the bedroom through the door, so David held the ladder while he got in through the window.

'Funny sort of burglars,' the window cleaner said to the police, later. 'They'd thrown everything about, furniture, clothes, the lot, all upside down and everywhere. The wardrobe was wrong way up and blocking the door. And the carpet! Great heavy thick thing. They'd picked it right off the floor, and wrung it out as if it was a dishcloth, and wedged it between the floor and the ceiling. The Rev and three strong men were all morning trying to untwist it but they couldn't. Now what sort of burglars can do a thing like that? If you ask me—' which they didn't, of course. They wrote the matter down on their files as U.P., or Unexplained Phenomena.

'She was a very strong woman,' said David to his new young lady organist. 'She did all that to my things and then somehow got out by the window. She wanted to frighten me, and make me believe in ghosts. That was the level of her spiritual potential, I'm afraid.'

Later they were to marry, but had no children, which as he was growing older was something of relief though a disappointment to her, and to the parish.

Fred Urquhart

Witch's kitten

Cyn and I sat on top of her coffin and watched the mourners enter the kirk. Muriel Brunton and Nurse Abernethy sat in a back pew. In a wee while Bessie Dodds crept in and sidled down beside them. I had never seen Mrs Dodds wearing a hat before. She had worn the same green and red headscarf over her curlers all the years I'd known her. Two women from the village that I knew only by sight had a confabulation just inside the door, then they chose a pew about the middle of the aisle where they could miss nothing. Old Mr Nisbet, who used to do the garden before he had to give up with his rheumatics, hirpled down near the front on his stick. He sat with his head down, biting his straggly smoke-browned moustache. A couple of middle-aged women I didn't know sat behind him and studied their hymn books. 'They were great pals of Kathy's,' Cyn said. 'I can't see why they've come – except from curiosity. They're women I never liked.'

I could not resist a merry mew when Mrs Drummond and Mrs Jarvis-Waddell, two great galleons full of importance, sailed slowly down the aisle to the front pew as chief mourners. Nan Drummond, all solicitude, hovered over her friend like a mother hen, holding her elbow and settling her as she'd set precious porcelain. I mewed again hysterically, knowing the Jarvis-Waddell woman needed no help, knowing only too well to what lengths of devilment she would go.

'Wheesht!' Cyn hissed.

'They cannie hear me,' I said.

'How do you know?' she said. 'You haven't been dead long enough yet to know what they can hear and what they can't.'

I was a few months short of eleven when Cyn died. The vet did me in, at Mrs Jarvis-Waddell's command, the same day. So I missed becoming seventy years and seven, which I would have attained if he'd left me alone. I know how old I was because often in the last year I had heard Cyn say: 'Anne of Austria is seventy. She has reached her allotted three score years and ten.' And always I'd heard her give a sad wee cackle after that, implying that it wouldn't be long now before the fairies got me. She never seemed to remember that she herself had long syne passed the same life-mark. It is true that she'd said from time to time, on her 85th, her 88th and her 89th birthdays: 'I'll not see another birthday.' But a year ago, on her 90th, I'd noticed she hadn't repeated this.

I looked around the kirk with interest while we waited for the minister. I had never been in a kirk before. Cyn had not set foot in a kirk for many years either, and this was the Drummonds' way of getting their own back on her instead of having the funeral service at the graveside like other decent Presbyterian bodies.

'Not a bad turnout,' Cyn said. 'Ten mourners. Better than I expected. Though I'm surprised the lawyer-mannie isn't here to grace the festive board.'

'Surely you don't want him?' I said.

'Why not? I'd like him to see the damage he's done. It would be something to nag at his conscience for the rest of his days.'

'I doubt he's got a conscience,' I said.

'You should have more faith in human nature, Annie,' she said.

'How can I? I'm only a poor wee cat that's been ill done by.'

I could not help giving another wee skirling mew when Miss Beanie Gilmour garred the organ give an extra loud peal, and the Reverend Snotty Drummond came sweeping in from the vestry wearing his long black gownie with its purple and white accessories. I had never seen him in his Sunday togs before. I looked close to see if he had the usual snotter at the end of his neb, the reason for Cyn christening him this. She thought the nickname was a secret between her and me, but one day, in excitement, she let it out to Bessie Dodds, and it hadn't been long before the minister got it back. It did not endear Cyn any more to him and nosey Nan.

'Wheesht!' Cyn cried again. 'Be quiet and you may learn something that'll be of advantage to you in the afterlife.'

Cyn's name was Miss Cynthia Isobel Mackenzie, and she was a poet. It was because she was a poet and didn't give two hoots for them that Nan and Snotty Drummond disliked her. She never tried to hide her contempt and anger for their manipulation of Miss Kathy and their responsibility for her dreadful Will. The Drummonds came religiously once a week to visit her after Miss Kathy died, and Cyn aye received them with icy politeness, but they never dared call her anything but Miss Mackenzie. Only a few folk close to her called her Cyn. They were all ladybodies of her own generation, and most were dead now, too. Some folk called her Miss Mac. She didn't like this, saying she was Miss Mackenzie to the *hoi polloi* or nothing.

So Miss Mackenzie she'd been to everybody for years. Except to Mrs Bessie Dodds, the cleaning lady whose husband drove a tractor at the Barns of Dalbogie. Mrs Dodds aye called her Miss Mac behind her back, and often to her face. It was a kind of running battle between them. When first she came to be the daily at Seven Yewtrees, Mrs Dodds, a sonsy young farm-wifie, had been what Cyn called overfamiliar and had kept calling her 'Miss Mac, hen' and 'Miss Mac, m'dear' every half dozen words until Cyn had put her foot down. 'My name, Mrs Dodds,' she said in that loud upper-class voice of hers that could have filled a drill hall, 'is Mackenzie. M.A.C.K.E.N.Z.I.E. Miss Mackenzie to you, if you please. And if you don't please, you can ask Miss Brunton for your wages and depart in peace. But if you do please, you must mind not to say "Miss Mackenzie" ower often. There's nothing worse than having one's name continually deeved in one's lugs.'

'Okay, Miss Mac hen,' Mrs Dodds said, fell affronted. And she tossed her head with such abandon that the curlers she aye wore ablow her headscarf rattled. Mrs Dodds was a great head-tosser, and when she was having her mid-morning cup of coffee and biscuits in the kitchen with Miss Brunton and Nurse Abernethy her curlers clattered about so much you'd have thought she was conducting an orchestra. And they aye rattled waur than usual after she and Miss Cynthia Mackenzie had a bit tiff about names.

Years long syne Cyn had been in love with a sailor called 'Sin', short for Sinbad. They had aye called themselves 'The Two Sins' and said it was the film they were starring in. They were introduced by an admiral, for Sin was a high-ranking officer, and so they'd had their great love story. But it was a story that turned out badly for Cyn Mackenzie. Sin was drowned at Jutland. I never heard what his real name was.

I got mine when I was a month old. I used to be a twin. My sister and I were called Penny and Twopence by the village wifie whose black cat had kittened us. Miss Mackenzie bought us when she heard we'd been born in May. 'In olden days,' she said to the scandalized cottar-wifie, 'witches would never have any but May kittens. They vowed they made the best familiars. They're stronger and more cunning than most cats. I hope these two will help to keep my broomstick in control when we're flying in a high wind.'

Cyn's sister, Miss Kathy, was still alive then. She was as scandalized as the cottar-wifie when Cyn, a keen student of history, rechristened us Anne of Austria and Caroline of Naples. 'It's more in keeping with your new status as gentry,' Cyn told us.

'Havers,' said Miss Kathy, a bossy body who was aye laying down the law. 'Carrie and Annie they'll be from henceforth. And I'll have you know, Cynthia Mackenzie, that your royal ladies will have to be a lot cleaner in their habits if they're to remain in my house.'

Miss Kathy always called Seven Yewtrees 'my' house. She would never have dreamed of saying 'our', although truthfully it was as much Miss Cyn's as hers. Seven Yewtrees was built in the early eighteenth century to house a large family, and it had stood in the middle of an estate of several hundred acres. But the acreage had dwindled like the family fortunes, and by the time Miss Cyn and Miss Kathy were born it was standing in a garden of three acres and a paddock. It was occupied then by the girls' parents, General 'Buffy' and Mrs Mackenzie and a staff of five indoor servants, a nanny and a coachman. By the time I came to it as a kitten the paddock had been sold; the house was well weatherbeaten and needed repairs; most of the garden was just rough grass; and only the two old sisters and their housekeeper, Miss Muriel Brunton, lived in a few rooms, the rest of the house being dustsheeted and deserted.

When the General died at the age of ninety-four he hadn't mentioned the house in his will. Miss Kathy had been Buffy's favourite, for he couldn't abide Miss Cynthia and her poetry and what he called her whimsy-whamsies; so he left seven thousand pounds to Miss Kathy, and the remainder of his possessions to be divided equally between her and Miss Cyn. But Miss Kathy always chose to forget that Seven Yewtrees and everything in it belonged to both of them. Since she was ten years younger than Cyn – there had been a wheen miscarriages and two babies that died in between – Miss Kathy fully expected to live long after Cyn, who was delicate and had a bad heart. Cyn was encouraged, therefore, to spend her money by paying all the household bills. Kathy hung on to her own.

Miss Kathy was seventy when Carrie and I came to bide in 'her' house: the age I am now, the age I suppose I'll be for all eternity. She was seventy-three when she died, so I had plenty of opportunities to watch her in action; I ken how true it was that Cyn did all the paying-out while Miss Katherine, as she insisted on being called by Mrs Bessie Dodds and others of the lower orders, sat back jocose and watched her own bank balance rise higher and higher. Miss Katherine, who deemed herself appointed by God to manage her older sister's affairs, was absolutely certain that Cyn would die long, long before her. Cyn would not be able to take her money with her, and nearly all of what she left would be taken by a rapacious government; so it was only sensible, right and proper that Cyn should pay the household bills, the gardener's wages, Miss Brunton's wages, the charwoman's wages, and the rates and taxes and insurance, forby the income tax, so that Kathy could hang on to her own money, and it would be there, in readiness, when the time came and she was left to cope on her lonesome.

Not that she would be on her lonesome. She would have her dear cousin, Willie Jarvis-Waddell, to be her staff and prop for the rest of her days. Willie Jarvis-Waddell was a third cousin of the Mackenzie sisters' mother. He was a big bug in the Foreign Office and had a mansion in Yorkshire and a house in Belgravia, which Cyn told me is a fashionable part of London. The Mackenzies' money had dwindled through the decades, but the Jarvis-Waddells had kept an iron grip on theirs. They were what Cyn called stinking rich.

Willie visited Seven Yewtrees twice or thrice when he was a bairn; then they didn't see him until Buffy's funeral. He was a good looking young man of twenty then, and Miss Kathy, aged fifty-four, a repressed spinster though she would never have admitted it, fell in love with him. For the rest of her life Cousin Willie was her god. Even when he married, it didn't make any difference to Kathy's great pash. She was aye inviting him and his wife Bertha for holidays, which were paid for, of course, by Cyn. Nothing was too good for Cousin Willie and Dear Bertha. Crates of champagne were stocked. Expensive foodstuffs were sent up from Harrods and Fortnum & Mason. All on the account of Miss Cynthia Mackenzie, who had to hide it from Kathy if she was rash enough to buy a book that wasn't a paperback. A lot of the wines and foodstuffs got wasted, for Willie and Bertha never stayed for the full term that Miss Kathy had invited and expected them for; they always had some excuse and, after a couple of days, would hasten away farther north into the Highlands so that Willie could do a little fishing and shooting on some great estate. Yet, no matter how they abused her hospitality and invitations, Kathy always gushed about 'My cousin Willie in the F.O. – such a brilliant administrator who's always travelling abroad with the Foreign Secretary.' If Cyn spoke about him she only said he was a distant cousin – 'a very distant one, and the more distance there is between him and me the better I'll like it.' Cyn aye called him and his wife 'Waddling Willie' and 'Bitchy-faced Bertha'. They did not like Cyn either.

I heard all this from Cyn in the long hours she used to lie in her bed with nobody to talk to. And over and over again she told me about the time Willie and Bertha came for a week and stayed only one night because Willie had to dash – he said – to Balmoral to confab with the Queen. This was a memorable night in Cyn's life, the night all the evil and damage was done.

That night Miss Kathy had invited the Reverend Snotty and Mrs Drummond to dinner to meet her famous cousin. The Drummonds had just come to the parish, and a great all-absorbing friendship had sprung up between Nan Drummond and Miss Mackenzie of Seven Yewtrees. Nan Drummond was a big stout body with a big damp face that aye had beads of sweat on the temples and upper lip. Her large protruding eyes had great bags under them; the irises were so pale a grey and the whites were so unhealthily yellow, they looked like cold poached eggs that had got stale from lying in the pantry. Nan Drummond fair oozed sympathy and affection for those she thought in want of it. Kathy Mackenzie was a natural target.

When she wasn't directing Miss Kathy's life, Nan Drummond was tripping over with good works. In olden times she'd have been able to use up all her energy in saving village girls in trouble, poking her nose in where it wasn't wanted when they had bastard weans; but in our day the village girls wouldn't admit to belonging to the village at all, and they were all on the pill and too cute to get caught. So Nan Drummond would have had a very lean time in our parish if it hadn't been for Miss Katherine Mackenzie.

It was she who egged on Kathy to make yon Wicked Will.

This was after she met Waddling Willie and Bitchy-faced Bertha. Mrs Drummond was tremendously impressed by Willie, who hadn't started to run to fat yet. Like her buddy, Kathy, she fell for his diplomatic palavers. And when he was called to the phone in the middle of dinner and came back to say Lillibet wanted him to go to Balmoral the first thing next morning to help her and Tinker sort out a crisis in the Middle East, she was that overwhelmed by joy and pride at sitting next to a man who was on such intimate terms with Her Majesty and the Foreign Secretary that she never once thought of the inconvenience and the waste and the cost caused by Willie's shortened visit. Nor did Miss Kathy. She beamed at her cousin and said: 'We'll be so glad to look after Bertha while you're away, dear. Rest assured she'll be safe with us.'

'Bertha is coming with me,' Willie said. 'Lillibet insisted on it.'

Only Miss Cyn failed to be impressed. She neither believed that Willie had been summoned to Balmoral nor that he was on christian name terms with the Queen. 'I jaloused that he and Bitchy-Face were going to a hotel in Aberdeen or Strathpeffer or to the home of whatever man Willie had got to phone him,' she told me. 'They couldn't bear biding at Seven Yewtrees for any longer than I could bear having them in the house.'

Like Kathy, Nan Drummond was so unsuspicious of Waddling Willie's deceit that he and Bertha could scarcely have reached whatever haven they'd chosen before she started to agitate for Kathy to make her will in Willie's favour. The whiff of Willie's presence, the powerful scent of a man who could speak so nonchalantly about his Sovereign Lady, was like gunpowder in a charger's nostrils to Nan Drummond. She saw herself becoming one of Willie's bosom pals. If she could be so chief with Willie's cousin, then she could be as chief with Willie himself – *and* his wife. Already Mrs Drummond saw that when Miss Kathy joined her ancestors – Miss Cyn would be away long before that, needless to say – she would become the greatest pal of the Jarvis-Waddells when they settled down in Seven Yewtrees, and – who knew? – she might become intimate with the Queen, too.

Until Nan Drummond broached the subject, Kathy Mackenzie had not thought about her will since the time thirty years ago when Buffy, straight-backed and bristly-moustached, had ordered his lawyer to make wills in which each daughter made the other her sole heir and executor. Now, with Nan breathing so vehemently in her lug, pointing out that Cynthia couldn't last much longer with her weak heart, Miss Kathy was only too ready to summon the family lawyer.

The lawyer who'd drawn up their own and Buffy's wills was dead. His place had been taken by his son, Mr Ronald Glossop-Macleod, a smarmy wee shaver who fancied himself as a ladies' man. He fair buttered up Miss Kathy and, with Nan oozing advice at her elbow, he drew up what Miss Cyn aye called the Wickedest Will in the World.

In this will Kathy left Seven Yewtrees (forgetting half of it belonged to Cyn) and her jewels and all her money – except for two thousand pounds to her dear friend Mrs Nan Drummond – to her beloved cousin William Eric Jarvis-Waddell, appointing him her sole executor. Then Mr Ronald Glossop-Macleod said that *maybe* she had better make the will a little longer than this. 'All of us are at risk, Miss Mackenzie,' he said (these were his exact words, Cyn told me, for she'd sat there in the drawing room and heard it all from A to Z). 'It isn't at all likely, but there is always the possibility, of course, that Miss Cynthia *might* outlive you' – and he gave Cyn one of his extra special heart-warming smiles, like a melting marshmallow – 'so I suggest that in case this happens you leave your property and money to her in trust for her lifetime, allowing her the income from your funds but not allowing her to touch the capital, until such a time as she, in turn, will hand them over – and her own funds too, I trust – to Mr William Jarvis-Waddell.'

Cyn protested that she had no intention of leaving Waddling Willie a halfpenny, but she was ignored. Miss Katherine said she agreed wholeheartedly with Mr Glossop-Macleod, and she thought that maybe as her sister's own capital would be depleted should Cyn outlive her (and here she shook her head affectionately at Cyn to signify that, naturally, she didn't believe this) she would make it a condition of Cyn being allowed to stay on at Seven Yewtrees and to utilize the income from her own estate if Cyn would leave certain sums to charities in which she (Kathy) was interested. And she gave Master Ronald a list of these charities, saying she would have left them the money out of her own estate, except that she wanted as much as possible to go to her dearest cousin Willie.

Master Ronald obligingly put this conditional clause in Miss Katherine's will and she signed it, despite all Cyn's protestations. 'I can't see why you're making all the fuss, Cynthia,' she said. 'You'll be dead long before me, so it doesn't need to worry you. Willie will see that the charities get their legacies from what money you've left to me.'

Nobody knew how really wicked the will was until Miss Katherine Mackenzie kicked the bucket a great many years before it was expected. Cyn knew right away how dire it was when Willie and Bertha came to Kathy's funeral, and Bertha collected all the jewels. The sisters had some very precious ones that had belonged to their grandmother, who had bequeathed them equally to both sisters, though Kathy always claimed the lot. Bertha put the jewel case under her oxter, saying: 'Legally I shouldn't take them till you die, Cynthia, but I know you'll never want to wear them – it's hardly likely in the short time you've got left – so I might as well have them now. Jewels improve with wearing.'

Miss Cyn never stopped talking about these jewels and the will for the next seven years. Day after day, night after night, when she couldn't sleep, she went over the will and what it was doing to herself and her dependents. 'And that means you, Annie,' she would say. 'You're my chief dependent now that your poor sister like my own sister is away.' For my twin, so grandly called after Queen Caroline of Naples, had been killed by an Alsatian dog belonging to one of the village brats when she was only a year old. 'You and Muriel Brunton and Bessie and Nurse Biscuits, you're all my dependents and I want to provide for you all after the fairies take me away. You can rest assured that Waddling Willie won't provide for you.'

The only thing that gave Cyn any joy over Miss Katherine's will was the fact that Waddling Willie and his avaricious wife couldn't lay hands on Seven Yewtrees and the rest of his legacy until she died. 'It's what keeps me alive, Annie,' she said. 'Just to spite Willie I've told the fairies I won't be ready to go with them for a long time yet. Though, mind you, I'd fain often be away to join my dearest Sin, it's the thought of doing Willie down that keeps me here.'

She talked like this not only to me but to Miss Brunton and Mrs Bessie Dodds and Nurse Abernethy, the district nurse who, in the last years of Cyn's life, came in every morning to attend to her. There was always a tussle when 'Biscuits' gave Miss Cyn a blanket bath. Cyn hated anybody washing her face, and poor Abernethy had to keep saying: 'Now be a guid lassie, Miss Mackenzie, and let me give your phisog a wee dicht. Surely ye don't want to look like a smoked-out tinker when the doctor comes?' 'I don't care what I look like,' Cyn would say. 'The doctor 'll just have to thole it. Better folk than him have seen me with a smut on my nose. I remember once when the Countess of Dalwhinnan came to call on my mother ...'

When she wasn't talking about the Wicked Will and how little siller she had left in the bank and how it would be depleted even more when yon charities got what by rights should come out of Kathy's or Waddling Willie's money, Miss Cyn recited poetry. She would recite her own poems, and she would recite screeds and screeds by a man called Browning. But her favourite poets were Emily Dickinson and Alice Meynell. Hardly anything ever happened without giving occasion for her to remember some apposite quotation from one or the other.

A morning came when she was talking about Sin, her sailor laddie, and the good times he and she had had, and she said: 'Maybe Emily Dickinson kent more about sailors than any of us when she wrote: "Can the sailor understand/the divine intoxication/ of the first league out from land?"'

And when she sighed and said: 'Now, let's be quiet for a wee while, Annie. I'm going to sleep.'

I went to sleep, too. When I woke, Miss Cyn was still sleeping, so I slipped through the open window and foraged in the garden. When I returned, she was lying on her back, very straight and stretched out, and there was a hankie over her face. I sprang up on the bed, but I didn't curl up beside her. I was debating whether I'd have another wee nap or whether I'd go and see if Bessie Dodds had a titbit for me when Miss Cyn said: 'Annie! Now that I'm away, I want you to be a good wee cattie until your own time comes. And I want you to give Waddling Willie's fat legs a real good scratching when he comes to the funeral. But mind he doesn't kick you!'

I looked round and there was Miss Mackenzie standing in her nightgown behind me. She was that thin and worn-away I could see right through her. I looked from her to the Miss Mackenzie on the bed, and I cried: 'Guidsakes, mistress, what's ado?'

'A stupid question, Annie,' she said. 'You ken fine what's happened to me. You ken that I'm a ghost just as well as I ken that you can speak like this when you feel like it.'

It was then that voices made me notice that the door, which was always open, was now shut. Nurse Abernethy and Dr Duncan came in. Dr Duncan walked through Miss Cyn and bent over Cyn on the bed. 'I'm glad she went so quietly,' he said. 'Her old ticker just conked out.'

'I'll old ticker him!' Cyn said to me. 'When I think of all the heart pills that gowk's garred me swallow in my time!'

After the undertaker and his men had carried out Miss-

Mackenzie-on-the-bed in a funny-looking purple blanket-box affair, Cyn and I joined Miss Brunton and Bessie Dodds and Nurse Biscuits in the kitchen. Miss Brunton and Bessie were still snivelling, putting their hankies to their eyes, and Abernethy kept trying to jolly them. She cracked a wee joke, and after a while Mrs Dodds tucked her hankie into her apron-pocket, saying: 'Ah well, it has to come to us all. Puir Miss Mac, rather her than me, though. I'm no' ready yet.'

Biscuits cracked another wee joke, and they were laughing when the phone rang. Miss Brunton answered it. Cyn and I could hear every word that Bitchy Bertha said at the other end. 'Mrs Drummond has just phoned to tell me that Miss Mackenzie died last night,' she said. 'Why was I not informed earlier?'

'Miss Mackenzie died only two hours ago,' Miss Brunton said. 'I phoned Mrs Drummond at once, and she came to look at Miss Mackenzie before the undertaker took her away to the mortuary.'

'Who are you?' Bertha demanded.

'You know perfectly well who I am. If you had deigned to visit Miss Mackenzie even once in the seven years since her sister died you'd perhaps have known me better. I'm Miss Muriel Brunton, the housekeeper.'

'Why haven't you left? You've no right to be in the house now that the body's gone. I asked Mrs Drummond to give you notice. You will lock up the house at once and give Mrs Drummond the keys.'

'I'm staying until Sunday to look after the cat.'

'Have the cat destroyed,' the voice said. 'Immediately.'

'Miss Mackenzie wanted the cat to go to a good home,' Muriel said. 'We're going to find one for her, and I don't leave this house until we do. We haven't decided which day the funeral is to be yet, but no doubt your friend Mrs Drummond will keep you well informed.'

And she banged down the phone. She and Bessie and Nurse Abernethy started to discuss me. Mrs Dodds said she'd be more than glad to have me, but there were some collies at the Barns and she didn't think I'd take kindly to them. 'I'd have her,' Biscuits said. 'But a district nurse's house is no place for a cat. There are always interfering folk who'd complain about it being insanitary.'

They were still arguing back and forth when the phone rang again. 'If it's that woman,' Muriel Brunton said, 'tell her I've left for Hong Kong.'

'Hello,' Biscuits shouted into the mouthpiece.

'This is Mr Glossop-Macleod. I'm so sorry to hear about Miss Mackenzie's death. Who are you? I've just had Mrs Jarvis-Waddell on the blower – all the way from Yorkshire. She says there are strangers trespassing in her husband's house, and she orders you all to be gone before this evening. Will you kindly hand the keys to Mrs Drummond? Mrs Jarvis-Waddell also told me to inform you that she has a complete inventory of all the furniture and valuables in the house and she will check this with the contents as soon as she arrives for the funeral.'

'She's feared we nick something,' Biscuits said. 'I've aye had my eye on yon picture of the wifie in the red cloak in the hall, but I doubt, I doubt ...'

'It's the inventory,' Miss Brunton said. 'I went round with the agent at the time, and I remember him taking notice of it. It's not worth anything, but it's better not to take any chances with that woman.'

Mrs Dodds said: 'I'd have liked a wee memento. Could I no' take yon wee blue jug that's ahint Buffy's photy on the drawingroom mantelpiece? It would never be missed. I deserve somethin' after workin' here for donkey's years.'

'That jug's lapis lazuli,' Muriel Brunton said. 'It's one of the first things she'd spot. Anyway, you've been left a good few hundreds in Cynthia's will.'

'Ay, if Waddlin' Willie lets me have it,' Bessie said. 'I bet he'll try to stop us all gettin' what Miss Mac put in the will she made last year.'

Biscuits said: 'He can't do that. She was in her right mind, and what money's left of her own has nothing whatever to do with him.'

They were having lunch when Alick Buchanan, the vet,

arrived and said a strange wifie had phoned from England and told him the cat was to be put to sleep. 'Instanter,' he said, lifting me and giving me a cuddle. 'It'll be all right, Annie my wee doo, one prick and Bob's your uncle.'

The three women set up a great hue and cry, but Alick was adamant. 'It breaks my heart,' he said. 'But orders is orders. I not only had the strange wifie. I had Mrs Drummond on the blower forby, telling me to get on with it.'

The vet didn't come to the funeral, but the lawyer did. He arrived as the coffin was being carried out of the kirk. Ronald Glossop-Macleod was carrying a wreath. He held it behind his back, not knowing what else to do with it, when they all gathered round the open grave and Snotty said a long prayer. I had a keek at the wreath, and it said 'To Cynthia with love from Ronald.' She had never called the man 'Ronald' in all her life. She had called him a lot of names, but never Ronald.

The undertaker began to dish out the cords so that the coffin could get lowered. He handed the first cord, with a bow, to Mrs Jarvis-Waddell; then he handed the second to Mrs Drummond. The third went to Mr Glossop-Macleod. Then the undertaker hesitated, looking about to see which other mourner seemed most worthy to get the fourth, and after a pause he handed it to Mrs Bessie Dodds. But he didn't bother to bow to her. He was busy looking at his men to give them the signal to let the big ropes drop, which they did in a fell hurry, and so Cyn's coffin tumbled down into its last resting place.

'I'm sorry Waddling Willie wasn't able to come because he's in some Bongo-Bongoland with the Foreign Secretary,' Cyn said. 'I'd have liked fine to put a cold hand on the nape of his neck when he was kneeling in the front pew.'

'Never mind,' I said. 'Maybe the Blacks 'll pop him in a pot.'

'No such luck,' she said.

'Would you like me to rub against Bertha's legs and make her topple into the grave?' I asked. 'I'd fain like some revenge.'

'No, no, Annie,' she said. 'We must think of something better than that. Something more lasting.'

*

For the next two days Cyn and I watched Bitchy-faced Bertha and Nan Drummond rake through Cynthia's and the family's papers, screwing them up and throwing them into cartons that they carried out and emptied in a heap on the lawn. Drawer after drawer, cupboard after cupboard were emptied and the contents carried out. All the family photographs, their birth certificates and wedding licences, photographs of friends, letters that went away back to Cyn's great-grandparents – for the Mackenzies had been great hoarders – were picked up, glanced at and thrown on to the scrap heap. All the manuscripts of Cyn's poems and the letters Sin had sent her were laughed at and torn into smithereens. And while they destroyed several generations of family love and pride, the two women talked and talked. Bertha kept telling Nan Drummond about all the grand times they would have when she and Waddling Willie took residence in Seven Yewtrees, but Cyn and I, who could see right into her evil mind now that we were ghosts, knew this was just a ruse to keep Nan sweet in the meantime, for Bertha planned to sell the house and all its antique furniture and pictures as soon as she could make arrangements with a big firm of London auctioneers.

By the second evening the two women were exhausted by their rummaging and destruction, and an enormous bonfire of papers, letters, birthday and Christmas cards, old clothes, children's broken toys, photographs, postcards, all kinds of cherished keepsakes, everything that had gone into the creation of three or four generations of Mackenzies, was standing six or seven feet high on the rough grass that once had been a well-kept lawn. And as the sun was almost setting over the Grampians, Bertha went to the scullery and brought out a can of paraffin oil. She sprinkled about half of it over the wreckage. Then both women struck matches and threw them onto the pyre. The bonfire flared up and was soon going merrily.

Bertha said: 'Well, that's a good day's work done.'

'It is that,' Nan said. 'Now, dear, let's go home to supper and a nice wee drinkie to celebrate your inheritance.'

Cyn stood by the bonfire, moaning and wringing her hands. 'The years of love,' she cried, 'the years of joy that are going up in smoke!' I spat venomously in the direction of the manse, and went to find something to eat. I hadn't known ghosts got hungry. I was enjoying the remains of some fish when I noticed the half-empty paraffin can left on the back-door step. The stopper wasn't screwed on properly.

I don't know where the idea came from. But I acted at once. I leaned against the can and knocked it off the step. In a jiffy I had got off the cap with my paws and teeth; then I started to roll the can towards the bonfire. The paraffin spurted out every time the can rolled over.

Cyn stopped moaning and watched my efforts to trundle the can. At first she watched with sad amusement; then she watched with irritation. 'You'll hurt yourself, you silly wee pussy,' she said. 'Aren't we in enough trouble without you doing that?' And then, suddenly, the purpose of my activity dawned on her.

'Oh, what a wonderful idea!' She clapped her hands and laughed. 'What a smashing idea, as your friend and my friend, Mrs Elizabeth Dodds, would say: "Right smashin' guid, eh, Miss Mac hen?" I do wish our good friend was here to shout encouragement from the sidelines. And maybe to help kick the can!'

Cyn shot out her foot, newly rejuvenated by death, and sent the can two feet nearer the bonfire. I dunted it with my head and pushed with my forepaws, sending it another inch towards its destination. Cyn gave a wild screech of laughter and gave it another kick.

'It breaks my heart,' she said. 'Poor old Seven Yewtrees! I feel like the Vandals and the Visigoths sacking Rome.'

In a few seconds the fire rushed along the oily track I'd left and licked the back door. It was not long before the flames were thrusting into the house. The sun went down as the kitchen became one big fiery oven. Before it had been dark for an hour Seven Yewtrees was a blazing mass.

Cyn and I flew up and sat on the roof. I was nervous of the flames licking up towards us, but Cyn said: 'Don't be a fearedy-gowk. You must remember you're a ghostie now and you can't be harmed by fire, water, heat, snow, any of the elements you like to name. You're invincible and invisible.'

Still, I was nervous, and so I pranced about, thinking I could feel the heat seeping through my paws. It was all very well being a witch's kitten, but I didn't care for fire. At first Cyn said: 'Stop dug-dancing about.' Then she began to get excited, too, when the flames got higher and folk from the village started to arrive. Some of them stood and watched the blaze, standing like stookies and doing nothing. Others rushed away to get the police and the fire brigade and pails of water that they flung on the fire – as if their paltry contributions could help quench such a gigantic furnace.

By the time three fire brigades came Cyn and I were dancing skyhigh above what was left of the roof, gurgling with glee at the sight of Bitchy-faced Bertha and Nan Drummond holding onto each other and wailing in the front of the crowd, which, by this time had swelled to well over a hundred. Cyn took higher and higher leaps in the air, and she shouted down to them: 'An eye for an eye, and a tooth for a tooth! Greet awa', my bonnie dearies. I aye knew I'd have the last laugh on you.'

They couldn't hear her, of course. But that didn't make her revenge any less sweet. 'Even if they do get the insurance to cough up,' she said, 'it'll not be as much as the property was worth. And I'm not sure that the insurance will pay. The insurance folk may say it's arson, for there's that can in the middle of the bonfire. I wonder if their fingerprints are still on it? Wouldn't it be fun if Bitchy-face and Nosey Nan were stood up in the dock and sentenced to twelve months hard! It would serve Nan right for wanting so much to be a guest of Her Majesty.'

Cyn gave a few skirls and a few leaps, then she cried: 'I feel just like Anton Dolin! What a pity it is that you never saw the ballet, Annie. You'd have loved it. You'd have loved Dolin in *Hymn to the Sun*. But what am I havering about? It's not Dolin I feel like. It's Nijinsky! I'll never forget him in *The Fire Bird* ...'

Janice Elliott

Figments

'Who is that woman in blue, on the beach? And the girl?'
'That is Sandie Outram with her ghost daughter.'

Every morning Ms Sandie Outram, the novelist and person, wakes early in her beach-house, rises clear-eyed and switches on her electric kitchen. Though she is a good waker, the light from the sea is too bright before ten so she does not open the blind and the sun is received through slats. Wearing caftan and towelling mules, she plugs in the coffee pot, the liquidizer, the toaster, the air conditioner, the waste-disposal unit to gobble up last night's detritus, which is fishy, this being the seaside. Her kitchen hums. Pug-pug says the coffeepot. Soon Ms Outram will switch on the filter that cleanses every day the little blue pool, hardly bigger than a tear among the chain of pools that are preferred, on this coast, to the sea.

She flicks on the radio and cannot be doing with hijacking of jumbo jet by Japanese terrorists before ten o'clock. Radio off, television on without sound. There is the big, fat plane roasting on the tarmac. She had noticed a 'hard line' lately. It will be stormed. Snipers already wait, probably, though God knows where on that lunar landscape.

Her own breakfast finished, Ms Outram lays a pretty tray, with toast and orange juice and milky coffee. At the last moment she adds a fuchsia head in a narrow liqueur glass and Sandie Outram carries the tray out of the kitchen, down a short corridor to a small white room. Sandie puts down the tray at a certain angle on the cane sidetable and says to her ghost daughter: 'There has been some terrorism.

'It will be a glorious day. I have decided that you prefer toast to brioches. You will wear the orange shift today, for the beach, though of course you will change for the party tonight. Or perhaps you will refuse to change and we will quarrel. I shall have to think about that.'

The girl steps naked from the bed and walks around the room eating toast (she would have preferred brioches). She is thin and brown, her hair striped by the sun, a touching little backside but breasts, thinks Ms Outram, too heavy, much too knowing for such an innocent. Though perhaps that is right? Time will tell. Mrs Outram has learned to trust her instinct.

The ghost daughter is always dreamy before ten, not exactly sullen. She opens the shutters and yawns at the sun. Really, Sandie thinks, smoothing the pillow and shaking the single duvet, she is very fond of the girl, quite devoted. On such a splendid day it would be good to give her a treat. Perhaps they won't quarrel. Maybe they will take a delicious picnic to the beach: crab and crisp salad and half a bottle of wine. But, of course, the daughter needs company of her own age, Sandie has been thinking about that; she has given it a lot of thought, not that the girl has ever complained.

She touches the ghost girl's breast, smiles, brushes cheeks, promises.

'Perhaps this is the day you will met your daemon lover!'

Along this little strip of coast, in the rich beach-houses between the scorched hinterland and the polluted ocean, Sandie Outram's ghost daughter has long been accepted. There was curiosity at first, of course, and there is still gossip. When Sandie sleeps, Marianne, the ghost girl, disappears, naturally, and the first time this happened in public at one of Muriel Crosby's duller dinner parties, there was comment. But waking, refreshed, as she always does, Sandie Outram carried it off. Whatever you say about Sandie, she has style. Besides, there is always some new scandal to distract, this summer as any summer. Herman Trailer and his second wife have axe fights on the beach most nights. Since April there have been two suicides, one breakdown, one vasectomy, a quite serious shark scare, several shoals of sea fish washed up polluted to death on the sea shore, and Herman Trailer is said to have had carnal knowledge. That is probably flattery but it is true that Trailer leaped on Marianne behind a rock at a beach party, and might – given a fair wind – have penetrated had not Sandie Outram at that very moment, poised to write the rape of her ghost daughter by a world-famous boxing playwright, yawned and dozed off over her typewriter, leaving Trailer on the rocks.

Marianne, who was Marie until Mu Crosby said that sounded like an *au pair*, picks her way through the rock pools, as far as she can get from Sandie and Mu knocking back bloody Marys up by Jake's beach-bar. Sandie's having trouble with chapter four and Marianne is accordingly enervated. It seems to her sometimes that she has no future; she looks into the still pool and sees no reflection: molluscs, albino spider-crabs, are better off. Even Trailer might have been better than nothing. How wearisome it is, Marianne thinks, to be the victim of a writer's block. She suspects (actually she peeked at the typescript) that Sandie is torn between the long-promised daemon lover and anorexia nervosa. Or perhaps first the one followed by the other. Neither option attracts Marianne who, given self-determination, would probably be a sweet, rather quiet girl, inconspicuously happy. Marianne with her toe sets all the tiny, urgent forms of life dashing around their murky pool and, round-shouldered, almost invisible, wonders if fisherboy-barman Jake has noticed her. No daemon lover he – though many old rich women would have him. But Jake for her? No, Mother Outram would never allow such simplicity. Life now, it seems, has sad endings.

There she is, calling Marianne to heel.

'Marianne, don't stay too long in the sun.'

Mu Crosby is Ms Sandie Outram's best friend. That is: they play bridge together, exchange recipes, gossip about other women and irritate each other in a companionable way. Everyone but Mu is a little in awe of Ms Sandie Outram. Mu Crosby is in awe of no one and, in the way of rich, healthy women, cares nothing for anyone's opinion. Unlike Sandie, she dresses expensively and badly and eats too much. Wearing pink stretch slacks, she sits now at Jake's beach-bar before a plate of fat pink prawns. Shellfish will probably kill Mu but not yet.

Mu says: 'The poor girl. I don't see why you can't give her a reflection. Sometimes I think you're quite brutal, Sandie.'

'You'll kill yourself one day with shellfish. A reflection's out of the question.'

Mu shrugs. 'Well, she's your daughter, Sandie. So to speak.'

'You know I'm quite devoted to her.'

'You've a strange way of showing it. Letting her drift like this – look, she's getting quite round-shouldered. I think, Sandie, a girl needs companions of her own age.'

Sandie frowns at the sun. 'I'm aware of that, Muriel. But I have a block.'

'Hard cheese.'

Sandie sighs. 'Writing is not tinning pilchards, Muriel. Sometimes I wish it were.' Not that Sandie will moan. She cannot be doing with moaning writers, with any of the self-regard that so often accompanies the creative act. If Sandie were a man, she would probably dress for work like a stockbroker. When he was alive she used to approve of T. S. Eliot because he had worked in a bank and once she met him posting a letter on Cheyne Walk just round the corner from his flat, and he did not look like a poet at all.

Muriel is saying: 'Jake for instance. He's a dear boy.'

Sandie, preparing to leave, drops into her tapestry hold-all, menthol cigarettes, lighter, Sylvia Plath, Mu's recipe for *taramasalata*, sun barrier-cream and fluoride toothpaste Jake has brought her from the drugstore in town (all you can buy by the ocean is beach balls, pizzas from Jake's take-away pizza bar, sun oil, sun hats, snorkels and flippers, postcards and the sort of shell jewellery Mu Crosby wears, which is her own business, but she gives it to people for Christmas; once Sandie did find among the rubbish one beautiful whalebone pendant which she may give to Marianne when she decides what to do with her).

The sporting crowd has taken over the beach. Some young Germans are playing a complicated ball game. The sun is high. Wearing singlet and trunks, Herman Trailer jogs along the fringe of the sea. It is a very beautiful, shimmering picture. Sandie shivers.

'A ghost walked over my grave.'

'Goose,' says Mu.

'Geese what?'

'Walk in graveyards. Though I can never see why the hell.'

Jake is preparing the barbecue for the Trailers' party this evening. Though he is too sweet ever to think so, it is Jake really who runs the beach. He has long blond seaweed locks and may love Marianne. That would be natural. But he is shy of her, sees her as something odd and unaccountable: a revenant. A fish who will slide, sad-eyed, through his fingers, slip the net, mermaid wife.

'No,' says Sandie Outram, firmly. 'No, Jake's a good boy but no daemon lover. Not at all.'

Ghosts. The light shifts. Dusk on the beach, no chains rattle or doors creak but Sandie Outram broods in her room above the ocean, smokes too much, accepts the Trailers' party as inevitable, for Marianne's sake, and thinks I am tired, I would like to be an ordinary woman, but I am writing a story. It seems to be a ghost story. Perhaps we are all haunted, one way or another. There are fishing boats going out, hardly a fleet any more, they'll be out all night. I should wax my legs. This is a nice room on the beach. The window is black like a curtain, pierced by the little, fish-frying fires. Beyond the horizon one might tip over the edge of the known earth into darkness, or so it looks tonight – the fires as brave as beacons outstaring the deadly sea.

'Look!' calls Ms Outram to her ghost daughter. 'Look, aren't the fires pretty.' And they stand, the mother and the child, arm in arm, cheeks to the dark window, while one by one the barbecues are lit to announce the finest party of the season, down that coast.

'What do I do like tonight?' asks the ghost daughter wistfully, since mirrors do not serve her: though she can, if Sandie wills it, walk through walls.

'I think,' says Sandie, 'you can't make up your mind what to wear, you put on too much make-up, change half a dozen times, then at the last moment slip on the pale green and scrub your face. No jewellery – except perhaps this whale-bone pendant.'

'We quarrel?'

'Not tonight.' Sandie shades her eyes, though it's dusk and the lamps are discreet. 'I have a migraine coming, I think.'

Sandie does look tired and Marianne is sorry. The ghost girl's ties with her mother are stronger, after all, even than flesh and blood.

'Lie down. We don't have to go to the party.'

'You're a dear girl. I don't deserve you. I don't know how I ever thought of you. But we will go to the party. At your age you must have fun. And it will be good for my block.'

Where does Marianne go, Sandie wonders, when I am sleeping? We have had some good dreams together and a nightmare or two. But sometimes I don't dream or I dream of others and where does she wander then, poor ghost? And all my dream people? Mu said once when I asked her: to one of Herman Trailer's parties, where else? But that's how she talks, that's Mu.

The party of the season starts in the Trailers' beach house which is not exactly a changing room or even a studio like Sandie's, but a wonderful cantilevered structure poised in mid-air reaching out at different levels from the sheer rock so you could look up from the beach and see the beautiful people dancing apparently like angels on air. Though structurally it is perfectly sound, a pupil of Nervi says. And there was nothing Nervi did not know about cantilevers.

Mu Crosby in an unsuitable pants suit says, 'I'm not dancing on fucking air. Where's all this fish food? Lead me to the lobsters.'

Sandie yawns. 'Do shut up, Mu. Mimi Trailer looks doped. She usually is. D'you think she'll get out the axe tonight?'

'Not before din-dins I hope. Herman's got to cook that fish.'

Marianne comes up with a plate of *vol-au-vents,* looking very pretty in her mermaid green. She longs to ask if Sandie plans for Herman Trailer to be her daemon lover tonight, and hopes not.

'I thought I might help with the cooking on the beach?'

'Of course, if you'd like to,' says Sandie and Marianne bends down to kiss her cheek. I could keep her with me forever, thinks Sandie, my ghost daughter. But I'll have to let her go, I always do, how sad. The oncoming migraine confuses her. She wonders how many at the party are her phantasms: maybe she made it all up, summoned from the fruitful dark this coast, these people, this season? The one world nudges the other. Once a suicide she had dashed off carelessly telephoned in the middle of the night to say he'd thrown up the sleeping pills and was stuck in purgatory, which was rather like a wet Sunday in Wales – would she please settle the matter one way or the other. Gas was no good because he'd been converted, and he didn't fancy all those dready Mishima freaks so *seppuku* was out. So Sandie blew him up with his own bomb in a Boeing in the paperback edition and got a nice postcard; airmail, of course.

Pull yourself together, Sandie Outram, this is not your style.

Mu cuts in. 'Off you go, dear girl. Leave the grub.'

At this point in the party there is a lot of kissing. My God, thinks Sandie as Herman Trailer nibbles her ear, I could never have invented you.

Herman sits at her feet, fifty-year-old ex-boxing playwright dressed as a boy. Makes much sexy play of the creativity he believes himself to have in common with Sandie.

'She's lovely,' he says, meaning Marianne. 'It'll be a great book. Can I have her?'

'Ah,' says Ms Outram, with the smile of an elegant crocodile. 'That's the point, Herman. Can you?'

'You bitch. Just because I've gone off-Broadway.'

'Oh, Herman, Herman,' says Sandie Outram taking his hands. 'I want the best for her, you see. A daemon lover.'

'You're a violent woman, Sandie Outram.'

'Break it up, you two,' says Mu Crosby. 'Come on, Trailer, fry that fish.'

At that last, best party of the season, there are a number of realities, none of which is necessarily absolute.

For instance, Herman has asked some tiresome characters from his last play, or they have gate-crashed; anyhow, axe-woman Mimi can't stand them and becomes terribly drunk railing against these ratty, spaced-out girls and pot-smoking faggots, as she so elegantly puts it before Herman hits her and she shrieks he is written out. Why doesn't he go off and screw that Outram woman's ghost daughter if he can. Which he does.

Or, Herman and Mimi Trailer are touchingly reconciled. He is naturally tempted by Marianne, but then suddenly weary of the chase, of all this young flesh from which he can borrow nothing. In an excess of tenderness he sees how time has smudged too Mimi's keenness and brightness. They have been too frantic. He takes her glass, whispers in her ear and they walk hand in hand by the sea.

(That version would have to be very well written to hold water.)

Then there is another version in which Mimi catches him behind a rock with Marianne and chops off his hand. Now Herman is the only known left-handed ex-boxing playwright off Broadway. (In the out-of-town try-out Mimi posts the bloody hand to Trailer's agent but the mail service complains so this *grand guignol* coup is written out – anyhow there is nothing special about Herman Trailer's right hand nowadays, as Sandie Outram says, what with all these people being kidnapped and the post over-burdened with fingers and ears.)

The beach is soft and dark. There is a grace, now night has fallen, to this last party. Even the gate-crashers are hushed, someone is playing a guitar, Sandie and Herman, fellow soldiers, exchange wry salutes across the fire. Oh well, they mean what a life: writing. Mu Crosby cracks a lobster claw. There's sand in the crab.

Marianne says to Jake the beach-boy as they explore each other's salty bodies, 'I do hope she doesn't fall asleep.'

'You're not quite solid.'

'Hush,' she says. 'My mother might see.'

'I could put my hand right through you.'

'But I'm fond of her.'

'All we have to do,' says Jake, 'is go and tell her. We're not playing her games any more.'

'She means no harm. She wants the best for me.'

'Is Herman Trailer your daemon lover?' Jake's suddenly furious.

'Do you believe in ghosts?' she says. 'You must believe in me.'

In one draft Marianne and Jake go off together and live happily ever after in an abandoned coast-guard station, even out of season. For a while anyway. He gets used to it in time: her being a ghost and the way she can walk through walls. They are quite cosy, almost bourgeois, and after a few years Marianne, Sandie Outram's ghost daughter, puts on weight and no longer disappears though she is quite ill the night Sandie Outram dies.

Alternatively, Marianne is raped by Herman Trailer, out at sea in his Chris Craft, and washed up in the shape of a lobster Mu Crosby eats. Mu dies screaming of crustaceans and hauntings and phantasms, but then Jean-Paul Sartre believed, after he had taken some drug with empirical intent, that he was followed by lobsters and he got over it, and he's as sane as anyone now.

The only thing that is certain is that this was the last party of all on that coast. Afterwards there was the salmonella, and the pools were drained, then everyone went away. Christmas cards were exchanged for a few years but the beach houses were empty. The sea was declared officially poisoned, on the beach a rash scavenger might pick his way between the cola tins, the french-letters, the tar, the detergent, the ruins of the holiday.

'Flotsam and Jetsam' (murmured Ms Sandie Outram the novelist returned for the sake of old times) 'played the music halls for many years and some summer seasons.

'There's a dead cormorant. Silly bird.'

Sandie made the sun to set and shivered, though not with cold. Sat in her car, decided not to smoke, wished Jake's bar had not closed down, missed Marianne. Even Mu.

She put out the lights round the coast, one by one, dowsed the moon, and consigned the world to darkness.

Then she drove off, though there was nowhere to go, no one to meet on the road, no road.

Donald E. Westlake

The girl of my dreams

Yesterday I bought a gun.

I'm very confused; I don't know what to do.

I have always been a mild and shy young man, quiet and conservative and polite. I have been employed the last five years – since at nineteen I left college due to a lack of funds – at the shirt counter of Willis & DeKalb, Men's Clothiers, Stores in Principal Cities, and I would say that I have been generally content with my lot. Although recently I have been finding the new manager, Mr Miller, somewhat abrasive – not to overstate the matter – the work itself has always been agreeable, and I have continued to look forward to a quiet lifetime in the same employment.

I have never been much of a dreamer, neither by day nor by night. Reveries, daydreams, these are the products of vaulting ambition or vaulted desire, of both of which I have remained for the most part gratefully free. And, though science assures us that some part of every night's sleep is spent in the manufacture of dreams, mine must normally be gentle and innocuous, even dull, as I rarely remember them in the morning.

I would date the beginning of the change in my life from the moment of the retirement of old Mr Randmunson from his post as manager of our local Willis & DeKalb store, and his prompt replacement by Mr Miller, a stranger from the Akron branch.

Mr Miller is a hearty man, cheeks and nose all red with ruddy health, handshake painfully firm, voice roaring, laugh aggressive. Not yet thirty-five, he moves and speaks with the authority and self-confidence of a man much older, and he makes it no secret that some day he intends to be president of the entire chain. Our little store is merely a stopover for him, another rung on the ladder of his success.

His first day in the store, he came to me, ebullient and overpowering and supremely positive. He asked my opinion, he discussed business and geography and entertainment, he offered me cigarettes, he thumped my shoulder. 'We'll get along, Ronald!' he told me. 'Just keep moving those shirts!'

'Yes, Mr Miller.'

'And let me have an inventory list, by style and size, tomorrow morning.'

'Sir?'

'Any time before noon,' he said carelessly, and laughed, and thumped my shoulder. 'We'll have a great team here, Ronald, a first-rate team!'

Two nights later I dreamed for the first time of Delia.

I went to bed as usual at eleven-forty, after the news on Channel 6. I switched out the light, went to sleep, and in utter simplicity and clarity the dream began. In it, I was driving my automobile on Western Avenue, out from the centre of town. It was all thoroughly realistic, the day, the traffic, the used car lots along Western Avenue all gleaming in the spring sun. My six-year-old car was pulling just a little to the right, exactly as it does in real life. I knew I was dreaming, but at the same time it was very pleasant to be in my car on Western Avenue on such a lovely spring day.

A scream startled me, and my foot trod reflexively on the brake pedal. Nearby, on the sidewalk, a man and girl were struggling together. He was trying to wrest a package from her but she was resisting, clutching the package tight with both arms around it, and again screaming. The package was wrapped in brown paper and was about the size and shape of a suit carton from Willis & DeKalb.

I want to emphasize that everything was very realistic, down to the finest detail. There were none of the abrupt shifts in time or space or viewpoint normally associated with dreams, no impossibilities or absurdities.

There was no one else on the pavement nearby, and I acted almost without thinking. Braking the car at the kerb, I leaped out, ran around the car, and began to grapple with the girl's attacker. He was wearing brown corduroy trousers and a black leather jacket and he needed a shave. His breath was bad.

'Leave her alone!' I shouted, while the girl continued to scream.

The mugger had to give up his grip on the package in order

to deal with me. He pushed me away, and I staggered ineffectively backwards just as I would do in real life, while the girl kicked him repeatedly in the shins. As soon as I regained my balance I rushed forwards again, and now he decided he'd had enough. He turned tail and ran, down Western Avenue and through a used car lot and so out of sight.

The girl, breathing hard, still clutching the package to her breast, turned to smile gratefully upon me and say, 'How can I ever thank you?'

What a beautiful girl! The most beautiful girl I have ever seen, before or since. Auburn hair and lovely features, deep clear hazel eyes, slender wrists with every delicate birdlike bone outlined beneath the tender skin. She wore a blue and white spring dress, and casual white shoes. Silver teardrops graced her graceful ears.

She gazed at me with her melting, warm, companionable eyes, and she smiled at me with lips that murmured to be kissed, and she said to me, 'How can I ever thank you?' in a voice as dulcet as honey.

And there the dream ended, in extreme close-up on my Delia's face.

I awoke the next morning in a state of euphoria. The dream was still vivid in my mind in every detail, and most particularly did I remember the look of her sweet face at the end. That face stayed with me throughout the day, a day which otherwise might have been only bitter, as it was on that day Mr Miller gave the two-week notice to my friend and co-worker Gregory Shostrill of the stockroom. I shared, of course, the employees' general indignation that such an old and loyal worker had been so summarily dismissed, but for me the outrage was tempered by the continuing memory of last night's wonderful dream.

I never anticipated for a second that I would ever see my dream-girl again, but that night she returned to me, and my astonishment was only matched by my delight. I went to bed at my usual hour, went to sleep, and the dream began. It started precisely where, the night before, it had ended, with the beautiful girl saying to me, 'How can I ever thank you?'

I now functioned at two levels of awareness. The first, in

which I knew myself to be dreaming, was flabbergasted to find the dream picking up as though no day had elapsed, no break at all had taken place in the unfolding of this story. The second level, in which I was an active participant in the dream rather than its observer, treated this resumption of events as natural and inevitable and obvious, and reacted without delay.

It was this second level which replied, 'Anyone would have done what I did,' and then added, 'May I drive you wherever you're going?'

Now here, I grant, the dream had begun to be somewhat less than realistic. That I should talk with this lovely creature so effortlessly, without stammering, without blushing, with no worms of terror acrawl within my skull, was not entirely as the same scene would have been played in real life. In this situation in reality, I might have attacked the mugger as I'd done in the dream, but upon being left alone with the girl afterwards I would surely have been reduced to strained smiles and strangled silences.

But not in the dream. In the dream I was gallant and effortless, as I offered to drive her wherever she was going.

'If it wouldn't be putting you out of your way—'

'Not in the least,' I assured her. 'Where are you going?'

'Home,' she said. 'Summit Street. Do you know it?'

'Of course. It's right on my way.'

Which wasn't at all true. Summit Street, tucked away in the Oak Hills section, a rather well-to-do residential neighbourhood, was a side street off a side street. There's never any reason to drive on Summit Street unless Summit Street is your destination; it leads nowhere and comes from nowhere.

Nevertheless I said it was on my way – and she accepted, pleasantly. Holding the car door for her, I noticed my car was unusually clean and I was glad I'd finally got round to having it washed. New seat covers, too, very nice looking; I couldn't remember having bought them but I was pleased I had.

Once we were driving together along Western Avenue I introduced myself: 'My name's Ronald. Ronald Grady.'

'Delia,' she told me, smiling again. 'Delia Wright.'

'Hello, Delia Wright.'

Her smile broadened. 'Hello, Ronald Grady.' She reached

out and, for just a second, touched her fingers to my right wrist.

After that, the dream continued in the most naturalistic manner, the two of us chatting about one thing and another, the high schools we'd attended and how odd it was we'd never met before. When we reached Summit Street, she pointed out her house and I stopped at the kerb. She said, 'Won't you come in for a cup of coffee? I'd like you to meet my mother.'

'I really can't now,' I told her, smiling regretfully. 'But if you're doing nothing tonight, could I take you to dinner and a movie?'

'I'd like that,' she said.

'So would I.'

Our eyes met, and the moment seemed to deepen – and there the dream stopped.

I awoke next morning with a pleasant warm sensation on my right wrist, and I knew it was because Delia had touched me there. I ate a heartier breakfast than usual, startled my mother – I have continued to live at home with my mother and older sister, seeing no point in the additional expense of a place of my own – startled my mother, I say, by singing rather loudly as I dressed, and went off to work in as sunny a mood as could be imagined.

Which Mr Miller, a few hours later, succeeded in shattering.

I admit I returned late from lunch. The people at the auto store had assured me they could install the new seat covers in fifteen minutes, but it actually took them over half an hour. Still, it was the first time in five years I had ever been late, and Mr Miller's sarcasm and abuse seemed to me under the circumstances excessive. He carried on for nearly an hour, and in fact continued to make reference to the incident for the next two weeks.

Still, my hurt and outrage at Mr Miller's attitude were not so great as they might have been, had I not had that spot of warmth on my wrist to remind me of Delia. I thought of Delia, of her beauty and grace, of my own ease and confidence with her, and I weathered the Miller storm much better than might have been expected.

That night I hardly watched the eleven o'clock news at all.

I stayed until it ended only because any change in my habits would have produced a string of irrelevant questions from my mother, but as soon as the newscaster had bid me good night I headed directly for my own bed and sleep.

And Delia. I had been afraid to hope the dream would continue into a third night, but it did, it did, and most delightfully so.

This time, the dream skipped. It jumped over those dull meaningless hours when I was not with Delia, those hours as stale and empty as the real world, and it began tonight with me back at Summit Street promptly at seven, and Delia opening her front door to greet me.

Again the dream was utterly realistic. The white dinner jacket I wore was unlike anything in my waking wardrobe, but otherwise all was lifelike.

In tonight's dream we went to dinner together at Astoldi's, an expensive Italian restaurant which I had attended – in daylife – only once, at the testimonial dinner for Mr Randmunson when he retired from Willis & DeKalb. But tonight I behaved – and felt, which is equally important – as though I dined at Astoldi's twice a week.

The dream ended as we were leaving the restaurant after dinner, on our way to the theatre.

The next day, and the days that followed, passed in a slow and velvet haze. I no longer cared about Mr Miller's endless abrasion. I bought a white dinner jacket, though in daylife I had no use for it. Later on, after a dream-segment in which I wore a dark blue ascot, I bought three such ascots and hung them in my closet.

The dream, meanwhile, went on and on without a break, never skipping a night. It omitted all periods of time when I was not with my Delia, but those times spent with her were presented entirely, and chronologically, and with great realism.

There were, of course, small exceptions to the realism. My ease with Delia, for instance. And the fact my car grew steadily younger night by night, and soon stopped pulling to the right.

That first date with Delia was followed by a second, and a third. We went dancing together, we went swimming together, we went for rides on a lake in her cousin's cabin cruiser and for drives in the mountains in her own Porsche convertible. I kissed her, and her lips were indescribably sweet.

I saw her in all lights and under all conditions. Diving from a tacketa-tacketa long board into a jade green swimming pool, and framed for one heartbeat in silhouette against the pale blue sky. Dancing in a white ball gown, low across her tanned breasts and trailing the floor behind her. Kneeling in the garden behind her house, dressed in shorts and a sleeveless pale green blouse, wearing gardening gloves and holding a trowel, laughing, with dirt smudged on her nose and cheek. Driving her white Porsche, her auburn hair blowing in the wind, her eyes bright with joy and laughter.

The dream, the Dream, became to me much finer than reality, oh, much much finer. And in the Dream there was no haste, no hurry, no fear. Delia and I were in love, we were lovers, though we had not yet actually gone to bed together. I was calm and confident, slow and sure, feeling no frantic need to seduce my Delia now, *now*. I knew the time would come, and in our tender moments I could see in her eyes that she also knew, and that she was not afraid.

Slowly we learned one another. We kissed, I held her tight, my arm encircled her slender waist. I touched her breasts and one moonlight night on a deserted beach, I stroked her lovely legs.

How I loved my Delia! And how I needed her, how necessary an antidote she was to the increasing bitterness of my days.

It was Mr Miller, of course, who disrupted my days as thoroughly as Delia soothed and sweetened my nights. Our store was soon unrecognizable, most of the older employees gone, new people and new methods everywhere. I believe I was kept on only because I was such a silent enduring victim for Mr Miller's sarcasm, his nasal voice and his twisted smile and his bitter eyes. He was in such a starved hurry for the presidency of the firm, he was so frantic to capture Willis & DeKalb, that it forced him to excesses beyond belief.

But I was, if not totally immune, at least relatively safe from the psychological blows of Mr Miller's manner. The joyful calm of the Dream carried me through all but the very worst of the days in the store.

Another development was that I found myself more self-assured with other people in daylife. Woman customers, and even the fashionably attractive newly-hired woman employees, were beginning to make it clear that they found me not entirely without interest. It goes without saying that I remained faithful to my Delia, but it was nevertheless pleasurable to realize that a real-world social life was available to me, should I ever want it.

Not that I could visualize myself ever being less than fully satisfied with Delia.

But then it all began to change. Slowly, very very slowly, so that I don't know for how long the tide had already ebbed before I first became aware. In my Delia's eyes – I first saw it in her eyes. Where before they had been warm bottomless pools, now they seemed flat and cold and opaque; I no longer saw in them the candour and beauty of before. Also, from time to time I would catch upon her face a pensive frown, a solemn thoughtfulness.

'What is it?' I would ask her. 'Tell me. Whatever I can do—'

'It's nothing,' she would insist. 'Really, darling, it's nothing at all,' and kiss me on the cheek.

In this same period, while matters were unexpectedly worsening in the Dream, a slow improvement had begun in the store. All the employees who were to be fired were now gone, all the new employees in and used to their jobs, all the new routines worked with and grown accustomed to. Mr Miller seemed also to be growing accustomed to his new job and the new store. Less and less was he taking out his viciousness and insecurity on me. He had, in fact, taken to avoiding me for days at a time, as though beginning to feel ashamed of his earlier harshness.

Which was fine but irrelevant. What was my waking time after all but the necessary adjunct to the Dream? It was the Dream that mattered, and the Dream was not going well, not going well at all.

It was, in fact, getting worse. Delia began to break dates with me, and to make excuses when I asked her for dates. The pensive looks, the distracted looks, the buried sense of impatience, all were more frequent now. Entire portions of the Dream were spent with me alone – I was *never* alone in the early nights! – pacing the floor of my room, waiting for a promised call that never was to come.

What could it be? I asked her and asked, but always she evaded my questions, my eyes, my arms. If I pressed, she would insist it was nothing, nothing, and then for a little while she would be her old self again, gay and beautiful, and I could believe it had only been my imagination after all. But only for a little while, and then the distraction, the evasiveness, the impatience, the excuses, all once more would return.

Until two nights ago. We sat in her convertible beneath a swollen moon, high on a dark cliff overlooking the sea, and I forced the issue at last. 'Delia,' I said. 'Tell me the truth, I have to know. Is there another man?'

She looked at me, and I saw she was about to deny everything yet again, but this time she couldn't do it. She bowed her head. 'I'm sorry, Ronald,' she said, her voice so low I could barely hear the words. 'There is.'

'Who?'

She raised her head, gazing at me with eyes in which guilt and pity and love and shame were all commingled, and she said, 'It's Mr Miller.'

I recoiled. *'What?'*

'I met him at the country club,' she said. 'I can't help it, Ronald. I wish to God I'd never met the man, he has some sort of hold over me, some hypnotic power. That first night, he took me to a motel, and—'

Then she told me, told me everything, every action and every demand, in the most revolting detail. And though I squirmed and struggled, though I strained and yearned, I could not wake up, I could not end the Dream. Delia told me everything she had done with Mr Miller, her helplessness to deny him even though it was *me* she loved and him for whom she felt only detestation, her constant trysts with him night after night, direct from my arms to his. She told me of their planned meeting later that very night in the motel where it had all begun, and she told me of her bitter self-knowledge that even now, after I knew everything, *she would still meet him.*

Then at last her toneless voice was finished and we were in silence once again, beneath the moon, high on the cliff. *Then* I awoke.

That was two nights ago. Yesterday I arose the same as ever – what else could I do? – and I went to the store as usual, and I behaved normally in every way. What else could I do? But I noticed again Mr Miller's muted attitude towards me, and now I understood it was the result of his guilty knowledge. Of course Delia had told him about me, she'd described all that to me during her confession, relating how Mr Miller had laughed and been scornful to hear that 'Ronald the sap' had never been to bed with her. 'Doesn't know what he's missing, does he?' she quoted him as saying, with a laugh.

At lunchtime I drove past the motel she'd named, and a squalid place it was, peeling stucco painted a garish blue. Not far beyond it was a gunsmith's; on the spur of the moment I stopped, I talked to the salesman about 'plinking' and 'varmints', and I bought a snub-nosed Iver Johnson Trailsman revolver. The salesman inserted the .32 bullets into the chambers, and I put the box containing the gun into the glove compartment of my car. Last evening I carried the gun unobserved into the house and hid it in my room, in a dresser drawer, beneath my sweaters.

And last night, as usual, I dreamed. But in the Dream I was not with Delia. In the Dream I was alone, in my bedroom, sitting on the edge of the bed with the gun in my hand, listening to the small noises of my mother and sister as they prepared for sleep, waiting for the house to be quiet. In last night's Dream I had the gun and I planned to use it. In last night's Dream I had not left my car in the drive as usual but a street away, parked at the kerb. In last night's Dream I was waiting only for my mother and sister to be safely asleep, when I intended to creep silently from the house, hurry down the pavement to my car, drive to that motel, and enter room 7 – it's always room 7, Delia told me, always the same room – where it was my intention to shoot Mr Miller dead. In last night's Dream I heard my mother and sister moving about, at first in the kitchen and then in the bathroom and then in their bedrooms. In last night's Dream the house slowly, gradually, finally became quiet, and I got to my feet, putting the gun in my pocket, preparing to leave the room. And at that point the Dream stopped.

I have been very confused today. I have wanted to talk to Mr Miller, but I've been afraid to. I have been unsure what to do next, or in which life to do it. If I kill Mr Miller in the Dream tonight, will he still be in the store tomorrow, with his guilt and his scorn? If I kill Mr Miller in the Dream tonight, and if he is still in the store tomorrow, will I go mad? If I fail to kill Mr Miller, somewhere, somehow, how can I go on living with myself?

When I came home from work this evening, I didn't park the car in the drive as usual, but left it at the kerb, a street away from here. My mind was in turmoil all evening, but I behaved normally, and after the eleven o'clock news I came up here to my bedroom.

But I was afraid to sleep, afraid to Dream. I took the gun from the drawer, and I have been sitting here, listening to the small sounds of my mother and my sister as they prepare for bed.

Can things ever be again as they were between Delia and me? Can the memory of what has happened ever be expunged? I turn the gun and look into its black barrel and I ask myself all these questions. ... 'perchance to Dream.' If I arranged it that I would never Awake again, would I go on Dreaming? But would the Dream become worse instead of better?

Is it possible – as some faint doubting corner of my mind suggests – even remotely possible, that Delia is not what she seems, that she was never true, that she is a succuba who has come to destroy me through my Dream?

The house is silent. The hour is late. If I stay awake, if I creep from the house and drive to the motel, what will I find in room 7?

And whom shall I kill?

Celia Dale

Tenants

I have to tell someone. But who? They'd think I was mad. Or that Nicky ... I'm frightened, frightened. And I'm not that kind of person at all really. People always say I'm so capable, so level-headed. And I am. That's why now ... So if I write it all down perhaps I'll be able to see that it's all imagination, that it's not really ...

Nicky and I started a thing together about two years ago. I was living with two girls and he was in some sort of a grotty commune thing, so it wasn't all that easy for us to be together. I simply can't do private things in semi-public – people in the next room or due back in half an hour. Nor could Nicky really, although he pretends he could. The thing is, we've both been brought up 'proper'. And although he really has broken away (he left Marlborough before taking his A-levels and then he dropped out of LSE because he had this fantastic offer to help start up a sort of pop art magazine, but it only came out once), I honestly haven't. I left home and got a job, of course, and went through various phases, but underneath it all I really like to be tidy and organized, and I daresay that's why I got such a good job that really interests me and pays a bomb.

And really, actually, I'd like to be married. I know it's silly and no one does now unless they're having a baby or something, but I can't help it. I've been conditioned and I just should awfully like to be Nicky's legal, lawful wife. Of course I've never said so, absolutely never so much as hinted. But I suppose he might have sussed.

Because I really do love him. It's not just that I think he's beautiful – he's sort of fine-boned and ethereal, as though his skin was transparent somehow, although he's as strong as a horse – but I love even his faults. He's terribly moody and highly strung, especially when his work's not going right. Then he just goes into a silence. Absolutely withdrawn. It's horrible, but I do love him and I have to try and help him sort of come back to me. Usually I can – could.

So to go back to what I was saying first, I decided – we decided we had to find a place together on our own. The idea didn't grab him at first, but after we'd talked it over a bit he said, 'Great.'

Well, I looked and looked and honestly, you wouldn't believe the grotty places people think people will pay to live in. Basements you could grow mushrooms in, attics the rain came into, crumby bits of furniture, filthy old gas stoves. I looked and looked and if there was ever anything halfway decent it had gone before I got there. I began to get really frantic. You know how it is if you finally decide you want to do something, you simply get frantic if you can't do it at once. Nicky said give it a rest, we'd look again later, but I really did want to be with him on our own. Besides, he hadn't been well – bronchitis or something – and he was looking more and more as though made of glass. I longed to take care of him and fatten him up a bit and cosset him and – well, just love him. I do love him.

Then I found it. It was the first floor of one of those terribly ugly Victorian semi's in north London, yellowy brick and a portico, laurels in front with the dustbins, a straggly garden at the back. Two decent rooms and a bath with a cover over it in the kitchen, and a few bits of not too grotty furniture. The road was dreary but opposite they'd built a new school, all glass and flat roofs and lollipop ladies, so we could see the sky instead of just other ugly houses. Somehow I'd managed to be there first and I had to decide at once, so I did. I took it and paid six months in advance and we moved in the next week.

Nick was funny about it. He prowled around like a cat, sort of sniffing the atmosphere. 'It's got a funny feel to it,' he said, 'sort of – I don't know – echoes.'

'Vibes?' I said, sort of pulling his leg.

'Yes – maybe. It's sort of . . . cold.'

'Of course, it's cold, it's been empty. An empty place is always cold.'

We painted it up a bit and moved in our own bits and pieces. Nick hadn't much but I'd got – or soon bought – quite a bit – some rugs and I made curtains and we had big cushions to sit on, a kitchen table. I'd got a lot of saucepans and china because I like cooking, and Mummy and Daddy gave us a bed – which was jolly nice of them really because I don't expect they really approved, but they never said a word.

Oh, it was heaven! I'd get up early and clean and polish before ever Nick woke up, and think what we'd have to eat. I'd leave him just waking up, with coffee and an apple (that's all he ever wants) and go off to work simply longing to get back. I'd hurry home in the evening with lovely things to cook and jobs to do like cushion covers or shelves or something, and he'd be there. Sometimes he'd be in a mood and I knew he'd not had a good day, but sometimes we simply fell in each other's arms and went to bed then and there and had our meal afterwards. And almost all our nights were full of love – real lovely warm loving connubial love – that's a lovely word, connubial. Solid. Secure. Like my parents.

And he really seemed content. Sort of stretched out and relaxed, as if he liked this way after all. It was bliss. For a little while.

He'd always had moods, I knew that. I hoped that with me they'd grow less because he was as happy as I was. But they didn't. After the first week or two they began to come back. You see, I was out all day and he was there on his own and when I got back he was often all pent up and I'd get it all. Sometimes it was just silence. I hated that. He'd just sort of grunt if I said anything, sagged down on the cushions, not reading, just sort of shut away. But sometimes he'd be restless, walking about with a sort of listening look, although he wouldn't listen to *me*. The restlessness was new; before, he'd always been passive, sunk down in his own gloom.

We'd been there about a month when one day he suddenly said, 'I hate this place.'

I was using the blender and couldn't hear properly and shouted, 'What?'

He absolutely yelled back. 'I hate this place. I hate this bloody place!'

I switched it off. 'Nicky – you can't! It's lovely, it's perfect ...'

'It's a bloody prison. It hedges me in. You've not been alone here all day, listening, wondering ...'

'Wondering? What about?'

'Everything. What we're doing here, what people did here before. What goes on.'

'Nothing goes on except us. It's ours.'

'Is it?' He gave me a funny look. 'It's yours maybe, not mine. I hate the bloody place.' Then he went silent and wouldn't speak again for a long time.

I thought I knew what it was. You see, in a way he was right, the flat was more mine than his because I earned more money than he did. Well, actually, I earned it all because I had this fantastic job which I really loved and paid a bomb and Nicky earned nothing at all. He's a writer – that magazine thing was just the beginning, really he was writing two things, a novel about being a student and dropping out and finding yourself, and then this fantastic television series, sort of plays which acted out all the various philosophical concepts in terms of modern economics that he hoped BBC2 would do, only it was taking ages because it was all so deep, and he didn't know anyone in TV to give him encouragement.

Of course he couldn't possibly have done a job at the same time as all this writing, so naturally I paid everything and that was fine. I mean, what does it matter who pays, it was *us*, wasn't it, and lots and lots of men live off their women – that sounds horrid, it's not like that a bit. I mean, I had the money, I was earning, so what the hell, me or Social Security? I loved him to, I wanted him to.

Only the thing is, although he agreed in theory – well, you can't have parents and schools and upbringing like ours and get rid of it all as easily as that. I mean, look at me and my feeling I'd like to be married. I mean, what difference does it make whether we are or not? I mean, how silly can you get? But I suppose that just as I felt about that, Nicky felt about me being the breadwinner, deep down. I suppose that was it.

We'd got plenty of friends and they'd all loved the flat and said how lucky we were and all that. We'd been there about six weeks and Ben, who I've known for ever, and this friend of Nicky's were there drinking coffee. It was late, after midnight, Nicky never wants to go to bed (not to sleep, anyway) and Dicky never does either. That's his sort of nickname – he's Nicky's oldest friend, like Ben is mine, they were at school together and went to LSE together, only Dicky stayed on; they got called Nicky and Dicky (Derek really) because they were always around together. He's very good-looking, sort of like the blond one in 'Starsky and Hutch', and very masculine, which is jolly odd because I'm absolutely certain he's gay as a bird. I've never dared say this to Nicky, he'd be furious, but Dicky's got that sort of mocking, amusing, light way about him which makes people laugh but is spiteful underneath very often, especially about me. I've never said anything because maybe I've imagined it and Nicky'd be furious. But I've seen the way Dicky looks at him sometimes and the way he looks at me, and he's always calling me 'the little home-maker' or 'our career lady', two things that Nicky absolutely doesn't want.

So we were all there that evening with our mugs of coffee and Ben said something about going home and Dicky said something about 'hard to leave the cosy nest' and then, 'You really have done wonders, love, no one would ever know. And it doesn't bother you?'

'*What* bother us?' I said.

'Why – what it was.' Then he paused and looked round at us in a sort of mock concerned way. 'You can't mean you don't know?'

'Know what?' asked Ben.

'Well . . .' Dicky paused again. 'This is where that murder was. A few years back.'

'A murder?' Only Ben spoke.

'Yes, an 'orrible murder. You can't mean you didn't know?' He knew we didn't. 'Feller strangled his wife, then stuffed her in the cupboard – that one, I shouldn't wonder.' He waved a hand. 'He went on living here, going to work every day, then he killed himself. Neighbours found him, police found her. You must remember, it was the juiciest since old Christie – the Haylett Road murder.'

Ben had gone scarlet and shouted. 'You bloody oaf, what d'you want to say that for?' but I couldn't say anything and Nicky simply sat there, staring at Dicky with his mouth half open and an awful sort of glazed look on his face.

Well, after that the absolute nightmare began. Actual nightmare for me. I'd struggle awake trying to scream, nothing but mumbles and twitches to help me out of the horror, and when I managed to thresh myself awake I'd find Nicky lying there beside me with his eyes open, wide awake as though looking at something, listening to something, far far apart from me. If I clung to him he'd respond absently, as though he wasn't really there. And in the morning he'd sometimes pretend to be asleep when I left.

We never talked about what Dicky had said. I couldn't. I couldn't even think about it, except that I thought about it all the time I wasn't actually at work. I thought about the fury and terror of the thing itself but more I thought about the days and nights afterwards, the horror and fear and grief when that man was here alone, pretending to the outside world, living with his inside hell, cracking . . .

I shut my mind against it, I busied myself more and more on making the flat our own, bright and clean and new, and I wrapped Nicky round with all the love that was in me to blot out his thoughts too. I thought about moving and looked at advertisements in newspapers and notice-boards – I even went to see one or two without telling Nicky, for I couldn't let him see how upset I was, all my thoughts were on calming him, pretending it hadn't happened, we'd not been told, there was nothing to know. But housing was even more hopeless now than when we'd found the flat. And we'd still got nearly four months paid for. How could we leave? As soon as we could, we would. I'd go on looking. But not say anything to Nicky, not let him know how frightened I was by what Dicky's words had done to him.

He was so silent, much more than before. Or else very gay – the old use of the word. A sort of frantic gaiety that seemed to glitter and flash as though he were made of metal. I guessed he'd been seeing Dicky when he was like that – I don't know what he did when I was at work all day, but he wasn't writing.

When I asked him about it, he looked at me oddly and said, 'I can't write now, I'm not that sort of person any more.'

One evening I came back and he was just sitting in the dark. He didn't say 'Hullo' or anything, just sat there looking at me with a peculiar sort of laughter in his face as though he had some private joke which was – I don't know – spiteful somehow.

He watched me a bit and then he said, 'They weren't married, you know. They were just living together – like us.'

'Who?' But I knew.

'Ted Frensham and his girl. The former tenants.' He grinned. 'She was pregnant.'

I blurted out, 'I'm not pregnant.'

'Great. But she was. I read it all up in the library back files of the newspapers. She was nagging him to get married.'

'I don't want to hear about it.' I made as much noise as I could with the supper pots and pans. He just sat there, grinning.

'He left a note when he killed himself – on the mantelpiece, I expect – there.' He gestured towards ours. 'He said he felt hemmed in. Trapped. I can understand that.'

'I can't. He could have gone away.'

'Perhaps he didn't really want to.' Then he got up and came over to me and put his arms round me, and for a little while he was the Nicky I'd loved for ever.

But that was the last time. Bit by bit it was as though a shadow was growing somewhere – it was at the back of his eyes when he was in one of his silences; and it was somewhere just behind me sometimes just out of sight – a shadow, a shape, a feeling. I knew it was all imagination. Dicky had done it on purpose, to break up Nicky and me. He knew how suggestible Nicky was, even if the story hadn't been true. But it was true, and he'd made sure Nicky went and checked up on it. Ted Frensham had murdered his girlfriend in Haylett Road seven years ago, and how could we not believe that the echoes could still be heard?

'You're a great pair,' said Dicky, 'the stuff the Empire was made of. Horror movie into love nest with a wave of the home-maker's wand. No ghostly tappings or moanings, mysterious chills in the night. No malign presence – love conquers all.'

'Belt up,' said Ben. He got fearfully uptight about it all and tried to shut Dicky up if ever they were there at the same time and Dicky started picking and digging away at it, as he did, always. 'When people are dead they're dead, it's over and done with.'

'You don't believe in ghosts? In "sensitives" that can pick up the violence left behind?'

'No, I bloody don't.'

'Nicky does.' Dicky smiled. 'Nicky's a sensitive. He knows things get left behind when murder's been done ...'

Ben hit him. Not very hard because they were both sitting down, but he cut Dicky's lip. Nicky simply went white and sat there, silent, but Dicky said spitefully, 'There, you see – violence is still here.'

It's hard to describe the next bit. It wasn't just Nick, it was me too. The flat wasn't ours any more, it was as though there was always someone else in the next room, keeping quiet, holding their breath, listening. Listening to Nick listening. Some of the time I didn't feel it – I had to be out all day, I made myself busy and cheerful when I got back, we played records and had friends in or went out. But when we were on our own, if we were quiet, then, behind the next room's door, outside in the passage, the listening began again. I'd get up and go into that room or the passage, banging my feet, terrified but determined to face it out. The room was always empty, quite silent. But presently, in a different place, the listening would start again, the shadow grow again.

That's all I ever heard – the listening. But Nick heard and saw more. He didn't tell me but I knew. I could see him begin to draw away from me, just sitting, his eyes alert, flickering as though trying to follow something, trying to hear something. When I tried to get near to him he almost snarled at me. He wouldn't eat the things I bought specially because he liked them. When we made love, which was hardly ever now, he didn't care about me at all, it was just quick and savage as though he hated me. A different Nicky looked out of his eyes and hated me.

At last I said, 'Nick, let's leave. Let's go away for a bit. We can go to a hotel even. I can pay.'

'I'm sure you can,' he said and his face and his voice were horrible. 'You've got me by the short and curlies, big earner, big boss lady. Why not ask Daddy to buy us a nice little semi with room for a pram in the patio? You go if you want to – go on, piss off if you want to.' I began to cry. He just stared at me. 'That's right,' he said, and his voice wasn't a bit like his but rough and with a sort of accent, 'you always cry, don't you, you cow. That's how you got me, isn't it. That's how you bloody tie me down . . .' Then he slammed out of the room.

The listening closed in on me like a fog and through it all there seemed to run a sort of snigger.

I should have gone. But I loved him. How could I leave him on his own in that place with whatever, whoever it was creeping in on him, taking him over, my poor unhappy love? I was stronger than he was, tougher. I suppose he resented it, resented all the things I was and he wasn't, like being successful and earning a lot and being efficient and level-headed and, well yes, conventional, even if not by Daddy and Mummy's standards. But it was more than that now. He was changing. He was Nicky, yes, high-strung and insecure, but he was someone else too, someone ugly and vengeful and bottled up, whose violence lurked in the empty rooms, behind closed doors, under the floors, listening, whispering, reaching out to enter and take possession . . .

At work I was promoted. I was given a whole small section of my own. It meant more money, and I went out without telling Nicky and I found us a super bed-sit, kitchen and bath in a modern block of flats with no character and no ghosts, and I mortgaged my pay for a month's rent as from the following week. We would be free again. Ted Frensham couldn't follow us there. Nothing could follow us there, we'd be on our own as we'd been before and Nick would start writing again and love me again and all would be well. We still had two months to run on the flat but I didn't care.

I went home and told Nicky.

He was sitting in the dark as usual – twilight really, because the days were getting longer, and the birds were still settling down in the trees outside the window. I took the things through to the kitchen and came back, taking off my coat. 'So we'll pack up at the weekend and be out of here Sunday. We can use Ben's car, he won't mind going backwards and forwards. We can leave what we haven't room for until we find a really permanent place, and start from there.'

He got very slowly to his feet. 'You bitch,' he said. 'You bossy, arrogant, interfering bitch.' He came towards me. 'D'you think I'm going on poncing off you? D'you think you can tie me up and lug me off like I was a piece of furniture? D'you think I'm going to be tied to you and some squalling filthy little bastard for the rest of my days? I've had enough, d'you hear me, I've had a bloody enough!'

He reached out and he put his hands round my neck and he began to choke me. I couldn't scream and I pulled and pulled at his fingers but they were like wire biting into me, his whole body was trembling as though a current was passing through it and up his arms and into his fingers, pressing, and pressing, and his face was sort of swimming above me as my knees gave and I began to fall but was held up by those wiry trembling arms, and his face with the lips drawn back like a dog snarling, a dog intent on a bone, fixed and savage and quite, quite without . . .

The telephone rang. It shocked. For a moment we hung there, he and I, frozen – me on my knees with my hands trying to undo his, he bending over me, wiry arms braced to the fingers. A dazed look came over his face and he dropped me. I fell to the floor, choking and sobbing. In a daze he stared at the telephone as it rang and rang. Then he crossed the room and lifted the receiver. A voice squawked in it.

'Yes,' Nick said thickly. 'Yes. You what?' His gaze moved to me and a kind of horror began to thaw the mask that had been his face. 'Gone? I see. Well, thanks . . . Yes, sure, I'll tell her. I'll tell her.'

He put down the receiver though the telephone still squawked, and stood staring at me, his face seeming to break up, disintegrate like something under water.

'That was Ben,' he said. He sat down slowly. 'He checked

at the town hall. The Frensham house was opposite. Where the school is.'

I had pulled myself to my knees. 'The school ... ?'

'The Frensham house was pulled down. It's gone. He never lived here.'

I croaked, 'Never lived here? No murder? Nothing ... ?'

We stared at each other. It was dark by now, but a street lamp shone in. He was a black shape motionless against the window.

He said dully, 'He never lived here. He was never here. There was only us.'

H. R. F. Keating

The spirit of service

They were late arriving at the dark bungalow. The hired jeep had not been running perfectly sweetly and when they had halted for lunch Poppa had decided to correct the engine timing. 'I guess Indians just don't understand machinery,' he had stated, with all of three weeks' experience of the subcontinent behind him.

But really it was simply because there was nothing he liked better than getting his hands dirty stripping down a motor and carefully reassembling it. Otherwise he would hardly have forgotten that he was now an enthusiast for all things Indian. 'Nowhere, but nowhere, do past and present co-exist so darned dramatically.' He had often said it. During the three weeks of their holiday, and even before.

Momma, in the time they had been in the country, had lost most of the enthusiasm she had originally shared with Poppa. The prospect of showing the colour movies at her coffee mornings, once so beguiling, had faded in face of the absence of hot water for baths at many of the places they had stayed at since getting out of Calcutta – and she had not been able to do that too quickly when she had seen the sprawl of swollen-legged beggars on the pavement right outside the hotel – as well as the occasional absence of ice for drinks and, one experience to be forgotten completely if possible, an absence of drinks for ice.

So she was just about ready for the modest comforts of the *dak* bungalow as described to them by the Block Development Officer whom they had, with some difficulty, tracked down – 'You have to remember Indian bureaucracy is the last legacy of the British,' said Poppa – when they had started to make arrangements for this particular part of the trip, the viewing of the elephant herds. 'It is not at all hotel. Kindly bear that in mind. But the *khansamah* there, a fellow who has been in charge since the British days, you know, is a damned first-rate cook. That I can promise.'

Junior, at thirteen, was just taking it all as it came.

But the building had come into sight at last, not very large, perhaps two big rooms, whitewashed mud walls, a low thatched roof, a wide veranda. It lay about a hundred yards back from the haphazard, cart-rutted earth road, shaded by a huge belu tree in a compound surrounded by an ineffective looking fence made of criss-crossed logs.

They pulled up with some triumphant but rather unnecessary hooting on the horn, since in the quiet of this remote place the sound of their engine must have been audible for perhaps as much as the past quarter-hour to the *khansamah* and whatever other servants there were. The Block Development Officer had indicated that there were more servants without being particularly specific. 'Water and bathroom and all that sort of thing, no problem, no problem whatsoever.'

Which made it a little strange that no one had come out to greet them.

'What if the place is empty?' Momma said. 'What if there's no one to do anything for us? If they've just locked up and gone away? I mean, it's a crazy way of doing things, keeping servants waiting here just in case anybody should come by.'

'It's the way they have in India, honey,' said Poppa. 'I guess I don't too much like the idea of being waited on hand and foot like I was a rajah or something. But they have one hell of an employment problem, you've got to remember.'

'Well then, why don't we get some service, goddamnit?' Momma said.

Junior said nothing. He just sat at the back of the jeep and looked out at the bungalow with its small signs of decay, the patches where the whitewash was stained, the areas of disarray in the reed thatch, at the enormous pale sprawling trunk of the belu tree, at the distant thick dark green line of the jungle and the more distant dark blue of the hills. And he sniffed in the scents of the end of day and absorbed the sounds, the tiny cheepings and callings of the birds, the yet tinier squeakings and whinings of the innumerable insects.

'There is somebody here,' he said suddenly into the short silence that had fallen. 'There's a fire. I can smell the smoke. Kinda sharp.'

'All right then.'

Poppa jumped down and headed determinedly towards the steps up to the sleepy-looking hushed bungalow.

But he never reached them.

From around the corner of the building, from where indeed a little smudgy smoke from a dung fire could be seen drifting to nothingness in the intermittent puffs of breeze, there hurried a man. He was a person of some impressiveness. But not much. Grey-moustached, broad shouldered, turbaned, but with his white tunic and whitish shorts much mended and drooping with age.

'No, no, no, no, no, no,' he said, running forward with outstretched hands.

Poppa stopped and looked at him.

'Is this the *dak* bungalow?' he asked, though it could be nothing else, there had been nothing else for miles. 'Are you the whayamacallit, the *khansamah*?'

'Oh, yes, sahib. I am *khansamah* for *dak* bungalow. For many, many years I have been.'

'Ah, good. Yeah. Yeah, well that's just fine. That guy, the Block Development Officer – that what he's called? – told us you'd be here. Said you were a darned good cook.'

'Sorry, sahib. Full house today.'

The *khansamah* stood squarely in front of Poppa, between him and the steps up to the veranda.

'But the guy,' Poppa said. 'But the Block Development Officer. But he said. He told us there'd be no one else here. Not at this time of year.'

'Oh, sahib. Block Development Officer is Indian fellow. Sahib, he is knowing nothing at all. This is Colonel Sahib's *shikar* time, sahib. First to fourteen February. So it has always been.'

'You mean there's a Colonel in residence? What is he, a Britisher? But he won't want the whole place, will he? I mean, I guess if I could have a word with him. There's Mrs Algren out there. I'm sure the Colonel, if he's a British gentleman, I'm sure he'd be willing to have us share his accommodation.'

'No, sahib.'

Poppa's eyes seemed to jerk forward a tiny bit in his skull. He very nearly dealt with the situation as if it was one of the many obstacles he had bulldozed down in the course of a business career that had taken him to the top in his city, right to the top. But then he remembered that this was India, and that he had great respect for the Indian way of life. For what it was.

'Yeah, but if I could just see the Colonel,' he said.

'Sahib, Colonel Sahib "Not at Home".'

It could not have been more definite.

Poppa scratched his ear a bit and then turned and tramped back over the dry dusty earth of the compound to the jeep and began to explain.

'You know, we have got that emergency tent,' he concluded a little doubtfully. 'We could set it up, I guess, and sorta camp right here.'

'Gee, Poppa, could we do that?'

Junior was so plainly delighted with the idea of camping that even Momma sank her objections – and they were many – and agreed.

Though later that night, when Junior was safely asleep, her doubts, and fears, all rose up again.

'Honey, I don't like it out here.'

'It's all right, honey. Well, kinda.'

'It isn't. It is not. There's a damned mosquito right in here with us.'

'Yeah. Yeah, I know. But if I open up the tent there'll be fifty more just waiting to get in.'

'And I heard a sort of howling just now. Honey, I think it was a ghost.'

'Nonsense, hon. Nonsense. I guess it was a jackal. They're only something like a small coyote. They won't harm us any. I read about them in the book.'

'That book. You and India. Honey, I wish to God we'd made it Florida again this year.'

'But think of the film we've got already. And tomorrow there'll be the elephants. Sure ain't no elephant herds in Florida.'

'And there ain't no ghosts neither.'

'Honey. I said that wasn't any ghost.'

He laughed a little in the darkness. A tentative laugh.

'You can always tell an Indian ghost,' he said.

'What do you mean "tell"? And keep your voice down, you'll wake Junior.'

'Tell them. You can tell if they're a ghost. I read this too. Ghosts in India have their feet on backwards. Said it in the book.'

'Oh, for heaven's sakes. Go to sleep.'

And, mercifully, sleep came.

Next day they might well have altered their schedule and moved on – if the elephants had not been so successful. Or so very nearly so very, very successful.

They saw a big herd moving in and out of high elephant grass, with two huge tuskers keeping guard and at least three mothers with the sweetest young ones beside them, just where the Block Development Officer had told them they would and they shot a lot of film. But at the very moment it had looked as if the great romantic grey-backed lumbering fleet of them was going to come out into an open area in perfect camera range something had alerted them – Junior privately thought it must have been the yucky smell of the insect repellent Momma insisted they smear all over themselves – and the whole herd had sheered off, calmly but implacably.

So there had really been no question but that they should stay on at least one more day, despite the difficulties not having the use of the *dak* bungalow presented (Momma had not taken kindly to cooking for them on the little butane stove nor to washing in cold water standing beside the plastic basin instead of luxuriating in the hot tub ready filled for her which she had seen as one of the services she could expect in the bungalow).

But Junior was delighted to be there. When, fairly early in the day after the disappointment with the elephants, they had arrived back he prowled happily all round the bungalow, despite some agitated signalling from Momma who would rather the family either met the still invisible Colonel formally or not at all. Junior made friends, as far as the language barrier allowed, with the little boy he discovered rhythmically heaving on a long cord disappearing through a small hole in the bungalow's back wall from behind which could be heard the steady swish-clunk of a cloth punkah presumably keeping the invisible Colonel cool in the afternoon heat.

And when, exploring a little further, he peeped in at the slit-narrow low doorway which was the sweeper's entrance to the Colonel's bathroom, and saw not only pails of water ready for the doubtless lean and athletic Briton to swish over himself but also an inexplicable dark teak-wood box on four sturdy legs in one corner, it was the little boy who, daring to abandon the *punkah* cord for a few moments, showed him in extremely vivid pantomine what the box's purpose was while repeating over and over again with tremendous glee the English words 'thunder-box'.

And, eventually leaving the boy to his draught-producing task, Junior went on, too, to make friends with the ancient sweeper.

'Guess he gets to do pretty well everything, 'cept cook,' he told his parents later. 'He was slurping water all over those sorta blind things they have over the windows when I first saw him. Y'know, like made outa grass stuff. Kinda pity they were there too, or I'd have got to see that Colonel guy.'

'Junior,' said Momma with some sharpness. 'You are not to pry.'

'Yeah, but I'd like to see him. He's a hunter, a really great hunter, y'know. Or I think he is, if what that sweeper guy sign-talked to me was true. Anyways he said "Tiger, tiger" lotsa times and made kinda shooting signs.'

'Well, the Colonel can't be shooting tiger any more,' Poppa said. 'India today is operating a full-scale conservation programme for the fast-disappearing breed. Yes, sir.'

But neither Junior nor his parents caught so much as a glimpse of the tiger-shooting (or not) Colonel that evening. They were much too busy trying to get a fire going in the sudden cool of darkness, partly to keep warm and partly to fend off the mosquitoes against which Momma's insect repellent did not seem to offer complete protection.

The Colonel, it looked, had a good fire inside the bungalow. A cheerful glow could be seen through the still-lowered blinds and once the sweeper carried inside a load of neatly chopped wood. And that morning they had seen the mosquito net for the bed spread out to dry after washing.

Poppa's fire, despite what he had had to say about camping in the Adirondacks when he was a boy, sulked abominably.

They went to bed early and Junior could be persuaded only with difficulty to wash his feet last thing in boric lotion, as had been recommended in the *Guide to India*. And next morning when they woke to find themselves enveloped, at least to shoulder height, in a layer of thick white mist, they were just plain cold.

'I'm sure the Colonel would let me step inside a few minutes to get warm,' Momma said. 'Have the servants get a cup of coffee and maybe light a fire.'

So Poppa, dutifully, went up to the bungalow to ask. But he did not meet with any success. At his approach the *khansamah* came shooting out from the kitchen at the rear just as he had done when they had first tried to claim the bungalow as their own. He said, with considerable firmness, that the Colonel Sahib had 'gone for *shikar*' before it had been light and that he could not allow anyone to enter the bungalow in his absence.

And a day that had begun badly went on by chance to be, if not worse, at least tantalizingly unsatisfactory. Once again they saw the elephant herd – it looked as if there were four calves, not three – but this time the creatures kept well inside the tall elephant grass and Poppa was hardly able to shoot any film at all. Yet he felt sure that, with a little more luck, and maybe just a slight change in their own position, he would be able to get some truly magnificent footage next day.

So they had returned, not very cheerfully, to their not very comfortable camp within sight of the increasingly tempting *dak* bungalow.

'If that Colonel's gotten back before us,' Momma said, 'I'm going to go straight up there and ask him outright if those servants can look after us too.'

'Yeah,' said Poppa.

But the Colonel was not to be seen. Only on the veranda, when with sudden caution, they had crept up close, they spotted on a small wooden table beside a long lounging cane chair a book in a faded dust-jacket turned open on its face at a place about halfway through.

'Well, I guess he'll be coming out again soon by the look of it,' Momma said. And she turned back to the tent and the chores that over the past forty-eight hours she had come to hate.

But the Colonel, apparently, had decided to pursue some other activity than reading because he did not come out on to the veranda again. Just before darkness fell Junior actually explored right to within a yard or two of that inviting chair and was able to tell them at least what the Colonel's abandoned book was.

'It said on the jacket it's "the newest Agatha Christie",' he reported.

'The newest Agatha Christie,' Momma said with sudden excitement. 'Maybe when he's finished it he could have that *khansamah* bring it over. What was it called, honey?'

'I don't— Yes, I do. It was *The Hollow*. Yeah, *The Hollow*. The hollow what? Pretty stupid name for a book, I guess.'

But Momma let this aspersion on her favourite author pass. Something else was fully occupying her mind.

'But that's not the latest Christie, *The Hollow*,' she exclaimed. 'That was years back. Yeah, let me see ... It was – yes, got it. It was the 1946 book. I remember. I was reading it when I graduated. I can see it now. So why does it say it's the latest Christie?'

All her vexation at being kept from the unseen but vividly imagined comforts and service of the bungalow seemed to have got transferred to this apparent error in the evasive Colonel's reading pattern.

'But, honey,' Poppa said, 'the book might have been just stuck in there on some shelf ever since it came out. You can't blame the guy for that.'

'Well,' Momma answered, the rage once released submitting to no check, 'I blame him for hogging that place then. And those servants. When all the time he knows there's a lady out in the cold – or in the heat.'

'But he may not even know you're here,' Poppa said, still ready to defend any circumstance in romantic India. 'We haven't seen hair nor hide of him. Maybe he hasn't seen hair nor hide of you.'

'I should hope he hasn't,' Momma said, remembering her awkward ablutions by the plastic basin just inside the tent.

They began then to build a fire to heat the supper they would make from the supply of cans – mostly beans – they had brought with them on the advice of the *Guide to India*. But the prospect was not improved by the sight of the sweeper coming trotting along the road from the direction of the little village a few miles further on swinging a chicken by its legs, and by the fearsome dying squawk they heard a few moments later.

'A whole chicken cooked just for one man,' Momma said.

'Your Indian chicken is a rather scrawny bird,' said Poppa.

But the exculpation was not well received.

And next morning, when again there was a four-foot layer of chilly white mist to contend with and the mosquito bites of the night were blotchy and bumpy in all the tenderest places, Momma had worked up a truly unquenchable hate for their fellow white man in this wide unvisited locality.

'He oughta have come and paid a call on us,' she announced. 'A courtesy call. That's the darned least he could have done. Damned snooty comfort-hogging Britisher.'

'Yeah,' said Poppa placatingly. 'But remember, honey, the British in India had their traditions. They were like maharajahs, you know, waited on from dawn till dusk, not even having to put on their own shoes. I read that.'

'And who let them be maharajahs?' Momma stormed, digging with furious nails at the bumpiest of bites, the one right round in the small of her back. 'Who let 'em be? Your precious Indians, that's who.'

'No, hon. It's just that the Indians has a different attitude to being ruled over. The book said—'

'Damn the book. Damn India. Damn—'

A bite behind her left knee suddenly forced itself itchingly on her attention.

She bent and scratched. Dig, dig, dig. And drew blood.

'Damn it, damn, damn, damn it. Get me some of that stuff before I get infected for God's sake.'

And it was while she was rubbing in the soothing antiseptic, with not a little savagery, that all her frustrations during the whole snag-beset three weeks – even the time when there had been no drinks for the ice – came seethingly to boiling point in a mind-reversing revelation.

'And what's more,' she shouted, rising so abruptly from ministering to the back of her left knee that her head struck the low central aluminium rod of the tent and all but collapsed the whole flimsy structure. 'What's more – oh, damn it – I don't believe there is any Colonel. I believe those stinking Indians of yours have just made him up. So's not to have to look after us as they're bloody well paid to do. That's what I believe: they're inventing the bloody Colonel.'

'But, honey . . .'

'Gee, Momma . . .'

They sat in a row then on Momma's bed and held a council of war. Could it be true? Had they been the victims of a colossal fraud?

They examined the evidence, scrupulously. And certainly there was nothing that proved directly that the Colonel existed. The little boy operating the punkah, the sweeper's sign-talk about shooting tigers, the water he had swooshed over the grass blinds to cool the room inside, the fire to warm it in the evening, the drying mosquito net, the Agatha Christie left open on the little wooden table, the scrawny chicken and the spicy cooking smell they had later been driven almost mad by – none of them was proof positive.

And, besides, wasn't it curious, the way the Colonel had gone off hunting so very early? And they had never heard the faintest sound of a shot coming from anywhere, not while they were at the bungalow before setting out nor while they were waiting for the elephants in the stillness of midday.

They were almost at the point of going storming up to the bungalow there and then, and forcing their way in to prowl and poke till they had got solid proof one way or the other. But then Junior, looking up and out through the tied-back tent flap, said 'Look.'

What they saw was the sweeper. The old man – he seemed to be about eighty, but Poppa had explained that Indians were apt to age very early – was making his way from the corner of the bungalow where the bathroom was, carrying a zinc pail with a swinging wire handle. And it was plain from the way the pail swung – it could only be the inner pail of the 'thunder-box' Junior had looked at with such awe on that first day – that it was not empty.

And somehow that evidence, even if it too was not absolutely direct, carried a conviction that nothing else had, not even the flapping punkah, not even the carelessly laid-down Agatha Christie.

'Listen, we ought to get off our asses and get after those elephants,' Poppa said. 'We arrive there a few minutes late and they'll scent us.'

'Yeah,' said Momma. 'I can't wait till I show those movies.'

'But tonight?' Junior asked. 'Tonight we go up and see him just to make sure, right?'

'Right.'

'Right.'

However, the elephants, once again, put paid to their plan. This time it was not by moving infuriatingly back inside the tall elephant grass just when they were at their most promising. It was by doing exactly the opposite. The beasts came right out into the open and there behaved like so many film stars. One after another they positioned themselves at the very best distance for the camera, and put on every party trick in the repertoire. The two great tuskers lifted up their trunks and roared at each other. The four calves – there was no doubt now that there were four of them – played like kittens. The huge cows laboriously knelt down and then rolled over and lay lazily waving their trunks as if they were girls sunning themselves on some beach trying to attract a little attention. 'You wait,' said Momma. 'You wait till I show them these back home.'

And so they had gone on filming till abruptly darkness had fallen, and then they had had some trouble finding their way back.

So there could be no question of the three of them going up and insisting on meeting the Colonel, just to be sure.

And, in any case, before long that seemed not to be necessary. While Momma was attempting to fix supper over the little butane stove – but tonight when it would anyhow be the last time it seemed more of a laugh than a chore – Junior wandered off for a final look round. And there, plain as plain, he saw the mysterious figure who had up until then so oddly eluded them.

The blinds were rolled up this evening and inside the bungalow the Colonel was sitting eating his supper. Or, no. Even Junior recognized that the ceremonious meal he was witnessing was something more than supper. The Colonel was eating dinner. He was dining.

The *khansamah* was serving. In the light of the softly bright Petromax lamp his battered and mended white tunic looked smarter than it had done out in the harsh sunlight. His turban, which in the daytime had seemed a little floppy, looked now stiff as a peacock's spread. He was standing upright behind the Colonel's chair, every now and again bending to offer another dish or to refill the tumbler. When, as Junior watched open-mouthed, one course appeared to be finished the grey-moustached old man marched across to the doorway that led to the kitchen and there, waiting on anxious tiptoe, was the sweeper, ready to hand forward the next. And Junior could just see from the angle at which he was standing that squatting by the kitchen fire, peering at it with tremendous intensity, was his little six-year-old friend, the *punkah*-puller, whose duty now it plainly was to make sure that the dishes cooked earlier were keeping warm and safe over the glowing embers.

Junior watched and watched. The ceremony of it all fascinated him. He felt himself, though he could not have put the feeling into words, caught up by the sheer concentration, by the devotion, there displayed. He felt even, though it was not until afterwards that he realized this, not in fact until many years afterwards, that he too would like, would give a great, great deal, to have a share in serving that quite simple meal. To want each item, and each part of each item, to be just exactly right, as those three waiting on the severe upright figure of the Colonel – he was every bit as lean and athletic as such a hunter of tigers ought to have been – so plainly wanted everything to be, desired everything to be with every inch of their bodies, with every thought in their heads.

Only at last did he realize that Momma was calling.

'Junior. Junior. Chow time. Junior. Chow. Chow.'

He walked back in a daze to where on the little plastic-topped camping table three red plastic bowls of pork and beans were set with a folding camping-spoon inside each.

'Junior, wherever did you get to? It's been ready ten minutes. For heaven's sakes get it down you.'

He took up his spoon and shovelled up the thick, appetizing stuff. It was only after his bowl was empty that he told them that he had seen the Colonel.

Poppa was very good about it. He never once ribbed Momma about her crazy idea, and he even managed to say nothing more, at least for that night, about how wonderful the Indians were.

Perhaps it was as well. When next day they were far on their way back, nearly at the little town of Satnagar where they were due to call on the Block Development Officer to report on their stay at the *dak* bungalow, Junior told them one other thing about that scene that he had stared and stared at the night before. Indeed, after the pork and beans he had told them very little, just that he had seen the famous Colonel and that he had been eating his dinner. He had somehow not wanted to say more than that. It had been all he could do to let them know that they definitely had not been victims of a plot. The scene he had watched was too vivid, too intense, too meaningful to be exposed in ordinary words. It was not, in fact, until years and years later that he himself realized why that was and what it had been about the simple ceremony that had so stamped itself on his memory.

But now, just as the jeep reached the new tarmac stretch of road leading into the little town itself, he felt he could mention just this one other small thing.

'Yeah, the Colonel,' he said suddenly into their companionable silence. 'Y'know, there was something darned funny about him. Darned funny, I'd say. It was his feet. I saw them under the table. Didn't realize it at the time, but you know something? His feet were backwards. They were on his legs backwards.'

Peter Tinniswood

On the train to Chemnitz

On the train to Chemnitz in 1922.

My wife, my child, myself.

Where is Chemnitz?

Why Chemnitz?

Why 1922?

The compartment is stuffy.

We have it to ourselves.

Or have we? Curious feeling I have.

My child sleeps in the moses basket. My wife, russet-maned, peers sadly out of the window.

In fox fur she is superb.

We clatter.

We see foothills askew with pines. Smoke from a lazy village. A harrier quartering a buxom lake.

The minute package strapped to my armpit nags.

My wife will not take coffee.

I pitch and toss alone to the luncheon car.

Coffee and schnapps.

Ja, fein.

In a corner of the car sits a woman.

Only she and I are present.

She inclines her head towards me and smiles.

Firm teeth. Full mouth. Smoke-blonde hair atumble to the shoulders. Hazel eyes. Straight nose. Pale skin at the neck. Firm breasts.

'Yes?' she says.

'I did not speak,' I reply.

'No?'

'No.'

She rises from her chair and leaves the car.

Swish of silk. Her perfume coils round my nostrils.

Coffee and schnapps dispatched, I return to my compartment.

The curtains are drawn.

Curious.

I pull the handle of the door.
It is locked.
I rattle it.
'Inge,' I shout. 'Inge, Inge.'
I heave at the door to slide it open. I tug. I pull.
'Allow me.'
It is the woman from the luncheon car.
A soft smile. A gentle incline of the head.
A tap at the window.
She opens the door.
'There,' she says. 'There you are, my dear Mr Pender Brandon.'
I look inside.
My wife and child lie dead on the floor.
Throats slit.
I scream.
I turn to the corridor.
The woman has disappeared.
No trace.
On the train to Chemnitz in 1922?
How curious.

It is 1978 and I am younger now.
Hoskins, my boss, is most solicitous about the trip I am about to make.
'Don't fuck it up,' he says.
'Sure.'
'I mean it, you twat – don't fuck it up.'
The package is concealed in my left armpit.
So small I hardly notice it as I drive to the airport, Berlin-bound.
Later it will nag.
Beside me sits my wife, russet-maned.
Sadly she peers out of the window.
On the back seat my child sleeps in the moses basket.
Why Berlin?
Why 1978?

Three days in Berlin.

Not bad.

I meet a Jewess with plump thighs and a tidy thicket of hair.

On the morning of the fourth day a telephone call comes to the room of my hotel.

'Mr Brandon?'

'Yes,' I say.

'Mr Pender Brandon?'

'That's me.'

'Thank you.'

The phone clicks and is dead.

A minute later a knock at my door.

I open it.

'Allow me to introduce myself,' says the man, stepping inside.

'Certainly,' I say.

'My name is Brandon,' he says.

'I see.'

'Mr Pender Brandon,' he says. And then he repeats himself very slowly:

'My name is Pender Brandon.'

Six hours later.

Six days later, maybe?

Six years perhaps?

Who cares?

We passed through Dresden a good and precise half hour ago.

The rain hisses on the bonnet of the car. Black bonnet.

The wipers heave.

I sense mountains.

I hear the fleet foot of goat. I smell wild thyme. I see the flash of dotterel.

'Your hotel in Berlin was good?' says the driver of the car.

'Yes,' I reply.

'It was a pity about Mr Pender Brandon.'

'It was,' I reply.

'It is never nice for a man's throat to be slit.'

'It is not,' I reply.

'Shall we take coffee?'

'Yes,' I say. 'And schnapps?'

'Coffee and schnapps – *ja fein*,' says the driver of the car.

We stop in the centre of a small town.

'Freiberg,' says the driver.

We get out of the car.

The wind shivers from the mountains, scattering pigeons, furrowing puddles.

The driver takes me by the elbow and ferries me across the street.

We enter an inn.

It is warm.

We sit in a corner and order coffee and schnapps.

The driver takes off her cap, and her russet mane tumbles and tosses.

'I love you, Mr Pender Brandon,' she says.

We reach Karl-Marx Stadt at dusk.

In a mean part of the town we find the apartment block.

It stands isolated from its fellows, crumpled and hang-dog.

We climb resentful wooden stairs.

We enter an apartment.

The foyer is bare.

A door opens and a voice summons us inside.

The driver pushes me gently but firmly in the pit of the back.

I turn to her and arch my eyebrows.

'No, you must go alone,' she says. And then she smiles. 'And remember this, Mr Pender Brandon – I love you very much.'

I move slowly towards the room.

A man servant in aged alpaca jacket, scanty at the elbows, bows softly. Hairless pate crisscrossed with wadis of wrinkles.

'Enter, please, my dear sir,' he says.

I enter.

An opulent room.

Jade pieces on the mantelshelf. A glass case with stuffed squirrel and hazelhen. Turkish rugs on snow white carpet. An escritoire. Chaise-longue. Armchairs arumble with comfort. Heavy velvet curtains.

'The mistress will see you at once,' says the man servant.

And immediately the woman enters.

She inclines her head towards me and smiles.

Firm teeth. Full mouth. Smoke blonde hair atumble to the shoulders. Hazel eyes. Straight nose. Pale skin at the neck. Firm breasts.

Swish of silk. Her perfume coils round my nostrils.

'Mr Brandon?' she says.

'Yes,' I say.

'Mr Pender Brandon?'

'Yes.'

She smiles slowly.

'My name is Inge,' she says.

Every second I grow younger.

Every day I grow older.

Every week ages me.

Every month youthens me.

By the year I grow older and younger.

By the decade happiness withers and love runs slow and cold.

'Mr Pender Brandon, I love you. Mr Pender Brandon, I adore you. Mr Pender Brandon, I want every part and particle of you.'

The heavy velvet curtains are drawn.

Her body is white in the moonlight.

Her hazel eyes flash.

Her hand weaves spells in my groin.

My tongue spills the juices from her body.

Her mouth encloses me softly, and my back arches in time to the slide and flow of her lips.

Inge, Inge, Inge.

Her thighs writhe round my cheeks.

Inge, Inge, Inge.

We break apart.

She swivels on her knees to lie beside me face to face.

She whispers:

'I love you, my darling Mr Pender Brandon.'

Dawn grows stronger.

Birds' feet rasp on the guttering.

Sunlight laps at the escritoire, purrs on the plump brocade of the chaise-longue, sparkles in the eyes of the long-dead squirrel.

Rugs over our naked shoulders we face each other, cross-legged, holding hands.

'Inge,' I say. 'Inge, where am I?'

'Chemnitz, my darling,' she says.

'And what is the year?'

She smiles softly.

'My darling, Mr Pender Brandon, the year is 1922.'

'You fucked it up, didn't you?' says Hoskins.

I lower my eyes.

'Look at me.'

I look at him.

'What were you doing in Chemnitz, you bastard?'

'I don't know.'

'And why 1922? Jesus Christ, you turd, it's 1978.'

I nod slowly.

'You fucked it up good and proper.'

'Yes,' I say.

'Get out, you cunt.'

I leave the room.

It is chill outside.

The streets of Berlin are not yet aired.

Why Berlin?

What year is it?

I find myself on the banks of a lake.

Pochard are there. How I love their russet heads.

I sit on a bench.

The package nags in my armpit.

Curious.

I am joined on the bench by an aged man.

He wears a ragged fox fur overcoat that slobbers over his ankles. The collar is frayed. He wears a fedora of bottle green.

'Mr Brandon?' he says.

'Yes,' I say.

He smiles.

No teeth. Fig-pink gums and a thin yellow tongue.

'Mr Pender Brandon?'

'Yes.'

He nods his head happily.

Widgeon sail on the lake. Gulls yap. A string of barges waddles across the milky horizon.

'I am Inge's husband,' he says.

I nod my head.

'A curious woman,' he says. 'Most beautiful, I assure you. Her hair so russet. A russet mane, I call it.'

I nod once more.

'Did I tell you how I met her?'

I shake my head.

'We met on the train to Chemnitz.'

'I see.'

'The year was 1922,' he says and sucks at his sagging cheeks.

A light aeroplane banks steeply and hurls its reflection across the surface of the water. The pochard remain serene.

'You like my overcoat?' says the aged man.

'I do.'

'Fox fur. My wife's. How superb she looked in fox fur. She wore it that day we met on the train. She was alone in the compartment with a child in a moses basket. I sat opposite her and she smiled at me. She leaned forward and took hold of my hand. She pulled me towards her and very firmly she bit my neck.'

The wind is chill. It rasps.

'We alighted from the train before it reached Chemnitz. We alighted at Freiberg in fact. Three days later we were married.'

He stands up and doffs his fedora of bottle green. He exposes a hairless pate crisscrossed with wadis of wrinkles.

He hands me his visiting card and limps away, the hem of the fox fur coat trotting at his heels.

I read the card.

It says:

'Mr Pender Brandon.'

Where am I?

Chemnitz?

Karl-Marx Stadt?

Berlin?

London?

What year is it?

What is the colour of her hair? What is the colour of her eyes? What is her name? What is the strength and fervour of her love?

Who cares?

I do.

Jesus Christ, I do.

'One last chance, Mr Brandon.'

I nod.

'You will take this package to Chemnitz.'

'Yes.'

'You will strap it beneath your armpit.'

'Yes.'

'Your travel documents will indicate that you are a representative for a firm of manufacturers of textile machinery.'

'Yes.'

'We think it will be rather amusing for you to have a wife. I take it you have no objection.'

'No.'

He rings a silver handbell.

Behind me the door opens and I hear the rustle of women's clothing.

'Mr Brandon, may I introduce you to your wife.'

I rise from my chair and turn.

I see a tall woman with a mane of russet hair. She wears a fox fur coat. Superb.

She extends a hand.

Her grip is firm. Her stride is confident as we leave the room together, arm in arm.

'We have a child, too, Mr Brandon,' she says.

'I see.'

'My name is Inge.'

'I like it.'

She smiles.

'Well then, Mr Pender Brandon, till the train to Chemnitz.'
'Till the train to Chemnitz.'

The crossing of the channel was smooth.

The child slept soundly in its moses basket.

We stayed overnight in Paris.

My wife gave herself to me with strength and fervour.

Her russet mane tumbled and spilled across my chest.

And now the exhaust of the locomotive rattles.

Its smoke is black. It trails its shadow over fields of maize, foothills askew with pines, a buxom lake.

On the train to Chemnitz in 1922.

My wife, my child, myself.

The door of the compartment slides open.

An aged man in a ragged fox fur coat and fedora of bottle green stands there.

He doffs his hat to expose a hairless pate crisscrossed with wadis of wrinkles.

'I hope I do not intrude,' he says, and with a stiff bow to my wife he settles himself in a corner of the compartment next to the bucking corridor.

My wife glances at his overcoat and then at her own.

She gives me a whisp of a smile.

'Do you wish to take coffee, my dear?' I say.

She shakes her head.

'Would you object if I did?'

She shakes her head.

The aged man looks up and smiles at me as I brush past his knees.

'On a day like this, my dear Mr Brandon, a glass of schnapps would be the perfect accompaniment to a cup of coffee,' he says.

Coffee and schnapps.

Ja, fein.

I pitch and toss to the luncheon car.

There is only one other occupant.

A woman.

She inclines her head towards me and smiles.

Firm teeth. Full mouth. Smoke-blonde hair atumble to the

shoulders. Hazel eyes. Straight nose. Pale skin at the neck. Firm breasts.

The train wheezes into a station and halts.

I rub at the window.

'Freiberg,' says the woman.

'I beg your pardon, madame?'

'The station is Freiberg.'

'Danke.'

'Bitte.'

I turn away from the window and idle with my glass of schnapps. It is the third glass.

Whistles and shouts. Hiss of steam. Clank of couplings.

I look out of the window.

Jesus, Joseph and Mary.

Three men in leather coats drag my wife along the platform.

Her russet mane is adrift. She struggles. She claws at them. Through the silent windows I see her scream.

Behind her two men carry the moses basket.

I leap to my feet.

'Sit down, Mr Brandon.'

I turn to the window.

She points a revolver at my chest.

'Please sit down, Mr Brandon.'

I sit down.

The train gathers speed. The carriage rocks. Cups and saucers and glasses of schnapps clink.

'And now, Mr Brandon, back to your compartment, if you please.'

The muzzle of the revolver is pressed gently but firmly to the pit of my back as I stumble along the corridor.

The curtains are drawn across the windows of my compartment.

I pull at the handle of the door.

It is locked.

I heave at the door to slide it open. I tug. I pull.

'Allow me.'

The woman taps softly at the window.

'You may enter now, Mr Brandon,' she says, and with a whisp of a smile she disappears.

I pause.
My heart pumps.
My hand trembles.
Slowly I pull back the door.
I see lying on the floor two women.
One has a russet mane. One has smoke-blonde hair atumble to the shoulders.
Their throats are slit.
I scream.

'You fucked it up.'
'Yes.'
'Bastard.'
I lower my eyes.
'Give me the package.'
I take out the package from beneath my armpit.
It is minute.
He peels back the breath-thin oilskin.
He takes out a silver box inlaid with mother of pearl.
He snaps open the lid. He shakes out the contents. Diamonds. They clatter to the table top. Still for a moment. And then they move. They form themselves into a word.
LOVE.
And then they move again. Hiss and rasp across the table as they re-align themselves. Three words this time.
ILL-SPENT LOVE.
And then they move again. Quickly this time. Sparkling in the dawn light, purring, lapping at the table top. Two words this time.
DEAD LOVE.
The door opens.
I hear the rustle of women's clothing.
I turn.
I see two women.
One has a russet mane. The other has smoke-blonde hair atumble to the shoulders.
They advance towards me, arms open.
I cower.
Nearer and nearer.

Their lips part. Their breasts heave. Their hips swing and writhe.

They pass straight through me.

They disappear outside into the chill wind, which rasps and furrows.

'Now you know it all, you turd.'

'Yes.'

'Bastard, you're just a fucking ghost.'

I turn to the window and look at my reflection.

I see an aged man with hairless pate crisscrossed by wadis of wrinkles.

I scream.

On the train to Chemnitz in 1922.

My wife, my child, myself.

The door of the compartment slides open.

An aged man in ragged fox fur coat and ...

I scream.

I shall always scream.

James Hamilton-Paterson

The party

Towards nightfall Tod and Andrew reached a desolate plain of stubble and pitched their tent. It glowed like a yellow beacon in the dusk as they moved around, bent double, looking for wood to make a cooking fire. There was nothing but dried grass and some scattered chips of concrete. Crossly they ate cold beans out of a tin with a shared spoon.

'If you hadn't lost our only canister of gas,' said Tod, 'we'd have the stove going.' It was not the first time he had said it.

'Okay,' said Andrew. *'Sorry.'* He could offer neither explanation nor apology. He was made uneasy in the empty acres of stalks, wishing there had been some way of inducing Tod to go on at least as far as the line of dying elms on the horizon.

'Still,' Tod said, unwrapping a squashed fruit cake in a polythene bag, 'I'm glad we stopped. If we'd left it any later the light would have gone and we'd have had to put the tent up in the dark. It's a bit rough here but it won't kill us just for one night. If we start early tomorrow we can get to that hostel place. I could do with a shower.'

By the time they climbed into their sleeping bags it was practically dark. Glancing out through the flap of the tent Andrew could barely make out the only nearby landmark: the square ruin of a concrete building. Only the first few feet of the walls appeared still to be standing; it was just possible to see where the sills of the ground floor windows had been. But even as he looked he could not be certain, for the last light drained suddenly away. Uneasily he pulled the flap closed.

'Aren't you ever going to sleep?' demanded Tod wearily from the back of the tent.

'I was just looking ... It's sort of sad outside. A bit sinister, too.'

'I couldn't care what it's like outside as long as there aren't any more damned cows like last night.'

Andrew did not remember falling asleep. He opened his eyes suddenly and saw a circle of greenish dots close to his face. It took him a dazed moment to recognize the luminous dial of his own watch. It was ten to three. Gently he knelt and opened the tent flap. Outside in the moonless dark, at a distance impossible to judge, a faint light was burning. It seemed to come from the direction of the ruin he had been looking at before going to sleep. It lit nothing, shone on nothing; it was merely a yellow point in the night. In the intervening distance the wind sighed through the stubble.

Andrew felt an inner surge of melancholy. He was surprised by his own lack of fear, but at the same time could not have explained exactly the mixture of apprehension and curiosity which made him inch cautiously out of his sleeping bag and into the night breeze outside the tent. As he eased on shoes greasy with damp Tod made soft sleeping sounds behind him.

The clatter of his feet through the dried corn stalks emphasized his isolation as he set off for the light. He went stumbling across the uneven land, jarring his head whenever he came down too heavily on his heels in unseen holes. The light became clearer and soon he reached a concrete path of sorts. It was only then that he wondered if he could ever find his way back to the tent. Anxiously he turned and strained to make out its small triangle perched on the landscape but it was so dark he could not even separate sky from earth. There was no horizon, no friendly silhouette, nothing but to go on. Whatever self-confidence he had once was now vanished and as he approached the light his steps became slower. Whenever he kicked a loose stone he winced at the sound.

Finally Andrew reached the blockhouse he had seen before falling asleep although it now seemed less ruined than it had from a distance in the twilight. It turned out to be quite a large building with an outside iron staircase slanting diagonally to an upper floor where the light was. Gingerly, he set his foot on the bottom step, impelled by the need to borrow a torch and by a fearful curiosity to see who was there. It seemed unlikely enough that anyone should live in a grey concrete ruin in the middle of an ocean of stubble. He reached the top of the stairs without making a sound and crept along an iron balcony which appeared to run all round the outside of the upper floor until he came to a door that was half open, yellow light spilling across the threshold. He sidled up and peeped round the jamb.

The light came from an oil lamp on a long table. The room was bare except for what seemed to be charts and maps around the walls. The white face of a clock hung above a notice board. Andrew was about to take a half-step forward into the room when he saw with a shock that he was not alone. In the area beyond the lamp he could now make out the shape of a wide window and in front of this, as if staring out at the invisible landscape, was standing the figure of a man. Although he had made neither sound nor movement Andrew sensed that his own presence was known, and this feeling frightened him irrationally.

'Sir?' queried the man. It was hardly a whisper, the voice of someone infinitely tired and waiting to be relieved of a heavy burden. Unwillingly, Andrew let his feet carry him forward. The figure by the window still made no movement but remained with his back to the room. Andrew thought he was wearing some sort of cap.

'My name's Andrew,' he said.

'Andrew, Andrew.' Then, tentatively, 'Andy? Awful how you forget names, but it was all so long ago. Of course, you must be one of Jocko's crew?'

'No,' said Andrew. 'Who's Jocko? I'm nobody you know.'

'Then what do you want? Why are you here without the others?' came the whisper, dull now.

'I'm lost. I can't find my tent. I came to borrow a light to find my way back.'

'Oh.' The voice was despondent. 'So you don't know the Groupie and you're not here for the party?'

'Party?' blurted Andrew, completely baffled. He was becoming aware of an appetizing smell in the room which reminded him vaguely of roast pork. From outside the building came the lonely unvarying noise of breeze moving through flat acres of stalks.

'Oh well . . . Since you're here you may as well stay until the others come. It's early yet. I don't know who the hell you are but at least you seem to know what it's like being lost.'

'Are you lost?' asked Andrew.

'I suppose I must be,' said the man. The lamp on the table between them made it difficult for Andrew to get much impression of the person he was talking to, for it sent out a dazzling glow which made the shadows beyond it deeper. However, the stranger's voice indicated that he was still standing with his back to the room.

'Do you know what this place is?'

'No,' Andrew told him.

'It's a control tower. This used to be one of the busiest airfields in East Anglia,' the muffled words came out of the dark. 'We were flying Lancasters all over Europe – three, four, sometimes five nights a week. At least, some squadrons in Lincolnshire and Suffolk were flying all over Europe,' he corrected himself. 'This particular outfit seemed to have a curse on it. Apparently we were doomed to go on bombing the Ruhr heavy industries while it was the other lucky devils who just dropped mines into the North Sea or stooged around the Dutch coast. Every time we sat in the Ops Room for pre-flight briefing we kept our fingers crossed for a milk run. You'd see men actually praying when the Intelligence Officer came in with the CO to announce the night's target. We were all hoping to God we wouldn't have to face the worst flak in Europe again, you see; the squadron was taking heavy casualties and we all needed a break. Just a bit of a breather to get our nerve back, really. But then it came again – Essen, Dortmund, one of those big places. "Happy Valley", we used to call the Ruhr. So we'd take off once more on the off-chance of killing a few wretched German shift-workers or putting a factory out of action for a day or two.'

The voice stopped. Andrew had the sense of being present at a private confession. He wanted to say something, to make a hurried excuse and go, but no words would come and the man resumed his story.

'It sounded glorious the way they told it. Even *we* didn't know that RAF bombing at that time was very inaccurate and that in any case a large percentage of the bombs we did drop failed to explode. Now they're saying that the output of those German factories went on going up and up until 1944, so we couldn't have been very effective, could we, in our Lancasters and Halifaxes and Stirlings and Wellingtons ... But I'm getting off the point.

'We had this amazing station commander, Group Captain Reid. He'd already done three complete tours on Lancs so there wasn't much he didn't know about flying raids. He was famous throughout Bomber Command: ninety operational flights and never once injured except for a few scratches. He'd come back with his aircraft hanging together by threads, often with half his crew dead, and all he ever got was cuts from smashed instruments. "Reid's luck", it was known as, and you would see chaps touching his machine before climbing into their own in the hopes that some of his luck would rub off.

'Himself, he would curse it. The more raids he flew, the more of his friends didn't come back and the more guilty he would feel for coming through unscathed. Landing after a night op. is a strange affair. If it's summer the sun will probably be rising and you come in through greyish mist and suddenly there's the airfield below, all dark and wet and you never expected to see those camouflaged hangars and line of crash tenders again. At first everything's very unreal and all you can think about is that you made it once more whereas some didn't, but you're too tired to do anything other than get de-briefed and roll into bed. Group Captain Reid, though, would never go to bed until everyone had returned or been accounted for. You would see him standing at Dispersal in that cold dawn air while the grey overhead became pink and the mist lifted, hands in his pockets, silently watching the sky. Somebody told me once he didn't have a wife and that his family had been killed in an air raid early on in the war, all except for one brother, so perhaps that explained it.'

The dark figure fell silent once more and Andrew shifted his weight. He was conscious of the cold; the sweater over his pyjamas did nothing to keep out the chill of the room.

'I'm boring you,' said the man. 'I'm sorry.'

'No, you're not,' Andrew contradicted him. His voice came out as hushed as the stranger's.

'Oh well, it's not a long story. It's not even *much* of a story, except that it really did happen. Eventually they took Reid off missions. He'd survived ninety raids when few ever made more than fifteen, but he was practically off his head with exhaustion and nerves and ... well, he'd seen a lot of the boys go. So they gave him a rest and promoted him Group Captain. Then with one of those bureaucratic idiocies typical of Air Ministries they posted him CO of this very station. So now he had to sit around and send out what was left of his old crews without being able to go with them.

'Meanwhile, I suppose I was having some pretty fantastic luck, too. I'd completed twenty-nine trips of my first tour and I hadn't even had my twentieth birthday. I'd never been seriously hurt, either. A few shell fragments in one leg and a touch of pneumonia after we had to ditch off the Dogger Bank in midwinter, but otherwise unharmed. You know most of the crews carried mascots? Well, I became a sort of mascot myself although I was just a mere Wireless Operator. By my tenth trip I was the only member of the original crew still flying and people were in two minds about whether I *was* lucky to have around. But they couldn't overlook how I kept on coming home in one piece, and chaps would feel that perhaps I was slightly immortal myself and so were glad to have me in the aircraft.

'The funny thing was that the Group Captain noticed this, too. We were sort of drawn to each other, I suppose. Perhaps he knew I didn't have any family either. I often saw him watching me as we walked into Ops after a raid. Once he said, "People like us should stick together, with our miserable good fortune." He said it jokingly, but he looked so down in the mouth himself it made me forget the horseplay going on all around us. About an hour later I learned my pal Dan Summers had been posted missing, and all of a sudden it seemed too pointless for any victory ever to make up for it – sending loads of teenagers over another country to drop high explosive on men and women and children and then hearing that *their* teenagers had done the same thing over here on the same night.' There came a faint derisive laugh from the darkness.

'Anyway,' the man resumed. 'One day the rumour went round there was to be a really big one that night – probably Berlin, for a change. At the last moment I learned we had a new rear-gunner assigned to our crew because the one we'd had on the last four trips had gone down with appendicitis. Well, we all went into briefing and I met the new chap Tim – very pink and fresh out of Training School and nervous as a cat. After the briefing the Group Captain came up to me.

'"Last trip of the tour for you, isn't it?" he asked, although he knew very well that it was.

'"That's right," I said.

'"No problem about tonight," he said. "Don't worry, in eight hours' time you'll be standing right here in this very room. Chaps like us were born to come back to empty Nissen huts."

'I didn't quite get what he was driving at; he'd never sounded so serious before. Mind you, I know he felt Dan Summers' death as much as I did: he'd flown with Dan and by now there weren't many left he'd flown with.

'"Your new rear-gunner, that youngster Tim," he said. "You'll get him back in one piece, won't you?" He was very insistent, very earnest. "It's his first trip," he added, as if that made any difference. "You won't let me down. Some of our hateful luck can bloody well be made to rub off, can't it?" It was as if he and I were hatching a conspiracy to defraud death.

'I pointed out that W/O hardly had much control over how an aircraft was flown, as he himself knew perfectly well. Still, I promised him that it would be a specially lucky trip. Stupid, really, but it seemed to be what he wanted to hear and he looked relieved. Then he said something I've never forgotten. He said: "Tonight's show is the sort of affair that starts anniversary reunions, isn't it? You know, in memory of the big one on Berlin, that sort of thing. Everybody – us – surely we can't just all disappear, can we?"

'I still couldn't fathom why he was talking like this except perhaps he thought if he fixed a reunion it would somehow make it more likely that we'd all survive. You get like that if you're a veteran – a sort of mixture of fatalism and superstition. Quite frankly, he was making me a bit jumpy. But I suppose he was right in a way – there really was some kind of atmosphere of finality.

'"I'll be back," I told him. "Just to prove that some people do have all the luck. But even if I find myself spending the duration in a German PoW camp I'll be here on this same damned airfield on this same damned night for ever afterwards if you're throwing a party and buying the beer."

'"Consider that an order," he said, and laughed. He wished me luck again and then at the last moment he produced this live .5 inch machine-gun round and gave it me. "I've had it with me all the time," he said, "and I'm still here. Pretty silly sort of mascot, I suppose, and it's no use to me now that I'm chairborne. Keep it, Ken; you can give it me back at that famous party." That's the mascot on the table, by the way,' added the voice from the darkness.

Andrew noticed for the first time the object on the table beside the oil lamp. He leaned forward and picked it up curiously. It was about five-and-a-half inches long, the brass cartridge and copper jacket of the bullet shining dully from much handling. He saw that the tip of the bullet was painted red, indicating that it was a tracer round. On the bottom of the cartridge case was stamped *SL 42*, the code for the place and date of its manufacture.

The quiet voice went on with its story. 'I wasn't very superstitious myself. I mean, there's no such thing as good or bad luck, just the laws of physics. But I took his mascot and it wasn't until we were out over the North Sea that I discovered our new gunner was the Group Captain's own younger brother, the sole surviving member of his family. Typical of me not to have found out his surname before take-off and typical of the Groupie not to have said. Funny thing was, it gave me a bit of an uneasy feeling.

'However, there wasn't much time to worry about that because pretty soon we ran into some bad flak over Leiden way. The skipper was throwing poor old "S" Sunday around the sky and some of my radio gear went u/s. Still, we pushed on and now and then I'd call up young Tim Reid and ask him how things were at the back. He said he was frozen and felt airsick but that he'd had a crack at a night-fighter he thought he'd seen. Eventually we were over target and went in to bomb.

'We were in the second wave: the Pathfinders had already

been over, and what with marker flares and beacons the place was hard to miss. Explosions everywhere and a dozen serious fires. You've no idea how frightening it is hanging in the sky with nothing between you and their guns but a thousand yards of thin air and few millimetres of fuselage. Coming in slowly on a steady course for the bomb-aimer and all lit up by flares and searchlights, you feel naked: it's like swimming over a sudden outcrop of sharp rocks with the skin on your stomach crawling. Mind you, they can't have been feeling too happy down on the ground, either.

'We did our run and felt "S" Sunday lurch as Mickey Mullard shouted "Bombs gone!" Then this terrific explosion nearby threw me into the gangway on my back. I remember looking up and seeing something extraordinary. I had a perfect view up through the dorsal turret past our mid-section gunner's legs. About two hundred feet above us there was a burning Lancaster – I never did find out whose it was. In that instant I knew what I would do if I were that pilot: I'd jettison my bombs quickly and find somewhere to bale out other than over the blazing city. And that was exactly what he did. He couldn't see us. He dumped his entire load and we were smack underneath.

'I tried to shout but my intercom had come unplugged. I could see the 500-pounders miss us but we were hit by a shower of incendiaries.' The dark figure gave a sigh and a shoe scraped. It was the first time Andrew had heard him make the slightest movement. 'The whole inside of "S" Sunday lit up like day. I could see all the serial numbers stencilled everywhere, every bloody rivet. I couldn't hear anything from the tail of the aircraft, of course, because my phones were dead. But there'd have been nothing to hear in any case because suddenly there *was* no tail section: just a bang and then a black rectangle of night a yard or two from me with some lights dancing in it and a cold gale of slipstream. Then the glare all around got a lot stronger. I think I was getting pretty badly burned but I never can remember what happened then.' There was a silence.

'Go on,' prompted Andrew, his own shivering forgotten. The

machine-gun round in his hands felt heavy with its own life.

'That's it,' said the voice apologetically. 'That's the end of the story. We got blown to hell by one of our own chaps, didn't we? It was the end of the old "S" Sunday, the end of young Tim Reid, of Jocko, Catesby, Mullard, all of them; isn't that enough?' His voice became muffled. 'I could have spent my twentieth birthday off active duties. As it was ... As it is ...'

There could be no doubt: the stranger was crying. Andrew could see him more clearly now because the window at which he stood had become a shade lighter. The grey summer dawn would soon spread over the stubbled wastes outside just as it once had as the first returning Lancasters, heavy with exhaustion, wallowed in over the perimeter fence. Andrew had a sudden inspiration.

'Tonight's the anniversary of the raid, isn't it?' he asked.

'Yes. I forget which anniversary it is, but it's been a long time now. I come here each year; I've never missed one.' The voice was distant. 'Nobody ever turns up. Perhaps tonight, though. You see, I *must* tell the Groupie what happened over Berlin. I've come to tell him that it wasn't my fault that his brother got killed, that all our luck ran out at the same moment. I came to tell him that I'm sorry. He was like a father to me, you see, for all that he was only about ten years older. I came to tell him that, too, and also that I've kept coming here each year as I promised I would. It was a sort of order he gave, wasn't it? And anyway, I've been looking forward to this party for God knows how long.' Stiffly, the figure raised its left wrist.

'Late as usual,' he said as if to himself. 'But he's on his way. They all are: they'd never miss a party, not that lot. They'd go anywhere for free beer. I wonder how the Groupie's bringing it all? Gallons of it, he'll need ... Listen,' the voice broke off in an excited whisper.

Such silence fell that Andrew could hear the faint hiss of the lamp wick as it burned low. The grey light beyond the window was strengthening and the details of the room were clearer. The charts on the wall were operational maps of Europe; baize-covered boards held schedules and notices.

There was a telephone by the window and a field phone painted emergency red next to a signalling lamp in one corner. A pair of binoculars dangled from a hook.

'Do you hear that?' asked the man, excitement in his voice. 'That's them, all right. After all these years it just has to be them.'

Half unwillingly Andrew listened intently, the hair at the back of his neck beginning to stiffen unaccountably, but still all he could hear was the lamp and the soft dawn wind outside.

'Merlins,' cried the voice exultantly. 'Those are Lancaster engines. The party's on: the Groupie's on his way!' With a sudden movement the figure at the window turned round. 'He is coming, isn't he? You must be able to hear him too?' he asked with urgent doubt. 'Please tell me you can.'

For a moment Andrew thought he was wearing a mask. Then he could see that the young man was so hideously burned that there were no defined features left on his face. The livid sheet of tissue glistened as if smeared with jelly. The roasting smell which Andrew had noticed earlier grew pungent.

'Please stay.' The pleading words came from a strained black hole. 'You've brought me such luck. I know you'd like the Groupie: he's the most remarkable man in the world.'

Andrew turned and ran as if his feet moved of their own accord. An electric panic drove him out along the balcony and down the iron staircase in a clattering rush.

There came a wordless cry from the room overhead but Andrew was already running away from the building towards the dim yellow pyramid of the tent, now just visible far out across the sea of stubble. It seemed there was no end to running and tripping, sprawling on outflung hands in the sharp stalks. There may have been another cry behind him, but he could never be sure. He might also have heard the distant hum of heavy engines rising and falling on the breeze, but the wind in his ears and the sound of his own gasping breaths made it impossible to be certain. At last the tent drew close, dew sparkling on the guy ropes, and he threw himself into the warm gloom.

'What on earth's got into you?' demanded a crotchety voice.

It was Tod, rudely woken, his face crumpled with sleep and annoyance.

'Quick, we've got to get out of here,' moaned Andrew, shivering as he drew his sleeping bag to him. 'There's someone in that building.'

'So?' enquired Tod. 'We're not doing him any harm.'

'But he's mad and burnt and he thinks there's going to be a party there.'

'Oh, for heaven's sake. Where?'

'In the control tower.' Andrew buried his face.

Tod raised himself wearily and peered out of the flap, blinking in the dawn light.

'You're joking,' he said. 'In that place? There's no one out there. Anyway, who would want to hold a party in a ruin?'

'I've been inside it,' came Andrew's muffled voice. 'He's upstairs with a table and a lot of maps.'

'Oh sure,' said Tod scornfully from the mouth of the tent. 'And there's a banqueting-hall with chandeliers too, I suppose?'

Andrew put his face in trembling hands and pressed hard. He was cold and ill. Surely he could not have invented that piercing atmosphere of loneliness, nor that sickening smell of roasting.

'Hey, where did you find this?' Tod was asking, jogging his leg. Between thumb and forefinger he held up a gleaming live tracer round. Shocked, Andrew came to squat beside him.

'Group Captain Reid gave it to him . . .' he began, and his voice died as he looked out. Far away across the stubble hunched the concrete remains which he had seen the night before. They looked small and forlorn, and suddenly he saw they were no more than a shell of nearly-demolished walls. In the early light the texture of the tilled land revealed where the main runway had once lain its weight in a broad ribbon of concrete past these remnants of the control tower and on towards the distant skyline. Now only the shadow of its imprint still survived the plough. A small flock of lapwings rose heavily from the field with sad cries and the rising sun bloomed like fire behind the empty ruin.

'The poor man,' whispered Andrew.

Steve Stern

The gramophone

Arnold Siripkin broke the thermometer and dropped tears of quicksilver into the boiling cauldron.

'This here is azoth from the sorcerers of Babylon,' he intoned, pushing his thick spectacles up on to the hump of his nose. 'Now Stymie Cohen,' he commanded, indicating that someone should shove forward a sullen boy who was lost in the contemplation of the swimming mercury. The boy was resentful.

'This here's whatever you said,' he sulked, tossing a seagreen marble into the gurgling tub.

'An eye of newt!' said Arnold, losing patience. 'Now Dumbo Klotwog.' A fat kid with enormous ears began giggling unhealthily.

'This is what you said is snake venom,' he wheezed, emptying a bottle of rusty liquid into the tub, 'but what is really the Sloan's Liniment what my mama rubs on my fadder's ...' A sharp glance from Arnold and Dumbo subsided into a chortling fit.

Then it was Phoebe Schutz's turn to utter an incantation, prompted by Arnold, as she squeezed the tube of pimple ointment which she'd stolen from her big sister's drawer. Other contributions were submitted from the rest of the kids assembled in that blind alley between the pharmacy and the kosher butcher. Into the cauldron they consigned such items of personal fetish as moth balls, suet, blackstrap molasses, a pair of dentures, a photograph of Itzhak Perlman, a wishbone, a pubic hair, noodle pudding, a potted hibiscus, shaving cream which Arnold insisted was foam from the mouth of a madman. When all of the sacred ingredients had been added, Arnold left off stirring the broth with his boat oar and lifted his eyes to heaven. This was a gesture borrowed from Rabbi Fisker, under whom Arnold was currently studying for bar mitzvah. His adam's apple was prominent, and his tuft of coarse red hair was a burning bush atop his forehead. It was difficult to tell whether the bush had set fire to the orange October sky, or vice-versa, but suddenly it was dusk.

'Nathan!' Arnold's voice echoed in the alley. 'Bring forth the candidate for resurrection.'

Nathan, Arnold's younger brother, had been watching the proceedings with rapt fascination from outside the circle of children. Summoned, he came forward smiling stupidly, holding a dead tabby cat.

'We gotta go home in a minute,' he said sheepishly, as Arnold snatched the cat away from him by its stiff tail.

'This cat was once a priest of Moloch ...' he began, examining the tyre tread across the animal's greasy fur.

As he listened to his big brother recite the history of the cat's reincarnations, Nathan was full of pride. Though he had no feeling for the solemnity of such occasions, he believed implicitly in his brother's wisdom. If Arnold said that the tin washtub, mounted on a folding cot over a fire fed by gutted theatre seats, was in fact the magic cauldron of Bran, then it must be true. For Arnold had read it in a book with snuff-coloured pages which he claimed was older than God. It told how the ancient Irish had flung the bodies of their dead warriors into such a cauldron, how the warriers had leapt forth with vacant eyes to fight again.

Arnold let go of its tail, and the cat plopped into a vat of seething debris.

'Let us pray,' he exhorted, inclining his head. Nathan closed his eyes tightly, while the other children, exchanging elbows in ribs and trying not to laugh, watched him. The fire about which they huddled took the edge off the chilly evening and augmented the atmosphere of conspiracy.

'Behold!' shouted Arnold, and Nathan opened his eyes in time to see a cat somersault through the air, land on all fours, and sprint out of the alley. It made no difference that the cat was a tortoiseshell, unlike the original tabby, or that Dumbo Klotwog, wheezing dangerously, had just risen from where he was crouched behind the washtub. These things, though he noticed them, did not interfere with Nathan's wonder. Arnold had proclaimed that the holy resurrection was accomplished, and Nathan, applauding with wide-open mouth, was convinced.

The other kids howled themselves dizzy over Nathan's gullibility. 'Nathan's a nudnik!' 'Nathan don't know nuttin!' 'Nathan's so naïve,' this from Phoebe Schutz. But eventually, when they were sore from derision, a kind of reverence set in. They gathered closer round the cauldron and peered into the churning swill, a little spellbound as they listened to Arnold droning something about the soup primeval. Nathan's conviction was not without its influence, and this was what Arnold counted on.

His little brother was such a willing dupe. Only three years younger, he worshipped Arnold this side of idolatry. His only recreation lay in observing his older brother and anticipating his next project. At night he sat vigil in their bedroom, while Arnold dragged mouldering tomes from the Lucy Street library into bed with him, where he read them by flashlight beneath the sheets. Not content to let his world remain cramped between cloth bindings, Arnold felt compelled to set it loose upon the neighbourhood. On these occasions Nathan, his brother's loyal famulus, would practically volunteer himself for bait.

There was the time after Arnold had read the volume on the Spanish Inquisition, whose pages had crumbled like dead leaves and earned him a substantial library fine. He had convinced Nathan that it was in his best interests to be strappadoed. In a derelict factory the children bound Nathan's hands behind him and hoisted him to the ceiling with a winch, while Arnold, his parka hood pulled over his head, appealed to the dangling Nathan to abjure his false faith. Nathan's general good humour was impaired by the near dislocation of his arms. His small frame flinched like a marionette, and his outsized pink head lolled grotesquely. The children shuddered as he spat out the words that Arnold had put in his mouth:

'I will not be forsworn!'

Then Arnold read *Tales of the Prague Ghetto* and led a few friends by candlelight up into the loft of the old Stuyvesant Street synagogue. There Nathan had been waiting patiently for several hours in the dark, standing where Arnold had planted him amid a pile of Union hymnals. The candle discovered his tiny eyes and his body, naked save for his underpants, dusted in talcum powder. Hebrew letters were scrawled in charcoal across his forehead.

'Behold the *golem*!' cried Arnold. When the boys in Arnold's party were recovered from their fright, they took their indignation out on Nathan. They knocked him over and kicked him until he soiled himself, then left him where Arnold said he would lie forgotten for another seven hundred years.

Lately Arnold had turned to mythology – ritual murder, premature burial, magic cauldrons and the like. Today his victim was merely an alley cat; tomorrow he might be more ambitious. To be honest, Nathan had reservations about being hurled into boiling muck from which he would emerge a zombie. Still, if his older brother should expect it, Nathan would never let him down.

Arnold and Nathan lived in a brownstone walk-up on Henry Street with their widowed mother and their grandmother, who was dying in an alcove off the parlour.

'This is the living room,' Arnold was fond of saying, standing outside the alcove curtain, pointing, 'and this is the dying room.'

There was an unstable Negro nurse named Frieda, who attended the old woman on weekdays, while Mrs Siripkin worked in a millinery shop. Each afternoon the nurse departed and an hour elapsed before Mrs Siripkin returned home, removing her shoes and complaining that she was so goddamn tired. During that hour the boys were required to look after their grandmother, whom Nathan called Memaw and Arnold called whatever should happen to enter his head.

She was little more than a death rattle in a flannel nightgown. She had a pair of rheumy eyes which drooled from a ruined face that was as populous with silver hairs as the top of her head. In sleep her mouth, which was toothless and surrounded by a pink stain of *borscht*, made a sucking motion like a baby or a fish. She seldom spoke, except to say *oi* or *gott* or, on days of unnatural vitality, *oi gott*, while being washed behind her floral curtain. When Nurse Frieda, who belonged to a fanatical religious cult, promised her that soon she would be in the bosom of Jesus, she said: 'God forbid.' Occasionally she farted with the sound of a playing card fastened to a bicycle spoke. Her only diversion, before Arnold broke it, had been the antique gramophone that she brought with her from Cracow.

Watching his grandmother die was for each of the boys a separate and unique experience. Nathan retained a fondness for his Memaw, who, with her *borscht* breath and Yiddish lullabies, had been the companion of his infancy. She had played him her gramophone, cranking the handle slowly and savouring her old record of Strauss waltzes which sounded as if the orchestra were treading upon their instruments. She had called him Mosche Pupik and given him pennies, when he was known in the neighbourhood as Nathan the Noodle for his ponderous head. Where his brother had his unquestioning allegiance, his grandmother had his affection. When she slipped on a herring and broke her hip – the broken hip in the Siripkin family being a traditional prelude to death – Nathan sat at her bedside with the gramophone. Moribund, she was sacred to him, like an old toy.

Arnold, on the other hand, delighted in the old woman's dying. He studied her slow passage and took advantage of her decrepitude to perform what he called experiments. These were conventional enough at the outset. He might tickle her nose with a feather as she slept, or dip her hand in warm water until her bladder let go. Becoming intrepid, he might hold a mirror beneath her hirsute nostrils, place coins on her eyelids, speak to her from behind an armchair as Jehovah. Discarding all scruple, he might wave his callow member at her, saying: 'Hey, Medusa, looka my schmuck.' After which the invalid hissed *gevalt* and spat up her cottage cheese. And recently Arnold had broken his grandmother's gramophone.

Nathan told himself that his brother had not done it on purpose. Still, it was hard to explain how Arnold, in stumbling, had managed to fall so mightily, to crack the turntable and mangle the copper speaker so thoroughly.

'It was an accident,' he protested, grinning with gapped

teeth as he removed himself from the wreckage. Later that evening the grandmother, through whimpering and Yiddish gutter slang, was able to communicate to her daughter the crime of her momzer son.

'I'm so goddamn tired,' complained Mrs Siripkin, massaging her instep, while Arnold suggested that the old lady was maybe confusing him with the Czar.

In any case Nathan had salvaged the record of Strauss, and he knew of a local pawnshop in whose window there was a similar gramophone. He was certain that his brother, with his greater allowance, would buy it to replace the other. Nevertheless, his feelings were hurt. Though he said nothing, he felt it unworthy of his brother to stoop to abusing the helpless Memaw. Such pranks did not become his native dignity. Still, it made Nathan sick to doubt his older brother. 'Arnold knows best,' he thought, presenting himself for further proofs of loyalty. Besides, his persecution might distract his brother from tormenting the dying woman.

Arnold held several unflattering theories concerning his grandmother: that her veins were full of glue, that her bowels would not move, that she was becoming a fossil for which the museum might offer a tidy sum. On a hopeful note he'd asserted that she was an hermaphrodite soothsayer and, abandoning that, that she was a man.

'She don't wear pants,' ventured Nathan, not wishing to gainsay his brother's authority. But Arnold pointed out that she had no particularly distinguishing female characteristics and that her whiskers argued in his favour of masculinity. Nathan conceded the truth in this, though it bothered him profoundly.

On the evening of the cauldron the boys arrived home after sunset. Nurse Frieda, in her haste to get away, had neglected to close the alcove curtain while holding the grandmother over her bedpan. The invalid, saying *oi* and *oi*, had hoisted her nightgown above her hips. Amber water trickled from the cobwebs between her legs; it tattooed in the pan like a tin drum. Hearing the boys enter, Nurse Frieda drew the curtain. In a moment she emerged, mopping her brow and saying goodnight, adding: 'Soon dat ol' woman gots to be washed in de blood o' de lamm.'

'Why don't you try disinfectant,' said Arnold, disappointed at the revelation of his grandmother's true sex. But as the nurse left, he saw that Nathan, still fascinated, continued to stare at the faded curtain across the alcove.

Then Arnold had parted the curtain again. The old woman, exhausted from the effort of her pee, was snoring despondently. The air around her bed smelt of buttermilk and gas. Crooking a finger towards his brother, Arnold told him come here, and Nathan dutifully complied. He obediently bent his bloated head, so that Arnold could grab it by the curls and shove it towards the hem of the grandmother's gown.

'I'm gonna introduce ya to the jaws of hell!' declared Arnold, losing enthusiasm in mid-threat, because Nathan didn't really seem to mind. Hell was just another aspect of the education with which his big brother was providing him.

The invalid drowsily opened her eyes, then shut them again, preferring nightmares. Exasperated, Arnold let go of Nathan and stamped into the kitchen. Nathan scarcely had time to speculate on the mysteries to which he'd nearly been initiated, when his brother returned, carrying a bowl of viscous, mouse-grey gruel. It was customary for Arnold to feed his grandmother a little something before his mama arrived. Holding the bowl aloft with one hand, he reached with the other into the pocket of his baggy trousers and produced a test tube full of violet food colouring.

'The spinal fluid of a loup garou,' he pronounced, 'mixed with ratsbane to make the victim claw out her *kishkas* and eat her own tongue. When she's stiff we can throw her in the cauldron.'

He uncorked the vial with his teeth and prepared to pour it into the gruel, when Nathan did the implausible. Charging forward, he intercepted the test tube and swallowed the alleged poison. Stunned, Arnold spat out the cork.

'Whadja do that for!' he gasped.

'I'm sorry,' said Nathan, bewildered by his own temerity. Arnold's features contorted as though outrage were a pie in his face.

'It won't work on you anyway,' he muttered; 'you're too dumb to die.'

Nathan stood for a moment digesting this food for thought, while Arnold spooned the ropy mess into his grandmother's mouth, smeared it over his cheeks and chin. Downcast, Nathan went to bed. It was not that he doubted his older brother or that the tasteless poison had made him nauseous in the least. It was just that he wanted – no offence towards Arnold – to be murdered in place of his Memaw.

So he closed his eyes and thought of a skeleton in a black robe, swinging a long-handled scythe. He lay corpse-like until suppertime, when his weary mother came in and, seeing him in his posture of sham rigor mortis, said, 'This I don't need.' She brought him a frozen dinner which he refused to acknowledge, brought him a laxative in a bottle called a McSomething's Cocktail. Unable to stir him, she left the room, saying, 'I got headaches enough without this.'

Nathan kept his eyes closed and thought of angels. Eventually he dozed and awoke hours later to the frustrating fact that he was still alive. Sitting up, he spoke to the adjacent bed.

'Arnold,' he said to the light beneath the sheet. At these times Nathan felt he was talking to a ghost.

'I'm immersed in the study of hermetic lore,' snapped Arnold.

'When you gonna buy Memaw another gramophone?'

'I'm saving my dough for *The Cabbala Unveiled*, edition of nineteen aught six, top shelf on the left hand wall of Kaplan's in Apple Street,' said Arnold. 'And anyway, we can throw the old witch in the cauldron tomorrow.'

Something quietly falling to pieces inside him, Nathan began to sob.

Nathan continued sobbing through the night, and in the morning he said that his heart was sore and he wished he could spit it up. Mrs Siripkin said that he had no fever and was just malingering and should be in school. Asking herself if she needed this, she answered, 'Like a hole in the head,' and then she went to work. Nathan felt a little better.

He spent the day spying on Nurse Frieda as she read her

Bible and administered morphine to Memaw. At one point he called her ('Psst, Psst.') to his bedroom door from behind which he whispered,

'Don't let her out of your sight.'

'You crazy,' said the nurse, returning to her Scriptures and her sardines and crackers.

Towards the middle of the afternoon Nathan's restlessness got the better of him. Satisfied that his Memaw was resting comfortably, he cautioned the nurse once again to be vigilant and left the flat. At the top of Henry Street, among kids who were returning from school, he could make out the indigo parka that belonged to his big brother Arnold. He was doubtless on his way to stoke the cauldron.

Nathan ducked down a windy sidestreet and ran three blocks to Novack's pawnshop. The large front window of the shop was frosted in swirls of cleaning wax. Nathan stood on the pavement panting, watching a rag inside the glass wipe a circle whose diameter spread to the width of the window. Items materialized: toasters and radios, clocks and guitars, a consumptive pawnbroker, a gramophone with a speaker like a giant tiger lily. Impervious to the pawnbroker, who signalled him first to come in and then to get lost, Nathan coveted the gramophone for an entire half hour.

Then he wandered for an indefinite time, talking with an imaginary Arnold.

'I know where there's a gramophone,' he would say.

'So tell me,' demanded the make-believe Arnold, 'and I will buy it for the Memaw to make her happy.'

It was nearly dusk when Nathan arrived at the alley. A couple of kids were tending the fire, while Arnold and his trio of lieutenants, bored from a surfeit of magic, reclined in the theatre seats that were not yet kindling. There were a few token jeers which ebbed to indifference at Nathan's approach. Dumbo Klotwog was occupied in using Phoebe Schutz's pigtail for a moustache. Phoebe was eavesdropping on Arnold, who was suggesting to Stymie Cohen that the birthmark on his cheek was cancer. No one noticed that Nathan sought an audience with his brother, until he was tugging at Arnold's coatsleeve.

'Don't soil the material,' said Arnold, turning back around to Stymie who was begging for a cure.

'Arnold,' said Nathan, but Arnold was busy prescribing a spider swallowed whole in maple syrup.

'Arnold,' a little louder, but he was recommending an albatross talisman. Nathan persisted.

'I know where a gramophone is.' This earned him a half-hearted reply.

'So what? I told you already we gonna throw the old lady in the cauldron.'

Nathan shook his head, too excited by his brother's words to note that his voice carried little conviction. He understood only one alternative.

'Throw me,' he urged, 'not Memaw. Throw me in the cauldron.'

Suddenly interested, Arnold arched an eyebrow and gave Nathan his full attention.

'We can't throw you in the cauldron.'

'Why cantcha?' It had seemed such a simple solution. But Arnold was frowning as if Nathan were of insufficient quality to share a washtub with superior refuse.

''Cause you ain't dead yet,' he explained, 'that's why.'

Nathan felt confounded, trapped again by the familiar technicality.

'Neither's Memaw,' he offered feebly, already anticipating Arnold's,

'She's as good as.'

He was right of course; Arnold was always right. And Nathan was surprised to find that he didn't care. All he wanted was to die in the cauldron for Memaw, and it was too bad if he couldn't be reborn from the steaming sludge for Arnold. He was glad, as he lurched towards the fire, to be depriving his big brother of a zombie.

He had one foot on the folding cot and one foot poised over the smouldering washtub, when the pair of stokers grabbed him. Punishing his presumption, they pulled him on to the cobblestones and pressed his face into an oily puddle. Dumbo Klotwog waddled over and, brandishing the wooden boat oar like a white hunter, perched a heavy brogue on the small of

Nathan's back. Arnold rose slowly from his seat, his eyeglasses full of the setting sun. Officially, he raised the hood of his parka, so that his hatchet-thin face was framed in fur. As he spoke, he swayed like a cantor, his voice breaking frequently in its first throes of puberty.

'We gonna steal her corpse outta the mortuary. We gonna roll her in a carpet and bring her to the alley. Then we gonna throw her in the pot without no clothes on. We gonna boil her old *knish* in the sauce of resurrection. We gonna cook her till she comes alive again, till she walks around at midnight with her false teeth chatterin' like some kinda man-eatin' clam.'

Because he could not hold his ears, Nathan flapped his head from side to side and said shutup. 'Shutup shutup shutup!' he shouted, until the word was as empty of meaning as a prayer in a foreign tongue. Thus he was unable to hear his older brother, who was cataloguing where and on whom they would set loose the undead grandmother. In the *mikvah*, the subway, the high school cafeteria; on the organ-grinder, the rabbi, the congregation of the Church of the Holy Communion, cousin Myra's wedding. 'And we'll serve up the soup at Passover,' he finished. Then, remarking that Nathan too was silent, he began again.

'We gonna put her in the pot,' he taunted, 'where it's as dark as her old you-know-what.' Pleased with his impromptu rhyme, he repeated it with more concision.

'In the pot where it's dark as her you-know-what.'

The other kids took up the chant. 'In the pot ...'

Nathan closed his eyes and was someplace mysterious and warm. He was under his Memaw's nightgown; he was at the bottom of the cauldron. He was dreaming, and in the dream he was not Nathan but an Irish warrior, come to avenge his dishonoured grandmother. The warrior was tranquil, despite the fat boy who was sitting on his spine and the surrounding litany: '... dark as her you-know-what.' Nathan knew that it would be dangerous to open his eyes, but he was lonely in his dream, and he missed his brother.

He was not yet shed of his tranquillity when he started to scream. It was a sound which escaped him like a pent-up genie from a cracked urn. Everything happened in the space of that scream. His captors spread out to give him more room. Dumbo Klotwog rolled from his back in fright, relinquishing the oar which Nathan, springing to his feet, took up and swung above his pomegranate of a head. Arnold had just enough time to ask himself the first half of a rhetorical question: 'Who does the little *schlemiel* think he is?' He omitted the second half (which went: 'Samson with the jawbone of an ass?') because his curiosity had been terminated by the edge of the oar which caught him at the base of his neck. His spectacles flew off and his head, before he folded on to the cobbles, was cocked to one side, as if he were listening to music.

Arnold's friends and disciples evacuated the alley, calling for their mothers and stumbling over those who had fallen. Some of the fallen crawled on their knees rather than stop to pick themselves up. Then Nathan was alone with his brother, whose face was coming to resemble the blue of his parka. His meaty lips were, as always, bemused, but his eyes, green and bulging, contained an unlikely innocence. Dead, Arnold inspired in his younger brother something that went deeper than respect. And Nathan embraced him like a long lost friend; he lifted him beneath the armpits and hauled him towards the fire. With a passionate effort, he raised Arnold so that his knees rested on the folding cot and his chest lay on the rim of the washtub. Then it was a simple matter to heave him – quickly, before his trousers ignited – into the vintage broth. The displaced liquid sloshed over the side of the tub, sizzling in the flames, and Arnold, still hooded, lay curled in the murky soup like a baby with a caul.

Nathan stood back and made a wish, then, settling himself in a damp theatre seat, waited for the wish to come true.

The old woman, forsakenly snoring in her alcove, was awakened when Nurse Frieda, shrieking over her open Scriptures, fell face forward out of her chair in a swoon. Opening her yellow sleep-filled eyes, Memaw saw her grandson Nathan before her, beaming with his surplus of sympathy. Behind him stood the *meshugunah* brother in his soaking-wet parka to which shards of glass were still clinging. His narrow face, trimmed in a halo of ratty fur, was tallowy and distended; it was the face of a potato or a misshapen moon. His stench was more acrid than burning grease. In one arm he was holding an old-fashioned gramophone whose handle he turned with methodical slowness. The recording of Strauss crackled from the speaker, as if the orchestra were all eating toast. The grandmother endeavoured to smile at her grandchildren. Nathan, he was her *shany* kin, and Arnold she forgave for his mischief. How could she not when the tilt of his head said that he too was enjoying the waltz? The old woman rattled a sigh and floated a mottled hand in time to the music. For a moment she was unsure if she were in heaven or in a park in Cracow, young again and with a pair of suitors, under an umbrella in the rain.

Dulan Barber

Call

People often ask me why we at City Broadcasting discontinued 'The Loneliness Session'. Such is the shortness of the public's memory that they no longer ask about Simon Jacob – and that, I admit, is a relief. We did a deliberate and effective hush-up job on that and now, well, you'd be pretty hard pressed to find anyone who remembered his name. The other day, though, we received a letter at the station (one of the many asking if we could not please reinstate the programme) which enquired about Anna, if we knew what had happened to her.

The mailbag certainly proves the need for the programme, but that was never in doubt. Ironically, it was Simon's idea. He'd only been with the company about three months and was very much the new boy, but when he suggested 'The Loneliness Session' at a programme planning conference, we all pricked up our ears.

Up until then, Simon's show had been much like any other phone-in programme. He had what we call the entertainment slot – nine until one a.m. on Fridays and Saturdays. He had studio guests, usually actors and singers, the occasional author, and the programme was primarily light-hearted. Simon had been given the slot because he was an actor, although not a very successful one. Still, his background enabled him to put people from the entertainments industries at their ease, and he had good contacts. This was important because at that time commercial radio was in its infancy and a lot of likely guests needed to be persuaded that we had an audience worth reaching. But then Simon was a very persuasive chap.

Too persuasive according to some. If his new boy status did not count against him his success with women did. In the three months or so he'd been with us he'd had rather heavy affairs with at least three of the girls at City Broadcasting. He was discreet about them and always professional in his work, but it hadn't escaped notice that we'd lost one very competent (and very pretty) telephonist; one first-rate (and very attractive) trainee studio manager and that one of our best reporters (with a terrific figure) was in an emotional turmoil. In short, he was creating havoc among the female staff, and that was why we thought of Stefanie.

Stefanie James is, without any doubt, the best producer we have. We knew we'd been lucky to get her and we were always scared of losing her. She got a lot of very tempting offers not only from other commercial stations but from the dreaded Beeb as well. Fortunately for us, Stefanie was loyal and by upping her salary, giving her more autonomy, we managed to hang on to her. But there was more to Stefanie than professional brilliance. She was known in the building as the Ice Maiden and that was why, when the rumblings started about Simon's prowess with and depletion of our staff, I undertook to persuade Stefanie to take over Simon's show.

It wasn't easy. Stefanie's a hard-news and political controversy lady. She likes, as she puts it, the nitty-gritty of government, how it gets to the people. But I prevailed, largely, I think, because I played straight with her. Somebody had to keep Simon in line. I think she regarded him as a challenge to her Ice Maiden image. Anyway, there were a lot of sly grins the morning I announced that Stefanie was taking over the Simon Jacob Show. Office gossip had it that Simon had met his Waterloo, but that Stefanie's very evident attractions would keep him sufficiently interested to take the pressure off our more susceptible female colleagues (and give the other fellows a look in). In a way, we brought them together as a mutual challenge and, in a way, it worked.

Stefanie, of course, was solidly in favour of 'The Loneliness Session'. She'd done the research which backed up Simon's instinct. His theory was that a lot of the late-night callers rang into the programme not because they really wanted to talk to the guests (some did not even know who the guests were or what they did) but out of sheer loneliness. Stefanie had made a précis of several sociological reports and a lot of statistics about the increasing problem of loneliness in our large cities. Inevitably, London topped the ratings loneliness-wise. And, not surprisingly, this loneliness reached a peak on Saturday nights when, traditionally, the world and his wife (or mistress) is out on the town, having a good time. Stefanie persuaded us that there was a vast audience out there of lonely, even desperate people who wanted nothing more than somebody to talk to. The gimmick (there always has to be one) was honesty. According to Stefanie, we shouldn't pussy-foot around, hiding the light of our intentions under a bushel of soft-sell crap. It was to be a phone-in for the lonely. We were going to face the subject head-on, admit that the problem existed. Within the laws governing such programmes, the callers could talk about anything. The only qualification for getting through was that they had to be lonely.

We liked it. We liked the toughness and the honesty. It bore the Stefanie James stamp and that, in our books, spelt success. Only one inevitable question remained: could Simon handle it, or should we get in a specialist, a counsellor, an agony-column auntie?

'No way,' Stefanie said. 'If we do that we're just another problem programme, offering instant counselling. We already do that and so does every other station. This programme is for people who only have one over-riding problem – loneliness. They just want somebody warm and sympathetic to listen to them. Simon fills the bill perfectly.'

This last assertion (Stefanie doesn't make suggestions – she tells you) caused a few raised eyebrows, even the odd worried grin. Had the Ice Maiden thawed under the warmth and sympathy of the Jacob charm? We shook our heads. Impossible.

We agreed to run a three-week experiment. The last hour of the Saturday show would be 'The Loneliness Session', just to test it out. In fact it took off. By the second week the switchboard was jammed by 9.30 with callers only too willing to wait until midnight for a chance to tell Simon how lonely they were. (After all, they had nothing better to do.) On the following Monday morning, Stefanie predictably demanded that the entire show become 'The Loneliness Session'. We gave in gracefully because facts are facts. That segment of the show was the biggest thing to hit City Broadcasting – and that made everybody happy.

A lot of the credit must go to Simon. If some of the other presenters said he was too unctuous, even sentimental, you can put it down to professional jealousy. He was a hot property in a matter of months. Now it was Simon who was getting the tempting offers. For myself, I thought he handled the programme well: straight, direct and, when necessary, tender. I couldn't help thinking it odd that a man who seemed to be utterly insensitive to his women could be so caring and gentle when handling the distress of strangers. And as the show captured more and more attention, something else intrigued me. Ever since the idea had taken off, Simon had ceased to be a wolf. As far as we knew he was leading a totally celibate life, answering the thousands of letters that began to flood in. Whatever the explanation, we were relieved. Of course, it never occurred to any of us that the boot might be on the other foot.

'You know I'm in love with him, don't you?' Stefanie said, fixing me with those cold, challenging grey eyes that had withered many a better man than me or Simon Jacob. We were sitting in an almost empty wine bar where we had lunched together. It was nearly closing time and Stefanie, whose morning show had gone particularly well, had been quietly celebrating. Now she evidently felt like confiding in me.

'Who?' I asked, knowing the answer and praying that she would contradict me.

'Don't be so bloody stupid,' she snapped. 'Simon, of course.'

'And?' I said, after a bracing swig of hock, nicely chilled.

'Nothing,' she answered, her shoulders slumping.

'What's that supposed to mean?' It was inconceivable (and I admit I may be prejudiced) that Simon could be indifferent to Stefanie. She is simply the most desirable woman in the company.

'It means that I'm going the way of little Tessa and poor Jean and whatever that other kid was called. The trainee, you know.'

'Oh come on,' I said. 'Firstly, you're not the type. Secondly, you've only got to crook your little finger if you really want Simon.' But I hope you don't, I added silently.

'Thanks.' She treated me to one of her rare, dazzling smiles, but it was very short-lived. Playing with her glass, she said: 'It's nice to have a vote of confidence, but you're wrong. I've tried a hell of a lot more than finger crooking and he just doesn't want to know. No way.'

I tried not to look relieved. I tried not to think about what constituted 'more than finger crooking'. My motives were purely professional, of course, though spiced with a zest of the personal.

'Then there's got to be somebody else or he's turned queer,' I said, trying to make light of it.

She shook her head almost savagely.

'It's the programme,' she said miserably. 'He gets off on it. And do you know why he's so bloody good at it?'

'No. Tell me.'

... And that was the first time I heard Anna's name, though the story was more important than the girl at the time.

In a flat, almost monotonous voice, Stefanie told me what she believed was the secret of Simon's success, and of her failure. Anna was an actress. Simon had met her in some remote weekly rep and, apparently, she had fallen for him, just like all the others. Except that Anna had lasted for two years. According to Simon, more through her own tenacity than his desire to keep on with the relationship. She became dependent, almost pathologically so and when things got really hairy between them Anna forgot to take her pill and quickly became pregnant. Simon's reaction to this was to step-up his extra-curricular sexual activities, which sounded typical of what I then began to think of as 'the old Simon'.

'... Then, in her eighth month, he took off for a couple of days – and nights,' Stefanie added meaningfully. 'When he finally turned up again, she was dead. He found her. In the bath. She'd cut her wrists.' She lifted her glass with a shaking hand and drank greedily.

'Christ,' I said, 'but ...'

'Let me finish. And don't, whatever you do, let on that you know a word of this.'

I nodded.

'He moved flats and came to us. He was determined to make his life over, to push Anna out of his mind. Tessa and the others were all part of the plan. That's why he got tired of them so quickly. Some men would have got smashed, or turned to dope or something. Simon made out with women, compulsively, and every time he broke it up – always because he got bored and scared – he felt even more guilty.' She must have sensed an instinctive resistance in me for she pinned me down with that cold, challenging stare again and said: 'He feels guilty. It's all because of Anna. The women and now, most of all, the programme. He's haunted by her, by that night. No, listen. I've heard him. When he talks about it it's ... terrifying. He sees her, in his mind. Her loneliness, her desperation. He describes how she must have wandered around the flat. He's constructed the whole evening in his head, what she did, how she must have felt, until she took the razor blade out of the cabinet and got into the bath.'

I couldn't help shuddering. Some of Simon's fear had rubbed off on Stefanie.

'So you see, every Saturday night he ... expiates himself. Every one of those callers is Anna. He is making up to her, and if ever anything goes wrong ...'

'It won't,' I said firmly. 'After all, they're not in her state. It's just not like that.'

'It is for him.'

'But that must be good for him, no?'

She lifted her shoulders uncertainly.

'It only seems to make it worse. About Anna, I mean.'

'Are you saying we should take him off the programme?'

'No.' She almost shouted it. 'No, that would be disastrous. But I must come off it. I can't stand being, well, second to a phone call from some neurotic ... Sorry. Anyway, Simon doesn't want a woman any more. He wants phone calls. He wants to help. He wants to chip away all the guilt about Anna, bit by bit, every Saturday night. And I can't stand it any more.'

Stefanie was taken off the programme the following week, without a murmur of protest from Simon. It was part of my job to keep an eye on the new producer (a young guy, incidentally, whom Simon accepted without comment) and that gave me a chance to observe Simon. Any four-hour radio talk show is bound to be exhausting but Simon seemed half-dead after his Saturday 'Loneliness Sessions'. Hollow-eyed, gaunt-cheeked and bathed in perspiration, he would simply fall into a taxi and disappear. I was seriously worried about him and, without letting on that Stefanie had told me about Anna, I suggested that he took some leave. He refused point blank (he was, at that meeting, his calm, charming, healthy-looking self) but offered a counter-suggestion. He was willing to give up the Friday night spot.

'Why?' I asked.

'It doesn't interest me any more. If someone else wants it, okay by me.'

Well, I thought, at least it would take some of the pressure off him. If anything, though, the 'Loneliness Sessions' seemed to drain him even more after that, but his tiredness, his complete washed-outness never showed in his voice.

I switched on the radio that first fatal Saturday not to check up on Simon but to catch the midnight news headlines and I thought nothing at all of it when, after the commercial break, Simon's voice said:

Welcome back to the last hour of 'The Loneliness Session'. Now we're going over to Hammersmith, to talk to Anna. Hello, Anna. Are you there?

Her voice was very faint. She was obviously in great distress. Simon did most of the talking, trying to draw her out. All I recall of that first conversation was that she kept on saying how unhappy she was. Then my telephone rang. It was Stefanie, sounding as close to hysteria as I've ever heard her.

'I'm terrified of what it will do to him.'

Of course, I'd completely forgotten Anna's name and in my anxiety to calm Stefanie down, I didn't take it in for some minutes.

'It's bound to have been a shock. They lived in Hammersmith, you know. Christ, you don't think it's some kind of awful joke, do you?'

No, I did not. Our switchboard team were excellent at weeding out cranks. I had every confidence in them. I also refused to drive her over to the studio to see if Simon was okay.

'It's a coincidence, Stefanie, that's all. Hundreds of people live in Hammersmith and Anna is not an unusual name.'

I managed to pacify her at last, but I did give the studio a buzz and checked with Mike, the new producer, that Simon was all right.

'He's doing fine. What's the problem?'

'Nothing. Just checking. But keep an eye on him, Mike, there's a good lad.'

If that first call meant anything special to Simon, he made a damn good job of concealing it. In fact, Mike reported to me on Monday that he seemed less tired that night. And since my enquiries were causing puzzlement, I let the matter drop. After all, what Stefanie had told me was not my business as long as Simon was doing his job. And he was, superbly.

The rest of this story I pieced together later, from Stefanie, Mike and some of the others. You see I had some leave due, things were going well, so I took it and never gave a thought to Simon or 'The Loneliness Session'.

Meanwhile, three Saturdays in a row Anna telephoned the programme. Each time hers was the first call on the air after midnight. Now there was nothing odd at all in the same person ringing up week after week. There were many lonely 'regulars' and other callers as well as non-participating listeners took a genuine interest in their ongoing problems. Anna, in her small way, became something of a celebrity.

What *was* odd, of course, was that she got through to Simon at the same time each week, but a thorough enquiry later revealed no explanation. Some say that Anna's timing was good, others shrug and don't care to talk about it, but one thing is certain: nobody on the switchboard colluded with her. The records show that Anna, like everyone else who phoned in, was treated on the standard first come, first served basis.

In fact, I was ignorant of Anna's regular weekly calls until Stefanie invited me to dinner, on a Saturday. I accepted eagerly because along with those long legs and that amazing bust, Stefanie is a great cook. Also, I knew that she would give me an accurate verbal picture of what had been going on at the station during my hols. I enjoyed myself too much to notice that she stayed off the subject of Simon and I wasn't about to bring it up. The last thing I wanted was to encourage her thing for Simon.

It was after the meal (extra-extra even by Stefanie's standards) that she said, pouring me a large brandy:

'Of course you realize I had an ulterior motive in asking you round tonight?'

'I only hope,' I replied, 'that it's the same as mine in accepting.'

She gave me a quick smile which left room for hope.

'I want you to hear something.' She produced a tape recorder.

'Sure,' I said, thinking that the night was still young. I was more than willing to indulge her on the off-chance that she might later, with the aid of several brandies, come to realize what an irresistible guy I was.

She snapped on the machine.

Hello? Simon? A woman's voice, clouded with static. *This is Anna.*

Hello, Anna. How are you?

Bad. It's very bad.

I'm sorry. What can we do to ...

A pause. She was crying. I looked angrily at Stefanie but the expression on her face was enough to shut me up.

Anna, love, listen. It's all right. It'll help to talk. You're not alone. You rang last week, didn't you? I'm glad you called back. Really.

Are you? You don't mind? You see, I'm so lonely.

Can you say why, Anna? It helps, you know. And not just you, but all the other lonely people listening in.

It's my boyfriend. He's ... he's gone out again.

You live with him?

Yes.

And does he leave you alone a lot?

Silence.

Anna?

I can't stand it any longer. He's gone off me, you see, but I ...

No, no, Anna, he hasn't. Maybe he thinks he has but I promise you it's just a phase. He'll be back. Everything'll be okay.

I reached over and switched off the machine. Such promises, based on no knowledge, were strictly against the rules. I looked at Stefanie and asked why I hadn't been told about this the moment I got back.

'I reckoned you'd need a lot of convincing.'

'It's not your job to bring it to my notice. What about ...'

'I don't know,' she cut in. 'My guess is that like everyone else the staff are hooked on Anna. Listen. This is a week later.'

The spool whirled, stopped, Stefanie pressed 'playback'.

You see, Anna, the thing is – and I really do know what I'm talking about – men sometimes behave in ways that seem harsh ...

No. He hates me. He doesn't care if I live or die. There isn't anyone ... No one. You don't know what it's like. Just the four walls. I don't care either.

You mustn't talk like that.

I don't care if I live or die, either. Only, well, it's not just me.

How do you mean, Anna? You mean your boyfriend ...

Simon sounded breathless, tense, as though he was expecting something.

I'm pregnant.

Oh, Anna. Well, that's good. Listen, how long is it? I mean ...

Seven months.

There was a pause. If a silence can be startled, that one was. Then, almost hysterically, Simon spoke.

Anna? Are you there?

A muffled voice in the background.

Oh, right, well ... I gather Anna hung up on us. We'll take a break there.

This time Stefanie switched off the recorder.

'I'll sack him and everyone ...'

'No you won't. During the break he asked the switchboard for Anna's number. They hadn't taken it. No reason. Now listen.' She restarted the machine.

Before signing off I'd like to make a special appeal to Anna. I know a lot of you share my concern for her and will join me in urging Anna ... Anna, if you're listening, please call in again and leave your number, okay? Will you do that, Anna?

'And did she?' I asked.

'No.'

'But she rang again?'

'Yes.' Stefanie turned towards the machine but I stopped her. I'd heard enough.

'There's got to be a lot more, Stefanie. A lot more.'

'There is,' she said, lighting a cigarette. 'I knew you'd take a lot of convincing. The next week she left her number with the switchboard. Simon had ordered them to get it. She said she had been unable "to get through" earlier.'

I heard the inverted commas in her voice.

'So?'

'You'll see. Simon got the number and apparently nearly collapsed. The studio was going to call a doctor, but he managed to pull himself together and left.'

'How do you know all this?'

'I asked around. No, I'm not telling you. I don't want any heads to roll except mine, if it comes to that.'

'You don't trust me.'

'I don't know. It depends on your reactions. I got the number, too, and I checked it out. It's a flat in Grove Court in Hammersmith. I went round there. The flat's unoccupied. The last tenant was Simon Jacob. He lived there with a girl. They haven't been able to let the flat since ... "the accident", as the caretaker put it. He showed me round. The phone's still connected.'

'So it *is* a hoaxer, somebody who knows ...'

'I don't think so.'

'Then what?'

She didn't answer directly.

'The caretaker told me Simon had been back there. He said he thought he'd left something. The caretaker loaned him a key. Simon had a key made a few days later.'

'The same key?'

She shrugged.

'Well, even if it was ...' I didn't feel convinced and it showed.

'I did some more checking.'

'You have been busy.'

'I'm frightened.'

'What of?'

'This time last year Anna was seven months pregnant. Simon was barely living with her. He was ... "Always out".'

'Stefanie ...'

'And tonight, according to my information, Anna will be in her eighth month. And Simon won't be home. He won't be home until Monday morning and Anna will be dead.'

The silence was awful and my forced laughter did not help. I got up, sloshed a lot more brandy into my glass, drank and said: '*Was* – past tense, Stefanie. This thing's obviously getting to you, getting you down. I know how you feel and I agree – we've got to stop Simon, stop this once and for all. I'll do that, but don't ask me to believe ...' I couldn't bring myself to say it. 'Not you, of all people.'

Stefanie stood up and faced me squarely.

'I've got contacts in the Post Office.'

'Good old Stefanie,' I said. 'That's what we employ you for.'

'And I've had some very discreet checks made.' She picked up a folder and held it out to me. 'No calls have been made on that line – Anna's number – for a year. They ran a trace on last week's call. It wasn't made.'

I sat down heavily and opened the folder. Everything she had said was true. Doctors' reports. Post Office reports. The police, Stefanie was always thorough.

'Could he be making it happen?'

'Possible but not probable. We all hear her. People who don't even know Simon hear her. Even you've heard her. If he is doing it, then Uri Geller had better look to his laurels.'

I stood up again, a little unsteadily, and not because of the booze.

'What are you doing?' Stefanie asked.

'I'm going to cancel tonight's show.'

'Too late. It's gone eleven.'

'The last hour, then.'

'If you do, your head will roll.'

It was true. And I didn't want to lose my job. But Stefanie's attitude puzzled me.

'What do you suggest then?'

'Sit tight. If I'm right, Simon's got to see this through. If you pull him out now, the consequences to him could be terrible. At least, that's my guess. You see, whatever it is, whatever is causing this, it will come to a head tonight.'

'You want me to think it's a ghost, don't you?'

'Not want, no ... I'm glad you said it though.'

'Stefanie, I can't cope with this. It's just not possible and meanwhile the whole damn station's at risk, not to mention Simon.'

'It's all right. There won't be a call tonight,' she said calmly. 'And I intend to be at the studio the moment he comes off the air. I want you to help me to get him to a doctor. All right?'

'But you said it would come to a head tonight, so how can it ... How can you be so sure that she won't call tonight?'

She snatched the folder from me and pulled out a sheet.

'According to the autopsy, she died before midnight.'

I took the sheet from her.

'But how accurate can they be? It was more than twenty-four hours before he found her.'

She moved towards the radio. I asked her not to put it on. Not yet.

'It's okay. I've taken one precaution. *If* Anna calls tonight, the switchboard are going to ring me direct and they have instructions not to put her through to Simon. Does that satisfy you?'

I had to admit that it made me feel better. She switched on the radio and adjusted the volume. In addition to all her other qualities, Stefanie James is a very cool customer. I was trembling and not at all convinced that we were doing the right thing. I suggested that we should go to the station at once.

'No. Simon's still a professional. He'll get through the programme, but if he suspects we're snooping or something, God knows what it might do to him. We must be there, but not until one o'clock.'

I looked again at the folder.

'This is probably the best piece of investigation you've ever done,' I told her. 'Will you use it?'

'No way. I told you. I love him.'

There was no answer to that. I started to chew my finger

nails. Stefanie seemed perfectly calm and composed. Then suddenly, she pounced on the radio, increasing the volume.

A male voice. A caller.

I'd just like to say if Anna's listening, I hope she'll ring in tonight. There are a lot of people who can help her.

(Simon speaking) *Right. I've got a lot of addresses here, but really I think we can help her most.*

'You see?' Stefanie said. 'She's got something. It may be against the rules but the special relationship between Simon and her has really got to them.'

'But Anna doesn't exist,' I said.

'Maybe.'

'Stefanie, for God's sake ...'

'Sh. Listen—'

I'd like to say that we're waiting for your call. Anna. Simon again. *Not just me but lots of people. Why don't you call a little earlier. Anna? Before the 'witching hour. Please. I'd like that. So, if you're listening, Anna, get on the line and ... Well, we want to talk to you, sweetheart. Now, Deirdre's calling from West Hampstead. Hi, Deirdre. How are you?*

Stefanie looked stunned. I knew why. Simon was begging Anna to phone in early so that he could stop her. I caught myself out in the fantasy. He couldn't stop her. She was dead. There was even a copy of her death certificate in Stefanie's folder.

'Now do you believe me?' she asked. 'Whatever the explanation, Simon thinks she is *his* Anna, that he can change things.'

'I'd like to get my hands on the bitch who's doing this. Who knows besides us?'

'I don't know. I couldn't find out. Even the caretaker won't admit that she was a suicide. "An accident", he says. Well, he's got to let the flat.'

'Why hasn't he?'

'Search me. But it is odd, isn't it? But then, would you live there?'

'Don't be stupid. But then I know ...'

'Quite. And perhaps others guess or sense ...'

I turned away from her, tried to dismiss it. I went through the folder again.

'This key he had made – if it is the one to the flat, why?'

'I don't know. Maybe he sneaks in there ... I don't know.'

'You haven't been following him, checking?'

'I tried once, but he spotted me.'

'And?'

'He bought me a drink.'

'I don't like it,' I said. 'I don't like any of it.'

'Now listen. Nobody can die twice, right? If it is a hoaxer, against all the odds, one thing is for sure: she's not going to kill herself. All that can happen tonight is that Simon is going to have to face reality. Just try to get that into your head.'

'You know, Stefanie, you've always been tough but I never thought you'd get hard.'

'I'd do anything for him,' she said levelly. 'I intend to be there when he needs me.'

I said nothing. We listened to the 11.30 headlines and the extended sports report. Spurs had scored five goals, I remember, but it seemed a cold, irrelevant comfort. Simon took another call. I had some more brandy. Stefanie, watching me, announced that she would drive when we left. We waited, silent and tense. The midnight headlines. Stefanie heaved a sigh of relief.

'You see? No call. The switchboard would have been through to me by now.'

'Thank God.'

'Get your coat. We'll just listen and see how he reacts. We can catch the rest on the car radio.'

And now back to Simon Jacob and the last hour of 'The Loneliness Session'. A few bars of moody music and then:

Hello. Simon.

Stefanie and I were petrified. We stared at the radio, not trusting our ears.

Anna. Good to hear you. I want to talk to you very much.

Stefanie's hands became tight-clenched fists. She shook from head to toe. I couldn't bear to watch her.

It's no good, Simon. I know how you feel. I've made up my mind. All this time I've been using the baby as an excuse ...

I want the baby. I want to make it all right. This time. Anna ...

I know you don't care for me any more. I've got it all worked out. I just want you to know that I'm sorry. It was a rotten trick, getting pregnant. I'm sorry.

Listen, Anna. I want you to keep the baby. Listen, I love you. I want you and the baby. I know better now. I want ...

It's no good, Simon. I know you mean well but it wouldn't work. It never has, really, has it? Pause. *I'm going to the bathroom now ...*

No. He screamed it into the microphone, making us both jump. A moment of silence and then a familiar commercial. We began running, Stefanie and I, out of the flat, down the stairs. I put on the car radio. They were putting out music, moody-post-midnight music. Neither of us dared to speak. The music faded and Mike's voice came on.

This is Mike Brancer. I'm sorry but Simon Jacob isn't well. He won't be able to continue with the show. And in view of that we won't be taking any more calls tonight. Now here's some more music to take us up to the 12.30 news headlines. Stay tuned to City Broadcasting, the station that ...

'Get to a phone box,' I said, searching for change. I dialled straight through to the studio. Simon had left. According to Mike, who sounded really shattered, he had just snatched the headphones off and bolted out of the studio and the building. 'I'll get there as soon as I can. Say nothing to anybody about Simon and keep playing the music.' I hung up and sprinted back to Stefanie.

'Get in,' she said.

'I ought to go to the studio.'

'Sod the studio,' she snapped.

It was a terrible drive. God knows how many red lights we went through. At one point, Stefanie switched off the radio. We squealed around Hammersmith Broadway and came to a stop outside a block of elderly mansion flats. I took Stefanie's arm and held it tight. It felt as though she might collapse at any moment. We said nothing in the lift, nothing when we got to the flat. The front door was open.

'You wait here,' I said.

'No. It's okay. I'll ...' She didn't finish but walked into the flat, fumbling for light switches. We passed through one empty room to another. I noticed the telephone, the receiver resting innocently in its cradle on the floor. I never thought I would find a telephone sinister.

'The bathroom,' Stefanie said. Her voice sounded as though it came from a very long way away.

'I'll go,' I said and this time she didn't argue.

He was sitting with his back against the side of the bath. Later I was told that he was in a catatonic state, but at the time what scared me was the stiffness of his limbs. Legs sticking straight out. Arms held out before him. And his face ... *Nothing.* A white arrangement of flesh and bones, hollows and planes. His eyes did not recognize me as I bent over him. All the light had gone out of them. I spoke his name, but he was effectively deaf, certainly beyond reach.

It was as I straightened up that I looked into the bath. It was three-quarters full of water, discoloured water, a sort of pinkish-brown. Terrified, I grabbed Simon's wrists, but there wasn't a mark on them. Stefanie came in then and knelt beside him. I went to the telephone.

And that's why we cancelled 'The Loneliness Session'. Simon is still in hospital, in the country. It's a nice enough place. I visit him every three months or so, usually with Stefanie. He doesn't speak. It's as though he isn't there, as though he'd answered the call, wherever it came from.

One thing I've always regretted. Before the ambulance and the police arrived, Stefanie pulled the plug out of the bath. She says that she doesn't want to know what caused that strange discolouration of the water. Perhaps she's right. I often tell myself that it couldn't have been blood but ... well, I wonder what else, perhaps beneath the discoloured water, Simon saw before we got there.

There are only two other items to report. They ought to conclude this story, but in a sense they raise more questions than they answer. We played merry hell, of course, about the switchboard's failure to ring Stefanie, block Anna's call, and a fat lot of good it did us. Anna's call never went through the switchboard. They had been as surprised as us. Somehow, Anna, who or whatever she was, got straight on to the air.

We checked and we checked but that call was never made, never received. And yet we all heard it.

Stefanie took charge of Simon's affairs, when she felt up to it. She cleared his stuff out of his new flat. She came to my office one morning, months later, carrying a spool of tape. She insisted that I listen to it. I recognized the voice at once, but then I don't think I'll ever forget it:

What would it pleasure me, to have my throat cut
With diamonds? or to be smothered
With cassia? or to be shot to death, with pearls?
I know death hath ten thousand several doors
For men to take their exits: and 'tis found
They go on such strange geometrical hinges
You may open them both ways

Without telling Stefanie, I got a friend of mine to run a voice print on that tape and the one she had made of Anna's calls to the show. My friend is an expert and his report is adamant: the voices belonged to the same woman. The tape Stefanie found in Simon's flat was dated some eighteen months before Anna died, more than two years before Simon joined City Broadcasting. It is labelled 'audition pieces'. But to me it seems like a message. After all, if those exits open both ways, presumably you can come back.

Michael Stewart

The Lady of the May

Begin at the beginning. That's the sensible thing.

What was the beginning?

Was it his daughter Tessa sprawled across the sofa, her auburn hair falling on the black-red stain at her neck, so clear in the flickering moonlight of the television?

No, that was perhaps the end.

Or was it his wife Sylvia's phone call? 'Darling, it's my Evening tonight. Get Tessa to fix you something but don't keep her up. She's got a big day tomorrow.' It is her Evening because they do not like to speak of her seances. They do not quite see eye to eye over that.

Or was it much earlier? When they moved to the area, to the new house with two garages and its own driveway? When he changed his name from Chris to Christopher. Christopher and Sylvia Burton, At Home. Printed notepaper and a private school for Tessa.

Or again, did it begin just that evening, that Friday evening on the last day of April?

Perhaps it began then, at the office. Emptying the desk into the briefcase: the export sales figures and media coverage reports to join his *Angling Times* and the golf tees. 'Cheers, Christopher. Nice weekend. All the best for your girl – didn't you say she was something in your village May Day caper? Cheers. Don't do anything I wouldn't.' 'That gives me plenty of scope,' he returned the standard formula. Such backchat was the privilege of the managers.

No, it really began a little later, at the Lady May. The small whitewashed pub on the green just a couple of miles from his home. The Friday evening stiffener.

He felt good driving from town, down the country roads with the flattening sun firing at him low through the trees. His black car felt good to handle, smoothly commanding the road. Each year it was a better one, always picked for its miles per gallon and servicing costs. Practical reasons, for he was a practical man. Not an exceptional man, that he knew. That Sylvia told him often.

'There are Things Beyond,' Sylvia would say. 'You either have it or you don't.' Thus they tacitly had their separate provinces, his and hers. His worked like this car, governed by the logic of engineering, the laws of predictability. He was really more at home with his car than with his family. He would admit feeling comfortable in its solid explicability.

The green was staked out for the festivities to come. Ribbons demarcated parking lots for the coaches. Banks of chairs stood highstacked. Small tents for side-shows were being made ready and, in the centre of the white-lined circle, was set the tall maypole.

Twilight cast a calm over the whole campus as though upon the eve of a great battle.

There, at the far end, was the tavern, the Lady May, with its boxes of geraniums and the painted hanging sign. He noticed the strangeness of this sign as his tyres bit satisfyingly into the gravel of the carpark. 'The Lady May' was written in old floral script and, in the centre of an oval ring of multi-coloured rope entwined with flowers, was the picture of an old woman, bent nearly double, in a grey hooded travelling cloak. It had always been there, long before they did up the pub. No one quite knew who she was, nor seemed to care greatly. She had something to do with May Day. On every first day of May there had always been a gathering there, at the pub.

'Evening, Charles. How do, Jim.' To each in his own vernacular.

'Evening, Christopher. How's the motor?'

Christopher's week of sales conferences and policy meetings entitled him to speak knowledgeably on such important matters, to be critical of the little defects of suspension, the quality of the ride. Bit sluggish with two up, Henry. Maybe the tappets or the torque.

Henry pushed across his drink and Christopher sat on the bar-stool, his back to the window.

Reflected in the old mirror behind the bar, he could see the copper pans and old pistols stapled to the stone walls, the diamond-leaded windows and, beyond, the dusk encroaching on the green and sponging out the colours of the maypole in its centre.

Henry saw him looking at the mirror and said, 'Ugly old thing, isn't it? We had to leave it there when we did the place up. Couldn't budge it. God knows how the Davies got it there.' Henry's face suggested he had mixed himself too sour a drink.

The Davies were the previous owners. That much Christopher knew from local talk. That, and that Flora Davies had been a real beauty and died in a strange accident. On one of their May Days. People didn't seem to want to say much more and after all it was just a piece of outdated gossip.

Sylvia has joined the other four around the three-legged table. The nectars of the purple and dark magenta lilacs press into the room. The messages are coming in, thick as droves of pigeons. They come in through the open french windows, between the heavy velvet curtains and into the solitary pool of light over the circle of green baize.

Sylvia's hands are very white against the green cloth. Messages are coming for her.

She sees a young woman in a pale yellow coat, struggling with a man in a ditch beside the road. More like a girl, really. A pale yellow coat like Tessa's. Auburn hair, too.

There are two cars. Perhaps there has been a collision. One is a pale yellow also, an old model like her father once had. The other is some way off, and is dented. It is black, shiny. It is Christopher's.

He has forced the girl against a tree-root and is labouring her flimsy body powerfully. There is no sound. Her arms claw at his back but his neck is thick and unheeding, lowered as a bull's. Her legs spread at angles like a rag doll.

The rag body goes limp. The auburn head lolls to one side. A swathe of bright red starts out at the neck.

Sylvia screams.

'Same again, Henry. Bit quiet tonight.' The evening was mellowing. It varnished the glasses and turned the lights up a tone.

'Early days yet, Christopher. They're all getting ready for

tomorrow.' Henry returned the other's glass. He was raising it when suddenly his elbow was knocked and the thing spilled. Clumsy arse, he muttered, turning to see Mr Goodbody, white-faced, shaking, calling urgently, 'Double scotch, for Christ sake, Henry.'

Mr Goodbody the butcher. His whole vast frame was quivering as though an earth tremor were passing through his meat-hanging rooms.

'Can't make it out. Doesn't make sense. She was there one moment. I hit her, see, and then gone the next. Into thin air. I swear to God.'

Coming in his van from the shop, down the road Christopher took home, Mr Goodbody had knocked down a woman in a pale yellow coat. (Tessa had a pale yellow coat.) There she was, only a girl really, suddenly stepped out in front of him. Came from nowhere. Couldn't help it, couldn't swerve, no time for any of that. He felt the thud. He ran back up the road, but no sign of her. Road empty. Nothing in the hedges either side, nothing in the fields. No trace on the road. Nothing except this red scarf – Mr Goodbody held out a dark red swatch. (Tessa's was just like that, the one she bought for her costume.)

Better report it to the police. Henry was fond of being cool and wise in emergencies.

Can't be anything, Christopher said, and reassured Mr Goodbody with a sequence of sound reasoning. It was a pheasant, they concluded, and the scarf had been dropped by someone earlier. Gypsies were always up and down the road.

Christopher looked up into the mirror. Charles and Jim were disputing the merits of the A45 and the B29. Jim's grandmother was dying and, rightly, the discussion over the pint was about the best route to take. Beyond them, just inside the window, he began to make out the figure of an old woman. She was almost crouching and wore a grey cloak-like garment with a hood. He thought she was looking at him.

He turned to face her. But the seat by the window was empty. Only Charles, Jim and two others in the far corner. No old woman, only the little painted figure on the pub sign which he could make out softly in the fading light, swinging in a gentle touch of wind.

Trick of the light, he told himself.

Henry was competently pumping glasses into the rubber-fingered washer. He had been responsible for doing up the place. His was the wipe-easy laminated bar-counter, the little crested beer-taps, the gas log fire, the lamp affair with the coloured oils. His down-to-earth sense was in every part of this room.

'Nothing to worry about,' he told Mr Goodbody comfortingly, and added in confidence to Christopher, 'You get all sorts of stories in here. The things I've heard. Take the Davies – case in point.' He gestured to the mirror. 'They say funny things happened the night Mrs Davies ... had the accident. Never worried me.'

Henry took a cloth and dried the smaller glasses. 'Lovely woman, though. Her old man used to get jealous as hell, but reckoned it brought the business in. Show you what I mean.' From under the counter Henry pulled out an old photograph. 'Taken the day of the accident.'

The Davies couple stood behind the bar. Mr Davies' hands were on the china beer-levers, hers on the mahogany counter. He was looking at her, while she posed to the camera. She was certainly a beauty: auburn hair, green eyes, dressed in her May Queen costume with its red scarf and white head-dress. Behind them is the old mirror and the photographer himself reflected. But Christopher could also make out a greyish form behind him, a figure slightly hunched, the hood quite sharply defined against the window.

Instinctively Christopher looked up at the mirror. No old woman.

Mr Goodbody had taken the photograph. 'That's her!' he cried, stubbing out his finger on Mrs Davies' picture. That's her, he kept repeating, as though that would convert the unbelievers.

Now we all know what it was, Mr Goodbody, Christopher reminded him. This is getting tedious, he thought. He remembered Tessa at home. And the reports to be done. Better be getting back. Set him up another, Henry, and here's for one in the stable.

Mr Goodbody's van was next to the black car. Christopher

looked at it condescendingly. Its lowliness exalted his own by simple contrast. Then he noticed the dent. Definitely fresh. Must have been a pheasant. Just as he thought. Didn't he say so?

He nosed the black car on to the road and round the green. Evening had cast its fine-meshed nets over the tents and benches, over the small figures hurrying to catch the light and over the tall maypole in the centre. He breathed in the flirtatious scent of the trees and hedges. Their fresh leaves throbbed with an internal glow.

Then he noticed a rasping noise behind him. The wheel-bearing again, and maybe the axle needs greasing. All week-end to fix it.

But the rasping became more like a wheezing. He looked up in the rear mirror, a routine check on the road behind.

She was there, in the car, right behind him. Weathered boniness of the face in the hood. Little eyes, bright juniper berries of eyes, filled the mirror.

He spun round, hard on the brakes and shrinking towards the windscreen. He only got a glimpse but saw that the back seat was empty. Quite empty.

Suddenly, it was too late to avoid the car in front, parked beside the road. He was already on top of it. A woman was coming out from behind, more of a girl really. A pale yellow coat and the auburn hair fired by the low sun behind her. 'Tessa!'

Christopher hit the brakes harder and swerved, catching the back of the pale yellow car with his wing. He had stopped and was already bounding back up the road. His feet crunch on fragments of plastic and glass.

The girl was waiting for him, one foot on the long running-board. She did not look surprised. She was smiling, her green eyes holding his fast. It was not Tessa.

He reached for her hand. Are you all right? The hand was cool. Its ring he noted with great clarity – a knotted cord entwined with flowers. Her neck bore a livid finger of colour. As he looked into her face the horizon behind her began to revolve. It drew him closer, into the vortex of her eyes.

She smiled, and a swollen sweetness rose in him. She laughed, and galaxies returned the low echo. Her hand was the touch of the corn and the wind. She drew him to her with the pull of the rising sap.

Rooks wheeled their pagan cries above them. He reached towards her and she receded, against the fleshy tree-roots in the ditch, against the rich wet humus and into the very earth.

Sylvia screams again.

She has upset the table, scattering the cards and the tumbler. My little girl, she shrieks.

The lights go on, shrinking the spirits into the wallpaper with a catch of the breath.

Madame is on her feet. Fetch water. Everyone calm. It is nothing!

But no, Sylvia cannot be held back. She fights the invisible ropes holding her to her place. Fiercely she kicks her way through the tangle of clinging hands and exhortations, through the door and out, out into the garden, out into the street and is scrabbling for the keys to her car.

Flung past the pub on the green she notes that Christopher's black car is not there. She sees fleetingly the green all laid out for the morrow's festivities. She'll make a pretty Queen. Tessa, my child!

Down the road to home she swerves to avoid some broken glass. Fresh tyre marks. No time to think about anything but her Tessa.

Up the drive she sees Christopher's black car. She skids on the gravel and leaps out, leaving the car running, and flies into the house.

No lights. Sounds coming from the living-room. Pushing the half-open door, Sylvia gasps.

Tessa, lying there, sprawled on the sofa, lit by the flickering moonlight of the television. A dark red stain is spreading from her neck.

Noises of Christopher approach. Blundering through the back of the house, slamming the fridge door, dropping a glass and cursing. Closer they come. Already shuffling in the corridor as Sylvia sees the decanter. Outside the door as she picks it up. His hand is groping for the light switch as she raises the object.

The lights burst on. Darling! exclaims Christopher, what are you doing?

Sylvia is impaled in the bright light.

On the sofa the silent body stirs. Tessa sits up with a jerk. Mother, are you all right? The red scarf falls from her neck to the ground.

Sylvia has dropped the decanter and is crouched, sobbing. Tessa runs over to her while Christopher replaces the decanter on the mantelpiece. In the mirror he catches sight of his own frown and then suddenly the old woman, there, at the back of the room, eyes bright as juniper berries burning from behind the grey hooded cloak.

He whips round. On the couch by the window is only the May Queen costume that Tessa will wear the next day.

A bright, youthful day. Tessa and her mother had already gone into the village early. Christopher was taking his time, relishing the sounds and scents of the season coming of age.

Shaving, he saw a line of blood on his face. A briar must have caught him. Must have slipped in the road adjusting the lights or the wipers to get his shoes in such a state. The phone rang and he answered with his manager's tone of practical efficiency.

Once again Christopher got into his black car with a sense of satisfaction with the world. Leaves were unfurling their tight canopies and young flowers poured out their seductive scents to the air.

Down the road to the village, he avoided a patch of glass. Clumsy idiots, drunken as likely as not. Still, what matter on a day like this?

The Lady May was full and his usual space taken. But the air was full of pleasure and expectation and he shrugged off his slight annoyance and passed in among the happy faces of merry-makers. Outside, the coaches had arrived and families were well encamped on their tartan rugs around the white circle of the green. The band was in position and testing out their reeds and tubes. Across the green he saw his wife's car. Tessa was arranging her head-dress and had wrapped the bright red scarf gaily about her. She waved to her mother and went off to join the others, all highly decked with coloured silks and bells and ribbons.

Tessa looked very lovely with her full, auburn hair.

He pushed to the bar. Henry was besieged by jocular appeals for glasses to be refilled. It was full of people Christopher had not seen before, people from the nearby towns on a day's outing. He gave old Mr Goodbody a slap of encouragement. He was slurring, damned if it was a bloody pheasant.

The band had struck up and people were moving outside. He'd join them in a moment. The place was better now it was emptier. Henry, same again please.

Christopher watched the procession in reverse in the mirror over the bar. He could see them, their heads bobbing above the spectators who lined the green, beer mugs and crisps in hand, punching each other in play. The dancing began and the light sound of the bells added itself to the music and the shouts. He watched the top of the tall maypole being wrapped and wound by slow degrees as the dancers wove in and out beneath with their coloured traces.

The room seemed to join the dance, keeping time with the pump of the deep trombones. It's really going with a swing, Henry.

As he looked more, he saw again the grey figure emerge from the shadow by the window. Suddenly it had swept up its cloak and was moving away, towards the doors.

Christ, not again. He turned in horror and anger. But no sign of the old person. He turned back to the mirror to check again, but something seemed to be missing. The maypole, it seemed to be no longer there. He looked up to the painted hanging sign outside. Inside the oval ring of coloured ropes and flowers – nothing! The grey old lady had disappeared from it.

Then the scream.

It comes from the crowd outside. The music stops. More screams come in on top, other people's now. The crowd presses forward to the centre of the green. The dancing has stopped.

Christopher rushes outside and sees Sylvia far away, fighting through the press. They reach the cluster of dancers together. The dancers are bending over one of their number.

Tessa is lying, limp as a rag doll, pinned to the ground by the maypole. Down her neck a red stain is slowly flowing.

He clasps her hand and sees the ring. It is a ring in the form of a twisted rope entwined with flowers.

Dulcie Gray

Four Ash Cottage

The summer was exceptionally fine. Day after day the sun blazed down from a cloudless sky.

My mother had been killed in 1942, during the war, attempting to escape from Singapore, and had left me a thousand pounds (nearly all she had) in her will, and in 1948, having just got married to a writer, I had decided to use the money to buy a small cottage in the country. House prices were low in those days.

Tony had been demobbed two years previously. He had had quite a bad time as a prisoner of war, and he now found towns too claustrophobic, and since I am a painter, I can, within reason, do my job anywhere.

We had settled on Dorset as a likely place to live. It was still unspoilt and a good distance from London, and we both thought the coast might suit us as we loved the sea.

We scoured the county in our little car, looking for our dream cottage, armed with lists from estate agents. The lyrical descriptions they gave roused our hopes to fever pitch each time, but we were always disappointed; so disappointed, in fact, that we decided to look further inland.

On each list, right at the bottom, a property called Four Ash Cottage was going for sale very cheap indeed, and though it was apparently in good repair, it didn't sound suitable as it was advertised as having 'cement paths', 'modern windows', and as being 'detached'. We wanted an old cottage, thatched, and remote from the world.

One radiant early June day, we had visited two cottages and a house, and had thought all were quite dreadful. The first cottage was certainly miles away from other houses, but it was situated on a corner of two roads, from which you could see the local buses and indeed all the traffic as it thundered past on one or other of the very straight roads. The old woman who owned the place considered this her greatest sales asset. It was fairly near the sea, but that was all. The second cottage was right on the cliff's edge, but it was run down to such an extent that it was beyond our means to repair; with money spent on it, it could have been made respectable. The house was much too big, and gloom personified. It was also modern, fake-beamed, and jerry-built as well, so we turned sadly for home. Gloomily I glanced at the agent's list before putting it away, and noticed that our little friend, Four Ash Cottage, was still unsold, and that we were heading straight for it.

'Look, Tony,' I said. 'We're only a few miles from that cottage they're always advertising.'

'So what?' asked Tony. 'It's getting late, and I'm worn out.'

'Please! We can't go on living with your mother in London for the rest of our lives,' I said. 'You hate it.'

'So do you,' retorted Tony.

'All the more reason to look at this place. We'll be driving right through the nearest town.'

'Okay,' replied Tony unenthusiastically.

'And by the map,' I went on excitedly, 'we come to Enderby Common before we get to the town, so we can't be very far away.'

'Okay,' repeated Tony.

We drove on for a further three miles, then found a signpost pointing to Enderby Common to the right. 'We're here!' I exclaimed, and for some reason I felt as though I had come home.

The Common was to the left of the road, and as we rounded the corner we came on it suddenly.

It was enchanting! True, everything looks its best on a fine day, but this was pretty by any standards. It was large, and in the centre of it, surrounded by red May trees still in flower, there was a pond with white ducks swimming on it. A row of white cottages was on the righthand side of the road, and to the left at the far side of the Common there were four more, but these were some distance apart. Beyond the row of cottages on the righthand side and looking fairly affluent was a farm, set well back and with a large sprawling white farmhouse, and beyond that again, there were hedges on both sides of the road.

'I wonder which it is,' I said, eagerly.

'The list said just beyond the Common on the right, next door to a farm,' replied Tony.

'Isn't all this beautiful?' I demanded happily. 'Oh Tony, how wonderful it would be if Four Ash Cottage was our dream house after all!'

'What about the sea?' asked Tony, laughing. 'I thought your dream house had to overlook the sea.'

'It's not that far,' I answered. 'We can get to the coast in under half an hour.'

Tony was now driving slowly and peering at the name boards on the cottages.

We passed the farm, and came to the hedges, and immediately beside the farm, behind the first hedge, was the prettiest thatched cottage either of us had ever seen. There were two gates to it. One led past a garage by a cemented path. One, by an old brick path, led directly to the front door. A white name board stated 'Four Ash Cottage', and underneath was written 'Beware sharp dog'. We both laughed, and Tony stopped the car.

We got out, and leaned over the gate, and our excitement grew. It was perfect.

Although the agent's list said we could only view by appointment, the cottage had a deserted air, so, with a wary eye lifted for the 'sharp dog', we decided to risk looking round the garden.

The place seemed all that we had ever wanted. The garden had been beautifully kept, and was a typical 'cottage garden' with lupins and roses, a small stream with an old apple tree in full blossom leaning over it, a little orchard, now a mass of blossom, and a vegetable patch. The cottage itself seemed in excellent condition. The thatching was almost new, and so still light in colour, and had been charmingly finished off with scalloped edges near the top of the roof. Everything looked completely spick and span, and the building, at a guess, dated from the seventeenth century. When we peered in through the 'modern' windows we saw whitewashed walls and black beams. At the back, the view over the hills was crowded with sheep, without another habitation in sight, and a huge oak tree in full and fresh green leaf stood just outside our boundary to the right. There was no sign of the four ashes of the name of the cottage.

'Well?' I asked confidently.

'It was made for us,' replied Tony, fervently.

We wandered round hand in hand making absurd plans, and when it was time to go, we dragged ourselves away with the utmost reluctance.

By the gate, at the head of the brick path, I stopped for one last look, and to my surprise saw an old man standing under the apple tree on the lawn, looking at us. I waved, but he didn't move; just stared.

'Come on,' urged Tony, getting into the car.

'There's an old man under the apple tree,' I said. 'I wonder if he's been here all the time,' I looked back, and the old man beckoned. 'He's beckoning to us,' I went on.

'We can't stop or we'll be late,' said Tony.

'I'm so sorry we can't come now. We didn't mean to trespass,' I shouted. 'Please forgive us, and we love your cottage.'

The man didn't answer, and vanished.

I rubbed my eyes. 'He's gone,' I remarked stupidly.

Tony opened the car door. 'Hop in,' he said firmly.

Three weeks later we owned the place.

The agent had no explanation why the property was so cheap, and the owner was nothing like the old man I had seen, but we didn't let it worry us, and the Sunday before we were due to move in we took a hamper with us to picnic in the cottage garden. We were now so besotted with it that we could hardly bear to be away from it.

As usual that year, it was a brilliantly sunny day. We sat on a rug on that little lawn by the stream. Scarlet poppies blazed up at the sky. Bright blue delphiniums, crimson rambler roses, hollyhocks, phlox, lavender and peonies of all shades rioted down the narrow garden beds, in a splendour of colour. The stream, clear and swift running, chattered as it ran, and the old apple tree dappled the grass with sunlight and shade. It was peaceful and happy, and we felt as if we were alone in a quite untroubled world, when suddenly from the back of the cottage there came three people: two girls and a young man. They were as surprised to see us as we were to see them. One of the girls was beautiful. She had red hair, a very white skin, and huge blue eyes. The other was almost as plain as the first was beautiful. She had mouse-coloured hair, brown eyes and a bad complexion. Her arm was round the young man's waist, and he was handsome, blond and blue-eyed, but with a certain vaguely unattractive swagger.

It turned out that the mouse-haired girl, whose name was Norah Heskethson, was the daughter of the next-door farmer, and that she was engaged to be married to the young man, Ron Hatley, who was a farm hand. The beauty was called Ellen Lowther. She was a life-long friend of Norah's who lived locally. The three of them apologized for intruding and explained that the cottage had been for sale for such a long time that they had developed the habit of walking through the garden when they felt like it. They seemed delighted to hear that we were to be neighbours, and asked us to tea on the day we were to move in. They also said they would give us any help they could.

For me their intrusion had cast a sort of blight, but Tony had enjoyed meeting them.

'It's the young man,' I said. 'He depresses me somehow.'

'Nonsense,' laughed Tony. 'What's wrong with him? He seems okay to me.'

On Wednesday we drove down to await the removal van, and I received a shock. We met Mr Heskethson, the farmer from next door. He was the old man whom I had seen beckoning to me from under the apple tree. When we were introduced I told him that I thought we had already seen each other, but he denied it, seeming genuinely surprised at my remark.

'Are you sure?' I asked in amazement. 'You didn't wave to me from under our apple tree on the first day we saw the cottage?'

'Certainly not,' he said strongly. 'I've never set eyes on you until today. I don't go into other people's property like these young things here.' He indicated his daughter and her friends. 'I believe that what a man owns he owns, and that is that.'

Norah and Ellen seemed amused that I had accused Norah's father of waving to strange young women, and there the matter had to rest. All the same I noticed that, when he thought I wasn't looking at him, Mr Heskethson stared at me oddly from time to time.

The next few years were eventful both for us, and for those at Ash Farm. Norah married Ron Hatley, and Ron moved into the farm. Tony wrote a couple of novels and began to make a small name for himself, and I began to sell some of my paintings. Then we had a child; a daughter called Jane. Our marriage was all that we had hoped for, and the cottage ideal. We enjoyed country life enormously, and had a wire-haired terrier wished on us by friends, on which we all doted. Norah's marriage didn't seem to go so well. Her relationship with Ron seemed tempestuous, and at times extremely strained. Old Heskethson hated his son-in-law, and made no bones about it. There were fierce rows which were embarrassing to hear, but which luckily we only did hear when the wind was from the west, and rumours began to spread that Ron was seeing the little red-head, Ellen. People said that he had always been sweet on her, and had only married Norah for her money, and for the farm which would one day be his, through the marriage.

During the whole of this time I was only visited by what I now laughingly called Heskethson's *doppelgänger* twice; once on the day of Norah's wedding, and once on the day our child was christened. Both times were in the garden, and each time our dog, Benjie, saw him too, and his hackles rose.

We grew very fond of the farmer and Norah. Tony quite liked Ron, and they would go out rabbit shooting from time to time but, like his father-in-law, I simply didn't trust him. Old Heskethson had the added disappointment that there were no children. He wanted grandchildren badly.

One day Ron took Norah by surprise by saying he had business to attend to in Scotland. An aunt of whom Norah had never heard was dying, Ron said, and she had always been good to him, and had promised to leave him something in her will. In spite of the fact that Heskethson was now his father-in-law he hadn't made Ron a partner in the farm, and Ron said he would like to achieve some financial freedom if possible. Norah offered to go with him, but Ron wouldn't hear of it, and then it was found out that Ellen would be away from home at the same time. 'Going to Cornwall for a holiday,' she explained. The gossips made a good deal of it, and Norah became increasingly unhappy, though she never discussed her troubles with us. She did however visit us a good deal while her husband was away, and since she was a great help with Jane, I was delighted to see her.

She talked to us a bit about her childhood, and of going to the village school with Ron, and she told us a good deal about her mother, whom she had adored, and who had died when she was seven. 'Uncle Jack and Dad brought me up together,' she said. 'Uncle Jack was Dad's identical twin, but though they looked as alike as two peas, two men were never more unlike in nature. You know Dad. Well, Uncle Jack was a proper old woman, and a miser too. I suppose that's why he never married.'

'Did he live at the farm with you?' I asked.

'No. He lived here. He was the eldest, but he didn't like farming much, so he turned the farm over to Dad when my grandparents died. He made all this garden into a vegetable garden, never bought any new clothes, and took all his meals with us and, except for Dad and me, he didn't bother about anyone. But he was marvellous to me, and I adored him, I was heartbroken when he died.'

'Didn't he leave the cottage to you when he went?' I asked. 'If it had been mine like that, I couldn't ever have parted with it.'

'He didn't leave a will. It was very odd, so we just went on living at the farm with no bother from anyone. We sold the cottage and divided the proceeds between a few relations, and everyone seemed satisfied.'

Ron was away for two weeks, and he sent Norah a couple of postcards from Perth. He also telephoned her twice, sounding very affectionate. When he returned, though, the quarrels at the farm intensified, and it was obvious that things were going from bad to worse. Then the old man fell ill. He had some sort of gastric trouble, and he looked terrible. Ron took charge of the farm, and his arrogance with the other farm hands created difficulties. I used to go over there to sit by the old man's bed on the bad days, but Ron didn't like it, because by this time he didn't like me. He seemed to be trying to make it up with his father-in-law though. He waited on him hand and foot, and when the old boy was really weak, he even fed him, himself. Norah was grateful and touched, but Heskethson was obviously wary and suspicious. He remained ill all that winter, though sometimes he seemed to improve for a few days and, when he did, he insisted on getting up to have a look at how things were going on the farm.

The winter was one of the coldest on record. The snow lasted for several weeks. There were blizzards and black ice. The pond on the Common froze over, and small birds died by the hundreds.

It was during this winter that I had a series of quite horrible dreams. Heskethson (or was it perhaps Uncle Jack?) figured in all of them. Sometimes he gibbered at me from the foot of my bed. Once he attacked me furiously, clawing at my face, and once he attempted to throttle me. I woke up each time, sweating and trembling. Twice, too, when I was awake the *doppelgänger* returned. Each time he came straight through the outside wall of the bedroom in the middle of the night, moving slowly from right to left, shaking his head sorrowfully, and then just before he passed through the second wall, beckoning to me. Each time the temperature of the room seemed to drop so low that my teeth chattered with cold as well as fright. Neither time did Tony wake, but each time Benjie growled softly in his basket.

I told Tony, and he didn't like it, though he pretended to make light of it, saying that, because my own father had died when I was very young, I had got a father fixation for the farmer. Then I found I was pregnant again, and we both hoped that perhaps it was the pregnancy that was affecting me in this extraordinary manner, though it didn't exactly explain Benjie's behaviour.

Spring came, and the old man's health improved. The weather was mild, the farm was thriving in spite of Ron's lack of common sense, and Norah seemed happier. I became enormous, and presently Charlie was born. Old Mr Heskethson suddenly sickened again, and at the end of August he went into a coma. He died on the first of September. Norah's grief was dreadful to see, but Ron didn't attempt to hide his delight. He had now inherited the farm. For Norah's sake the other hands had agreed to stay on, but it was clear that they had even less time for Ron than they'd had before, and the rest of the people round the Common really disliked him. Ron didn't care. He'd got what he wanted. He bought a new sports car, put a telephone in the farm and, like several of us, he changed from oil lamps to electricity. 'Hauling the old place into the twentieth century,' he said, gleefully.

The terms of the will, which was found in the back of the top lefthand drawer, in the chest of drawers in Heskethson's bedroom, had shocked us all. The old man had left the whole place, lock stock and barrel to Ron, and only a yearly allowance to his daughter. It seemed utterly out of character.

Ron openly showed his feelings for Ellen now. They could be seen together at all times, roaring round the countryside in his little sports car, or wandering round the farm, arm in arm. They treated Norah as the paid housekeeper; she did all the cooking and domestic work, and if it hadn't been for Ron's fear of losing all the help on the farm, both Tony and I believed that Ellen would have moved into the house.

Obviously the situation couldn't last like this, and it didn't. Norah said she wanted a divorce.

She came to tell me about it one morning, when I was sitting on the lawn reading, with the baby asleep in his carrycot, and Jane playing at my side. Tony was out with Benjie. The leaves on the old apple tree were turning yellow and orange, but they hadn't yet begun to fall.

Norah was very calm now that she had made her decision. 'I've known all along that he was sweet on Ellen,' she said. 'Right from when we were all children together he was mad for her, but I loved him so much that I thought I might change him. More fool me, so it's all my fault, really. I suppose I tried to buy him, and it didn't work.'

'Where will you live?' I asked anxiously, then I added, 'I simply don't understand your father leaving the farm to Ron! He wasn't a fool.'

At that moment I saw him, Heskethson or his brother. He

was standing in his usual place, under the tree, right beside Norah. 'Look, Norah!' I said excitedly. 'Look beside you!' I pointed a shaking finger at the old man.

Norah turned round to where I was pointing. 'What at?' she asked in amazement.

'Can't you see him?'

'Who?'

'He's right beside you.'

'Who is?'

'Can't you see anyone at all?'

'Where?'

Heskethson vanished. 'It's too late,' I said stupidly.

'For what?' asked Norah, bewildered.

'Never mind. Go on with what you were saying.'

'Are you all right?' Norah sounded worried. 'You can't have got sunstroke at this time of the year. What's the matter?'

'Nothing,' I said. 'Nothing at all. I simply thought I saw a strange old man just beside you. He seemed a bit sinister and it gave me a shock.'

'Me too!' laughed Norah.

'I think I was asking you where you'd live,' I said, firmly changing the subject. 'You haven't got too much money, have you?'

'Practically none. He'll have to support me, but I can always get a job somehow,' answered Norah. 'Besides, anything is better than staying on here under these circumstances.'

'I wish we had room for you in the cottage,' I said, 'but we haven't.'

'And a good thing too,' said Norah briskly. 'It wouldn't work, and I've got to learn to stand on my own feet.'

Once again I began having bad nightmares about old Heskethson or whoever it was, and on the day Norah came to tell me that she was actually going to leave the farm the following Friday, I felt cold and ill all day. In fact I looked so wretched that Tony persisted in calling in a doctor, who found nothing wrong with me, but suggested two aspirins and a couple of days in bed, if I was sickening for a cold, and a tonic if I wasn't.

That night, warned by a growl from Benjie, I saw the Heskethson *doppelgänger* for the last time, and I have never been more frightened in my life. He came through the bedroom wall, from the right as usual, and as usual the temperature dropped with his arrival, but this time he seemed as angry with me in spirit as he had been in those hideous nightmares. He kept on pointing at me, and gibbering. His eyes seemed to be starting out of his head, and when he wasn't waving his arms about, or beckoning me to follow, he was wringing his hands. He began to cry and swayed from side to side, then he wrung his hands again. Suddenly he pointed at me and slammed his fist into his hand in exasperation. I sat up in bed, shivering and staring at him. The hairs were standing up on my scalp. I knew he was trying to tell me something, but what it was, I was too scared to understand. Tony was sleeping soundly, and although I tried to call to him, I found I couldn't utter a word. I couldn't even open my mouth. Then Heskethson shook his fist at me, suddenly spat in my direction, and slowly glided through the wall on the left.

I couldn't sleep for the rest of the night, and the following day I had a fever and had to remain in bed. I lost consciousness from time to time, and more than once became delirious, but by nightfall the fever left me and I suddenly felt completely at peace. Tony was half out of his mind with worry, and even suggested that we should leave the cottage if it was going to have this effect on me, but I told him that I was sure the ghost of Heskethson had gone for good now.

'You call it a ghost,' said Tony. 'Ghosts don't walk when the person is still alive, as old Heskethson's did, you say.'

I hadn't told Tony about Uncle Jack, and my theory that the ghost could be either of them. 'Well, he's gone now,' I said equably.

'How do you know?'

'I just feel it,' I said, and with that Tony had to be satisfied. He left it for the time being, but when I was out with the children in the morning, he rang Mr Thomas, the previous owner, and asked him if he had ever seen anything odd in the cottage or grounds. Reluctantly Mr Thomas said he had sometimes seen an old man lurking about in the garden, and then even more reluctantly he confessed that he had sold the cottage because the old man had begun to trouble him too much. 'The first time I ever saw anything was when Norah got engaged to young Hatley,' he said. 'From then on he almost pestered me.'

'Did he look like Mr Heskethson?' asked Tony.

'Yes, and it worried me, because he was alive and living just over the hedge from me, and I couldn't understand it.'

The end of it all came very quickly. I heard about it from Norah later.

Two nights after Heskethson had appeared in our bedroom, Norah was lying asleep in the little single bedroom she now occupied at the farm. The windows were open, and the curtains drawn back so that a brilliant shaft of moonlight illuminated the room. She had cried herself to sleep, to the accompaniment of the unmistakable sounds of love-making going on in what was once her marriage bed, next door. Suddenly her father (or was it her Uncle? It was hard to be sure in this light) walked in through her window. He came over to her, in her dream, and told her loudly and very clearly not to worry. 'You won't have to leave the farm,' he said, 'and when it's done, you'll find it.'

'Find what?' she asked.

'Don't worry,' repeated the visitor. 'I'm taking care of it.' And before she had time to reply, he faded away.

When she awoke in the morning, she felt happy. She couldn't understand it. Nothing in her situation had changed, but she felt on top of the world. It was Monday, and she was due to leave the farm on Friday. She ought to be sorting and packing her things, but she didn't feel like it. Her father (?) had told her in her dream not to worry, so she wouldn't. She'd believe in miracles. She'd believe that at the last moment something would stop her from having to leave the house where she had spent nearly all her life, something her visitor must have meant, that would bring Ron back to her, and send Ellen, her lifelong friend, away from their lives for ever. What would it be? How could such a thing come about? She went round the farm filled with a kind of euphoric anticipation.

Nothing happened on Monday or on Tuesday or on Wednesday. By Thursday the euphoria was fading, and she hastily began to do the sorting and packing that she should have done all week. Tony was going to drive her to her new house the next day after lunch, and help to get her settled in. She hadn't said goodbye to her friends on the Common, and had made no arrangements for stores at the new house. She worked quickly and anxiously.

Ron told her that he and Ellen would be out that night as they felt that she would prefer to be in the place alone. This depressed her inordinately. She had so desperately wanted to spend the last evening in her old home with Ron, but he said that he and Ellen had arranged to go to a dance that very evening, long ago, and they wouldn't be back until all hours. 'Sorry and all that, Norah,' he said cheerfully. 'Too bad things have turned out this way for you, but what will be, will be.'

At seven o'clock he and Ellen left her; Ellen looking her loveliest in a low cut figure-hugging white dress. Ron looked handsome in a dark blue suit.

Norah cooked herself a lonely meal, then went through to the sitting room to have a last look round. She noticed that the desk was slightly away from the wall, and tried to push it back, but it was too heavy for her. She wandered through all the rooms, to give them a silent goodbye, feeling desolate and a little ridiculous, then went back to the kitchen, washed up, took off her apron, and slowly went up the stairs to sleep in her bed for the last time at the farm. She fell on her knees and prayed for a few moments, which was something she hadn't done for years, after which, feeling strangely tranquil she got into bed, and almost at once, fell asleep.

She woke with a start, horribly scared, and sat up in bed. It was still dark, and the luminous hands of her clock stood at four o'clock. It was bitterly cold and she shivered. There was a man in her room. She nearly screamed aloud, but he put a finger to his lips, and she saw with anxiety that it was one of the twins. 'Dad?' she enquired, tentatively.

He shook his head at her, and stared intently out of the window. He seemed to be waiting for something.

For what?

It seemed hours that the two of them waited together in

silence, but when she glanced at her clock again, she saw that it was ten minutes past four. Suddenly the visitor tensed, and she heard it too.

The road from Enderby Village, which ran past Four Ash Cottage and the farm before it reached the Common, was dead straight. You could hear the cars coming along it from nearly a mile away. One was coming now, and instinctively she knew it was Ron's before she heard the special sound the sports car made. What was going to happen? The visitor had told her not to worry in her dream, now here was this ghost clearly waiting for the sound of this particular car. It must be Ron. No doubt of it.

Had he and Ellen quarrelled at the dance? Was everything going to be all right after all?

The ghost turned to her, gave a ghastly smile and walked out of the window. She jumped out of bed to follow its progress. It seemed to be walking down the side of the house as though it were walking down a stairway. It went briskly across the lawn towards the entrance to the garage, through the garage gates, and out into the middle of the road, where it stood stock still. How she could see it so clearly on such a dark night, she was never afterwards able to explain.

The car came nearer and nearer. The ghost didn't move, and then just as the car was almost on it, it turned into a sheet of white light. With a scream of brakes Ron swerved to avoid it, and ran into the iron gate post. The car burst into flames, but Ron and Ellen were already dead.

The sequel to these events came about two years later.

We decided to enlarge the cottage – both of us were by now quite successful in our careers – and to enlarge the cottage we had to pull down the kitchen wall, with its old ranges and bake-ovens. In the lefthand bake-oven we found a will made by Uncle Jack, leaving the farm and all its contents to Norah. A letter explaining what he had done was found in a secret drawer that Norah had never bothered to look into, in the very desk which she had found standing away from the wall in the farm sitting-room on the night she had been proposing to leave her home for good.

Experts found that the will that Ron had 'found' in Hesketh-son's bedroom had been a forgery.

Norah still lives at the farm. She has married again; this time happily.

Giles Gordon

The necessary authority

Hal Marcus took one last look at himself in the mirror which covered almost an entire wall of his dressing-room, then squinted his eyes to look at the photograph of himself in make-up and costume pushed into the frame of the mirror. If he ever lost his voice, or it declined substantially in quality or character, he could surely eke out a living as a make-up man or dresser. He would leave the opera house in a few moments and once beyond the stage door and the surrounding streets no one would recognize him as Mephistopheles.

He found it easy to tolerate anonymity in the street, in the outside world, only because he dominated in the house – both the stage, the other singers and the audience. Oh yes, he'd been booed at bit at the end of every performance of this new production, and admittedly the press notices hadn't been ecstatic about either his voice or his acting but, well, audiences and critics were surprisingly unsophisticated about these matters. He knew they were booing the devil not him, Mephistopheles not Marcus, the role not the singer. It showed how convincing his performance had been. Besides, he was American, and the British seemed to have a prejudice against singers from his country.

He stood up from the chair in front of the make-up table, with the mirror behind it, the dozens of pots and tubes and sticks of grease paint and gauze and hair and cotton wool on it, and walked the five or six paces to the door of the tiny dressing-room. He wasn't sure whether it was number one, two or three: his name was on the door, and Charles Hammond and Hilary Fenn, the British singers who were Faust and Marguerite, had their names on the other dressing-room doors on the same landing. He unlocked the door, opened it, looked at his watch, clicked off the light, went out of the room, shut the door and locked it. He walked along the corridor, away from the other two dressing-rooms, then proceeded down three flights of metal stairs.

He made his way towards the stage door, smiling a little at

the people standing around just inside the door – stage hands, he supposed them to be, or members of the orchestra, or of the chorus, or friends or fans of singers waiting to meet them. He acknowledged their collective presence sufficiently that they wouldn't take offence at having been ignored, but no more than so: he didn't want to become engaged in conversation. Above all, he didn't want anyone commiserating with him about the booing, for he wasn't – really he wasn't – remotely put out. Let any of those standing about or who had been in the audience try singing and playing the role. Merely because they had bought their tickets they thought they could call the tune. It wasn't even as if they paid the proper price for the seats, hugely subsidized as they were.

Hal Marcus nodded to Ed, the stage door man, who leant out of his glass-fronted box, and Marcus moved his lips up and down without saying anything, as if to wish him goodnight.

'Goodnight, sir,' the door man responded.

'Who's he?' someone asked when the singer had passed.

'Mephistopheles,' said Ed.

'You'd never guess to look at him,' said Big Ron, a dwarf of a man, renowned throughout the stage hands' world for his strength, and the care with which he handled delicate pieces of scenery.

'He's American,' said Ed. 'They're usually all over you with chat, but not him. Keeps to himself.'

Just ahead, as he almost reached the door and felt the night air pushing in towards him, Hal noticed Charles Hammond, his Faust, greeting a woman. They were not more than ten feet in front of him. She had been standing there, obviously waiting for Hammond, and she smiled as he moved towards her, as quickly as he could given the number of people packed together in the confined space. Hal despised Charles Hammond. The man had made nothing of the part – the opera was named after his role in it, too – and the audience at the end of each performance acclaimed him uproariously. His voice was adequate but he put no feeling or characterization into the part, he had no panache. At curtain call he bowed and scraped and the ingratiating smile was off his face the second the audience was hidden from view. What sort of girl would he be meeting? Hal wondered, without particular interest, and looked from Hammond to her.

The older you become, the less likely it is that anything will move or disturb you. You are largely immune to new experience because you have experienced everything before, emotionally at least. Thus you are unprepared for a sensation which you haven't know for decades, a feeling of such intensity that you can only vaguely recall its equivalent in your distant youth.

Hal Marcus was in his early fifties, and his life was settled. He knew what he could do and his limitations. No overweening ambition any more. He could afford to adopt this stance because he knew he accomplished successfully whatever he undertook: was he not singing Mephistopheles in one of the world's foremost opera houses?

His wife had died five or six years before. The coroner had recorded a verdict of suicide while of unsound mind but how could he have known what Anna was like? He'd encountered her only as a corpse. She'd been happy enough with her lot, though she might have been more fulfilled had they been able to have children. Admittedly she had been examined by the doctor twice, and he had found nothing wrong with her. Hal had refused to see the doctor, not because he thought there was anything wrong with him – he didn't – but in case the doctor had discovered something.

Increasingly he had been away from Boston a great deal of the time, to Vienna, Paris, Munich, or elsewhere in the States. Anna had, during the early years of their marriage, accompanied him to what they had both regarded as exotic cities. But having to spend long evening after long evening in second-rate hotel rooms waiting for him to return after the performance soon lost its excitement, and in the last ten years of her life she and Hal had spent far fewer nights together than apart. Whether Anna had had a life away from him, he didn't know. He would have been surprised but not shocked. For her sake, he hoped that she had, but he doubted it.

For years, long before she died but after their relationship had gone sour, he hadn't devoted more than the minimum of attention to women. He spent much of his life rehearsing with them, singing with them, touching and embracing them on stage. But he'd preferred, as far as his private peace of mind was concerned, not to strike up particular friendships with them, let alone anything that might have been regarded as more intimate. He preferred to depend on himself, to rely on no one else.

But this woman meeting Hammond: undoubtedly she had upset his equilibrium. Which was ludicrous, as he'd only glimpsed her for a second. To describe her face is not the point. It was the face that Hal would have spent his life searching the world for had his imagination ever dared conjure such perfection.

He had stopped, he realized, inside the stage door, riveted to the spot, surrounded by a crush of people. His legs, hands, his whole body was shaking. 'Excuse me, mate,' someone said, and squeezed past him. He was glad there were so many people as it was unlikely that anyone would notice the state he was in. His eyes were glazed as he focused on his memory of the face. He shook his head suddenly, as if to return himself to the present, and pushed his way past eight or ten people, back towards the door man in his box.

'Do you know who that lady was with Mr Hammond? I thought she looked ... familiar. Someone I once knew.'

'What, the lady waiting for him? Comes every night he's singing. That's Mrs Hammond. Lovely lady. Always waits for him down there, never goes up to his dressing-room.'

'His wife?'

'Yes, that's right. They haven't been married very long but that's who she is. They've got a sweet baby too. She once brought him here. None of the snob about her. Or him.'

Hammond's wife, thought Hal. He heard little of what the door man said after that. The situation was appalling, he thought, his mind and emotions as uncoordinated as his physical movements. He was a maelstrom of indecision.

He remembered the door man, who was staring at him.

'Oh, thank you,' he muttered.

'Any time, sir. Any time,' said Ed.

Unseeing, groping his way by instinct, Hal went out of the stage door and stood on the pavement. Again he shook his head suddenly, as if to bring it to its senses, determined to regain control of himself. He peered to the right, and then to the left. There were groups of people talking and laughing, raising their feet in the cold, then banging them down on the street again, trying to keep warm. It was after 11.00, and the performance had ended forty minutes ago.

He couldn't immediately see Hammond or his wife. Which way had they gone? Without thinking (not that thought would have assisted him) he stumbled to the left, dazed and excited, through Covent Garden, looking for the couple. They might have gone for a bus, or a tube, or most likely in search of a taxi. Maybe they had their own car parked nearby. He didn't know where they lived but presumably within reasonable access of London, if not in the city itself. He stopped in King Street, wondering if he should have gone down Henrietta Street. But what difference would it make, what would he do or say if he did run into them? He hadn't thought about that. He was utterly confused. Yet he had to find her, whether with or without her husband. The line 'Sweet Helen, make me immortal with a kiss!' slid into his head, uninvited, uncalled for, unsummoned. And it began to have the force of a command, to dominate his thought processes, his free will. It was as if he was being compelled by external forces, as if to kiss her – whether or not he desired to do so – was necessary for his survival.

A clock struck. He looked at his watch. Midnight. Probably Big Ben, he thought, knowing it wasn't that far away and for all he knew the wind might have been blowing in his direction. He knew that he should be back in his hotel room. He was hungry, his throat was parched, he'd been wandering about – he realized – searching for Hammond and his wife for nearly an hour, passing the same drunks, beggars and even policemen without registering the fact. For the first time since he had left the theatre he was aware of how cold it was. His coat and scarf seemed not remotely adequate protection against the windy November night.

Confused between wanting to return to his hotel, and find the beauty, he again understood that not only would he not know what to say to Hammond's wife should they encounter each other but that with her husband there he wouldn't be able to speak to her at all. At least, not in the way he would want to; and any other way would, in the circumstances, be ... meaningless, irrelevant. Hammond, no doubt, would have introduced them, and pleasantries would have been exchanged. All of which would have made it difficult for him to meet her on her own at a later date. And that he should do so had become essential, the point of his existence, his very being.

He walked through King Street, into Garrick Street, out into the bright lights and traffic of St Martin's Lane. He waved his arm at a taxi, and at another, and at another. The third empty one he hailed stopped and swallowed him up to disgorge him outside his South Kensington hotel.

Faust was being sung again three nights later. When Hal arrived at the theatre he asked the stage door man to give Mrs Hammond, if he would be so kind, a note as soon as she arrived to meet her husband at the conclusion of the performance. Ed said that he would and took the note in its envelope, at the same time making a gesture of the forelock-touching type. Hal slipped him a fiver, and asked him not to reveal to anyone (the implication being least of all to her husband) that Mrs Hammond had gone up to his dressing-room, because – Hal confided – that was what she would surely decide to do when she had read the note. He also asked Ed not to allow anyone else up tonight (not that he had had any visitors except after the first performance) and Ed said that he completely understood, you leave it to me, Mr Marcus, thank you, sir.

At the end of the performance that evening Mephistopheles was booed even more than on previous occasions. Hal smiled at the audience from behind his greasepaint and bowed low, as if acknowledging a greater ovation than he'd ever received. When he blew a kiss to the gods booing and hissing redoubled in strength, although there was some laughter in the auditorium as well. When the audience's response to the opera and its performance had died away and the curtain was still, Marcus hurried up to his dressing-room, relieved to encounter neither Hammond nor Hilary Fenn on the way, and unlocked his door. Inside, he looked around. The flowers were as he had arranged them beforehand, and the box of jewellery was where it should be at the back of the table. She wouldn't know whether the jewels were real or not.

Only then did he allow himself to look in the mirror. How very evil he looked, no wonder they booed so heartily, he thought. He was pleased with his appearance and grateful that he perspired as little as he did. He was nervous just a little. He should, he thought wryly, be relaxing after his performance but how could he, with the most crucial performance of his career about to commence?

He glanced at his watch. She would arrive any minute. He couldn't keep still. He checked that the champagne was still on ice – that the ice hadn't melted – and that the glasses were ready and polished, though he'd seen to all this in the last interval and no one had been in the dressing-room since. He placed the ice bucket and the glasses on the make-up table. He made sure that the room was as tidy as it could be: no dirty clothes to be seen. At last, breathing heavily, he sat down in front of the mirror. He adjusted his position so that when she knocked on the door he would be able to see the door without moving, although she would be on the outside.

He thrust out his left hand and pulled open the drawer in the table. He moved copies of Marlowe's play and of Goethe's poem, and the score of Gounod's opera, and withdrew from beneath them the copy of the letter he'd drafted so many times. *'Dear Mrs Hammond,'* he read. *'It is so long since we have met. I was surprised to see you at the stage door on Wednesday evening. I won't make you late for meeting your husband but if you would do me the honour of visiting me in my dressing-room immediately after the performance tonight I'd be honoured. Mine is the first door on the same floor as your husband's.'* He'd signed the letter with his own name. He was pleased with that act of defiance though at first he'd not wanted to use his name but realized there was no alternative if she wasn't to be made suspicious. As it was, she could obviously go past his door and Miss Fenn's and see her husband first but Hal believed she would not. He was confident in that belief.

He sat for two or three minutes looking at the letter, but not seeing the words any more. Had he made a mistake? Had he been affected by something other than her face? Had it been a trick of the light in the dark of the stage door? He was insane, at his age and his life being what it was, to tempt fate in this way. The likelihood of the woman being prepared to have anything to do with him was, to say the least, improbable.

There was a small knock on the door, and he pushed the letter into the drawer, closed it quickly. He stood up, strode across the room, opened the door. She stood there. He thought he'd never breathe again. He held his breath, couldn't, couldn't release it. Paralysed. He couldn't even invite her in, so overcome was he.

'Mr Marcus?' She thought it preposterous that he should still be wearing his make-up and costume.

He'd been handed a cue. He would speak:

'Mrs Hammond? Come in.'

'I ... got your note. But I don't recall ...'

It would be terrible if Hammond heard her and opened his door, saw her standing there, talking to him.

'Please,' he said, standing aside to allow her to enter. 'Do come in.'

'Well, just for a minute. My husband ...'

'Yes, of course. Just for ... a few moments.' She entered the room. 'Do ... sit down.'

She half turned and smiled at him: 'Thank you.'

It was all much more formal, more straightforward, than he'd expected it to be. As she sat in the armchair, he closed the door, turned the key in the lock. He looked at her back view. She gave no indication of having heard. He looked at her in the mirror, as if to look directly at her face again would turn him to stone. She was gorgeous, utterly, unfairly beautiful. He felt, standing there in his costume, that he wouldn't be able to converse with her, that he wished he could disappear through one of his own trapdoors. How could he explain what he felt, declare his love at first meeting? Which was what he planned to do, albeit in a somewhat bizarre way.

'May I take your coat?' he said, playing for time; but aware that he was wasting what little he had with her.

She shook her head. 'Thank you. I'll keep it on. My husband ...'

He murmured understanding, and with his big, useless hands

gestured that he accepted her decision. Then he withdrew the ice cold champagne from the bucket.

'What is this?' she asked, in surprise and, perhaps, with a flicker of amusement.

'Moet and Chandon,' he replied, and poured two glasses, replaced the bottle in the ice bucket, and handed a glass to her. She accepted, silently, but didn't raise the glass to her lips until he raised his.

'Your ... health,' he said, and they drank. He was irritated with himself. This wasn't how he had intended it to happen. By this stage he should have declared himself to her, and the champagne been drunk in celebration. Time was slipping away, everything was slipping from his grasp.

She looked up at him, in the mirror. He seemed sunk in his own thoughts. She was now a little frightened which, she realized, was foolish. Charles had hardly mentioned Hal Marcus to her, except to say how sorry for him the other singers were because of the booing. It was, of course, unfair that he'd been cast in a role which he wasn't equipped to bring off. It wasn't even, she realized in the dressing-room, as if he was in his youth, with a voice of potential. Still, he didn't seem put out by his reception. Above all, though, he looked ludicrous dressed up in that costume and wearing make-up. She had been to the first performance and he had looked quite different on stage. The lighting and atmosphere had rendered him extremely sinister. But here he might at least have put on a dressing gown, and washed his face.

In her other hand, the one without the glass, she held his note to her, and the envelope.

'Please could you let me have that letter back?' he said suddenly. She looked surprised, but he had taken it from her before she could respond. Did he want to write something on the paper? He placed it in one of the pockets or recesses of his costume. Very odd, she thought; but she could hardly ask why he wanted it. He had written it to her, therefore he should have let her keep it.

He was becoming increasingly agitated, more annoyed with himself every moment. He hadn't thought about the note beforehand. What if she hadn't been holding it, or if he hadn't noticed? She might have left with it, anybody might have read it, especially her husband. Did she realize how nervous and distraught he was, or – as he hoped – did his make-up and costume disguise the truth?

'You say we've met before?' she said, as once more he had plunged into silence.

'Yes,' he said, 'but I hadn't realized you were married to Charlie Hammond.'

Charlie indeed, she thought. No one called him anything but Charles.

'Where was it we met? I'm sorry I . . .'

'An extraordinary coincidence.' He was smiling, then the smile evaporated and he looked almost bashful. 'Forgive me, I've forgotten your first name. Seeing you in these different surroundings.'

'Helen, but—'

'Helen! What a fool I am. Of course.'

He was really excited, agitated. She stood up, and as she did so champagne lurched from the glass, towards him. A small quantity landed on his shoe and his tights just above the left ankle. He withdrew his foot instantly, as if in extreme pain, as if he'd had a nail hammered through it. He winced and looked angry out of all proportion to the triviality of the incident.

'I'm terribly sorry,' said Helen.

He regained his composure, such as it was.

'Don't worry, dear lady. Don't worry about anything.'

'I'm sorry, but I must be going. My husband . . .'

Hal look at his watch. 'No, he'll be another ten minutes. I think I owe you an explanation.'

'I wish you would explain,' she said, more sceptical now than fascinated. The man was absurd, reacting like that to a little champagne accidentally slopped on to his foot.

'Please.' He gestured with his glass to the seat she had just vacated. She sat down. 'Your husband is Faust, I am Mephistopheles.' He paused, as if wanting confirmation.

'In the opera, yes,' she said, sensing he required her to respond thus before he could continue.

'Good,' he said calmly, obviously pleased with her reaction.

'I,' he pointed at himself, stabbing his finger five or six times at his chest, 'make it possible for him to love Marguerite.'

He's mad, Helen thought. Quite crazy.

'In his opera, yes,' she said slowly, emphasizing the qualification more than she had the previous time.

'His life,' Hal continued, 'was worth nothing to him without his love for Marguerite. Indeed, madam, had I not brought them together Faust would have poisoned himself.'

Madder and madder, thought Helen. She had to get away from the room.

He placed his glass on the table. He stood close to her, towered over her. His voice had an hysterical edge to it.

'My life ...' he paused before his climax, 'has no meaning any longer away from you. Sweet Helen, make me immortal with a kiss!'

Somehow she arose from the chair, deflected him from her without actually pushing him, took two steps towards the door.

'You're wasting your time. It's locked. I have the key. Look.' He withdrew it from a pocket, held it up. 'If you call out I'll muffle you. I will, I really will. I've nothing to lose, have I?'

Calm yourself, Helen, keep calm. Take control of the situation. He's insane, you're rational.

'Mr Marcus. You cannot keep me in this room against my will. There are dozens of people in the building near us, my husband a few feet away. What happens when we leave here? Let us forget the whole incident, pretend it hasn't happened. Now, will you kindly unlock the door?'

Was she not afraid of him, did he not have her in his power? What was she going on about, about his unlocking the door? Didn't she realize the context in which he held her? He would make certain there was no doubt.

'Helen. You don't understand. I am Mephistopheles.'

'You are an opera singer. Now clean the make-up off your face, change out of your ridiculous costume, and go home. And first please unlock the door and let me meet my husband. He'll be very annoyed if I'm not at the stage door when he's ready.'

Hal Marcus's belief in his own identity crumpled, as if he'd disappeared in a cloud of stage smoke. His face resembled that of a clown, or of an idiot, grotesquely exhausted by life. What was he but a worn out, dull human being, not even – he acknowledged to himself – any good as a singer, worse as an actor? He saw himself in the mirror, this time without intending to do so. He hated the fatuous costume, the absurd make-up, although it had the advantage of disguising his face from his own sight.

Helen no longer felt any fear, only intense sadness for this washed-out man. The strain of singing the huge part of Mephistopheles must have affected him. She wanted to move towards him, try to comfort him, but she knew that she mustn't.

Their eyes met.

'Could I ... ?' he faltered, 'beg one thing of you? Would you not tell you husband about our meeting, or anyone else; at least until after our last performance at the end of next week?'

She said nothing, just looked at him. He seemed to accept that the look acceded to his request.

'These flowers' – he waved his hand in their direction – 'were meant for you; and these' – he moved the jewel box from the back of the table, and held it open in front of her eyes – 'were for you, also.'

She looked into the box. Assuming they were real, and how could she tell at a glance, they must have cost a fortune. The whole business was incredible. What would he have stopped at? Did he have a knife, or a gun?

'They're ... gorgeous,' she said.

He closed the lid, pushed the box at her.

'Please. Take them. They're yours.'

'No. Of course not. I couldn't. But thank you.'

The way she spoke he knew that she wouldn't accept the gift. He placed the box on the table again where, once more, it merged into the world whence it came.

He seemed to have nothing more to say.

'We haven't met before, have we?' she said.

'We ... may have done. As a singer, one meets so many people, all over the world, and you are ... very beautiful.'

She bowed her head, perhaps blushed. His feelings towards her did seem genuine.

Then he thought of something quite different:

'Do you know if your husband has been engaged for *Faust* next season?'

She smiled, assumed a more matter-of-fact tone:

'They wanted him again but he'll be at the Met when it's on here.'

Hal smiled. 'You'll understand why I say I'm glad to hear that. I think they'll want me, and I'd hate to turn it down. You won't be here then?'

'No, I'll be in New York. Charles likes me and our baby to accompany him when he's singing out of England.'

Hal thought of his own past, and understood. A weight of sadness forced itself upon him.

'Really,' Helen said briskly, 'I must go now. I've been here far too long.'

'Yes, of course.' He walked to the door, put the key in the lock. 'You won't tell your husband?'

She smiled, shook her head. There was a lump in her throat, tears welling in her eyes. She suddenly felt compassion for everybody. She despised her sentimentality. Life was messy, impossible, ridiculous.

'No, I won't tell a living soul.'

He unlocked the door, opened it, stood back to permit her to leave.

'May I?' he said quietly, and she knew what he meant.

'Yes,' she whispered, and closed her eyes as dry lips touched her hot cheek. The greasepaint smelt stale.

'Thank you,' he said. 'And . . . forgive me.'

She was gone. He closed the door, locked it, leant the weight of his body against it. He hadn't remembered that he could, off stage, cry. Real salt tears. His body shook with grief and despair as he slid to the floor, sobbing, imprisoned in his preposterous costume.

Two days later there was an accident immediately in front of the opera house. As he was crossing Bow Street to go home after the evening's performance, Ed, the stage door man, was hit by a speeding car, and died before the ambulance could reach the nearest hospital.

Four weeks later Helen was sitting at home in the living-room of their house at Esher, reading the paper. She expected Charles back for lunch at any moment. He'd gone up to London in the morning to see someone about a recording. Her mother, who lived with them and looked after the baby when they were away, was staying with friends for a few days.

Helen chanced to look up, in the direction of the window. Her face seemed to crack apart at what she saw. Her lips flew open as if fire had been plunged into her mouth to devastate the face. Her eyes bulged and surely would have cast themselves from their sockets had they strained any further. She screamed, and screamed, but apart from the child there was no one to hear. Besides, her screams were soundless.

The body hovered there, was suspended outside the window. It moved, as if in flight. The feet were not on the ground, or anywhere near it. It was his face, the same make-up and costume. Mephistopheles, that singer. What was it? How could it do what it was doing? She pushed herself with all her strength against the back of the chair, trying to escape from the sight at the window, from what was there, from – she remembered his name – Hal Marcus. She crammed her fist into her mouth, her other hand rubbed her eyes endlessly.

And then he was gone, there was nobody – nothing – there. She rushed to the window. Nobody, nothing. How could there have been? Hal Marcus had returned to America weeks ago.

The baby began to cry, a sudden, weird noise, as if all the feeling in his body was contained and concentrated in the single shriek. She hurried through the house, took the stairs two at a time. It was probably nothing, only a nightmare; but what could a baby know to frighten it to such an extent?

The sight that met her eyes as she entered the bedroom made her pass out at once.

Charles found her unconscious by the cradle ten minutes later.

*

At first Helen was thought to have committed infanticide but her finger prints were nowhere to be found on the child's neck. Undoubtedly the infant had been strangled, but there were no finger prints on the neck at all, and yet the neck was crushed.

Less than two years later, Helen died in a mental hospital, muttering deliriously about Mephistopheles, Faust and Marguerite.

On the day on which the baby died, Hal Marcus at home in Boston received a letter from the Royal Opera House, Covent Garden, regretting that they wouldn't be able to engage him next season to sing Mephistopheles. He was felt to lack the necessary authority.

Alex Hamilton

The loadstar

'Don't make it so obvious, Number One!'

The mate of the *Reina del Golfo* bent over the rail appraising the new passengers as they came aboard, straightened up and lurched backwards as guiltily as if he had been caught at a keyhole.

The captain guffawed, and nonchalantly slid into the mate's former vantage spot. He fired his saliva glands appreciatively. 'I've got to admit,' he said.

Others too were stopping work to watch the woman in the cherrypicker slacks walking briskly up the gang plank. From the customs shed to the quay, she had left a trail of erotic sensation quivering in her wake.

'Trouble,' moaned the mate.

'And we'll weather it,' said the captain. 'Don't be such an old woman, Mr Bensusan. Plenty of those about without you adding to their number.'

'Oh, didn't mean we couldn't handle it, sir,' the mate said hastily. 'But forewarned and all that. I'll have a quick word with chef and have him work a few bromides into the jungle juice. Better to damp down the fires before it breaks out into an inferno of lust.'

'Your language, Mr Bensusan! But as to lust, Mr Bensusan, this is a pleasure boat. Kindly remember that. Lust and pleasure have just about the same meaning. Or so I've been told.'

'Who was it told you that, sir? You wouldn't have had that for O-levels, I imagine, sir?'

'Your imagination is in good order, Mr Bensusan. It was not. It was the Swedenese that so informed me, at the time I worked on the Svenska Lloyd.'

The mate fiddled with his cap, and rearranged it several times on the back of his head. He went back to the rail, beside his superior, in time to see the cynosure of all eyes reach the deck. He grunted as she calmly halted, and took in the scene all round her, before proceeding. Then he remarked, 'Pretty short run, that one to Gothenburg, sir?'

'Ferry job, yes, but what's that got to do with anything?'

'Not much time for the, um, lust to take root?'

'Don't you believe it. It roots like lightning. Never saw anything like it for rooting. We had some pretty severe cases on that run.' The captain corkscrewed out over the corner of the bridge to observe the woman – youngish, by the tilt of her bow – move serenely along the deck towards the first-class staterooms, with a double ration of stewards in tow. 'Mind you,' he added judicially, 'that rotgut they drink, stuff the Lapps make from berries, can't remember what they call it—'

'Jalovina?' suggested the ship's doctor.

'Ah, doctor! Hope you found yourself among friends ashore. Can't say I care for Miami. But yes, thank you, that's it, yellow weaner. Great cure for lust. It dropped off 'em when they applied it, like ticks off a dog.'

'If it's a disease,' said the doctor, 'I shouldn't want to prescribe for it.'

'There you are, Mr Bensusan. The doctor don't care. However, you may be right in drawing my attention to danger. I thank you. I won't shirk the responsibility. Perhaps you'd pass the word along to the chief steward to see that the lady is seated at my table?'

He beamed at them both, and left the bridge.

'Old man seems to be feeling his oats,' remarked the doctor. 'Must have clicked in Miami.'

'He'd like you to think so,' replied the mate. 'I don't suppose he's had his leg over since VJ night. I'd say the best he could claim was that some old hooker kissed the gold braid on his arse up in the bayou.'

The doctor laughed. 'What's he done to upset you?'

'Oh, nothing to make an issue of. I just passed a remark to the effect that his bloody siren could be a cause of bother and he started on his perfect host routine. But have you seen her? Even if we ever got many good lookers on this cruise, she'd be noticed. No woman has a right to look like she does. And she knows what we're thinking. It'll be a pony to speak to her, you see.'

'If that were so,' the doctor said drily, 'she would find herself returning it with interest when she needed to speak to me.

But I think you may have her wrong. I haven't seen her but I can guess who you're talking about. If anything, I feel sorry for her.'

The mate eyed the doctor's placid face suspiciously. Then he burst out, 'Bloody hell! I don't believe it! She looks fit as a flea. She'll outlast the Rock of Gibraltar.'

'Oh, good heavens, man, I've no doubt she's robust. But women like her, who get talked about, and written about, can get sick of being hounded. I suppose it won't harm if I tell you her name: Yvonne Trillia.'

'You're sure that's not being indiscreet?' asked the mate with heavy sarcasm. 'Revealing the contents of the passenger list?'

'In your present mood, I'd think it indiscreet to recall what the public prints have said about her.'

'Don't bother,' said the mate morosely. 'You've said enough. As soon as I saw her I knew she'd be trouble.'

The first incident of the cruise that the mate could class as trouble came not, however, from Yvonne Trillia but from a citizen of Dallas, a Mrs Vanderveldt. All who had seen her join the ship swore that she had made the journey in an electronically-controlled limousine sporting no fewer than eight doors, and that each of these had disgorged a minimum of three items of baggage to sustain her during her holiday around the Caribbean. It was accordingly a great surprise to every witness of this spectacle of opulence when she stormed (some said limped, and both were accurate) into the captain's reception, held as Miami sank below the horizon, and declared at the top of her voice that she felt a fool having come on a cruise with only half her wardrobe. The captain said that this half was so far serving her well, that she looked prim in what she was wearing, and that her presence was in every particular an adornment to his party. She said in outraged tones that she brought two crates of shoes for the trip but the baggage handlers, obviously solid bone between the ears, had left one behind on the beach. Her tirade became general until it embraced all those who had recommended the *Reina del Golfo*.

The Captain fielded all this abuse as calmly as an elephant accepting buns. He drew forward a sleek young radio operator, and said that Sparks, a young officer whose expertise with radio signals was matched only by his wizardry with the samba, would immediately relay her views to the shore, so that her shoes, whether they were flown, conveyed by cab or in the last resort, walked there by themselves, would meet her at Tampico or Caracas. Pending this reunion – he put it to her – could she not make a brave show of managing on one crate? No, goddamnit, she screamed, she could not. Every mother-frigging, ass-kicking bit of footwear in it was a *left* boot, shoe, sandal or slipper! She hiked up her gown to her knees and pointed dramatically down. At the sight of her undeniably bare right foot, made all the more piteous by the splendour with which her left foot was shod, a chorus of sighs and exclamations of horror and amazement broke from the circle of guests clustered round them. A few hard hearts among the ship's company could not repress their laughter, until the icy stare of their commander caused them to turn away and busy themselves with replenishing their guests' drinks.

The captain, to win time while he considered Mrs Vanderveldt's brilliant if horny toes, and the dilemma they had placed him in, wondered aloud why she made this unusual division of her gear. She retorted tartly that only a seaman whose clogs were issued by a central agency and never went into a shoeshop could be so dumb. Wasn't it plain that shoes in pairs could be stolen, whereas separate they wouldn't be worth rancid lard? Someone, probably the purser, remarked that from here on after, she would always be caught on the hop. This comment did not, however, offend the captain, but it was made *sotto voce*, and was picked up only by Yvonne Trillia.

She had come early, sheathed in voluptuous folds of white silk ('totally wrong for the tropics but she gets away with it,' said one critic), but after some polite and negative exchanges with her hosts, had settled herself in one corner of the saloon, and sat detached with a glass of bubbly, her positively stencilled chin resting on the back of her hand, and looked so much like a temple vestal that even the third officer, renowned for rushing in where angels feared to tread, dared not approach her.

Now for the first time her unfocussed manner lost its opaque, dreamlike quality. She seemed suddenly to be alert and purposive. She showed that, after all, she could smile. ('Someone should tell her to smile more often, it makes her truly lovely,' said a generous soul from Kentucky.) She announced in a velvet voice that nevertheless carried with great clarity to every ear that either she was tight, or her shoes were. Everyone turned to look at her as, with great deliberation, she unbuckled first one shoe and then the other and cast them, one, two, out through the open porthole into the blue Caribbean.

There was a brief, electrified pause, when no one moved or spoke. Then, with a cry of pure exaltation a matron from Memphis followed her example. In a minute every woman present was struggling with her straps, hopping or crouching or resting her weight on a man, or proffering a leg to him so that he could officiate, and a fusillade of feminine footwear shot out into the sea, for inspection by the hovering gulls. A sense of warmth and gratitude and relief permeated the party. Mrs Vandervelt hesitated but was finally prevailed on, also, to take off her solitary shoe. She decided not to jettison it altogether, though, and placed it in her filigree reticule, reminding the captain that in due course its sister would be looking for it.

The mate, whose watch it was, missed all the fun. When it was reported to him that Yvonne Trillia had saved the occasion and indeed had given it a lift that was unique, and that only the Dallas bitch hadn't liked it, the mate said he didn't like it either. Interfering hussies like Yvonne Trillia, he said, always provoked trouble in the long run. The itinerary of the *Reina del Golfo*, he added, could be described as a long run.

The sky on the first day out was like a newly washed bowl, fresh and glistening, without a smear of cloud, without so much as a chip at the rim. The sea did not move a muscle. The wake of the *Reina del Golfo* was as straight as a Roman road. The officer for Games of Chance and Skill complimented Yvonne Trillia on her shrewdness in picking a high number for the sweepstake held on the day's mileage. 'Oh? Is that shrewd?' she said. 'It was random, I'm afraid. I didn't even think about it. I could just have easily have picked zero. As far as I'm concerned we could be absolutely motionless at the centre of any ocean you care to name.' The OGCS said that in that case it was very sporting of her to buy a ticket. 'No, I'm a rotten sport,' she said. 'But if I didn't buy a ticket, some chivalrous gentleman would buy one for me. You probably have no idea what a burden it is to a girl when men insist on turning her into a gambling mascot.' He hoped, all the same, that she would look in at the casino. Blackjack, chemmy, roulette, all tastes catered for, high stakes and low. He'd be at the slipper himself, he added encouragingly, and would save a seat beside it where she need be nobody's mascot. 'Thank you. That could be very nice,' she said, 'but I tend to win, which is boring for other people. And if I lose, well I can afford to, which is dull for me. On the other hand, I'm not after excitement. You're very sweet, and I don't want to be churlish. I might well be glad of a peaceful evening under your wing.'

The OGCS went away and told the mate that she knew one more than a monkey. 'The question is,' the mate said, 'who's going to be her monkey?'

It seemed, at the start, that there would be no shortage of candidates. When she went to one of the pools in her Speedo costume, and spread out a body which for sheer smoothness and symmetry could not have been bettered on a lathe, the swimmers swam arabesques for her, the divers risked themselves and the springboard, the gymnasts sucked in their stomachs and rippled, and those who could not do anything special splashed water in each other's faces and hoped some of the drops would daringly land on her exquisite skin. But she remained impervious to every exhibition. The lifeguard, himself as disappointed as any, said later, 'It was a miracle we didn't get hernias and slipped discs wholesale. She could've been marble. If the water had started to flow from a pipe in her mouth to fill the pool it would have seemed natural.'

'Likewise the joggers got nowhere,' the doctor smugly told the mate, 'except twice as many as usual round the promenade deck.' Mr Bensusan grinned back sardonically. 'Yeah. But run as far as they like, they can't run away, can they?'

There was a man among the steady drinkers, who wore a deerstalker hat and had no need to change for fancy dress events, who declared he would corral the wench, as a public service. It meant a personal sacrifice, he told his companions, because he would have to leave the bar for a few minutes, but when he came back from safari he'd have her in his gamebag. If they could tie one on her, she would present a different and more humble face to the world on the morrow. Somehow the plan miscarried. She was surprisingly docile in agreeing to a drink, and meek as mineral water in hitching herself up on a bar stool so that the slit in her caftan opened, as her escort put it, 'to a point above the eternal snowline'. And she was furthermore complaisant enough to drink without demur a Jabberwock, an Inca, a sweet Patootie and a Tanglefoot, a One Exciting Night and a New York – she doted on anything, she said, with an orange flavour – and might well have worked her way on through the exotica, had her host not slid ungraciously to the floor, to be carried rigid like a vanquished warrior, his hands clasped to the deerstalker on his chest, to his cabin. Nobody during this session learned much about her, save that she came from London and was on first-name terms with a number of vintners and makers of cognac. Yet in fairness no one could swear that she had been secretive, as the guy with the deerstalker had never stopped talking, mainly about the declining standards of drink to be found on European expresses, and the lady hardly had a chance to open her mouth.

So Yvonne Trillia went in to dinner on the second night – 'black tie, shoes optional' – having done nothing which could justify a charge of being directly provocative. 'She plays a dead bat better than old Trevor Bailey,' said the purser. She had blocked every thing and everybody, including the brash third officer. This man, ex-Navy, who had never lived down the reputation in the service of being 'too keen' when he paid out £180 for his ceremonial sword before being given his commission, had the nerve to suggest that she go with him after dinner to hear a film star descant on his career, by which means he was working his passage to Rio. But if that was too boring, they could always adjourn to discuss her career, and his, and where their meeting point might lie. 'Too boring?' echoed Yvonne Trillia. 'Of course it's boring. That's why I came.' The third officer realized he had been dismissed, without understanding how, and went off scratching his head.

The captain quizzed his underling, and upbraided him for

being too selective on the one hand, and not keen enough on the other. 'Mr Cassidy,' he said, 'we have aboard at least a hundred and twenty unmarried and no-longer-married ladies who would be glad of a particle of your attention. It's bound to cause unrest if the Trilla girl, without stepping out of line, gets one hundred per cent of the interest shown by every man on this ship. We are none of us used to having a beautiful woman with us, but we must learn, *muy pronto*, to take it in our stride. Or there will be a ruckus. I am thinking of putting it to her, tactfully, that she pretend she has been hired by the company to be photographed for the brochures and posters. But her personality suggests that she may not take kindly to the notion. In any case, Mr Cassidy, please from now on motor at top speed in all directions, and spread your well-known charm in all quarters like a balm.'

Resolving to set a good example, he carefully neglected her at dinner until the vichysoise was cleared away. But, as the food as well as the ship took a turn towards Mexico, and the enchiladas were served, he noticed that she sat silent, taking no part in the conversation based on the famous stories reproduced from old newspapers, printed on the backs of the menus.

He asked politely if she was enjoying the trip and if she liked the ship. She looked momentarily startled, as if her mind were far away, then she gave him an enthusiastic response.

'It's ideal!' she said. 'All these lovely quiet corners. And *two* libraries. I think that's smashing!' Her tone was quite childlike.

'Libraries?' He was nonplussed. 'Is that the best we seem to offer?'

'Oh yes, for me. The saunas and the Turkish bath and the beauty parlour and the casino and the lectures on hypnotism and gardening are all moderately banal, and that's nice, but the libraries are just perfect, full of books no one has heard of.' She swivelled and plucked up a book from her bag on the floor. 'And one can be quite alone. They're wonderfully remote from anything.'

'Not for long, though,' he warned. 'Tampico tomorrow. Twelve hours to punt around. First tender goes ashore at eight.'

He was about to enlarge on Tampico, when the OGCS made

a bell of his wineglass and rang for silence with his fork. He declared the Breakfast-to-Dinner Sweepstake won by ticket 283, and held aloft a basket of fruit and a giant teddy bear as prizes. Apart from its size it was a normal cuddly toy, except that a small diamond as a belly button and pearls for eyes gave it a faintly sinister look. The OGCS looked slowly all round, adding that, since no one in Tourist claimed it, the winner must be here. No claimant spoke, however, until the captain noticed that Yvonne Trillia's bookmark bore the magic number.

Prompted to her feet, she looked vaguely about her in a bewildered way. At that moment the doctor guessed that part of the cause of her aloof and mysterious bearing was short-sightedness. And then a hubbub broke out from the third officer's table. A stout middle-aged woman from Michigan leaped, as if she had springs in her buttocks, from her chair to the middle of the table, crashing candles and glasses as she did so. She flung her skirt up, smacked her plump thighs with her hands, and bawled, 'A hundred dollars to every man who makes a meal of *that* before Rio!'

By the time the disturbance was over, and the captain had vowed several times over that Tampico would be the terminal point of the journey for the lady from Michigan, the winner of the fruit and the teddy bear had disappeared to her cabin, saying she had no appetite, and leaving her prizes behind her. The kindly soul from Kentucky, helped by an enigmatic soul from Geneva, volunteered to take them to her, and see that she was all right.

They found Yvonne Trillia in tears. They were aghast at the spectacle of anyone so young and lovely in such distress. She apologized over and over again for being the cause of such a terrible scene. Try as she would to prevent them she said, they happened wherever she went. Their hearts overflowed as her story spilled out, it wasn't her fault, and they called her pretty thing, and poor thing, and washed her face and rang for the steward for brandy, and generally settled in with a drink for themselves too, to have a heart-to-heart and chase the blues away.

And the long and the short of it was, as it finally reached the mate's ears, that she wanted nothing better than to be left in peace. She had reached a crisis in her personal life, and she had come on the cruise away from anything and anybody she knew, to sort it all out. Her elder sister, whenever she had to come to a decision, used to camp out on an island, and Yvonne had thought that a cruise ship was the ultimate form of island. And best of all, it was an island which did not figure on the map. The decision she had to make was in essence quite simple: whether or not to marry this tycoon. But he kept harrying her, being, like everybody else, incapable of behaving like a Christian until she either said yes or brushed him off, only with a zillion times as much energy as other men put in to the hunt. So she had made this deal with him, that he would not pester her while she was on the ship weighing the pros and cons, nor would he send a private eye on board to check on her.

'Nobody wanted to believe me,' said the mate. 'But it's even worse than I thought. On the first night out we get a lunatic version of the Cinderella story, on the second it's Beauty and the Beast. I tell you, there's something weird about that lady, and he must be a pretty weird guy that wants to marry her.'

The pendulum of feeling swung sharply. The devotion of the men seemed to have been drained of all carnal content, and they treated her with the awkward respect they would have shown to a postulant not quite sure whether to take the veil. The women, by contrast, thawed out completely and swarmed all over her. Even women more than twice her age and continents apart sought her advice on maquillage, calorie counts, the side effects of the pill, what to read and the best tactic for fending off gropers in the cinemas. Only the attitude of the children towards her remained unchanged. They watched her curiously from a short distance, and left smutty anonymous notes and drawings where she would find them; while their conduct in general was execrable, what with fights, petty larceny and throwing toffees at the cabaret. Yvonne told her circle of new friends, whose numbers increased on an exponential curve, that she thought marriage and kids could not mix, and the sight of these was an argument against her suitor back home. On the other hand, as he was a man whose desire fed on the desire of other men, it was possible they would never come into the reckoning anyway. The OGCS began making a book on which point in the trip she would take her decision, all ports of call after Rio being odds on.

By the time the ship had lain at anchor for some hours at Tampico, where Yvonne did not go ashore until the forenoon, the mood was very cosy. It was universally known that the pretender had eyes of steely grey, got by on five hours' sleep a night, was always at his desk by six in the morning and was an avionics wizard. He flew himself from one business appointment to another in his own plane, which in Britain was thought eccentric and pushy, but certainly gave him an edge over his competitors. Yvonne found herself waylaid in every corridor and companionway, to be given hints and counsel and gossip which might have a bearing on her problem. She set off for a quick scurry over Mexican soil looking more relaxed and less of a threat than any of them would have thought possible. But one important element of her previous outlook persisted: she was determined to 'punt' around on her own.

So there was no witness of whatever adventure befell her in those few hours in Tampico. Something drastic must have happened, according to the few who saw her return. She was one of the last to do so. It was dark and the ship was making ready to sail to avoid payment of overnight dues. In the launch she huddled in the stern and barely acknowledged the greetings of the others. The third officer, keeping tally on the shore party returning, reported, 'She looked pretty ropey, and I wouldn't say on account of bashing the tequila, like some. She said "Goodnight" but she was looking straight through me, like it might have been "and sleep forever, you bastard". You know that look she has when her eyes could have been taped open. My guess is she wandered off the high street up some back alley, they're all the same these independent cows, can't tell 'em anything for their own good. And while she was dreaming it was the aisle and she was in white and all the washing was bunting, some shafter of a Mex popped up from behind a pair of socks and slipped her ring on his finger.'

'What a lurid imagination you have, Mr Cassidy,' said the captain. 'And may I remind you when you speak to your captain that you are not in the Navy now. Has Miss Trillia complained of any violation, or referred to an assault, of whatever variety?'

'No sir. But I'd swear something put the frighteners on her.'

'Ah well, let's hope it was no worse. And if she had a scare thrown into her, perhaps in Caracas she won't stray from the main plaza.'

This expectation was not realized. He was disappointed to see, on the arrival at Venezuela, that she had become more of a loner than ever. It was all the more poignant after the brief glimpse of enchantment – not too strong a word, he thought – they had had when the barriers came down. She was always by herself now, moping in the bows, roaming the library shelves, abstracted in the Quiet Room. 'It's like mental hibernation,' said the doctor.

She was very tense on the night before the *Reina del Golfo* put in at Caracas. People steeled themselves for another drama, like the one at Tampico. The kind person from Kentucky fervently hoped there might be one. 'I'm confident Yvonne is a truly vibrant human being,' she said. 'She'll come back to us.'

She did not 'come back' that evening. She was patiently brittle, but she did not break. People who diffidently suggested she might like to make up a party in Caracas were turned down with that strange finality which she seemed to have borrowed from British institutional life, and mastered as a personal technique.

In Caracas, it was said, she met a man. Descriptions of him varied, because the car had shades and dark glass. Some said that he was there, outside the dock gate, by assignation. Others were sure that he was a prowler, and that he had hardly halted at the kerb side before she skipped in through the door he held open. 'Oil,' said the mate. 'But to me that's good news. So long as she behaves herself afloat, she can make what trouble she likes ashore. That's what God made South America for.'

She rejoined the ship, just in time, looking utterly exhausted. Her steward said she was literally staggering the last few yards to her cabin. Next day, in the aftermath, she was still deflated.

The doctor came on her with her head in her hands at a kidney desk in the Writing Room. There was a litter of unmarked postcards of Caracas around her. 'A bit down?' asked the doctor. 'Would you like me to fix you up with a tonic?' She turned her head and flashed on a vivid smile. 'Oh, Lord, yes, doc,' she said, 'provided you could fix up a shot of vodka to go with it!'

When he brought the drink, he said, 'I shouldn't indulge you, I suppose. But I do. Can't help it. How's it going? Coming to the boil?'

'Already boiling,' she answered.

'Ah. I don't want to be heavy, but remember this is the tropics, if you're saying goodbye to the single life.'

'I'm doing that all right. What do you advise?'

'Salt.'

'Salt? You advise salt?'

He spread his hands helplessly. His tone defensive. 'I'm a doctor, not a psychologist.'

'Ah, but you are, really.' She put back her head and laughed, then said soberly, 'You see, you make me laugh about it. And how Harvey will laugh when I tell him the doctor prescribes salt to put on Harvey Sherrard's tail.'

'Sherrard.'

'Say I'm lucky. No, you don't need to. It's only that I resent the inevitability of it.'

'Nothing is inevitable.'

'You, a doctor, and you say that?'

'Take it easy in Bahia.'

'Can't promise. But I'll certainly take salt.'

Coming down to Bahia, as the menu turned Brazilian, the long Atlantic swell got under the counter of the ship. Some of the faces under the paper hats were a trifle wan. There was more room on the dance floor. Yvonne Trillia, whose intensity once again peaked as they approached a port, for the first time elected to dance. Her partners held her gingerly or boisterously and worked her outstretched arm up and down vigorously, like the handle on a parish pump. She laughed a lot, in a hectic way. Once she cried out, 'You can't dance to the band, you can only go with the sea!'

There was a man in Bahia. Some said he was black as the ace of spades, some that he was white as the meat of a coconut. Some said he was as big as a barrel, others that he was shrivelled like a prune. All agreed he must be a tyrant, and very demanding. She came back like a rag doll. 'Harry Flakers,' reported the second officer crisply. 'Cattle,' replied the mate just as tersely, 'and cattle means leather.'

After Vitoria do Espirito Santo, he said only one word: 'Minerals!'

On the reach down to Rio, on the eve of arrival at the port, the kind lady from Kentucky considered the wretched state of the girl and reckoned with alarm the effect of an overnight stay on her at this terminus of the outward journey. She felt it was her duty to risk a snub, and try to get through to the girl. She found her in her cabin superb in a Hawaiian outfit, which was her dress rehearsal for the Carnival ashore.

'Morals have changed since I was a girl,' the kindly lady said, 'and I wouldn't criticize you for purging your system, or whatever it is you're doing, but it's clear, my dear, that it's not doing you any good, you must feel that yourself, by going with all these men in every port.'

Yvonne Trillia faced abruptly round from her mirror, so that necklaces and beads rustled like shingle, and a myriad of lights sparkled off her baubles. 'Men?' she exclaimed sharply. 'Whatever gave you the idea of *men*?'

'Haven't you—?'

'Not men,' she said emphatically. '*Man*. One man!'

'I don't understand.'

'He's always there to meet me. Harvey, the daredevil Sherrard. Flies by the seat of his pants. Flies his own bloody Bulldog. He has his interests down here, like everywhere else. He makes his deals, and waits for the sea to deliver me up to him.'

'That's so un-British! He's breaking his word. Your bargain?'

'The bargain only applied to the ship. He thinks of everything. There's a Harvey Sherrard waiting for me in every port. He said to me, "I always wanted to have a girl in every port – how nice it's always you." I feel bloody surrounded.'

'My dear! Poor Yvonne. The bully! But why not stop on the ship? You could let him hop about and wait.'

'Yes, you'd think so,' said Yvonne slowly. 'The funny thing is, I just don't seem able to do that. I'm unable to help myself. Besides,' she added on a lighter but defiant note, 'I always wanted to see these places. Why should I let him spoil my holiday?'

And after dinner, she showed them how to enjoy themselves. 'She dances like a witch,' said the delighted captain. 'So does a witch,' said the mate.

Shortly before midnight, a steward caught a rainbow glint shining in the moonlight by the after rail of the boat deck. Investigating, he found a number of necklaces looped there and below them on the deck a grass skirt, butterfly bra and embroidered dance slippers, held down by a book. Their owner was nowhere in evidence. He took the little pile to the captain.

The captain read on the flyleaf: 'Tell the doctor I've gone where there's plenty of salt.'

The *Reina del Golfo* put about and searched for two hours, but Yvonne Trillia was not to be found.

The captain said to his officers, 'When we put into Rio I personally want to have a few words with this Mr Harvey Sherrard. And I'll have more to say to him than merely to give him the news of her death.'

But Sparks chimed in. 'Sherrard? Was that who her bloke was? Hang on. The name rings a bell. On the BBC I heard an appreciation of him, his contribution to export, what a loss he was to the industry.'

'His *obituary*?' said the captain.

'Yeah. Bit farcical. He was supposed to have had a heart attack when the colour coding on some new electronics box didn't match the machine it was meant to run. At some big sales demo.'

'When was this you heard it, tonight?'

'No, no. This was while we were lying off Miami.'

There was a long silence, while the officers stared at one another. Finally the mate pushed his cap forward on his head. 'I knew she was trouble. I never believed in her.'

'Well, you'd better believe in her,' the captain said angrily. 'She existed all right. She was real and you'll never see anyone else so marvellous. Not on this ship anyway.'

As day caught fire, the ship's siren saluted Rio harbour.

'So be it,' said the mate. 'But skipper, do you still want to give her lover a piece of your mind?'

Jennifer Jenkins

Alice

Alice was thin in a very English way. She took after her father, who was a tall handsome lean man. Alice was as tall as he, six feet, and the leanness with her became boneyness – and the bones were heavy in her face so that she had that look which the English call 'horsey'.

A pleasant girl, intelligent, thoughtful, generally cheerful, she gave little outward sign of the loneliness that she suffered because of her height and her plainness. Indeed, when she was in her early twenties, at teaching college, she had plenty of companionship; there were other young women, even occasionally a young man, to accompany her to a film or to share an energetic hour on the college tennis courts. It was only later, as friends got married or moved away to take up teaching jobs in other parts of the country, that she really began to feel her isolation. But she didn't let it impinge too much on her; her temperament was basically cheerful and optimistic, and she simply accepted that the companionship of the other teachers in the staff room during the week and the sharing with her students was to be enough.

At Elm Road School, she was lucky enough to find a friend in Susan Fleming, who was the same age, also lived on her own, and was happy to share a weekend meal and an excursion to the local cinema. It was still a quiet life for Alice, but the friendship with Susan made it fuller than before. The two even took a holiday together to Sicily one Easter, and planned to go away again for a week during the summer. Then, between one weekend and the next, Susan met Jack Burgen, an Australian, who was looking up family in the 'old country'. They fell in love and Susan went with him back to Australia.

A year later Alice went out to Australia on a working holiday. She first went to Brisbane, where Susan and Jack lived, and taught there for a year, but she found the heat didn't suit her at all and her skin reddened fiercely in the harsh Australian sunshine. Brisbane was then a rather simple country town; life was beer, sunshine and picnics rather than concerts and films. Alice was used to a life that included music and cinema, and she missed them more than she had expected.

She went on to Sydney, a more interesting and beautiful city, and found a good job there at a private school. She was teaching small children for the first time; she enjoyed the teaching and she was good at it. The Australians were friendly and hospitable – she had plenty of invitations to parties and barbecues – and she explored the varied bushland around the city with an amicable group of bushwalkers. She made friends and she found herself less of an ostrich than she had been in England: there were more tall men and even more women close to her own height, which gave her confidence. She still found the heat very trying, but that seemed a small price to pay for the comfort and ease of the Australian way of life.

She settled in happily and even began a hobby that sprang out of her new teaching: she began to write children's books. The first one was, naturally enough, set in Australia, and concerned a shy young English girl who had just emigrated there with her parents; the story described her problems settling into the new environment with all the natural mistakes that a newcomer could make. The book was lively, even funny in parts, because Alice had, through the circumstances of her upbringing and nature, come to have a discerning eye and a rather humorous, self-critical awareness that she was able to project on to her heroine. Her heroine had the virtues of stoicism and determination; an enduring spirit: the kind of character that was appreciated and valued in Australia. The book had whimsy, too, because the bush that Alice explored on her walks seemed to her to be full of quirks and oddities: plants that were so alive with white-tentacled blooms that they were called 'spider plants', bushes full of devils' heads, soft green 'flannel flowers', the hard wax waratah spearheads – so much more variety than she had expected from her first view of the khaki bush – and so disarmingly full of life and very, very un-English and unsettling. The book was a great success: it became the kind of children's book that adults also enjoy reading, and she found herself with more invitations and more friends to share her time.

Then, one hot November day, she received a letter from her mother, telling her that her Aunt Jane had died, and that Jane, who had moved to the village some ten years before to have company in her old age, had left her small cottage to Alice in her will. She saw the cottage in her mind: old stone, grey and golden, set back a little from the main street of the village, a small garden in the front, with lupins and wallflowers, hollyhocks and foxgloves, a small lawn at the back and then a vegetable garden. Two tiny bedrooms upstairs under the eaves, a stone-flagged kitchen warm with a Aga cooker, and a lovely sitting-room, always bright with sunshine and chintz, as she remembered it. And the quiet East Anglian village where she'd grown up, tucked away from the main tourist routes, just a village, not a picturesque postcard-viewed place at all – a small functioning village that muddled along quietly with enough work available in nearby Saxmundham to keep some of the men there in the village.

It was December, the end of the school year, and in the midst of marking exams and writing reports she kept on thinking of the soft green English countryside and the grey worn stone of the village houses and the gentle sunshine. And she decided that she would go back. She had been planning to go back for Christmas, anyway, to see her parents and to avoid the hottest time of the year in Australia. It was extravagant of her to go simply for six weeks, but she'd already decided to do so. Now she realized that, with the money she'd saved from her teaching salary, and with the cottage rent free, she could, if she lived modestly enough, have enough money to last her a year. And it was suddenly clear. She had an idea for a series of children's books: she'd not really had a proper chance to work out how they would develop. She could take a year off, and work on the series, not in distracted snatches of time, but in uninterrupted calm.

She explained the new situation to her headmistress and asked for a year's leave of absence. She stored her furniture, her books, her china and her casual summer Australian clothes, and left for England.

She had changed. She knew that as soon as she went back to the village. She was stronger, had a kind of inner confidence, a sense of self she hadn't had before. Born of her time in the sun, of her acceptance of friendship; probably, too, from her modest literary success. Physically, too. She was thirty-eight now, but looked younger than when she had left at thirty-five. She walked more cleanly, stood straighter, and had acquired a colour, a kind of bronzing that made her look more vivid and healthy than she had looked before, in great contrast to the pallor of her parents.

She explained her idea to them, and they were pleased that she would be there in the village with them for at least a year; her mother missed the ready company of her sister Jane and hoped to have some of that lack made up by the companionship of her daughter. Alice felt that she could share tea-times or lunch-times, short times in between writing, but she did explain the importance of her work: of her needing free time and long hours alone to concentrate, so that fringes of ideas could get a chance to grow and she could 'see things whole' as she hadn't been able to before. And her mother was eager to understand and accept this stronger daughter of hers.

They both wanted Alice to spend the first week at least with them – in the house where she'd grown up – but that had sprung from their thinking of Alice as a child. A confident woman she was now, and she insisted, after the greetings and the ritual tea, that she wanted to go and look at the cottage straightaway. Unless there were any problems, she wanted to move in that first night.

'There's no problem.' Her mother was almost indignant. 'All right and tight it is. Jane kept it neat and clean. I've been up and aired, to make sure it didn't smell of damp, or the mustiness of unopened rooms. No, there's no problem about moving in straight away; it just seems a shame ...' But Alice was firm. She let her father help with her luggage, and they walked down to the cottage, which was at the other end of the village.

It was as she had remembered. Warm with light and sunshine, even on this chilly December day, and the colours of the chintz echoed the green of the garden that came softly through the large back window.

'Oh, I love it ... I'm going to be happy here.' She glowed at her parents, wanting to whirl them and hug them in her pleasure, but they seemed fragile and old, so she contented herself with the words.

'Oh, thank you. Thank you. Thank you, Aunt Jane. Thank you Mother, Father . . .'

'Going on a bit, isn't she?' said her dour father.

'Leave her be. Would you like to settle in and then come back for supper, dear?'

She wanted to say that she'd like to settle in and then make her own meal here, here alone, in the lovely bright kitchen. But she knew she couldn't. The first day back – she had to have her supper with her parents. 'I'll come back down at 5.30,' she promised. When the time came, she was reluctant to leave. She'd put away her clothes, set up her typewriter in a corner of the sitting-room, made herself a cup of tea, and then she'd dozed gently in front of the fire. She'd flown straight from Sydney and she was still suffering from jet lag; her time was not the same as the village time. Here she was sleepy at four o'clock, had to shake herself awake at five o'clock. She knew she would have to force herself to eat, too, for her mother would surely not understand jet lag, but would think that her daughter had come to tea and no longer liked her mother's cooking. So despite her having had, it seemed, ten meals in two days, she would have another one. She was still the same thoughtful considerate girl she'd been. The new confidence had not made her brash or coarse: in fact it gave her a gentle strength.

Which she was going to need.

She was not sure later whether he knocked on the door, whether she got up from her half-sleep in front of the fire, too tired with food and travel to go to bed yet, too desirous of holding the warmth and peace of the house to herself, if she let him in. Or whether he had just opened the door and come in.

What she remembered later was simply that she woke up and that he was there, smiling at her. A big man, as tall as she was, no, taller, smiling down at her, warm and friendly, offering her his hand.

'I'm Alan Bennett,' he said. 'I used to live here.'

'My Aunt Jane,' she began.

'No, before her – long before her . . .'

'Ah,' she accepted. 'And . . .'

'And you're Alice Biddell.'

'Yes.'

'May I sit down?'

'Of course. A cup of tea?'

'No, thank you. Just the warmth of the fire would be nice.' And he sat down in the other armchair that was in front of the fire, relaxed, as comfortable in the house as she was.

She didn't ask him how he knew her name, or why he had come there. She was just pleased to have him there with her – beside the fire. It seemed so right that she didn't question it at all.

They talked of the garden, what she would plant, when she should dig the soil over. Even though it was winter, the earth should be turned, he said, and she remembered from her childhood that he was right. 'I'll do it tomorrow,' she said.

He asked her to read to him and she took a book of poems that she had brought from her parents' house and she read.

'I like your voice,' he said. The first intimacy.

'And I yours,' she said formally.

'May I stay?' he asked.

And she felt the compliment of his asking. He needn't have. She had known that he would stay, known from his first smile at her, warm and deep with love, laughter-webbed eyes, kind warm deep blue eyes, that he would want her, expect much of her, demand much from her. She'd known that she would accept the love he offered – the sweetness and the caring. She read from the poem by Dowson: *'Love and desire and hate / I think they have no portion in us after / We pass the gate.'* And he corrected that: 'Yes, love there is still – and perhaps the other. But not for me. And not for you.'

And she accepted that.

He spoke as if he knew.

And she accepted his love.

She'd lost her virgin shyness in Australia; she could respond to him and accept his body, could be natural with him. And loving.

When the wintry morning came, she cried softly that he must not go away.

He reproved her: 'Don't be greedy, Alice.' When she wept, he added: 'Or only if you must.'

To her silence, he talked gently: 'I only have a certain time. But perhaps *you* should choose. One month or one year or even ten ...'

And she half understood. Half couldn't understand, didn't want to.

He was offering her time.

'My mother said I was greedy because I grew up in wartime,' she said light heartedly. 'I didn't like rationing. I couldn't save the two chocolate bars and make them last. I would eat them straightaway.' She was trembling.

'And that is what you wish?'

'I don't know. How could I know?' But she didn't want him to go.

'I'll stay then,' he said. 'Stay quiet. No more tears.'

And he walked to her, lovingly, his hand soft on her hair, gently touching her.

That was the pattern of the days that began there in the cottage for Alice.

She felt a peace that came from his loving, asked no more questions. She just accepted him.

She started her life there, the housework, the gardening, and she set aside the afternoons for her own writing. She would look up and see him, feel his love and caring always there with her.

She hated Christmas lunch with her parents: the long meal, the ritual relaxation and tea after. It went on too long, she was too long away from him. It frightened her, that he might not be there when she got back. She was restless and awkward, impatient to go.

Perhaps her mother sensed that, perhaps she worried about Alice, thought that she might be missing friends, comparing this Christmas with the one in the Australian sun. Perhaps it was just a crisp sunny day and that made her decide to walk over to Alice's cottage. For whatever reason, she did come – in the afternoon. There was no phone in the cottage, so Alice had no warning. She hadn't said 'no visitors' but she had stressed that she needed her privacy. If this was true when she first moved in, how much more so was it now.

But her mother came, knocked on the door, and opened it, talking as she came in. 'I know you're there, Alice. I could hear you talking.'

Alice got up from the chair she'd been sitting in by the fire and looked at Alan. What could she say?

Her mother didn't seem to see him. 'There's no one here. Talking to yourself, was it? You know that's supposed to be ...'

'Just reading my book out, Mother,' said Alice quietly, her eyes fixed on Alan who had gone to stand at the other end of the room, by the window. He looked at her and shrugged a brief answer to her questioning look.

'Tea, Mother?'

'That would be nice. You know, it's lovely and crisp outside. You should get out more. You used to walk a lot in Australia, so you said. But you've hardly left the house here.'

True. But if she left, when she had to, she always worried if he'd be there when she got back.

'No, I've been working.' It was partly true at least.

'You know your father ...' and her mother settled down to a comfortable chat. Alice listened and squirmed and looked at Alan. She felt a surge of relief when her mother finally said, 'Well, better be getting back. Your father misses me when I'm not there, you know. Gets quite restless. Doesn't really like me out of his sight. Funny old duck.'

Then Alice *could* smile a sharing smile at Alan.

'What are you smiling at, think we're a couple of old fools, do you?'

'No, Mother.' She realized she must be more careful. 'No. I'll walk part of the way with you.' There was some comfort in what her mother had said. Or at least she felt it so. If her mother and father's love had endured so long, if they had kept their closeness and their love, then perhaps she could, too. It gave her some hope – some quite unreasonable hope. Perhaps it was the *quality* of love that was important, that made it last. Perhaps that was it.

'No, Alice,' he said, when she asked her naïve and sentimental question. 'And you must be ready, must be strong – to endure.'

'There'd be no reason.'

'There would be,' he assured her.

Better to be silent, not question, better just to accept, because she didn't want the cool logic of his answers.

Not even to ask, how long? Frightened of the answer.

She was sure she couldn't bear to say goodbye, but she didn't get the chance.

Did it seem later that he was more tender that night? Somehow quieter, more gentle with her? Did they talk longer, hold each other more closely?

She hadn't wanted to sleep, but she had, eventually.

And when she woke in the morning, he was gone. No point in searching the house, in calling. There was no presence there, no sense of him at all. Just she alone in an attic bedroom. No sign of him at all.

She wept.

No comfort. But she had to weep for loss.

She sat that day, empty-handed, her eyes empty, too, looking at nothing.

Then began a sad pattern. She tried to work during the day, and wept herself to sleep at night. In the morning, she got up tired, even sometimes so sick that she retched and vomited.

There came a time when she knew she could stop the tears; they had become self-indulgent. But she still woke up sick, often felt nauseous during the day, and her monthly bleeding had stopped.

Her mother commented: 'You were looking so well.' And that had been true: she knew she'd had the glow of a woman well loved; she'd lost her strong-boned plainness and her face had softened, become more fleshed out.

Now she was pale, her tan faded to a rather weak yellow colour: she was tense and sick and boney ugly again.

Then came another stage. The sickness stopped and she could feel the real growth inside her. The softness came back to her face. She was still a tall thin woman, but glowing, rather regal now.

The village had noticed. But she did not live for them or their comments. She went walking again. Every day for miles, walking for strength. She noticed no one, absorbed in herself.

She still visited her parents. She saw something in her mother's eyes, when the new change came, when she started filling out again. But the accusations and the bitterness, when they came, were quite unexpected, 'So that's why you came back, to have your bastard here!'

She didn't answer, but looking at herself realized it was time to see a doctor. Six months now and it showed.

The doctor was from outside the village. He accepted her version, her dates, her lies, without question. He wanted her to have tests. She was thirty-eight, after all. And it was her first child. He insisted on her going to the ante natal clinic. She said 'yes' quite easily – but she didn't go.

Her mother softened a little as the time came closer. It was her child, after all, her grandchild.

But she would try and question. And Alice wouldn't have that. She accepted the pram and the booties, the blankets and the toys; why shouldn't she? But that gave her mother no right to question.

When her time came, she let the pains run for as long as possible. She sensed somehow that the child would like as little of hospital as she could manage. So she waited till the pains came birthing close and then she went to her neighbour and asked her to phone.

At the small country hospital, they were a bit anxious. But she was such a strapping healthy woman – surely there was nothing to fear. The doctor watched for a while, left it to the nurse, and went to see other patients.

Alice felt her time coming closer, held the nurse's hand, strained against the brutal tearing pain, strained to force open the passage for the child, felt the child leave, felt the warmth of blood and then relaxed into a dark contented sleep.

Dimly she heard the nurse screaming, the questions from the doctor, the tearful answers from the nurse. Jangling sounds and a repeated 'Nothing.' 'It can't be nothing.'

'My God, I can't believe it . . .'

'But the blood . . .'

'I never . . .'

The doctor turned to a wardsman: 'You know I was looking after Miss Biddell. I'd say it was her age. A lonely woman on her own. Maybe it was a hysterical pregnancy. But . . . I heard the baby's heartbeat . . .'

Alice heard the anxious voices. 'What shall we tell her?'

She kept her eyes closed. Let them go away and leave her with the baby.

'I'm afraid the baby's dead.' That's what they decided to tell her, to save her the pain and the exposure.

She knew better.

'Let me go home.'

She knew he'd be there.

And he was, waiting in the cradle, wrapped in the clothes she had knitted during the long months – she so unfitted for those women tasks but forcing herself into that new loving role.

Her mother was kind, forgiving now of the misunderstanding, but Alice drove her out; she wanted to be alone with him.

She called him Alan – after his father.

He suckled greedily. And she held him close, loving him with the warmth of years of wanting to love.

He was a handsome baby, and looked like Alan. He had dark hair, a wide brow, and his eyes – the only part of him that seemed to come from her – were set far apart, the same deep steady grey as hers. So sometimes, as she looked at him and held him close in front of her, it was as if she were looking at herself – mirror eyes.

He had a sunny nature; he chortled and chuckled and blew bubbles of happy laughter when she tickled him. When she fussed over him in the pram, it was for the joy of fussing and not because he was querulous or demanding.

She became familiar in the village. But the villagers were tolerant, more so than if the child had lived. 'Touched' was the word they used as they watched her wheel her empty pram through the main road and out into the lanes.

She sang to her baby, talked to him, as mothers do, full of plans, full of joy. She knew that others didn't see him, but somehow felt that things would change. Maybe when he was a year old, maybe they'd see him then.

In the peace of his company, in the afternoons, she began

writing again. Praying that he'd stay long enough for her to read him what she was writing.

He slept a lot. Perhaps that helped. Not using up his time as Alan had.

And he might have longer.

Six months and she began to hope for so much more. But there was a pattern that she couldn't see.

Nine months to grow – and nine months to sleep and grow again.

A week before nine months, he stopped suckling, started to fade. His eyes started to lose their greyness, turned from grey to an opaque new born blue, and she knew she was close to losing him. He cried fretfully, for the first time, and she sat up all night, rocking him close in her arms and woke, rigid, to find her arms empty.

It was the same sense of emptiness she'd felt when Alan went.

This time she didn't cry.

She sat and tried to think what had happened to her, tried to decide rationally how to behave. What should she do? She even wondered whether she should confide in someone, explain to her mother, so that her mother would understand and, perhaps, forgive.

But she knew the disbelief, knew the folly of an attempt to explain.

She tried to think if she had been given some message, some mission.

She decided that she hadn't.

She'd just been loved. And love has its consequences.

Greedy and hopeful: she took the easy way. The tranquillizers from the hospital, which she'd never needed, and a bottle of brandy.

Willis Hall

Waking or sleeping

Breakfast-times had been getting progressively more difficult for some months now, and Emily knew, instinctively, that this morning would prove no exception. Reggie accepted the bowl of cornflakes without a word, splashed fresh milk all over them, and then sat staring at the bowl without even bothering to pick up his spoon. A few moments later he pushed the bowl of cereal away. Emily was not at all annoyed, but sat staring at her husband, sympathetically, over the teapot.

'It happened again then, last night?' she said.

Reggie nodded his head, slowly, without looking up.

'Why don't you call in and see Doctor Attercliffe on your way home from the office tonight?' asked Emily.

This time, Reggie Wormald shook his head, forced a wry smile, and selected a piece of medium-brown toast from the chromium toast-rack. He buttered the toast, nibbled along one edge, pensively, and then that too was put to one side along with the cornflakes.

'Was it the same as always?' said Emily.

'It's *always* the same as always,' Reggie's temper was short and he spoke pettishly. 'It's the same bad dream – *exactly* the same – every night.'

'You didn't have it the night before last, dear,' Emily pointed out.

'No. But I had it the night before that, *and* the night before that.'

'And last night again?'

'Yes!'

'Oh, dear!' Emily's voice expressed concern. 'Was it *exactly* the same as the other times? Were you locked up in that awful cage again? In that horrible cellar?'

'It's a sort of dungeon. I've told you often enough. It's a medieval dungeon – not just a cellar.' Mr Wormald chewed at his lower lip, suffering the memory.

'I really think it *would* be a good idea if you popped into the doctor's this evening, Reggie.'

'And tell him what?'

'Why, tell him the truth. Tell him about the dreadful dream you keep on having. Tell him you've lost your appetite; tell him you're losing weight. Goodness, I should think he'll only need to look at you to know that *something's* wrong. You're so drawn – *and* peaky.'

Reggie Wormald 'harrumphed' non-committally and thought to himself that 'peaky' was hardly the adjective that he would use to describe the mental torture he suffered during his sleeping hours. But he kept the thought to himself. 'And what do you think Doctor Attercliffe will be able to do for me?' he said aloud.

'Why, prescribe something,' said Emily. 'Something to take – probably a tonic.'

'I *don't want* a tonic.'

'You most certainly need *something*,' said Emily, pursuing her theme relentlessly. 'Doctor Attercliffe will diagnose what's wrong with you, and give you something for it.'

'I *know* what's wrong with me,' said Reggie. He paused and let out a deeply felt long-suffering sigh, before continuing: 'And I can hardly take up the valuable time of an extremely busy general practitioner, simply because I'm suffering from nightmares.'

'Night*mare*, dear,' Emily Wormald corrected her husband. 'The same horrid nightmare almost every night of the week. It's obviously something ... well, something in your mind, Reggie. Doctor Attercliffe will probably think that it might be good for you to see a ... a specialist.'

Mr Wormald clattered his cup noisily in his saucer and blew out his cheeks. 'What absolute rubbish, Emily,' he said. 'The fact that I'm having a recurring bad dream is not necessarily a sign that I'm ready for the nut-hatch.'

'I didn't say it was, dear.'

'You said that I needed a psychiatrist.'

'No, I didn't, Reggie—'

'Yes, you did—'

'*No*,' Emily's voice was firm though quiet. 'I said "specialist". All I said was that there's obviously *something* wrong with you.'

'Most probably indigestion,' said Reggie.

Emily, taking her husband's last remark as an intended slight upon her own cooking, rose from the table, and maintained a dignified silence.

The subject was considered closed.

Mr Wormald left for the office a few minutes later. He did not call in and see Doctor Attercliffe on his way home. That same evening, Mrs Wormald cooked the lightest of meals; steamed halibut and a milk pudding.

Mr Wormald ate the food without once referring to the nightmares or even to his digestion. The meal passed almost in silence. After dinner, Reggie decided against watching the television news – for fear that some disaster might have taken place that could set his subconscious thoughts racing. He went up to bed just after 10.30, taking with him a P. G. Wodehouse novel and, with only the slightest feel of trepidation, he switched off his bedside lamp at a quarter to eleven.

A beam of moonlight stole into the bedroom through a gap in the curtains. Reggie Wormald paused only to cast a resentful glance at Emily, who lay sleeping soundly at his side, and then he put his balding head on the pillow and tried to channel his mind into thinking comfortable thoughts.

It was well over an hour before he fell into a restless sleep.

He started, fearfully, aware that he was waking yet again from a fitful and uncomfortable doze. How long, he wondered, had his eyes been closed? An hour? A minute? Less than a minute? Certainly not more than an hour – for in the narrow confines of the metal cage, complete sleep was utterly impossible.

At first, as always, as consciousness returned, he was aware only of the chill and clammy damp that seemed to seep from the rags he was wearing through his flesh and into the very marrow of his bones. He held his breath and bit his lip in terror and foreboding of the pain he knew that was yet to come. And then it came, the cramp biting into his body like ugly, jagged knife-cuts. A scream shrilled out in the darkness and it occurred to him that it was his mouth that was open and that the scream was coming from somewhere at the back of his own throat. The only light came from the flickering torch on the wall. Not that he needed light. For in those awful, painful waking moments, his world consisted only of the narrow cage in which he was contained and he was fully aware of every single metal strip that formed the cage – for each and every one gnawed at his flesh. And he knew, by now, that in time the unbearable pain would become bearable and when it did, mercifully, that he might even doze again.

He tried to stretch his neck. It was an instinctive movement, for he knew full well by dint of long experience that the cage was far too small for him to hold his head upright. He was imprisoned in the cage with his knees tucked up tight against his chest and his head, locked, permanently it seemed, slightly to one side. His head, in fact, had grown almost accustomed to this awkward position – although the throbbing cramp in his neck was there all the time. Except, of course, for those precious moments, or minutes, or hours, during which he dozed. He had not the faintest idea how long he had been in the cage – apart from knowing that it had been a long time – but he did not know whether that time stretched into months or years.

Sometimes, in the still of the night, he would awaken from his dream. Not for long, but long enough for him to become aware of familiar sounds in the darkness of the room and beyond. The fretful whisper of the electric clock on his bedside table. The oh-so-regular breathing of Emily, sound asleep at his side. The faint sigh of the night wind in the branches of the cedar tree outside the bedroom window. And sometimes, should he remain awake long enough, he began to distinguish familiar objects, too, as his eyes became accustomed to the dark. The dark grey line that was the windowledge. A pale streak of light caught in the full-length wall mirror on moonlit nights. But then he would be sucked back in sleep again; pulled back in at the edges of his constant dream . . .

With extreme difficulty, he could move his rump a couple of inches in the rusting strips of metal that formed the base of the cage. Not that it gave him pleasure to move, for each time he did so it was as if a thousand needle-points gouged at his skin. But only by moving occasionally, by proving that he could shift himself, no matter how slightly, was he able to convince himself that he was actually still alive.

And every time he moved, the cage swung an inch or two, groaning a complaint on the rusty hook which was attached to the length of chain that disappeared in the darkness up above his head where he sensed, rather than saw, the dank, vaulted ceiling that formed the farthest edges of his universe. Beneath the cage, some three feet away, lay the damp, glistening, cold slab dungeon floor.

In addition to being able to shift his backside slightly, he could also raise his hands sufficiently to get them to his mouth, albeit with difficulty. It was good that he could do this, for otherwise it would not be possible for him to feed himself whenever the old woman brought him food. Thinking of food gave him a gnawing pain in the tight hollow that had once been his stomach and the thought also brought saliva to his mouth.

He tried to concentrate his mind on the old woman herself, and not on the scraps of food she brought with her. He wondered how long it was since the old woman had last been and, much more important, how long it would be before she came again? He had never been able to make up his mind as to whether she paid her visits to him regularly or irregularly? If she came to him regularly, how long was it between her visits? A day? Two days? Three days, even? And if she visited him irregularly, how long was the longest period she had left him alone with the pain and the dreadful thought that she was never coming back again? Four days? Five days? Even a week?

He did not know. He did not know who she was or where she came from or if she fed other prisoners out there in the dark corridors beyond the pale circle of light from the flickering torch. What language did she speak? Was it the same as the one that he had once used himself? And, if so, what language was that? For he had been hunched in the cage for so long now that he had no longer any use for words, or any recollection of a previous life before the cage. Occasionally, he made sounds. He grunted with pleasure when the old woman arrived with her scraps. He whimpered with sorrow sometimes whenever some of those same scraps fell from his clumsy fingers through the bottom of the cage on to the floor beneath, to be seized upon, almost immediately, by the scuttling, scuffling rats.

The old woman was the only contact that he had with the outside world – if there was an outside world. But in all the time that he had been in the cage, he had never had any communication of any sort with the crone. In all the years of his imprisonment, she had never so much as offered him one word, either in kindness or in anger. She had never once looked into his eyes.

In that dark part of his mind that contained the past, he seemed to recollect, vaguely, that there had been a time when he had *tried to communicate with the old woman. But, if his memory did not play him false, it seemed that she had never so much as intimated, in any way, that she had even* heard, *let alone understood.*

He wondered too, occasionally, why it was that the old woman brought him his scraps and filled his leather mug with water? He had never before heard of a woman jailor. Sometimes, he even wondered if she was his jailor? Perhaps she was a benefactress? For without the scraps she brought him, he would surely die. Perhaps she had taken the task upon herself? Perhaps she was just an old, old woman, without the means to free him from his cage, but who brought him the scraps she garnered from somewhere whenever she was able? Perhaps this was the only kindness she was capable of bestowing in the entire world?

And then again, on the other hand, could it be counted as a kindness to keep him alive in all this wretchedness? No, it was not a kindness. The old woman was not a friend, she was his jailor right enough. If she were a friend, the only possible act of kindness would be for her never to come to him again . . . He didn't mean it! *His cramped, pained body cried out to God, denying the lie. And, please, dear God, let her bring him the scraps soon! His belly ached for food and his parched, white lips were cracked in a dozen places for the want of water.*

He shifted again and the harsh metal bars of the floor of the cage jarred through the thin layer of rump-flesh and grated along his bones.

*

Sometimes, in the middle quiet of the night, he found himself in that half-sleeping, half-waking world where dreams and reality were mingled. He was in the cage, but it was not the old woman that brought him food, but the comforting figure of Emily, in a rose/pink nightgown, sitting beside him in the cage and holding a polished wood tray, covered with a snow/white cloth, and containing buttered toast and a pot of tea for one, neatly arranged with milk jug and sugar bowl and a starched white napkin in his own, familiar napkin ring. Or, again, he was stretched out cosily in his own warm bed but it was the old crone standing over him, with the greasy scraps of food in one hand and the cracked filthy water jug in the other. And sometimes, on such occasions, he woke to the slow recognition of his bedroom, with the quiet whirring of the electric clock and the reassuring regularity of Emily's breathing. On other more cruel occasions though, he did not wake, but drifted back into the awful dream world of the rusty chain groaning above his head and the shrilly whispering rats below his cage . . .

The sound of tiny feet scampering off into the darkness brought him out of his reverie and back into the awareness of the pain of the cage, but his heart rose in his skinny frame because he knew that the old woman was coming. A few seconds later, he heard the shuffle of her rag-bound feet across the dungeon floor. His dry, parched mouth was swelling up from the back of his throat at the thought of food.

He struggled to control his shaking hands, forcing them to obey the warning signals that his brain was sending out. He scrabbled urgently at the bottom of the cage for the leather mug and the bony fingers of one hand clutched at its handle. He willed his thin, scarecrow arm to raise the mug up, chest-high, before the old woman arrived. He jerked his other hand up past his body and his fingers spread out, slowly, awkwardly, instinctively after years of practice, into the position that was exactly the right one in which to catch the scraps of food – not too wide apart or the scraps would tumble through the gaps between; not too close together or some of the precious crumbs might spill over the side of his palm and out through the cage, on to the floor, to be snapped up hungrily by the scavenging rats.

The old woman arrived. He could just make out the lank tangle of grey greasy hair that fell over her face. He could dimly see the threadbare rags – no better than his own in fact – that hung from her grimy, wrinkled shoulders. He knew that he was whimpering quietly, like a helpless animal, but he could not stop himself even though he was ashamed. As always, the old woman paid him not the slightest attention.

The manner in which the old crone gave him his food was always the same. First, she thrust the neck of the jug between the bars of the cage, tipped it up, and filled the leather mug in his shaking hand. Next she pushed her own leathery fist, containing the scraps of food, between the bars and then dropped them into his open palm. It was a routine that they had played out together countless times, a routine that never varied, and yet on each and every occasion that it took place, it proved a terrifying and nerve-wracking experience for him.

Supposing the hand that held the mug was shaking so much the contents spilled over and trickled to the floor before he could raise them to his lips? What if he were to misjudge the width of the spaces between his outstretched fingers, or supposing the scraps of food were smaller than usual – either of these instances might easily result in him losing precious pieces of the only sustenance that would come his way for a couple of days at least, much longer perhaps.

But on this occasion, everything went according to plan. In one shaking hand he held a mug full of water; in his other fist he clutched the greasy scraps of food. The old woman shuffled away as silently as she had come. He was left to consider the treasure she had given him, and to decide in which way he would dispose of it. It was always a difficult decision, but one that he thoroughly enjoyed deliberating over. Whether to wolf down the scraps immediately and sip the water afterwards, slowly; or should he gulp down the water first, leaving the scraps in his lap to be nibbled at leisure? He usually chose the latter course, for it was easier to safeguard the scraps than it was to hold the mug of water on his trembling lap.

Settling himself gradually, keenly anticipating the feast to come, he held the mug close to his chest protectively with one hand, while he lowered the other and carefully placed the bits of food between his hunched legs. He sat as still as he was able for several moments, enjoying the possession of his hoard with miserly greed. Then, unable to hold back any longer, he slowly lifted the mug of water to his mouth and allowed the contents to dribble down his throat.

It was in this moment that disaster struck.

A single cunning rat, it seemed, had not scuttled off across the floor with its fellows when the old woman had arrived, but had hugged the wall, silently waiting its chance. The scent of food had drifted down from the prisoner's lap and crept into the rat's twitching nostrils. Now, suddenly, twisting and arching its body as it rose in an attempt to force itself clean through the bars at the bottom of the cage, the rat leapt upwards and its hard snout struck him at the back of his thigh. It was by no means the first time that a rat had attempted its way into the cage, but on this occasion it was totally unexpected.

He flinched, jerked his leg, and the precious food-scraps spilled from his lap and tumbled on to the bottom of the cage, some of them falling straight to the floor, others rolling on the metal bars before slipping through, beyond his reach. He let out a wild, strangled cry that pierced the darkness of the dungeon. Then, as he scrabbled in desperation with his free hand in an attempt to retrieve what food-scraps he could, the trembling hand that held the mug loosed its hold and his water spilled to the ground.

There was an ever-tightening knot in the pit of his stomach; his tongue was thick and dry and clung to the roof of his mouth. A moment ago he had owned both food and water, and now he had neither. Nothing. Nothing at all. It would be days – an eternity, it seemed – before the old woman came again.

Beneath the cage, the rat had dropped to the ground again and, to add to his hunger and frustration, he could hear the razor-teeth shearing into his food. The rat was attempting to devour all the scraps before the rest of the rat-pack returned. Already there was the brisk if tentative patter of needle-sharp claws across the slab floor.

His head sank further to his chest and his whole body

shook with self-pity. Had there been moisture to spare inside his head there would have been tears running down the hollows of his cheeks. He gave himself entirely to the despair that had been at his shoulder, it seemed, since time began.

'Reggie? ... Reggie?'

He opened his eyes, blinked, and closed them again against the unexpected glare of sunlight.

'Are you sure you're all right, dear?' said Emily.

He opened his eyes again, narrower this time. Emily's face swam into focus. She was sitting in bed beside him, fiddling with the automatic tea-maker and looking down at him, anxiously. He darted his glance about the room, taking in familiar objects, returning to reality, trying hard to dispel the terror that he knew was still visible in his face.

'I couldn't wake you, Reggie.' There was an accusatory note to Emily's voice. 'I couldn't – really I couldn't. I tried. You were making horrid noises, sort of in your throat – and sobbing. I tried three times to wake you, but it was no use.'

'I'm all right now,' he said, but the voice did not sound like his own.

'It was that nightmare again, wasn't it?'

'Yes.'

'It's no good, you know, Reggie,' Emily said, firmly. 'You really will have to see someone about it.'

He nodded, shivered at a sudden vivid recollection of the dream, and pulled himself up in bed. 'I'll call in at the doctor's on my way home from the office tonight,' he said.

'Not before time,' said Emily, handing him a cup of tea in a gold-rimmed teacup. 'It *is* sweetened, but not stirred.'

Doctor Attercliffe beamed at Mr Wormald across his surgery roll-top desk. 'Nightmares, eh? Well, well, well. We must put a stop to those chappies, mustn't we?'

'It's a night*mare*, doctor,' said Mr Wormald. 'It's always the same one. I'm suspended in a sort of medieval cage and—'

'Mmmm, mmmm,' said Doctor Attercliffe, scribbling illegibly on a prescription form; frowning slightly at the chatter that was coming up from the fifteen to twenty other patients that were still needing attention in the waiting room. 'That's not at all unusual, to keep on having the same bad dream, you know.'

'But it's so – *vivid*,' said Mr Wormald.

'Mmmm, mmmm,' muttered Doctor Attercliffe, handing the prescription to Mr Wormald. 'Those little beggars should do the trick. Take one at night, fifteen minutes before you go to bed. I've put you down for a dozen, but don't complete the course if you find that two or three nights of them have put you back in top form.'

Mr Wormald looked down at the prescription he was holding. 'I don't really have trouble in getting to sleep,' he said.

'Course you don't – course you don't,' said Doctor Attercliffe. 'But what you need is the right *kind* of sleep. Those little devils will put your spark out. Give me a ring at the end of the week, let me know how you're suited. Ask the next poor benighted blighter to come in, on your way out, would you?'

Mr Wormald had egg mayonnaise, green salad, and stewed apples and custard for dinner that night.

At 10.15 he took one of the red pills that Doctor Attercliffe had prescribed, and at 10.30 he was in bed.

'What did the doctor say those pills would do for you?' asked Emily who, as usual, was in bed before her husband.

'He said they'd put me spark out,' said Reggie.

'Good,' said Emily. 'I'm sure the doctor knows best.' And she placed her woman's magazine on her bedside table and switched off her bedside lamp.

Mr Wormald switched off his light too, and settled his head on the pillow, hopefully but not entirely without doubts.

The prisoner in the cage awoke, shivering violently. As always, he prepared himself for the violent cramp that he knew would bite into his body almost at once. But, after all these years, he was ready for it – used to it, in fact. He had dozed and awakened; dozed and awakened; day in, day out; month after week and year after month until now there was nothing that mattered beyond the narrow, rustling metal strips that made up the cage in which he ate and slept and lived. He no longer cared particularly about the old woman – if she came, all well and good; but if she seemed to stay away for days on end, he was prepared to wait. After all, what else was there to do but wait?

He no longer awakened from the dream. There were no more brief night-time excursions into that bedroom and the bed he had once shared – ages ago – with the woman called Emily. All that was in the far distant past.

The prisoner shifted, slightly, on the bottom of the cage, causing the whole metal structure to groan, complainingly, on the hook and chain by which it hung from the vaulted ceiling.

Beneath the cage, across the dungeon floor, he could hear the urgent, familiar pit-pat of tiny claws and the shrill whispers of the rat-pack. But he had long since ceased to care about the rats. He had grown too wily over the years to allow them to steal his food and his existence and theirs were two entirely separate things. They lived outside the cage; he belonged within. He moved his backside again, half an inch at the most, for, with time, he had finally come to terms with living in the cage. The man who owns a forty acre park may take great pleasure in walking across his domain – the man who lives inside a cage experiences supreme joy in shifting his backside an inch, even though it may also cause excruciating pain.

He never returned again now to that half-sleeping, half-waking world where dreams and reality were mingled.

The cage was reality.

Somehow, at some time, the dream had become reality. Reality had become the dream, and the dream had long since ceased to exist. No matter. He was not even aware that there ever had been any other world than the narrow one he lived in.

He was in the cage. The cage was his world. He would remain there for ever and all time. He sat quite still, gazing out at the darkness that was his sky. He smiled to himself. Things, after all, were not too bad. For the next couple of hours, he decided, he would think about the old woman, and after that – yes, why not? – he would shift his backside one half inch.

Kathrine Talbot

Game

They had abandoned the big and ugly mansion the old Lord had lived in and had built themselves a modern house near the castle ruins. I'd passed it on walks, but this was our first social visit, a dinner party, and I was nervous. As we drove through the autumnal park the deer stood in silent groups, indistinct as in an old tapestry, some grazing, some lifting their heads to look at the passing car, while black sheep, dark shapes in the gloom, grazed together near a clump of trees. The ruins themselves looked unreal in the half-light, a stage set, with the tall square windows framing black emptiness and the delicate gothic arches of the banqueting hall pointing into dark sky.

'I don't think I'd fancy it as a neighbour on a dark night,' my husband said.

'Ghosties?' I suggested facetiously. 'Nonsense.'

'Remember the abbess who cursed it.'

'Still, *this* wouldn't be subject to the curse.' *This* was indeed far removed from the sixteenth century. It seemed to me more likely to haunt than be haunted. The man who built that castle on land taken from the abbey and given him by the king himself could not have believed that so stark a white box could ever come to be its neighbour. It looked fine in the day time I had thought, if a little alien to the great park, but at night its straight lines and glaring whiteness were intrusive in the gentle dusk. Catching sight of it through the ogee window of the chapel it must look startling during the full moon.

Now the windows showed slits of light around the heavy curtains, and the front door, when it was opened, threw a bright rectangle on the path. But once indoors one immediately forgot the park, the ruined castle, the little town itself, full of old buildings and new, a nice higgledy-piggledy promiscuous conglomeration inside and out, most of the houses filled and furnished through long years of accumulated acquisition. Here everything was deliberately chosen: the modern, white furniture on the old faded carpets, the modern bright paintings on the white walls. Lights were hidden but brilliant, highlighting what was to be looked at, so that it was like a stage or film set and I felt I must behave as if thousands were watching me. This made me tongue-tied and awkward, and I admired my husband who was immediately at home, talked animatedly to someone he'd never met before and whose name I hadn't caught, and was able to fall into lively conversation with our hosts while I was still trying to remember what on earth was the right form of address.

We hadn't come late but were the last to arrive. I looked admiringly at the handsome clothes, a flame-coloured dress and a midnight blue one, two young girls in floating flowery skirts, the gentlemen in dinner jackets, very clean and very smooth. I thought for a moment that I might have preferred it if this had been a television play with no demands made on me, the spectator.

But once I got going it wasn't so difficult and I enjoyed acting my part. I had a glass in my hand and looked at our hostess, once an American heiress, very tall and straight and white-haired, and over her shoulder at a bold painting which looked like an explosion of colour.

I found myself talking about pheasants. It's extraordinary how much you can dredge up on any subject you thought you knew nothing of. The pheasants in the park were familiar enough, and nobody, after all, expected me to have been out on a shoot. I told them of a little niece who had thought they were dragons. Their raucous cry had contributed to that idea. We talked of the noise they made when they flew clapping and coughing from beneath your feet, imitating, one might think, the guns.

When we talked of their colours I realized suddenly that all the time I had been looking at a painting of a pheasant, that the fountain of colour on the canvas opposite was a bird, possibly at the moment of its final disintegration, possibly only caught in flight.

'Their great green neck bands,' somebody was saying.

And, 'Oh no, blue,' someone else objected.

How meek the hens looked and drab among the fallen leaves until you saw the feathers up close with their intricate designs.

When I had plucked one, killed on the road, had it been this good Lord's bounty?

'I heard a story about a pheasant shoot once,' one of the men began and got up to stand against the fire as if this were the natural stance for talking, his elbow looking unconsciously for a mantelpiece to prop against. 'Some place in Wiltshire, I forget the name.' He looked at his wife as if he wished for approbation for his discretion. 'A friend of mine went shooting there, splendid estate.' He stopped, self-conscious with all those faces turned up at him. Would the story repay all this attention? It was a common enough tale, but it touched me, faced as I was with that explosion of pheasant on the wall opposite, and after what we had said driving past the dark ruins.

They'd had a good day's shooting in mixed country; some good woods, and the beaters keen and well organized and everything just right, decent weather for early December when it could so easily be dashed wet. The dogs had picked up the pheasants as they fell, and the keepers had heaped them up as usual to be counted and put into the trucks, while the guns and their dogs got into the landrovers, and the beaters clambered on to the straw bales on the trailer behind the tractor.

'A splendid bag,' they all agreed, but every time the pheasants were moved, every time some more were loaded, the original pile seemed to have diminished, so that the final count was infinitesimal. 'I shot more than that myself,' the story-teller's friend had said *sotto voce* to his neighbour in the landrover.

'Is it a ghost story?' one of the ladies exclaimed. 'Do you mean something or someone took them away unseen? Or that they just vanished?'

'That I couldn't say. But my friend said it was damned queer, and that the keepers nudged each other, or at least looked as if they knew more than they'd say, as if the same thing had happened before. It was jolly awkward for my friend. They all kept saying what a good day's shooting they'd had, but there was hardly a pheasant left, he thought – for they were unloaded out of sight in the stable yard – by the time they all got out at the house. They each took a couple of brace home, but he said he wouldn't be surprised if they'd been bought somewhere else in advance.'

'What sort of a ghost would it be,' my husband asked, 'to pinch all the pheasants?'

We all laughed.

'Perhaps there was a curse on the shooting,' someone suggested while our glasses were refilled. 'Like the curse on the castle,' inclining his head towards the long pale curtains that hid the night.

'Nonsense,' our host said quite sharply. 'A lot of twaddle talked on that subject. Curse indeed. They had to invent one, of course, with a place like that.'

'You've never seen . . . anything there then?' one of the ladies asked, looking appealing.

'Never,' our host said emphatically. 'Ask my wife. Lot of nonsense talked . . .'

Then we went in to dinner.

The dining-room was equally austere but did not look cold. There must have been a little hint of yellow or gold in all that white paint, and the paintings were in deeper, more sumptuous colours. I recognized a Matthew Smith flower piece and the abstract painting opposite me was all velvety reds and a green that might almost have been blue.

I sat between two of the younger men and enjoyed their company. Talk was easier and I felt less alien, and both my neighbours seemed not at all overawed by our hosts, the company, or the surroundings.

The first course was delicious, a fish *soufflé*, and my lefthand neighbour spoke in a low voice when he asked, 'Do you really believe they've never seen a ghost?'

It hadn't occurred to me that 'they' might have dissembled. If there was a ghost in the ruins they'd be proud of it, surely. An ancestor, and anyway the sheer look of the place would be enhanced.

'Why should they deny it?' I therefore asked.

'Lots of reasons. Not very nice to have in the family, for one. Then also what a bore it would be to be asked endless questions. They might even bring cameras down and lights, and try to flush it out. Then again it might repel rather than attract, keep their guests away if there was a chance of coming upon the abbess staring out of the chapel window.'

'The abbess? I'd always heard that it was the first owner who was seen in the ruins at night, and one of the books says that when the castle was burned down the young heir was burned with it – some funny business, he was locked up somewhere – and that he walks about on a dark night looking for the cause of the fire or perhaps for the people who locked him in.'

'I'd like to see him, wouldn't you, or the abbess for that matter,' my young neighbour said. 'Or don't you believe in ghosts?'

'No,' I said. 'I really don't think I do. And when you see the children playing hide-and-seek in the ruins in the daytime, or dumping their clothes on the walls during a football match, it's hard to believe anything of the past is left there.'

'Would you like to see it rebuilt?'

'Oh no,' I said, while my husband, diagonally across the table and with no business to listen to my conversation, said, 'Oh yes!'

'It wouldn't make sense with all those big, cold rooms,' I defended myself, but, 'Oh, you're just romantic,' my righthand neighbour said.

Then they served the saddle of venison.

'How lovely,' I said, raising my voice to reach my hostess at the end of the table. 'I haven't had venison since I was a child,' and the name came unbidden into my mind: *Rehrücken*. For though I had long forgotten my native tongue as people had forgotten, or had never known, that I was a 'foreigner', a word would sometimes come back to me, and now I remembered how often we had eaten venison at home in Germany.

But it was only when I tasted the first piece that a whole part of my life came into mind, replacing for a flash – for I continued polite conversation with my neighbour – the light, modern room and the present company.

With that taste I was transported on to our kitchen balcony among the pots of parsley and chives, the box of shoe-cleaning stuff and the crock of dill pickles, where our dachshund liked to come and smell the air to save himself the stairs, and I was looking up – I was still quite small – at the hare and pieces of venison, saddle and haunches, that hung there every autumn. I would reach up and touch the soft fur of the hare which hung by its hind legs, its little face masked by a bloodstained bit of paper, and I knew that these were gifts from my parents' three hunting friends, and that they had arrived wrapped in sacking, sent by rail and delivered by a messenger on a bicycle who received a tip or a glass of schnapps at the kitchen door.

I had looked at them with interest, not repulsed by their dead-animal aspect but already savouring this taste that now came back to me out of the past, saddle of venison in cream, rich and tasty with the pieces of larding like marzipan in the dark flesh. Sometimes I had been allowed to help the cook thread the pieces of lard into the larding needle: square piece of lard into square aperture at its end, and watch the cook's muscles bulge under the short blue sleeves as she drew the needle through the tough, raw meat.

Throughout my childhood the game had arrived, regular as clockwork with the season, and regularly too postcards had come from the three hunters, almost illegible in green ink, either announcing the imminent arrival of gifts, their prey, or their own annual visit.

They hadn't looked incongruous in our dark drawing-room with the big carved furniture. Some of the carvings might even have been of hunting scenes or of the heads of animals, stag and boar. They had worn green jackets with horn buttons and plus-fours with high checkered socks, and 'English' brogues with lolling tongues, and had had a lolling-tongued dog with them, a German pointer bitch whom I loved and of whom I was afraid. She had sat when told, and her reddened eyes had followed every movement of her masters and ourselves, and I had been sent into the kitchen to fetch a bowl of water for her thirst.

They had been an ill-matched trio and quite outlandish in our household where visitors were always 'family' or the most intimate of friends. Maybe my parents had met them at some holiday resort and kept up with them for reasons of mutual advantage. Perhaps my father had known the eldest of them, Hugo, in the Kaiser's army in the Kaiser's war not long ended. It was he who wrote the illegible postcards and who was the accepted leader of the group, not at all in his first youth, small and spiky like his handwriting, with his hair tending to stick up, his nose and chin pointed, a sharp smile on his lips. In memory they were forever smiling, though the second of the trio, Benno, less so than the others, a stoutish man who looked preoccupied as if he were busy making his way in business or some profession and couldn't really spare the time for their escapades. He spoke less than the others, sounded a bit pedantic, but it was only too likely that when it came to the real object of their visit, down in the cellars, he wasn't long left behind the others and could sing as raucously (I'd heard them once or twice before I went to bed) and talk as much, and feel as awful next morning.

Under the yard and under the big hall where the presses stood, and under the neighbouring house and the street ran our wine cellars. They were places full of drips and of the rats our dog chased, and between casks and the huge racks of bottles stood the filters shaped like flat metal men, once painted red but mottled with use, frightening under the bare bulbs. And it had been to visit the cellars that the three friends had come.

My favourite had been the youngest of the three, Sepp, almost a boy still, so that with that instinctive knowledge of a child I had felt close to him although he stood six foot and towered above his friends. It was he who had owned the dog, he who had come to talk to me, his big hands spread on his knees, a grin on his good-natured face. He had shown me his gun once, down in the yard, and had pointed it at the cat and said 'bang-bang' which had frightened me though I hadn't shown it. When I had looked up at him, up and up, I had realized that it had been only in fun, that he wouldn't have shot a cat. 'Roof rabbits' some people called them, remembering perhaps the starving days of the end of the war, and the great Inflation a few years later. Those were things Sepp and I knew little about, and this had been another link: the way our elders bored us with their past.

Down in the yard Sepp had looked rather like our workmen, the cellar master who was shorter but equally sturdy and the others who carted casks about as if they were toys. Sepp had talked to them too, where Hugo and Benno preferred my father's company, and I could imagine him heaving the great hods of grapes on to his shoulders at harvest time, his great hands cleaning out the wine-presses, or how he would roll those big filters about down in the cellars.

I didn't like the cellars and seldom went there, only enjoyed the *frisson* of fear near the dark corners where the drips were (and presumably the rats) when I was with my father, my hand in his and his voice reassuring me and talking to the men. Later my friends suggested games of hide-and-seek, but the grown-ups' prohibition had been a good excuse to veto this without showing my lack of courage.

The wine itself was part of everyday life, drunk at every meal and endlessly discussed, my father's business and the family's livelihood. The cellars were full of it, casks, barrels and bottles, but it was never consciously connected with drunkenness, only with the enjoyment of its bouquet and its varied degrees of excellence and the far-away places it was sent. Even now, so many years later, we had drunk a pleasant Rhine wine with the fish *soufflé*, and I had craned my neck to catch a familiar name on the pretty label.

But the hunters, when they had had their sober visit in the drawing-room, drinking tea perhaps or just watching the dog drinking water, had said their polite farewells to my mother and myself and vanished with my father into the cellars. That had been the end of their visit as far as I was concerned. My father had come up again a little later, smiling and shaking his head indulgently, but I knew, having heard gossip or simply putting an unconscious two and two together, that they weren't likely to leave the premises until the early hours when they would convey each other as best they could to the hotel at the corner of the street where they always put up.

Then one year a more than usually illegible postcard arrived to announce that Sepp had died. It had been rained or maybe wept on, and my parents puzzled over it as they tried to decipher its shocking message. And because death, like drunkenness, was something not to be discussed in front of me ('*pas devant l'enfant*' was said long after I knew enough French), I was never told how he died, and because he was so closely connected in my mind with guns and shooting it never occurred to me that he could have succumbed to pneumonia or fallen downstairs, been in a train crash, or that he might have carried with him for years the seed of some fatal disease. I took it for granted that he had been shot like the hare and the deer, accidentally, and presumably by one of his friends, and I sometimes imagined Sepp coming unexpectedly out of a clump of trees, green as a bush in his hunting clothes, and falling to the ground, the report of a gun in my ears. It didn't really affect me deeply, but I was by then of an age when death was rather romantic when connected with the young, and I convinced myself that I mourned him. I asked my parents what had happened to his dog, but they didn't know.

And then the other two had arrived one day, presumably announced as usual, and we had all sat in the drawing-room and they had talked about poor Sepp. There had been a new dog, more frightening than Sepp's although I had been older.

At first their voices had been lowered, Hugo had patted me on the head and said how much I'd grown. Later things had got back to normal, jokes had been swopped, Benno had seemed livelier than I'd remembered as if to make up for the missing third.

I had been a bit offended by the levity, had told myself that grown-ups were 'awful', uncaring, excused myself and gone into my room to mope, trying to write a poem about a young hunter who had been shot. I had felt sad and poetic, but the lines wouldn't rhyme or scan. Later I had been called to say goodbye and had heard my father escorting the two friends down the stairs, across the yard, and I had stood on the kitchen balcony to watch them open the green double doors that led to the slippery and concave steps down to the main cellar, and seen my father come back after a while.

That evening our dog had gone missing. This happened often enough, he was a scavenger and often went to visit friendly dustbins down the road. But for some reason my fickle love – I seldom wondered where he'd got to – fastened on the dog, and I wouldn't rest until I'd found him.

'I'll just have a look in the yard,' I had told the cook, 'and see that he hasn't been shut in anywhere.'

But I hadn't been able to find him and it had occurred to me that he might be rat hunting in the cellars. When I opened the door to call him the familiar cellar smell of wine and fermentation and damp met me, and I called down the stairs rather feebly for the lights were on and a great noise met me down there where voices could echo and rumble and where I liked to whisper. Then I remembered our visitors and thought it unlikely that the dog would be ratting on such a noisy night.

But once on the top step of the stairs some impulse made me go down. I may have thought that I'd like to see what they 'did' down there, what the attraction was in drinking wine which had been drawn into a jug straight from the barrel, and all that singing and falling about which I knew, by gossip or conjecture, went on.

And there they were: Hugo and Benno, and the cellar master who had upended a box and was sitting as comfortably as in his own quarters, singing with a fearfully loud and raucous voice, putting the other two to shame. Hugo was leaning against an upright barrel and had lifted his head as if to make his voice carry better, while Benno, splay-legged and awkward, was filling a jug from a barrel. A bright electric bulb hung right above them making their shadows huge and black, duplicating and exaggerating their movements, enlarging and distorting their features. And in the background, at the end of the avenue of casks and in their shadow stood a filter, reminding me more than ever of a flat, thin human shape.

Oh how they sang! I wanted to clap my hands over my ears but needed one to hold on to the stair railing, for I was just about to turn and go back up the slippery stairs into the good air of the yard and to bed, forgetting the dog's nocturnal wandering and despising my elders for the fools they made of themselves.

Then I saw Sepp. His mouth was open in song like the others', his hand held a glass. He was just outside the glare of the electric light, in the half-shadow of a cask. His movements, when he lifted the glass to his mouth, bending his head to meet it, were as calm as they had always been, and though he seemed to be propped against the barrel, his legs didn't totter when he shifted them to redistribute his weight to take a long draft. I watched, fascinated, not afraid, wondering whether the others knew that he was there, whether they would refill his glass as if it were the most natural thing in the world. He bent down and put the glass on the floor, and there it stood in the glaring light, empty and so natural that the unnaturalness of its being there gripped me by the throat and I gasped. They started a new song. Hugo, bending down to pick up his own glass lost his equilibrium, and the cellar master put out a hand to help, half turned and saw Sepp. Sepp, bending down, and his hand half-way to the glass, seemed to stare at the sitting figure, a glass fell and exploded on the stone floor like a gunshot, and in a flash Sepp looked towards the stairs as if for an escape, met my eyes and fell straight into the brilliantly lit aisle, vanishing as he went down. But I had seen, as our eyes met for that fearful moment, a trickle of blood at the corner of his mouth.

Then I fled soundlessly, letting myself out into the yard, sitting down immediately in the open air against a cold wall, panting like a dog and wanting to scream.

But I didn't scream, for it already seemed that I could not have seen what I had seen, and I buried the memory deep in my nightmares. Then for a while I wouldn't eat hare or saddle of venison or any game that came to the table.

'What a pity,' my mother would say, 'that you've lost your good taste,' and I would be given yesterday's stew warmed up.

Now, at that table, with everyone talking animatedly, I remembered for the first time for years meeting those eyes and felt again that uncanny sensation of the crawling of the flesh and my hair lifting itself off my scalp of its own volition. For the eyes had seemed so very dead, two deep black holes into nothingness, yet there had appeared to be some living expression too as if Sepp had seen me and was trying to tell me something.

Now I went on eating, and my hosts and the other guests went on talking all around me, and I added a little word or two occasionally and hoped I hadn't gone pale at the recollection. They talked about ways of cooking game and then about the way the Victorians had painted dead animals, so horrendously dead sometimes. 'A trickle of blood at the mouth,' somebody said, laughing, and I felt really faint for a moment, holding on to the knife and fork as if they could save me. Somebody mentioned the French passion for eating songbirds, and somebody else complained they were being quite put off their food, and there was laughter because our plates, mine as well, were quite empty, and the hostess and the cook were being congratulated.

'A delicious meal,' I said again as we left. It was late, had been a good evening with a lot of interesting talk. We'd gone to look at the paintings in other rooms, our hostess, who had collected them, talked about the painters she had met in her native New York and here in England, and in France where she often went, famous names were mentioned and then some books were brought out, and finally we looked at a folio of prints of the castle, made in the last century before they cut down the ivy and took some notice of the lovely slender windows and cleaned up the carvings in the chapel.

'You must come again,' our hostess said, and we all went out into the misty autumn night and found our cars and called goodnight to each other and how nice it had been to get acquainted, while the front door shut, putting out that yellow carpet of light.

Then the car doors banged and engines started, lights sprang up, and the ruins vanished as the road was lit up by the first car drawing away. We followed. My husband had started to tell me about a conversation he had had with one of the other guests, then swore when he had to brake sharply. The couple in the first car seemed to be having some sort of trouble, perhaps the engine had stalled or the wife had remembered that she had left something behind. They appeared to be arguing. I looked at them, turned towards each other in the front seats, and then my eyes wandered to the castle ruins which stood darkly against the lighter sky. The headlights of the car in front lit up part of the chapel and I stared at it, listening to my husband.

'Should I get out and ask what's the matter?' he wondered aloud.

'Leave them to sort it out,' I said and then saw that the chapel wall was overgrown with ivy as in the old print, green and bushy and hiding the familiar stone, and as my eye travelled, amazed, over that unfamiliar surface I came to the chapel window, in deep shadow, and saw, as if it were resting on the sill between the slender arches, the pale round blob of a face. It was some way away, but the more I looked at it the clearer it became, until I could see the eyes, black holes boring through the intervening space, and a dark trickle at the mouth.

I shook my head, closed my eyes and said, 'Perhaps you'd better see whether you can help those two.'

My voice sounded quite normal, but when I opened my eyes there it still was, just beyond the bright green ivy lit up by those headlights, and the face of a young man stared and stared at me.

'Did he have a fall?' I asked involuntarily, 'or was he really burned with the building?' And I imagined him, the dead young heir of another century, not locked up as legend had it, but running along corridors, seeking a way out while fire crackled around him, finally falling or jumping from a high window, his broken body on the ground illuminated by that pyre, the trickle of blood at his lips.

'Did who?' my husband asked, and then the car in front finally moved and we went after it, passing the bare stone walls of the castle ruins where no ivy grew, the empty window of the chapel, leaving it all behind for the lights of the little town, driving fast into the autumn night, the park silent and empty of deer.

Alexander Cordell

The lovers

When the buzzer went, Julia gathered her notebook and pencil and walked quickly through the typewriting clamour of the editorial to the door marked 'Assistant Editor'.

Paul, with his feet on his desk, said, 'Julia, the old man wants you to handle this one. It ought to make a good ending to our *Fifty-Year Recollection* series.' He slid a file along the desk towards her. 'Somebody's given him this old police file; you'd better read it up.'

'From the police archives, eh?' Impressed, Julia turned the pages.

'Yes, and there's some pretty good reading in it.' Rising, Paul looked over her shoulder. 'Listen to this,' and he read from the file:

'I . . . I'm telling you the truth, Your Honour. I didn't kill her. Moira Doyle was my girl before this rich young chap come along, and she loved me. She used to light the lamp in the attic and I'd see it and go up there to "Windleash". I did her no harm I tell you, neither then nor later, when they moved down to Plymouth . . .'

Julia said, 'For heaven's sake who wrote that?'

'It's the evidence for the defence – Saul Moran's testimony at his trial. He was hanged fifty years ago today in Plymouth for the murder of Moira Doyle, a maid servant in Windleash Manor.'

'And the editor thinks there's a story in it?'

Paul nodded. 'The old man's no fool. He can smell a story a mile off. Good Home Office stuff, he says, and I want Julia to get into it.'

'Just another murder? Where's the angle?'

Paul replied, lighting a cigarette, 'I'll tell you. Although this Saul Moran was buried in a felon's grave in the grounds of the prison, a headstone's been put up to him in Dooley churchyard – consecrated ground.'

'Who put it up?'

He shrugged. 'The villagers, apparently – and look at this,

the inscription on the stone,' and he turned another page of the file and read,

'But I shall rise again
Before the people stand
In defiance of the law
That brought me to this grave.'

'Good God,' whispered Julia.

'I thought you'd say that.' He closed the file and gave it back to her. 'All this ties in with the *Gazette*'s policy of anti-capital punishment, so get after it – there's a yarn here somewhere. I've booked you a room at the Bell in Dooley – a double.' He kissed her cheek. 'Get out to the churchyard today, take this file; interview the villagers, see if you can come up with anything. And give me a ring when you get to the Bell.'

Julia said, 'So you're not getting tired of the girls around here!'

Paul waved her away, 'No, but I am getting tired of the *Halford Country and Commercial Gazette*. This is kids' stuff, Julie, and at times the old man acts like a crank. When he read this file he raised his arms to the ceiling like a fakir and shouted, "Rise from the dead, Saul Moran, and we will prove your innocence. What's good enough for the villagers of Dooley is good enough for me!" – it was like the raising of Lazarus.' He held up a key. 'This is the key of the front door of Windleash. The agent let me have it in case the caretaker isn't there – he's often out on the beer, apparently. You might like to take a look around if it isn't too eerie in the churchyard.'

'It even feels eerie in here,' said Julia.

Taking the file away she read it from cover to cover. The inscription on his gravestone seemed to lift Saul Moran up from the great concourse of the dead.

Julia found the church on the outskirts of Dooley. Rain was spitting and a little wind rising by the time she reached Saul Moran's headstone. The inscription was accurate with that in the file, otherwise it was unremarkable – the same as any other gravestone. But, near the lych gate, she met a man sitting on a milestone near her Mini.

'You been readin' about poor old Saul, 'ave ya, missus?'

Lifting his moleskin cap, he greeted her with a smile and a wink, his small eyes regarding her from under his bushy brows. 'Lots of folk been up to see our Saul recent – this being his anniversary, so to speak.' He got up from the stone and leaned on his spade; towering above her, his movements seemed drunk with strength.

'Anniversary?' But she knew what he meant.

'Ay, ay. Fifty year ago this mornin' they topped him, didn't they!' came the reply. 'I reckon as how that's a sort o' anniversary, ain't it? Though it's one the poor soul could have done without, I expect. And what's your business, may I ask?'

'I'm a reporter from the *Halford Gazette.*'

'Well now, ain't that interestin' ... and you aim to write a piece on poor old Saul, is it?'

The rain was quickening. Julia pulled up the collar of her mac. 'Only about him being hanged and buried in prison ... and yet he has a headstone here. That's strange in itself, isn't it?'

His little eyes moved over Julia's face with a darting apprehension.

Once, long ago, he had known a woman like this: one whose hair was bright and like flax in his fingers, whose body was soft to his touch: he would have liked to touch this woman as he had touched the other, but the punishment was fierce for such a transgression. Now he said bassly, raising his face, 'What's so strange about it, then? Folks was fair in them old days. Everybody in Dooley knew he didn't do it, and him buried in lime in the prison yard ... so they puts up a stone in holy ground ...'

'He didn't murder Moira Doyle, you mean?'

'Course he didn't. I mean, I'm only young – t'was before my time, of course, but nobody in Dooley reckoned they should 'ave topped him. You know the yarn about it, don't ye?'

As she was after information, Julia shook her head, and he said, 'Well, this servant girl, Moira Doyle, she were at the big house – Windleash ...' he nodded down the road. A dim light was burning among the wet trees in the distance. 'And poor ole Saul, he fancied her, ye see. He were a true brave young chap, and young Moira, she used to lead him on, you understand? Get him randy for her like – beggin' ye pardon, missus.

She'd leave the key in the front door when everybody else was out, and her coat over the banisters, and a light burning in the attic where she slept, like it's burning now. O aye, according to reports she were a real hot piece, if ye understand . . .?' He peered down at Julia.

'And then?'

'Then one day when Saul went up for his fun, she'd 'ave nothing to do wi' him. "Out, out!" says she, "no more o' this danged old rabbitin'," and she heaves him off.' His big, wet hands moved before Julia's face, warming to the tale. 'You see, she'd just come across some rich well-spoken chap – a writing fella he were, apparently, and she were staying with him in the Bell Inn in Dooley. Aye! Fancying it up, they were, as large as life and no shame, neither, and poor old Saul not gettin' any.' His puddle of a face stared down at Julia in the rain and the water was dripping from his beard. 'And Saul knew he'd collected himself a hussy, and said in the village that he'd kill this chap, and Moira, too, and the pair of 'em got frit, see, and ran to Plymouth for work there, and the tale goes that old Saul he followed 'em there, and killed Moira because she were having this chap's baby.'

'Oh, no!'

'Oh, yes, he cut her throat – ripped her up somethin' terrible, they said.' He peered about him in the rain. 'I got to go, missus. What time is it?'

Julia looked at her watch. 'Just turned eight.'

The man swung his spade over his shoulder. 'Gone eight? Gawd! I've got a grave to dig tonight.' He nodded towards the distant house. 'Sad really, ain't it? Up goes poor old Saul to the attic, all buttoned up and polished and ready for love, and that Moira gives him the boot. A bitch she were, I reckon. I'd 'ave done the same, mind – O, ah! I'd 'ave cut her up for it – and think no more'n cutting the throat of a little old sow. Ah!' He elbowed Julia, knocking her sideways. 'You think of it, if you was a man, missus. The key were in the door, her coat was on the banister, a light was burnin' in her attic and she hadn't a stitch on her. "Here I come, my lovely!" shouts Saul, and out him goes on his backside, begging ye pardon for the language, missus.' He shook his big head sadly. 'That fancy-pant writing chap, he'd got it all.' He straightened. 'Ah well, little lady – be seein' ye directly, God willing,' and he bowed low to Julia and left her, striding away over the sheeted road.

The rain was pouring down now; thunder was clattering over the world.

Pretty good weather, thought Julia, for a meeting with a gravedigger.

I'd 'ave cut her up for it ... *I'd 'ave cut her up ...*

Getting into the Mini, Julia shivered.

Thinking that she'd better first check in at the Bell Inn in Dooley, Julia drove through the gathering storm to the Gallows Cross. Thunder was booming and reverberating over the moor now, lightning slashing the sky in blue forks. Temporarily unable to see, Julia slowed the car before turning right for the village; instantly, in a gush of steam, the engine spluttered and died.

It was only then that she realised she was in the ford. Storm water was racing round the car wheels.

'*Damn!* Damn and blast it!'

Disconsolate, repeatedly turning the electric starter, Julia eventually sat in soaked misery, listening to the storm.

Julia held her watch against the glimmering red light of the ignition. It was ten o'clock; she had been there for two hours and, if anything, the storm was increasing in violence. There was no apprehension in her, only a healthy anger that she'd left the comparative shelter of the church and hadn't even had the foresight to put a blanket in the car for such an eventuality. Now she stared at her face in the shimmering windscreen; watched, with an eerie interest, its contours constantly changing on the beaded glass. At half-past ten she got fed up with this, got out of the car and into the flood-water and ran the quarter of a mile back to the church, but its doors were locked. For a while she sat in its porch, cursing the weather. Thunder, detonating overhead, drove her back to the car.

Now chattering with cold, she tried the starter again: nothing happened. Julia stared through the windscreen again, instantly seeing not the reflection of her own face, but that of another.

She rubbed her eyes.

Before her on the glass, in constant lightning flashes, was the bearded face of the gravedigger, the man she had met. Clearly she saw it; the little eyes that regarded her with a mocking concern, the broken teeth ... And then the apparition disappeared and the reflection of her own face took shape again.

Imagination, she knew, could play tricks: she was cold and tired and the man's personality was dominant. With cold practicality, Julia put it out of her mind, yet she found she was no longer looking at the windscreen before her lest the vision return.

She began to wonder what would happen when she didn't arrive at the Bell Inn to claim her room. Perhaps nothing. Lots of people booked hotel rooms and failed to claim them. It wouldn't be a national calamity if she didn't arrive at all, unless, of course, Paul phoned her there. And he would most certainly do so when she didn't telephone him. She wondered where he was having dinner that night, and couldn't remember. They usually stayed together at the Bell – once a month at least – for the past year, since they'd become lovers. She smiled at her thoughts as she remembered the Dooley gravedigger: what had he called Moira Doyle for staying the night with a man – a hussy, was it? Then, unsmiling, she thought it strange that both she and Moira should have stayed at the same inn with their lovers ... It could even have been in the same room. Perhaps the same bed ... The thought chilled her. Even the names Saul and Paul were strangely coincidental ...

Presently Julia sank into a shuddering, sweating drowse, to awake with a start, stiff and chilled. She felt sick with cold and loneliness, and, for the first time, fear.

This wasn't a normal storm, thought Julia, it was a cloudburst; an unending tumult of lightning and terrifying thunder. She looked at the time in the flame of her lighter. It was gone eleven and there was no sign at all of the storm abating. The car was rocking to the mad assaults of the wind, the flood level was rising in the ford: to her horror she saw the water lapping into the car; soon it was rising around her feet.

She remembered with a shock an article Paul had written about a woman and a child being drowned in such conditions. Oh God, she'd remembered: it was in this very ford! She would have to leave the car; before it became impossible to leave, she would have to run for it and try to reach Dooley. And then, she actually cried aloud with relief. Windleash! The house! Why hadn't she remembered it before – it was little more away than the church. What's more, she had the key of the door. Hadn't she seen a light burning there? Of course she had – the gravedigger had pointed it out. She cursed her forgetfulness. Fear was at the bottom of it, of course – she had panicked – she who prided herself on her calmness under stress. All she had to do was knock and the caretaker would let her in.

She tried to open the car door but the weight of water held it back. Gasping, she got her shoulder against it and braced her legs against the dashboard: the door swung back and the storm water roared in, instantly rising to her thighs. Gasping with the shock, Julia climbed out into the ford. She was standing waist high in a flood. Grabbing her suitcase, she forced her body against the head of water and gained the bank. There she sat in the mud, shivering, clutching the suitcase.

Why hadn't Paul come? she wondered. It was past eleven o'clock and he'd made no apparent attempt to find her. Perhaps, when she hadn't phoned him, he'd thought she didn't want him ...? She began to cry, her fingers forming a cage over her mouth. With the rain pouring down on the swollen ford, she sat there crying. After a while she rose and began a soaked, squelching journey towards Windleash.

Julia saw the attic light of the manor shining through the wet, flailing trees of the garden. With the rhododendron bushes of the drive towering above her, she limped up to the front door and fumbled in her pockets for the door key, pulling out the linings in her nervous agitation. And then, seeing the bell-pull, she jangled the bell within. Key in hand, she waited, then repeatedly crashed down the knocker. Nobody came. The light was still burning from the topmost room, but the caretaker didn't answer. She tried the key in the door but the lock wouldn't turn.

She began to whimper with pain and cold. Some fool of an agent had given Paul the wrong key. Desperately, she twisted and turned it, skinning her fingers. Suddenly, the big door burst open, projecting her headlong into the hall. Lightning flared, lighting a wide expanse of parquet flooring and the ghost-like drapes of sentinel furniture. Thunder hammered within the empty house.

Wearily, Julia climbed to her feet and backed against the door, slamming it shut.

She didn't realize that the key was outside, still in the lock.

Lurching up the broad stairs towards the glimmering light above, she paused on the landing to pull off her soaked mackintosh and lay it over the banisters to dry.

The servants' back stairs, uncarpeted, echoed as she climbed them to the attic. Outside the attic door, she knocked, calling softly:

'Anybody home?'

Her voice echoed down the stairs of the hall. She pushed at the attic door and it swung back, exposing a large, untidy room within.

Distantly, in a sudden quiet of the storm, Julia could hear the tolling of a bell. It seemed like a small greeting as she entered the attic, if a little doleful. The old house with its drapes and light seemed to beckon her with arms of warmth. And the feeling of kinship with another human being – the belongings of the absent caretaker – brought companionship. It was a big room, furnished with period high-backed chairs, a single bed used by the caretaker, his bedside table and, best of all, a small electric fire. On the other side of the room, facing the door, was a canopied sea of a bed with a hair mattress and piled brown blankets.

Still shivering, Julia switched on the fire and began to take off her wet clothes, draping them over a chair to dry them; while waiting, she sat on the bed and pulled the blankets about her naked body.

Silence.

It was the eye-silence of the storm: the vacuum of quiet within the tumult when all opposing forces were cancelled. A mouse was scuttling in the wainscoting; it seemed the only sound of the night.

Julia pulled a blanket about her shoulders and went to the attic window. Thrashed and sodden, the country below lay motionless under a faint, watery moon; nothing stirred. It was as if she were the only human left alive. But, even as she watched, the topmost branches of trees began to stir; the hedgerows rustled, the wind began again a sad crying. And Julia saw, in a quick blaze of the moon, a man standing in the courtyard below. Fearfully, she drew back into the shadows of the curtains. With a trembling hand, she opened them and peered. It was ridiculous, she thought; it was all ridiculous. Her eyes, her senses were playing tricks again: the man had disappeared. One moment he was there, hands on hips, staring up at a lighted window, next moment he had vanished.

Frowning, she returned to the fire and knelt before it, her hands out to its single red bar. She had to get hold of herself, she thought: an unusual fear touched her being and she shuddered. Bile rose to her throat – the old sickness again, and she swallowed it down. She was beginning to see things that were not there; hear unusual sounds; it was like a crawling madness. Had she seen the man in the courtyard, she wondered. The face on the windscreen – was that a spectral image? The man in the churchyard – was he real?

Even as she was thinking these things a telephone bell within the house began a fearful, strident ringing.

Julia leapt up. At first it seemed like some obscene magic come to torment her; then the very normality of the sound snatched at her, and she shouted aloud, joyously, 'Paul! *Paul*!'

Overwhelmed with relief and happiness, she wrapped the blanket around her and clattered down the servants' stairs. Of course, it was Paul! She shouted his name as she ran. It was Paul ringing her from Dooley – from the Bell. Perhaps they had even found the Mini. The imperious clanging of the telephone, echoing below her, drove Julia on, almost headlong down that broad staircase to the hall, to stand there, staring this way and that, seeking its direction. And finding it, she ran, with the blanket slipping off her in her frenzy: but at the moment she reached the telephone, the ringing stopped. Receiver in her hand, she clattered the arm, for the line was dead.

'Paul, Paul! I'm here. Is that you, Paul?'

Silence.

There was no sound in the house but the moaning of the wind.

Replacing the receiver, she picked up the blanket and drew it about her body, staring at the front door.

It was open. Unbelievably, the front door was wide open.

And bright footsteps of clay led from the door to the stairs. Sheet lightning flashed and she saw them clearly . . . Footprints going up the stairs.

She screamed. Hands to her face, Julia screamed, and, as she screamed so thunder clattered, detonating directly over the house in a vivid fork of lightning. The blanket fell to her feet. Naked again, she ran for the stairs, beckoned by the light of the attic. And her screams, as she stumbled up the stairs, were flung back at her from the bare rooms as a mockery of her manufactured terror. Whimpering, sobbing, she gained the attic and slammed the door behind her, vainly trying to jam a chair beneath its handle. Beaten, for the chair was too high, she threw herself on to the canopied bed and lay there moaning hysterically. The room was being lit by lightning of stunning brilliance, the thunder was crashing as if to split the heavens. And Julia lay face down among the scattered blankets, trying to obliterate both the noise and her terror.

After a little while the storm quietened.

Listening, she lay motionless.

Slowly, she pulled the blankets away from her face.

Her tear-stained cheeks stared into blackness. The light had gone out.

The small red glow died as the fire went out.

With tingling nerves, Julia listened.

She had heard a sound on the stairs.

Footsteps?

In the darkness her eyes opened wide. A board creaked.

Somebody was coming up the servants' stairs.

The moon was shining through the window now.

Transfixed, breathless, she was watching the handle of the door.

It slowly turned.

The door swung slowly open, and silently. Pausing momentarily, it swung shut, yet nobody entered.

But . . . and she was staring through the faint light . . . something was in the room.

Something was approaching the bed.

She smelled again the sweet, sad earth-smell that she had smelled in the cemetery.

Julia's heart was thudding against her chest; it was in her head, her brain, a thudding that possessed her. The moon brightened. Bright yellow. Footprints of clay were approaching her, staining the boards of the floor. Strangely, within the limits of her remaining sanity, Julia watched them, fascinated. Her mouth was open, her eyes horrified; hysterically shaking, she screamed: three times she screamed but no sound came forth; from her convulsed throat she could make no sound.

And, in the vacuum of her terror, as one hypnotized, she saw the corner of a blanket slowly rise, lifted by unseen fingers: higher, higher it rose, as a blanket rises when one seeks a bed. Next, the mattress sank beside her: she sensed a new coldness near her trembling limbs.

And, as Julia lay back on the bed in the knowledge of horror, a face made shape above her.

A face made shape which was not a face but a mask of clay: nor was it fashioned of itself but was lime-covered, as the whiteness of the ceiling; and, as this mask grew nearer it assumed human proportions.

The head and face of the man of the cemetery.

The beard Julia knew first, then his little eyes, furtively shifting, the broken teeth; and the whispering she heard was not of human voice, nor was the breathing that of human breath, but rancid with corruption.

She did not resist, she knew no strength.

But lay within a corpse embrace, living yet dead; a fraud of dying.

And knew a coldness.

Calling the name of her lover, which was Paul.

'Saul, Saul, *Saul* . . .' she said.

00.40 hours. The ringing of the telephone again brought her back to life. The ringing persisted, again Julia stirred in that embrace.

The ringing was a living thing and jangled in her deadness.

It tore her from the vice-like grip that chained her to the bed.

With flailing limbs she scratched and bit, tasting earth; and the substance between her teeth was of lime and clay and splintered bone: and the ringing commanded her so that she fought and shrieked within the abyss, driving all away. And in her growing consciousness knew one fact – that she was the living understudy in an obscene and horrifying drama that was being played to the end; the facts portrayed, she knew herself as a counterfeit lover of Saul; the *doppelgänger* of Moira Doyle, a girl long dead.

Even as she tore herself free and ran from the attic, the inevitable unfolded in her brain . . . the facts relayed – *the raising of Saul from his grave, the key in the door, the light invitation in the attic, the coat draped over the banisters.* She had even, as Moira Doyle had done, spent the night at the Bell Inn with a lover, and for this Moira Doyle had died.

It was a legitimate repetition, step by step, fifty years later, of all that had happened before.

Knowing all this, Julia was incoherent by the time she reached the telephone; naked still and only gibbering. And, snatching at the receiver, she reeled and fell against the curtained shelf, and came face to face with Paul who had raced across the hall from the open door. And, when he gripped her, she fought in his arms as she had fought in the arms of a corpse, while he called to her:

'It's all right, Julia! I'm here – it's Paul. It's all right, I tell you!' But still she fought, kicking and scratching, so that he held her away and slapped her face.

The blow would have angered a man.

Julia slipped into unconsciousness, and Paul held her, calling her name as she lay in his arms, her bright hair hanging down, her arms drooping as he lowered her to the floor.

'Oh, my God. *Julia* . . .!' he said.

Julia, in her hospital room, got up from her bedside chair as Paul came in with flowers. Twice before, during her recovery, he had come, bringing her pink and white carnations.

'The colour of your cheeks at last,' he said.

Julia smiled. 'Yes, I feel tons better. With luck, they tell me, I'll be getting out tomorrow. Anything happening in the office?'

Paul kissed her. 'Oh, you know, the same old journalese – the Ladies' Guild, the Women's Institute, cricket, tourists, births and deaths . . .' He glanced at her.

'And how's the old man behaving?'

'Same as usual. If he's sane, I ought to be certified.' Paul sat on a chair, watching Julia; he was speaking gaily despite his apprehension. For there existed within her normality an evocation of something unreal; as if, though present, she was inexplicably absent. He had noticed this when they first brought her in by ambulance three days ago: the laughing Julia had gone; left behind was the ghost of the girl he knew. He said, 'Oh, by the way, I wrote up the Saul Moran story as far as I was able. Do . . . do you feel ready to talk about it in detail yet?'

'No.' With the flowers in her hands Julia went to the window, looking out.

Now he was at her shoulder, speaking of trivialities, and watched her pale, sad beauty while he spoke. Her eyes appeared to be looking into the far distance.

Lightly, Paul said: 'You'll be pleased to hear one thing, though – first thing I did this morning was to put old Saul back among the obituary notices – the old man thought it was good story publicity, and for you it should lay his ghost, so to speak . . .' His voice faded; Julia clearly wasn't listening.

She was staring down at the hospital grounds where white-coated hospital staff were chatting with patients in the sun. And on the white iron railings that skirted the drive, with his arms folded and a straw cocked up in his mouth, sat the gravedigger of Dooley. Paul was talking again, but Julia did not hear him.

'It's got to be a joke, hasn't it, old girl? This is the way to treat it, I mean – like a joke. If we don't we'll both go round the bend.' He faced her, adding, 'It's got to be imagination – things like you've described just don't happen ...'

The gravedigger had seen her; he was smiling up at the ward window.

Paul said, 'Look, last night I called at the cottage of the real gravedigger of Dooley. He's nothing like the chap you describe – he's small, very old, and as gentle as a kitten – you might have met him, Julia, but he hasn't met you ...'

Paul wondered if she was listening, also why she was smiling. He continued, 'You left the key in the door, didn't you? Of course somebody could have got in – I did, when I arrived. But the wet footsteps over the hall floor were yours, my love ...'

Julia nodded. The gravedigger on the railings below nodded back, and Paul said, 'Now come on – get hold of yourself. Yes the telephone did ring, but it was me the first time and I thought you weren't there, and the second time it was the police, after they'd found your car. Ghosts don't use the telephone, you know.' He kissed her face. 'And the only ghost you're ever likely to have in bed with you is me ...'

Julia didn't appear to hear him; head on one side, she was smiling at the window. In growing desperation, Paul said:

'Okay, we'll forget it. Listen, dear, here's some headline news. We've had an offer – do you hear that. An offer by phone from a really big newspaper – and for the pair of us ...'

Julia heard his words and replied automatically; suddenly she was feeling sick again. And she was wondering if she ought now to tell him about their baby. Perhaps the coming of the child would interfere with his plans.

He cried, gripping her arms, 'Aren't you listening, Julia? It'll mean leaving this one-eyed hole and working in a city, and ...'

'In Plymouth?' She turned back to the window.

Paul was astonished. 'Why, yes – the *Plymouth Star*, but how on earth did you know?'

'Because ...' She shrugged, smiling again. 'Well, we've got to go to Plymouth, haven't we? It's all arranged, isn't it?'

Julia answered Paul, but she was looking down at the grave-digger of Dooley, and he smiled assent, pulled a knife from his pocket and held it up to the sun.

Then drew his finger across his throat.

R. B. Hart

Dust

Mildred is 'doing out' my room. All I want to do is to die in peace, but she has to 'do out' my room. But then Mildred always was an aggravating woman.

I stare at the ceiling, wondering if today she will notice that cobweb above my head. It has been there for three days now.

She flick-flicks with her duster.

'It's a lovely day,' she says.

I know. Even if I am helpless, I am not blind.

'And the cherry blossoms are all out in the front garden.' Flick-flick. 'Quite lovely they look.'

I close my eyes, try to shut her out, her and her interminable flicking.

'There. I've done. Can you see? All nice and clean again.'

I open my eyes. It all looks very much as it had before – except that she has re-arranged the top of the dressing-table and I can no longer see the face of the clock. Even when a man is dying, he still likes to keep account of the time; can't she understand that?

She comes to the bed, fusses with my pillow.

'Alice is coming to see you this afternoon, Norman. Won't that be nice?'

Nicer than you'll ever know, you dried-up old hag. My God, we had some times, Alice and me. Time was . . .

She interrupts my thoughts again.

'Mushroom or chicken today, Norman?'

She is in fact enquiring which of those two soups I would prefer for my lunch today. I exist only upon soup. She spoons it down my gullet with consummate care.

She remembers how the question must be put if I am to answer it.

'Mushroom?'

I blink twice. I had mushroom soup yesterday. I, a dying man can remember that; so why the hell can't she?

'Chicken then?'

I blink once.

She pussy-foots out, leaving the door slightly ajar because she knows how I hate an airless room.

That cobweb is distinctly longer today, six or seven inches now at least. I'm surprised she hasn't noticed it. She is a most fastidious woman as a rule.

For myself, I like a bit of dirt, a bit of muddle, and I don't really mind the cobweb.

Alice is coming to see me this afternoon. The thought elates me. Lovely, gutsy Alice, my beloved wife's sister and as different from old Mildred as chalk is from cheese. By gum, Alice and me – the things we ...

No sooner is Mildred gone, it seems, than she is back again.

'I've brought you some nice soup,' she says. She likes everything to be 'nice'.

She draws up a chair beside my bed and squats her skinny haunches down upon it.

A spoonful of chicken soup is dribbled between my lips.

'That nice Mrs Bates ...'

The young woman who lives three or four doors down the avenue.

'... she's had a little boy.'

Inevitable, that. As one dies, another is born.

'... Her hubby's just rung Mrs Murchison ...'

Our next-door neighbour.

'... from the hospital. Isn't that nice?'

Very.

Odd, how the revolting idea of giving birth can stir excitement even in a dry and fussy old crone like Mildred. Babies send her into a quite delicious flutter. Mind you, whenever the urge to procreate coursed through my loins Mildred became a creature of migraines and mysterious aches. Sex was always abhorrent to her.

She drivels on. '... seven pounds and a few ounces. And just like young Mr Bates. Isn't that nice?'

She wipes my chin.

In my mind's eye I am presently conjuring the image of young Mr Bates engaged in the conception of this new offspring. Mrs Bates is young and very pretty. From behind the safety of the net-curtains in the back bedroom, I had often watched her sunbathing in her garden on Sunday afternoons. Lucky Mr Bates.

The cobweb stirs in the draught between the open window and the door.

I have found that the best way out always is to feign sleep.

'He's no better then,' whispers Alice.

Silence. Mildred probably shaking her head with funereal solemnity.

'Poor old chap,' commiserates Alice. 'Wouldn't he be better off in a home? I mean there are some nice places about these days for geriatrics ...'

Geriatric? Well, I suppose I am; but neither of them is far behind. Mildred is seventy-two – and Alice must be rising seventy if she's a day, although she does not look it, and even more certainly would never admit to it.

'What's your secret, Alice,' I used to say.

'Waiting for Fridays to come round,' she used to say. 'And this.'

'How's that Mrs Bates along the way?'

'A boy,' exclaims Mildred delightedly. 'A quarter to eight this morning. Eight pounds.'

Either her memory is failing or the child is expanding like a balloon. By the time Mr Bates fetches it from the hospital he will probably have to hack down the nursery wall so that this monstrous baby can stretch its feet into the room next door.

'I'll stay with Norman, if you like, Millie. If you want a break,' suggests Alice.

'Oh, no,' protests Mildred. 'He's fast asleep. He'll be no bother. I'll go and do my bit of shopping and you can go downstairs and watch the telly.'

At all of this my ears prick. I should like to be alone with Alice for one last time and have her talk to me.

I let my eyelids flutter open.

'Oh, look, he's awake!' exclaims Alice. She smiles down at me. She has never let herself go to seed and is still a fine woman. She still paints her face, wears smart clothes. She could easily pass for a well-preserved sixty.

She bends over me. 'Hello, Norman,' she growls, with that

gravelly voice she has still. She perches on the edge of the bed – Mildred detests that, it rumples the covers – and leans down to kiss me. She kisses me full on the mouth. Earthy women like Alice do not recoil from the idea of death the way women like Mildred do. It is a warm kiss, soft.

'How are you, old sport?'

'We're as well as can be expected,' replies Mildred, who acts as my intermediary when such questions are asked of me. 'Aren't we, Norman?'

Are we, hell. We are sinking fast and we know it. But I blink for Alice's sake. Her face is still close. It looks a little more rough-hewn than it used to, but the paint and the powder do their best to restore it the way I remember it in the old days.

Mildred stares tetchily at Alice's ample behind crushing the covers. 'I suppose you can stay with him if you want to, Alice. It *would* give me a chance to go out and do a bit of shopping.' She finishes then on a note of martyred weariness. 'I get so little time . . .'

'Do then.' Very business-like, Alice peels off her gloves, gives each a tug to stretch it, then lays them neatly side by side atop my bedside cabinet. 'You go out for a while, Mill. We don't mind being left alone together, do we, Norman? It isn't as if we're likely to get up to anything is it, eh, Norman?'

She winks at me, lewdly and lasciviously, her back safely to Mildred.

Mildred loathes any hint of filthy talk, even in jest.

'All right,' she agrees, but now with a certain reluctance. Then, irritably, 'But please don't sit on the edge of the bed, Alice, it makes him uncomfortable.'

It does nothing of the sort. But Alice obediently stands up and goes across to fetch the chair from beneath the window.

Mildred goes. She part-closes the door with her usual stealth and makes her silent way downstairs.

Alice perches herself back on the bed, strokes aside a lick of hair awry at my forehead, then leans down and kisses me softly again.

'Hello, Norman,' she whispers. The whisper still sounds like pouring sand. 'I don't suppose you ever told her, eh?'

I blink twice.

'No,' she whispers. 'I didn't reckon you ever would.'

She leans upright again, but leaving an arm across me, her fingers splayed on the quilt. Her eyes take on a nostalgic glitter. She smiles down at me with a smug and complacent smile.

'Good days we had, didn't we, Norman, you and me.'

I blink. They were unforgettable days.

'Brighton, eh?'

I blink.

'The Belvedere? Remember the old Belvedere.'

I blink rapturously.

The summer of '30 it was. I had been but a year married to Mildred, but already had found her dry and arid and incapable of loving.

Alice lifts her right hand from the quilt beside me. Its index finger bears the ring I bought her that day. At the Belvedere, for that riotous, glorious week, she had worn it on her wedding finger.

'D'you remember, Norm – we bought it off that little Jew who had that emporium near West Street.'

I probably remember it better than you do, Alice. His name was Solly Mandl.

It was a Sunday, a summer Sunday. Mildred had gone off the day before to spend the week with her mother at Clacton, and on that Sunday, at a loose end, I had slipped into my best duds and taken a cheap-day ticket down to Brighton. I was going there with the deliberate intention of picking up a woman, any sort of woman, for my year with Mildred had left me with such unspeakable needs that almost any sort of woman would have suited me.

'We bumped into each other on the front, didn't we – by the West Pier.'

It was the Palace Pier actually, Alice. I may be utterly helpless, but my memory is still pin-sharp. It was the Palace Pier, Alice, the one across the way from the Aquarium.

I had quartered the seafront all the way to Hove and back, eyeing up the girls in their skimpy summer dresses and their white-canvas shoes and their kiss-me-quick hats. I had found none of these bare-legged flibbertigibbets to my liking, not one.

Then I spotted you, Alice, only I did not realize that it was you at the time, sauntering out ahead of me on your high heels and your silk-cased legs – you were always smart, Alice – holding down your skirts with one hand and your silly little cloche on with the other. There was a stiff breeze off the sea that day. See, Alice, I can even remember obscure little details like that.

I sniffed after you like a hungry dog. Other men kept turning to look at you, and I hurried to draw level with you, practising my overtures, fearful that one of them would pick you up before I did.

Then, as I drew level with you, I recognized you, didn't I.

'Alice!'

You whipped around, and you smiled, as if I were the one person in all of Brighton that day you had hoped to see.

'Norman! How lovely!'

So were you, Alice.

Brother-in-law and sister-in-law. We had always been so cautious with each other, hadn't we, like a couple of swordsmen warily circling each other, each of us dreadfully aware of our mutual attraction but totally unable to do anything about it. When we were first introduced I was already engaged to old Mildred, and engagements in those days were not broken lightly. A pity, that.

We did Brighton, didn't we? The Pier, Madame Tussaud's, the Aquarium. You held my arm.

Then we took in that *thé-dansant* at the Belvedere. All very decorous, so far.

'... Until that dam' foxtrot, eh, Norman,' whispers Alice, bending over me close again, her eyes alight and gleaming.

The foxtrot was always a smoochy dance, even in the early '30s. Holding Alice close I made the most of it. She wore a heady perfume that day.

'I didn't half lead you on, didn't I, Norman,' whispers Alice. 'But we always had been mad for each other, hadn't we.'

I blink. I had never been as crazy for any woman, Alice, as I was for you during that foxtrot. I shuffled you into that dark corner behind the bandstand, didn't I, and I kissed you.

'... And you waited to get your face slapped.'

For my gall, I thought you would, but you did not. You

offered up your painted red bud of a mouth to be kissed again – in those days your mouth was not quite so thin as it is now. It was full-lipped – and reminded me always of Theda Bara's – and I kissed you again and felt you melt into me. Then you lidded your doll-blue eyes at me and whispered, 'Let's go somewhere, Norman, away from all these people.'

And I said, 'Let's book in here.'

And you hung by your bare arms from my neck and whispered, 'Whatever you want, Norman. You just say.'

'... And we went out to the lobby to book in, remember? and we saw that notice in the desk that said nobody could be booked in without luggage.'

I blink. I remember. So we went out and found a leather-shop by the Old Steine and I bought a cheap, fibre suitcase.

'... Then you said we ought to have a ring, Norman, remember. Lovely old Norman. You were so anxious for my respectability. And we bought this ...' Alice shows me the ring again, '... at that Jew's place.'

Solly Mandl's Jewellery Emporium, Alice, that's exactly where we bought it.

'Then we went back to the Belvedere, didn't we, Norman, you with the suitcase, me with my wedding ring. And you told the clerk that we were Mr and Mrs Player ...'

Because I had just bought twenty from the machine in the vestibule, that was. And I thought, as a name, that it sounded rather grand. Much better than plain old Smith.

'... and they gave us room Fourteen.'

Fifteen, Alice, Fifteen.

'... And the clerk asked you how long you wanted the room for. And you looked at me and I looked at you – and you looked him straight in the eye and said a week. And I thought, my God, I'm going to be locked up in an hotel room with this lovely man for a whole dam' week, and I went weak at the knees with the thought of it. I did, Norman, really.'

So did I, Alice, so did I. I followed you up the stairs, consumed with lust, you with your silk legs and swinging hips. I could hardly keep my hands off you till we reached that room. But Fifteen it was, Alice, Fifteen.

Alice's eyes can still smoulder, even now.

'We didn't even get to the bed, did we, Norman? God, you were a savage.'

And you were not much less of one, as I recall, Alice. You went for me like a bitch in heat. You cried out so loudly that I had to slap my hand over your mouth lest we were heard by the people next door; remember that too, Alice. It wasn't all me, was it?

'... And we stayed locked up in that room for a whole dam' week ...'

The door is opening behind you, Alice. Shut up!

'... didn't we. Except for meals. We went downstairs for meals, didn't we, Norman, then couldn't wait to get upstairs again.'

No, we couldn't, Alice! But shut up! Shut up! Mildred is behind you! In the doorway! Look in the dressing-mirror. You will see her!

But Alice will not shut up. Her erotic memorabilia is in full flood.

'Remember how you used to like me to keep my stockings on, Norman. You said my legs used to drive you dotty ...' Alice chuckles fatly at this, my quaint predilection. '... And I did, didn't I?'

Dam' you, Alice, I rage my head. For Jesus Christ's sake, shut up! Mildred is not two yards across the room behind you! She has not gone shopping, Mildred! Not gone!

I try to warn Alice of Mildred's presence by blinking. She misunderstands. She thinks I am willing her on to talk more.

'... Wasn't enough, that one week, was it, Norman? So we had all those Friday nights at my place, didn't we? Nearly thirty years of Friday nights.' Her eyes are glittering like sapphires now. 'And she never knew, did she, old Mildred.'

No. But now she does, Alice, now she does. Please stop your drivelling, Alice – for God's sake.

I am looking with terror at Mildred. She is looking at Alice's back, her beady little eyes gone to slits.

'... I could never wait for those Friday nights to come round, you know, Norman. I used to live out the days between in a dream, and thinking of all the marvellous things we were going to do to each other ...' Alice shuts her eyes dreamily, as she recalls those Friday nights.

While Mildred, her face stony with anger, begins backing out towards the landing again, drawing the door to behind her.

Mildred knows, Alice, Mildred knows, I blink frantically!

'It's you and me who should have married, Norman; you and me. Because I'll tell you, Norman, those few hours of a Friday night were never enough for me, Norman. I wanted you all the time ...'

They have had tea. I can hear the clatter of crockery in the kitchen as they wash up. As a rule, they chatter like a pair of old hens. This afternoon I detect a chilly silence. Alice tries to break it sometimes but Mildred won't have any.

Now comes the moment I dread.

'Goodbye, Norman,' comes Alice's cheery voice up the stairs.

Goodbye, Alice. And it really is goodbye, for she'll never let you in this house again.

I hear them noisily kissing air at each other's cheeks, the front door opening, the clack-clack of Alice's heels down the front path, the click of the latch of the garden gate.

The front door is slammed shut, shaking the house. Through the open window I hear Alice's heels heading for the bus stop. And I know, without hearing them, that Mildred's tartan-slippered feet are padding softly up the stairs.

The bedroom door is flung wide, crashing back hard against the wall, and there, framed in the doorway, stands Mildred. Her pursey little mouth is working, the skin of her face is stretched white and tight. Her fingers are scrabbling like claws low down in the folds of her skirts as if she would do me to death with them. She is quivering with anger.

'Pig!' she spits. 'Filth!'

I shrink small beneath my sheets, quailing as she approaches the bed.

'So,' she begins again, looming over me, spitefully, rancorously. 'That's where you used to spend all those Friday nights.'

Her voice becomes as tremulous as her spidery body. 'With that slut. My sister!'

She shuffles even closer to the bed. Her eyes blaze like two live coals, her hand rises high. She is going to strike me. I cannot move. One blow, even from Mildred, will be the death of me. I widen my eyes, begging her not to hit me.

Blessed respite. She takes the hand down.

'No,' she sneers, her lips curling in her detestation of me. 'I won't hit you. It isn't worth it.'

She breaks her own cardinal rule. She sits down on the edge of the bed.

She leans over me. Alice had smelled of perfume and powder, glorious. Mildred stinks of her own body and stale cooking.

Across her face flits a smile of mean and gloating triumph.

'You weren't the only one, you know, Norman, with Alice. She was anybody's. Always was. When we were young and shared a bedroom, she used to come home from her parties and regale me with all her dirty stories. What she had done to this boy and what he'd done to her. Filth. She was always filth, Norman. You didn't know that, did you, Norman?'

Lies, of course. She always did like a gloat, did Mildred.

'I never did like you very much, Norman. An animal, that's what I always thought you were. All you ever wanted was sex. Well, you obviously got plenty of that with Alice – although I really can't imagine what she saw in you.'

Of habit, she plumps the pillow each side of my head, that mean little smile still playing about her slit of a mouth.

She clasps her hands on her lap, gives a little shake of her shoulders, looks suddenly smug.

'I've decided against cremation, Norman,' she says, looking hugely pleased with herself. 'I'm going to have you buried instead.'

Horror! The ultimate horror! I have always had a morbid dread of closed spaces. I must have windows open, air. Not buried, Mildred, please not buried. All those tons of earth, pressing, pressing, driving the air out of me in the dark, crushing me.

Please, Mildred.

She sees the terror in my eyes, gloats more, drools.

She strokes my cheek. My body shrinks beneath her hand.

Not buried, Mildred. Please. It was cremation. You promised.

'You'd like that, wouldn't you, Norman, you and your – what do you call it – ah, yes, claustrophobia.'

Oh, Mildred, you bitch, you bitch. If I had tears I would cry for you, beg of you.

'Well I'll leave you now, Norman – now that I've given you something to think about.'

I am lying awake, as I have lain awake all night, in a cold muck sweat.

All that weight of cold black earth. Pressing down ...

Oh, God.

She has not done my room at all today. For lunch, she brought me tomato soup, a flavour which I particularly detest – and she knows it too. It stings my gums and bites at my throat, makes me cough. It hurts me to cough. She poured it down with evident glee, like a joyous harpy.

'About a week the doctor told me yesterday morning – on the q.t.' said Mildred, spooning in the soup. 'Then we can see you all nicely boxed up, can't we.'

My heart was still thudding long after she had left me. She was capable of anything. Supposing she had me coffined and buried *before* I was dead. This thought more than any other consumed me with dread, being confined in a cramped box, my arms and legs imprisoned, screwed down, no way out, a ton of earth bearing down upon me, in a black and airless dark.

I try to take my mind off it by counting the cobwebs.

There are three today, and the one above my head is getting even longer and fatter and hairier.

She has neither done my room today nor fed me.

And she has shut the window and locked it.

The room is hot, the air unmoving and stifling, a taste, I suppose of the coffin in which she intends to inter me – for ever.

The top of the dressing table no longer gleams with beeswax. It is covered with a fine film of dust.

There are cobwebs, everywhere.

'Tomato soup,' she says, smiling evilly as she perches like a vulture on the edge of my bed. 'We know you like tomato soup, don't we, Norman?'

Were I not so hungry I would spit it out.

She spoons it down me, lets it run down my chin. I retch, want to vomit.

'Alice phoned this morning to ask how you were. She sends her love. But then you know all about her love, don't you, Norman?'

She rams the spoon hard into my mouth and pinches my tongue against my gums, then rips it out again. I think that she has cut my lip. It hurts.

More soup. It is cold and congeals upon the spoon even before it has touched my lips. My stomach heaves.

'I'm not going to do your room any more, Norman,' she says, with an air of finality. 'Filth you are and filth you'll be. I'm going to let it get dirtier and dirtier and dirtier. You'll like that, won't you, Norman?'

And she *has* let it get dirtier and dirtier and dirtier.

A week has passed and for all of that week I have lived on cold tomato soup. My bladder and bowels are fretting and she will not help me. I keep praying for the doctor to come but so far he has not, although he did, I believe, telephone yesterday.

'He's very much the same,' I heard Mildred say, to someone. 'No. There's really no need for you to come round. I'll ring you as soon as he gets worse. Yes – I'm quite well in myself, thank you.'

She had worn her simpering voice, so I guessed she had been speaking to the doctor.

Yesterday afternoon she let the cat into the room. I cannot abide cats. I believe it defecated somewhere near the bed. The smell is sickening. There is dust everywhere, cobwebs descend from every square foot of the ceiling.

How abominable she must find me to treat me like this.

Another day. Several others have passed but I have no idea of exactly how many. I lie amidst my own detritus. I am wretched. Yesterday she came in with her knitting and sat on the high-backed chair by the window.

'I've come to watch you dying, Norman. I've got so little pleasure out of you up till now.'

The room is thick with dust, layer upon layer of it. It covers even my quilt and my pillow, and the ceiling looks like the reprehensible underbelly of some vast and nameless beast. The first cobweb that I noticed is scarcely a foot above my head now.

It moves fatly and pendulously in whatever little draught there is.

The room is getting darker as the grime and dirt thickens on the window panes. I did not see her yesterday, nor do I expect to see her today. Dust is piled in each corner, a thick, grey, amorphous dust. The clock on the dressing table is enshrouded by it, so that I can no longer even hear its tick. And I did so enjoy the tick of that clock.

My fear of confinement besets my every moment. The room is now devoid of all light.

She came today. She came with a torch and scuffed her way through the dust to my bed. She held aside the cobwebs as casually as if they were curtains and tipped the soup down my throat without even a spoon. She upped the bowl and poured it into my mouth, over my face as I gagged and choked and coughed. Had I had hands to use I would have wrung her scrawny neck.

She spoke with the doctor again on the telephone. I heard her.

'No, Doctor. It's very kind of you to ring, but I really am coping. Yes – he's still jogging along much as he was. Yes – if he gets any worse I'll ring you at once.'

I am hungry and I stink and I am wretched. I can hardly breathe for the dust.

*

I am dreaming, in one of my rare and blissful moments of sleep.

I am in room Fifteen of the Belvedere with Alice. She sits astride me, mother naked. Her breasts fill my hands. I reach up and unpin the mass of her black hair – which I think strange, even in my dream state, for Alice, as was the fashion then, always wore her hair cropped short like a boy's – and all that lovely hair spills down over my face. I love it. I was always a sensual, rumbustious man.

She teases me with it, dragging it to and fro across my face in time with her hips. She is laughing, then she is not. Her eyes are screwed shut and her teeth are gritted and she is crying out, gasping.

Her hair fills my mouth. It becomes Mildred's. Scant grey, wispy locks.

Not even that!

Cobwebs!

I wake and my mouth is filled with cobwebs!

Oh! Oh! I spit them out.

I am revolted. I vomit the sparse contents of my stomach upon the sheets.

Oh, God, what an awful state I am in. So dark, so dark.

The world is mute. I hear nothing. Dust must have filled every nook and cranny. There is a great weight of it upon the bed. I cannot raise my ribs to breathe. My nostrils are clogged with cobwebs. I am inhaling them, slowly drawing them up my nose, down my throat, into my lungs. They are choking me.

They have enmeshed my face.

And oh, the weight, the dreadful pressing weight.

Someone, come. Someone, help me.

There is air, there is light!

They have shouldered the door open against the hindering rampart of dust.

Someone has come at last! Explain all this away, Mildred. Explain how you came to leave a dying man in this foul state. I've got you, Mildred, I've got you.

Someone is close, dragging aside the cobwebs, coughing. Quickly! Quickly!

There is a hand clawing the dust and cobwebs from my face.

The light is blinding. I cannot shut it out.

'Oh, ye gods.' It is a man's voice, filled with revulsion. It is muffled, as if his nostrils and mouth are covered. 'No wonder it stinks. This one's even more decomposed than the one downstairs.'

So it is all over. I am dead.

But so, by the sound of it, is Mildred.

They *cremated* me, Mildred. I've *beaten* you!

I did not care much for the roar of the furnace, mind, but this morning they sprinkled me out here in the rose garden near the chapel. The earth beneath the pile of fine white dust that is me is cool and moist. I have air, I have light, and I always did need air and light, didn't I, Mildred?

Oh, the bitch, the bitch.

Not a few minutes ago another little pile of fine white dust was poured down beside me, and at every breeze a few grains of it are lifted and wafted over to fall upon me. Another hour and it will cover me – smother me – blot out the light.

It smells of stale cooking, you see. And Mildred.

David Pownall

There's a time to stop looking

It was the usefulness of dreams to their pasts that made both lads pursue them in their presents. Old friends, having shared the same fifth-rate English public school on orphans' scholarships, they had often ridden the vehicle of imagination over the bounds of that drab monastery for juveniles and escaped. Ghosts had been their companions on these high-flying journeys – sitting grey in the moonlight of the summer dark while a whispered story was wound round the dormitory – but, not satisfied with such an intangible presence, Wally and Rhino had actually gone out looking for phantoms which they had not conjured up, but had an independent existence of their own.

In the graveyard of the small Saxon church where the school worshipped each Sunday there was a cross which stood at a drunken angle under a spreading yew. If that were touched by someone at midnight under a full moon it was an act of great courage. That it was dangerous was undoubted – but the penalty was unknown. It was felt by the boys that a change took place, a change that rang of defiance. Slipping out of the dormitory windows, climbing down to the playground, wandering through the cool fields down past motionless horses and cows, the braver and more aggressive boys shuttled back and forth to that cross, that summoning, praying for an alteration in the régime which governed their lives. Wally and Rhino went down at least once a week in the summer term, ghosts themselves in the country night.

They survived the school.

No ghost ever presented itself, but there was a conscious thought in both their minds: phantoms were allies, not enemies. They stiffened your resolve to be yourself. Respect for the supernatural was not something which diminished a man, it was a deep nerve of entertainment, a strange comradeship between the seen and the unseen.

Ghosts were *always* anarchists.

They existed in spite of everything that was dull, pedantic, brutal and self-righteous.

To those in trouble; the persecuted, the down-trodden, the young groaning under the fossilized weight of the old, ghosts were friends.

Both Wally and Rhino went on to the same university.

Here they were free and their own masters for most of the time. They changed, found different friends, drifted apart, came back together again, became involved with the same girls, argued, fought, did little work, wasted time, got drunk too often, all in the business of trying to reshape themselves to a real world.

Yet that practical place with all its smashing of taboos, its philosophical attacks on fantasy, its insistence on the material world and its values, did not alienate them from their old comrades.

While other students spent endless hours discussing extra-sensory perception, mediums, the possibilities of the spirit surviving after death and all the tantalizing stuff of the supernatural, Wally and Rhino remained aloof from the discussion.

They did not need intellectually to explore the central question.

Already they had the answer: *of course* ghosts existed. The only problem which they were interested in was – how to actually find one.

The university was built around a fine red sandstone Jacobean hall which had once belonged to a prosperous merchant family. When the estate was sold to the government during the Second World War, a camp for displaced persons had been built and the Nissen huts were now used as student residences. In hut 13 there was a room in which a Polish refugee had hanged himself from a crossbeam – thus spake a talkative cleaning lady who had worked at the camp in those days and was now on the university payroll. The man's ghost was supposed to appear on the anniversary of his suicide, which was why the room was now kept as a store and not used as a student's bedsitter.

Wally and Rhino paid the cleaning lady a pound to lend them the key for the night in question, then sat in two folding-chairs with the light off, waiting.

They kept their eyes fixed on the crossbeam, expecting to see the figure materialize in its final position at death. The headlights of passing cars played tricks round the room and at one point Wally thought he saw an initial knot and length of rope beginning to grow from the crossbeam: but they were to be disappointed. The Pole remained where he was, his anonymous, tragic story untold.

In October they hid behind rhododendrons by the broad terrace of the old hall and waited for a lady in white without hands. She had once been the wife of the lord and had been caught in adultery. Her husband had exacted his own retribution and each year she appeared at Hallowe'en, complaining, looking for her lover, her bleeding stumps held out in front of her.

Through midnight until the birds started to sing in the dawn, they sat on a groundsheet, peering up and down the terrace.

No amputated adulteress. No displaced Pole.

No friend, no anarchist, no confirmation of their *belief*.

They suffered moments of doubt about themselves. Why did the ghosts keep away? Was it them? Did it need more than faith? At no time did they ask – do ghosts exist? All their criticism was levelled at their own powers as *hunters*, contacts.

They planned a trip to Greece by scooter. Wally managed to buy a second-hand vehicle in reasonable condition and started learning to ride it. With the enormous supernatural riches of the Aegean before them on the map it was difficult to plot a route that would not take a year to complete; and they only had seven weeks, including driving there and back. The birthplace of Zeus in Crete was a must ... Troy, Hector was still wandering about there, pierced through the anklebones ... the ghosts of one-hundred-and-eight murdered suitors to Ithaca ... wasn't it Sicily where the Cyclops could have lived, and would now provide gigantic one-eyed hauntings?

Wally failed his driving test on the scooter. He took it in Birkenhead and on that particular day there was a demonstration of striking printing workers who had occupied two zebra crossings over one of the roads used in the test. Wally grew impatient when they refused to move and sounded his horn.

'No horn can be blown at a pedestrian on a zebra crossing,' said the pedantic examiner. 'You have failed.'

'Ulysses, where are you now?' Wally murmured unhappily, wondering how he would tell his friend the bad news.

That evening they decided to take a different holiday – there would be a risk, that of getting caught two-up on a scooter with only a provisional driving licence – but it would have less serious ramifications if they stuck to Great Britain. Greece would have to wait.

Plotting a route from Lands End to John o' Groats, they included all the ancient sites of druids, prophets, mighty dreamers, bloodbaths and sources of mystical power such as holy wells, caves and mountain tops, stone circles, burial grounds, tumuli and bottomless tarns.

It was a wonderful summer.

They knew that their friends, the anarchist phantoms, were with them. So many times they crashed; so many times they shot across the paths of oncoming vehicles, plunged through hedges, were blown over by sudden gusts of warm wind, piled into mounds of clamped potatoes, the backs of delivery vans ... and lived. There were more than two riders on this chariot, but the others remained ... unseen.

They *felt* them everywhere. At every place they stopped and tested their sensitivities on the legend, prayed to the past, opened themselves to every vibration, there was a definite response. They drew no blanks in those sunny days. Once they had the facts, knew their stuff, could visualize the scene where the ghosts *could* walk, Wally and Rhino were satisfied that they did ... sometimes. Whether it was the bright light, the long evenings, or even – they argued to themselves – perhaps they don't perceive a need to appear to us – they actually *saw* nothing, though their eyes ached with looking.

They reached the northern tip of Scotland and decided to extend their journey to Orkney, taking a passage on a sheep-carrier with the scooter lashed to the mast. As the ship drove through the calm green sea, Wally and Rhino raised their eyes on the approaching islands, hopeful for even a waft of a Valkyrie's wing or the slightest tap from Thor's hammer.

At the Ring of Brogar they were uplifted by the great standing stones as if the druids themselves were capering on their tops, welcoming the midsummer sun: at Skara Brae, a Pictish village in a remarkable state of preservation, they were haunted by short, dark violent figures in a flitting dream of a reconstructed, but not revitalized past. Exhausted with the effort of imagination again, they turned the scooter towards Kirkwall, the capital, already thinking of the cathedral of the Norse saint, Magnus, and his roving, buccaneer antecedents: an anarchist, at least.

As the tarmac flowed beneath the small wheels and the gulls swung over their heads in the summer wind they became increasingly conscious of the thought that their quest was becoming phoney. Nothing concrete had come their way. All was indulgence and escape. They had not travelled further than those nights creeping through the sleeping village to touch the pale, crooked cross which gave them strength.

Driving along the west shore of the long Loch of Stennes they fell into a morose silence. Usually there was conversation from driver to pillion-passenger and back; guesses, ideas, hopes, plans – but these now lay squashed and confused under a month's apprehended fantasies. In the grimness it occurred to Wally that here was a point in his life when childhood was leaving him. It was almost streaming out behind the speeding scooter like smoke from the exhaust.

As they came to a T-junction and a signpost to Finstown, Rhino rapped on Wally's crash helmet (badly scarred by now, this steel bucket), and pointed to a weathered marker which read – Maeshowe. Wally stopped the scooter and they looked up the name in their guidebook.

'One of the finest chamber tombs in Great Britain,' Rhino said tiredly. 'I suppose we have to give it the once-over.'

'Must we?' Wally responded. 'I think I'd rather get to Kirkwall, have an early dinner and go to the pictures.'

'It says it's one of the finest . . . the finest. I'd feel guilty about letting it pass. I can't see me coming back to Orkney.'

Taking a further left turn towards Dounby, as directed by a Ministry of Works signpost, they eventually found the track and drove down towards what was now the eastern shore of the loch. The tomb stood hunched in a field, some distance from the water. A car stood nearby.

They parked the scooter next to the car, took off their crash helmets and walked round the great burial place. They did not approach the entrance or think of going in.

Whoever was driving the car was inside the tomb.

They resented another presence. It made them feel as though they were standard tourists instead of specialists and true hunters of the eternal brotherhood. Sitting on the grassy shoulder of the big tomb they waited for whoever was inside to come out.

Over the field the loch lay in a broad silver glide between the low, undulating country. It was warm. They were tired. Within minutes both of them had nodded off, their crash helmets on their chests in the manner of soldiers slain in battle.

'Ha! Snoozing!'

They opened their eyes and focussed on a tall, thin, silver-haired woman of considerable age who was smiling at them, her mouth sketched across a long jaw, occasional teeth breaking the line. She wore bifocal glasses over which her small blue eyes gleamed merrily, and in her gloved hand was a shooting stick with which she rapped Rhino's crash helmet, bringing him, abruptly, into a sitting position.

'Whathehell ...' he gasped, 'careful!'

'Get in there, get in there,' the old lady commanded. 'Graffiti which is a thousand years old. You can't miss that. Can you read runes? I can. One says *Orm loves Ylva*, another says *Ivar is a rabbit*, the one near the entrance I refuse to translate and I'm sure it wasn't true, poor fellow ... it makes it all absolutely credible. If I hadn't read the runes then I wouldn't believe the story. Go on, waste no more time. It's the best site on the mainland here. I've been three times.'

Wally stood up, warming towards the intense, concentrated happiness that radiated from the lean and ancient Englishwoman. Once he had recovered from the rude awakening and her eccentric means of introducing – or not introducing herself – he found himself charmed by her enthusiasm.

'Runes? I thought the tomb was supposed to be much earlier ...' Wally started to say.

'Of course it is, dear boy. I would put it at twelve to fifteen hundred BC, later than some authorities, but I have my reasons. The only other tombs like it that I've seen are in Spain and in Menorca, and their Megalithic period is equally difficult to date ...'

'Orm loves Ylva?' Rhino asked politely. 'Is there actually a rune which says that?'

'Oh yes, it's appallingly romantic, hardly the kind of thing I'd expect from a Viking washed up from a shipwreck. I would have expected his mind to be concerning itself with more basic things.'

Wally invited the lady to sit down on the flank of the tomb while he introduced himself and Rhino. She was happy to, spreading out the top of her shooting stick and primly balancing the bones of her backside on the twin leather hammocks while she announced that her name was Josefa Winterton with an F, on holiday with her daughter who was back at the hotel enjoying an emotional turbulence.

'Poor thing, divorce you know. Archeology is the thing for her. It's a passion in itself, I said. Not that she takes much notice. Perhaps we should have gone to the Italian Riviera as she suggested ...'

Gently they turned her chatter back to Maeshowe, the runes, the shipwrecked Norsemen. With her parchment-pale hands gripped on her long thighs she launched into the tale, her blue eyes popping with pleasure above the bifocals.

'It's a legend, so let's give it an arbitrary date in the period of the Viking invasions, eight hundred AD suit you? Why not? That's reasonable. Their long ship came up Scapa Flow we'll say – of course the German navy's still down there you know, they scuttled their ships rather than let the British have them – balance of power you know, oh yes, and probably right as well. Lloyd George came near to being *too* powerful you know. I believe that he was preparing to take over the world ...'

Rhino tenderly took Josefa Winterton with an F back to the ninth century after Christ. The long ship? On its way up Scapa Flow?

'Right. A storm whipped up ... they do here, very quickly, and next thing they know they're driven on to the rocks, manage to get ashore, terrible night, raining cats and dogs, blundering around looking for somewhere to stay and bingo! Here they are. Perfect. Dry, room for a fire, just what they're looking for. So, they go in, very tired, poor things ... and go to sleep ...'

She paused, aware that she had completely enslaved her small audience. They sat facing her, their mouths open with anticipation.

'The next morning, when they woke up, they were all completely and utterly mad.'

Rhino blinked rapidly. Wally remained very still, waiting again.

'Mad. The theory is that that was the time when they scratched the worst runes ... the most objectionable ones ... they are quite frightful in their implications, and those poor women, God knows what kind of lives they must have had with those men ...'

'The tomb drove them mad?' Wally asked quietly.

'Or something *in* the tomb.'

'If they were all mad, how did any one of them decide that they were?'

'Would you repeat that please, young man?'

Rhino shook his head and said that it didn't matter. He did not even have to look at Wally, or make the suggestion.

He knew where they would be sleeping that night.

Josefa Winterton went back to Kirkwall an hour later, having increased her enchantment over Wally and Rhino. The old woman's knowledge of folklore and legend was encyclopedic and she had a great gift of sharing both her knowledge and her enthusiasm and a bottle of Glenlivet malt whisky which was in the glove compartment of her car.

The sun was starting to go down.

Enjoying an inner glow which nicely balanced the softly flaming sky, they gathered driftwood from the loch shore and lit a fire for their evening meal. In the panniers of the scooter were a large pork pie, a bottle of piccalilli, a tin of salmon, the remains of a sliced loaf and fourteen bottles of Newcastle Brown Ale. They laid these out, then turned to Maeshowe.

With the driftwood blazing at the entrance of the tomb they took their torch and savoured a cocktail delight in previewing their bedchamber. The stonework was splendidly done, the blocks well worked and slotted together to form a compact, arched roof. The earthen floor was bone-dry and even the atmosphere was fresh. On the side-walls they made out the runes which the lunatic seafarers had written. Deciphering them was a skill which neither of them had and they sincerely regretted this ignorance. Any madman must have taken a long time making his point, choosing his words, for the runes were bitten deep into the rock, and painstakingly done.

'Orm loves Ylva,' Rhino chuckled. 'I feel at home here.'

'I don't think they were mad at all. They were in a state of spiritual elation which the crude Orkney islanders could not understand at the time. It was probably a divine frenzy, having come face-to-face with a New Stone Age king, skins, fleas, the lot, speaking in grunts and groans ... the first ancestor ... that's it. He appeared to them. He'll appear to us. I know it. He must. It's our turn ... Rhino, I think we were meant to come here today.'

Rhino nodded and led the way back to the outside world, the fire and the familiar food. They worked their way through the pork pie, the salmon, spearing the piccalilli with metal skewers from the tent which they did not erect that night, and downed the bottles of Newcastle Brown Ale until there were two left.

'How do you feel?' Wally asked.

'Great.'

'Want to go in now?'

'No, let's wait a while. I reckon we should go in when the moon comes right up. And, more than that, we've got to go in with an absolute faith that the ghost is here. Do you believe that?'

'I do,' Wally averred. 'I do, I do, I do, I do!'

They lay in the tomb.

A red light from the fire's embers touched the stones around the entrance, otherwise it was pitch-black and silent in the hunched, grey grave.

Every move which they made in their sleeping bags seemed amplified many times; every cough, breath, scratch.

They talked as was their habit. Each word was an effort, an entity.

From the dormitory to this moment they had always talked, dreaming of revelations, secrets, ciphers, *alternatives.* There was another universe and a man could have a double life. To prove that dream was real, the dream only needed that New Stone Age monarch to rise within these stones and ten years of priesthood, quest and devotion would come to a fitting conclusion. He had been here, once, brought in by weeping servants and wives, some of whom had probably followed him, their throats cut by the cold white priests with their golden sickles. What scenes, what sacrifice, what strange, barbaric agony, all bound up in his big, turf-covered belly by the loch, this sturdy womb.

'He'd lie here with his weapons, probably his best horse ...' Wally whispered.

'Food, a jug of beer for the journey ...'

'It would be a sacred place. No one in the tribe would be allowed to come near it ...'

'On pain of death. And here we are!' Rhino hissed. 'Would you call this provocation?'

'Holding out the hand of friendship I'd say. The tribe was broken years ago. His world has disappeared. If he does come back then he's the newcomer, not us ... and he's the one who'd go mad in this modern day and age.'

Still talking, they drifted off to sleep with the beer and whisky dragging down their eyelids, slowing their tongues into the half-rhythm of snores.

In their hearts both men were trusting in the New Stone Age king not to come. They had finally lost faith and the ghost hunt was nothing but an intellectual game. The challenge had gone and they lay securely asleep, but off-guard ...

Dimly, in a far distance, Wally heard the sound of a runner.

Through his sleep came the panting, the thud of feet on the earth.

In his nebulous dream the sound stopped. During that pause he slipped away again, softly retreating.

It was the gasping which awoke Wally, a rattling breath

deeply sucked down, and underneath it a muttered, choking language, incomprehensible. Some dawn was lighting the entrance but most of it was blocked by the white figure with its streaming head and sides, weed hanging from its hair, wrapped round stout legs ... the stench of decay filled the tomb.

'No!' Wally screamed.

'Orm ... Ylva ...' grunted the huge, dripping shape, shouldering through the entrance.

'NO!'

A bout of manic laughter shook the figure. It thrashed its arms, sending the clinging weed flying to the walls, stamped its feet and shouted.

'Yurgh!'

Wally dragged himself up against the wall, hands outstretched to fend off the reeking form as it started to slide down towards him. He could frame no word, only mouth a soundless scream of terror as the swinging weed touched his face and he felt the hot breath of the insane in his face.

A cold white hand clamped on to his naked shoulder, gripping it with terrible force. Through the weed and streaming hair he saw the wide crazy eyes of the shattered past.

Out of the depths of his being was hauled a bellow of terror which shook every rigid bone in his body. It blazed from his staring eyes, sounded a shrieking pain at the back of his mind. Through the seismic disturbance of this horrible cry came the voice of the ghost again, the other part of his ageless torment.

'Hold on, hold on ...' it said, 'you're lying on the towel. Just shift over a bit. You want to try a swim in the loch, that'll clear your head, but don't go in at the nearest point. Walk along a bit to get out of the weed ...'

Forrest Webb

A walk with Harris

It began as an ordinary day. It rained slightly from a little after seven thirty this morning but cleared by nine, although the clouds didn't break at all. Matthew and I decided to drive to Winchester to do the week's shopping and cash a cheque at the bank in the High Street.

When Matthew retired we came to live at Cheriton in a very old cottage. Cheriton is a small Hampshire village, nestling in a valley in the rolling chalk downs. It's quite a beautiful setting: the hills are soft and the woods deep and attractive.

We're not a large community, but sometimes we manage to win the Best Village in the County competition. Mind you, among the half-timbered and thatched cottages that were once the dwellings of the workers of the surrounding estates, are a few modern houses and the odd sprawl of barns and farm outbuildings. And it doesn't always rain here ... only at the weekends when we've planned some outdoor village activity.

The next day, Saturday, we were holding the annual village fête. It's usually an enjoyable day, even though it's hard work for many of us. The Women's Institute run several stalls, usually those connected with handicraft; things like weaving, cooking, pottery. Some stalls, the more active variety, are as annual as the fête itself. The Porter-Williamses always run a skittle alley, and Mrs Jean Coster invariably turns out with a length of drainpipe and a couple of stuffed dusters, rolled like yellow sausages, for a 'catch the rat' game. This Saturday, because it was Jubilee Year, we had decided to dip into our funds and stage a battle.

Perhaps I didn't mention it, but we are actually *the* Cheriton ... the one of Civil War fame. We did have a *real* battle in the fields around the village, and King Charles had his headquarters not too far away in an old manor house which belonged to Sir Benjamin Tichborne. Sir Benjamin hid in an oak tree after the battle, and that famous picture of a Roundhead questioning a small boy dressed in blue – entitled 'When Did You Last See Your Father?' – was painted in Sir Benjamin's manor at West Tisted. The boy was Sir Benjamin's son. The Tichbornes have been around for a long time. Not too many years ago they fought a big legal battle against a claimant to their title; it cost them millions of pounds, and is one reason why there aren't too many ancient oak and hardwood trees left on the estate any more.

The new battle, to be fought the next day, was likely to be more inexpensive and far less bloody than either of the other two. It was being acted out by a society calling themselves by the grand title of the Cavaliers of King Charles. It seemed they were quite famous for re-enacting Civil War battles, and on the exact fields and hills where the battles took place. They fit themselves out in the correct uniforms of the period, and wear armour and carry weapons. They even have cannon.

Mrs Philip-Ware had seen them in action at Sedgemoor while she'd been on holiday the year before, and suggested the idea to our Jubilee Committee.

The battleground itself is supposed to have been below the wooded hangar bordering our village. If you stroll through the beechwoods you can see humps and furrows in the ground. They're the graves of the men who fell in the battle. I don't believe they've ever been excavated to prove the story, and I think if anyone tried they would come up against a lot of opposition from all of us. The dead should remain buried, and undisturbed.

A cannon was fired just as Matthew and I were walking to the car. It made me jump. I'm used to the sound of shots and gas-driven pigeon scarers, as we're a farming community, but this was much louder, and it seemed to last longer than the sound of a shotgun. It was a throaty explosion, and the sound echoed back from the hanger, and Cheriton woods.

Matthew laughed. A flock of starlings joined the birds circling above the trees, and then scattered as a second cannon exploded in a thicket on the hill. I thought I could hear cheering, but it might have been the cries of our colony of rooks.

We drove to Winchester, but as we left the village Matthew slowed the car beside the long meadows below the hanger. The barley was ripening late. There was smoke drifting in the damp breeze, down the slope of the hanger and across the field.

Matthew said: 'If they set foot in there, old Will Parkins will have something to say.'

'Will's always got *something* to say,' I replied. Parkins has a hundred-acre farm, and doesn't like trespassers on his land, even when it's not in use and lying fallow. Still, he'd have genuine cause for complaint if the battle rehearsal spilled over into his barley; it was almost ready to harvest. I could see movement beyond the first line of hedges and a splash of yellow clothing. Just as Matthew accelerated again towards the top of the hill, I could make out a couple of dozen men, carrying what looked like muskets, crouched in the hollow of an old marl-pit.

It pays to go into Winchester early on Fridays. You can always find a parking place in the multi-storey car park, but that means a long hike back uphill when you're carrying all the shopping, which isn't easy at our age. It's better to arrive early and park nearer the centre of the town. The bank was empty and we were in and out in five minutes. I shopped at Sainsbury's and Marks & Spencer, then we had a coffee in the shopping precinct and drove home.

I don't suppose we'd been away more than two hours. It was about half past eleven by the time we reached the outskirts of the village. As we crested the rise and the road dropped down the valley, Matthew slowed the car again and then stopped beside a break in the hedge. We heard shots in the distance.

'They take their rehearsal very seriously,' he said. Where we had first seen the cannon smoke below the hanger was a scattered group of men. They seemed to be resting. Some were stretched out on the ground, others had their backs against the trunks of the trees. They were about three hundred yards away and it was difficult to make out any details. There was a fire lit and half a dozen men seemed to be handing out food, or perhaps soup that had been cooked over the logs. 'They've got a few horses.' Matthew leant across the car and pointed. I could see the riders on Parkins' side of the hedge. They were well out into the field, and there must have been thirty of them. I could picture Parkins' face when he examined his barley field afterwards. Thirty horses can do quite a lot of damage to a crop, and these were in line-abreast, not single-file. They turned slightly, at a canter, and the move brought them closer to us. They wore the kind of uniforms you see on pictures of Roundhead troops; lobster-tailed helmets, and breastplates. It was a bit surprising they didn't carry lances, but I imagined perhaps it wasn't encouraged. It would be too easy to have serious accidents in a mock battle. I could see Parkins' flattened barley behind the troop of cavalrymen as they swung suddenly away from us and towards the group resting below the hanger.

Matthew had switched off the engine. Suddenly I could hear shouts. The men on the horses had drawn their swords; they glinted in the sunlight. They charged the hedge in one long line. The men who had been resting leapt to their feet. We watched them scatter. The line of cavalry took the hedge together.

'That was fine riding.' Matthew rides with the hunt himself, even though he's now retired and almost seventy; we had our thirtieth wedding anniversary this year. The cavalrymen reached the small encampment. I heard a scream as a rider brought his sword down on the shoulder of a scurrying footsoldier.

'I'm surprised they don't hurt themselves,' I said. It looked a very dangerous hobby to me. Hunting's bad enough, especially when the ground is iced and hard. The cuirassiers on their horses were now as scattered as the men they had surprised. I watched a lone rider following a running man as he spun and wove like a coursed hare down the meadow. The pursued man stopped abruptly, stopped and picked up some sort of pike. It must have been three times as long as the man was tall. He just had time to lift the point and press the butt against the ground when the horseman reached him. The point hit the rider mid-chest, for he was thrown backwards out of his saddle. The footsoldier had the pike torn clean from his hands, but he didn't wait to see if he could help the fallen man. He just bolted for the dense cover below the beechwoods.

Matthew glanced at his watch, then restarted the car: 'They'll give their money's worth tomorrow,' he said. 'They look very good. Better than I expected. I've seen far worse at the cinema.'

We drove home and I cooked lunch. Harris, our yellow labrador, was pleased to see us. Nothing frustrates Harris more than the sounds of gunfire when he's locked up at home. He's Matthew's gundog, but I'm usually left with the job of feeding and exercising him when the shooting season is finished. Harris is a typical Labrador, he loves people and shows it by bringing them gifts. He never arrives home empty-mouthed. He always has to bring something for Matthew, and delivers it proudly, his brown eyes smiling.

After lunch Matthew sat in his leather chair and began snoozing. Harris was bored and fed-up. I decided I'd take him out. The rain had kept away, but the clouds were getting lower and there was a decidedly thundery feeling in the heavy air. If Harris wasn't taken out now, then it seemed likely I'd have to walk him in a downpour later.

I saw Henry Jossel from the pub, a hundred yards away. He waved and I waved back. There aren't a lot of people around at that time of the day. The farmers are working their fields or stock, and apart from passing motorists there aren't many signs of life around the village. The pub was closed, and Henry Jossel's wife Margaret and the barmaid would be washing glasses and cleaning out the bars. Henry looked as though he was going down to his garden with a spade over his shoulder.

I walked Harris along the side of the main road, and then turned off on to the footpath leading to Hinton Ampner and Cheriton wood. I couldn't see a sign of the Cavaliers of King Charles, and there hadn't been any more sounds of their cannon. They'd probably completed their rehearsal, and had reconnoitred all the surrounding land. I wondered if they'd made their peace with Will Parkins. Someone would certainly have to pay for the damage, and if it wasn't the Cavaliers of King Charles then it would have to be the Committee, and the money would come out of tomorrow's profits.

When we were well clear of the main road, I let Harris off his lead. He paused for a moment but when I said, 'Go on,' he raced ahead up the steep slope, paused again briefly beside the bole of his favourite tree and then charged through the thickets in the hope of starting a rabbit, a squirrel and anything else chaseable – except farm stock, or game.

I kept walking up the path through the woods. It steepens a lot, and after wet weather can be quite treacherous. I heard Harris bark a couple of times, which usually means he's met another dog and wants to play. The sky was very dark, now, and across the valley I could see the rain falling. A sudden squall hit the beechwoods, and the trees shadowing the path tremored and shook themselves. I felt rain on my face. I shouted for Harris, but the wind carried my voice away behind me. I remember saying 'Damn dog' without really meaning it. I plodded further along the path, and the rain increased until I was forced to shelter beneath one of the trees. I could picture Harris, his fur soaking, shaking himself the second he was was brought into the house. Dogs make work even if they're good companions.

I was watching along the path and he came round the corner with his head up, and something in his mouth. I think I shuddered. Labradors are quite capable of finding the most appalling things, bringing them happily back to you, and expecting to be congratulated for delivering some repulsive object defying description in polite non-farming company.

When he came closer, I could see it was a glove in his jaws, a red glove ... a gauntlet. Obviously it had been dropped by one of the Cavaliers. Harris's tail was wagging with satisfaction, and his eyes glistened with pleasure. He brought it up to me and circled behind me as he does when he delivers a pheasant to my husband, then he sat just by my left leg. I held out my hand and took the cuff of the gauntlet. Harris mouthed it slightly, then spat it clear of his jaws.

The gauntlet was heavy; so heavy it slipped from my hand. I'd expected it to be light! I stooped and picked it up. There were metal studs along the fingers ... along the ...

As I held the glove, it seemed to move. Something slid from it and fell with a plop into the mud by my feet. Harris stretched his head forward. Automatically I bent again, then saw what lay between us. A hand; a blood-covered hand ... its nails and skin so white they might have been wax, but with shredded flesh drawn back from the yellow bones of the wrist, where it had been severed.

I dropped the gauntlet, jumped sideways as though the hand

were a viper, and screamed. Harris was startled and thought it was a game. He began jumping around me, barking excitedly, then grabbed at the bloody hand and began tossing it around, pouncing on it and worrying it as though it were a dead rat.

I shouted at him to stop. I was shocked, but not frightened at that moment. Something, probably what Matthew calls 'feminine curiosity', seemed to hold me. Harris dropped the hand and ran off up the track. I followed him. The footpath bent round a clump of thick elderberry trees, their branches heavy with fruit. There was bracken, waist high, in a clearing. Harris began barking again, hidden by the thick fronds. I pushed through them.

For a few seconds I stared down at the things in front of me. They looked like a jumble of ancient military equipment ... a jigsaw. The pieces suddenly fitted together in my mind, and I screamed. It had been a man, now it was just hunks of raw red meat, scattered and twisted, shattered and torn by some explosion. The bracken on which it lay was scarlet. A buckled steel breastplate reflected my movement, and brought me a moment of reason. There had been an accident; a terrible accident.

I turned, shouted for Harris to follow me, then began running straight down through the hanger towards the open fields below – the quickest direct way back to the village. I ignored the path. The bracken was dense and snatched at my legs. I crashed through a bramble thicket, the sharp thorns tearing my clothing. As I tore myself loose I saw a bundle of sacking half in half out of the brambles. It was another body; this time complete and instantly recognizable. It lay on its back with wide and sightless eyes staring up at the dark sky. Rain washed bright blood from a terrible wound that almost divided the corpse's head. I screamed again, ran, then stumbled on yet another body. A child, a boy, perhaps twelve or thirteen years old. He looked as though he had been praying, kneeling, but had fallen backwards with his legs doubled beneath him. His throat was cut and his blood seeped away in the bracken peat.

There were bodies all around me, and I screamed and screamed. I was shaking with fright, with growing terror.

I burst out into the open. My legs were weak and I was

hardly able to run in a straight line. I scrambled over a fence of barbed wire, one of the sharp spikes tearing my slacks from knee to thigh, and scoring a deep and painful wound. God knew where Harris was.

I don't remember reaching the cottage, but Matthew was there, his face pale, but his arms comforting as he held me. I think I sobbed for a long time before I was able to speak.

He telephoned the doctor. Perhaps Matthew thought I'd had a fit or something; I don't know. He'd made a pot of tea, anticipating my return in the storm, and he made me drink a cup. It was so sweet I was sick, and then I retched until my stomach hurt me.

I told him what I had seen. He helped me off with my slacks and cleaned and dressed the long wound on my leg.

I was stammering ... stuttering ... I know my speech was hard for him to understand.

'I'll ring Fred Jones,' he said softly. Jones is the local constable. 'As you say, there must have been some sort of accident during the rehearsal. He'll find out.' Matthew knows I'm normally a calm person. He left me lying back on the couch, feeling weak, still frightened, but somehow completely drained, mentally. I could hear him dialling the number of the police house, and then the murmur of his conversation. He came back a few minutes later, even paler than when I'd first arrived in the house. He knelt by my side and spoke slowly and carefully.

'I don't think there are any bodies, Alice,' he said. His voice was very gentle. 'You see, there was no rehearsal today. They never rehearse on the battlegrounds.'

'No bodies ... I saw them ... saw the blood. I touched ...' I was almost hysterical, but he put his arms round me and I felt better. Matthew has strong, sure, hands, the kind animals like, the kind that give people confidence. He was a bishop when he retired.

'Fred walked his own dogs through the woods less than an hour ago; if there had been anything there, half a dozen Jack Russells would have found it.'

I thought, desperately. 'The guns, Matthew. We heard them, together.'

He nodded, slowly. 'But only *we* heard them, Alice. Only

you and I saw anything. He said there were no unusual sounds in the village today ... no cannon, no muskets ... no soldiers.'

'But ...' I began, and then stopped. Matthew had the same look on his face I used to see when he was a very young man, in the pulpit of his first church.

The gate, a few yards from the window, rattled. 'Harris is back.' Matthew glanced into the garden and I saw him stiffen.

'Matthew?' I heard the dog scrabbling at the door, trying to attract our attention.

'Dear Lord,' said Matthew. 'He's carrying something ...'

Tom Caslon

Hyacinth

It is fairly common knowledge that the painter Frank Handley's sight began troubling him when he was twenty-five, some two years after his first successful exhibition. He spoke of little haloes of light bouncing off the white ceramic handles on the doors of his studio. These haloes, he said, had all the colours of the rainbow. In that time he could not work regularly and he became morose and fractious, like a child deprived of a favourite toy for some mischief he did not know he had performed.

Then, inexplicably, the light, as it were, went out and vision seemed perfectly normal. He resumed work with a renewed enthusiasm.

That was a happy period for Frank, when elation went hand in hand with the knowledge that life itself was its own solace. In the next two years his career flourished, enhanced by that extraordinary work, *Hyacinth.* People have remarked, for example, its astonishingly vivid colours, and I don't suppose there's a bedsitter in the land that doesn't have a copy in postcard or poster form – or, for that matter, library, doctor's or dentist's surgery, office, boardroom and even the lowliest railway station waiting-room. People still flock to the Tate gallery to see the original as if it had been done only yesterday. Dazzling colour brought dazzling wealth, and it was at about that time that Frank suggested we make a home together.

We had enjoyed our home, part of a cunningly restored warehouse near the Pool of London, for some five years when, almost overnight, his sight went into decline. He described the affliction as being a mistiness over his eyes, rather like condensation on window panes. He was only thirty years old and afraid that nothing could rub the windows clean. The diagnosis was dreadful: corneal dystrophy, as you may know, is an inherited defect of the cornea. Thankfully, it was operable, and, he was assured, there was an 80–20 chance of his sight being fully restored. It induced in Frank first panic, but, by the time I had driven him home, a strange repose which lasted several days, something he was never to enjoy again. He carried himself as if charged with some profound knowledge; that, suddenly, he had affirmed the truth of a unique discovery he may have made while even in the womb – but repose was all too soon to abandon him. I wish I could say the consequences were tragic: they were not. There was nothing noble about his going, and he took with him one of the few beliefs I held dear – that man is at his best when desperate.

When the condensation he described grew thicker over the windows of his eyes all work, of course, became impossible. We were told that surgery would best be performed in the 'nearish' future – that is the word the ophthalmologist used – so Frank and I decided to travel. He said that because I was a poet (his word, not mine) he could trust me not to fail him in my descriptions of things and places he had left it too late to see. He spoke as if admitting that all along he had believed pictorial images to be surrogate words. I said I thought the contrary was true and he laughed. It was a laugh from which I derive comfort even to this day. Job's comfort, perhaps, but – well, *comfort*.

We went first to Venice, thence to the Aegean, through the Middle East into India and on to Sri Lanka. We travelled to Malaya and the East Indies, to the Philippines and Japan. We flew to the West Coast of America and went overland to the coccyx of the Argentine. My impressions of those journeyings I have published elsewhere and run to four volumes, but they give no indication of how very much closer Frank and I became in that time. He depended on me, yes, but my dependence on him grew greater by the day. He was indomitable and went about things in a spirit of adventure and discovery, and I felt somehow humbled. Our return to England took us along the entire eastern strip of South America and, when we flew back to London from New York, he and I were inseparable.

The enterprise took seven years. By then Frank was thirty-seven. And blind.

We had left our house to occasional tenants, the last of whom, Frank sensed, had been grossly negligent, for he asked if the windows were as dirty as those on his eyes. I told him they were and he telephoned the ophthalmologist, blithely asking the receptionist if he could speak to the 'Window Cleaner'.

The ophthalmologist was a mild-mannered, bland curd of a man whom nothing I'm sure could ruffle. Frank had every confidence and that reassured me. It is perhaps trite to say that to go blind must be a dreadful experience for anyone, but it is a remark I shall risk. I shall also risk asking you to imagine, if you can, what blindness must do to a man who can be made to feel safe in life only by what he may see. Beethoven, they say, sawed the legs off his piano or took a tuning fork to his teeth. Frank had neither saw nor fork.

He insisted that I sat in on every consultation and demanded as much detail of the operation as could be explained in lay terms. 'Come on, Mr Window Cleaner, I'm paying you, aren't I?'

'I help to clean windows, yes, but in your case, Mr Handley, it's more like a bit of re-glazing.'

He explained that there would be two separate operations: if both eyes were done at the same time and became infected there was the risk of irreparable damage. A piece of cornea, six millimetres in diameter and half a millimetre thick, would be incised from the donor's eye. A piece of cornea, identical in size, would be sliced from Frank's. The donor's piece, once 'floated' into place, would next be sutured, the last step in an operation lasting merely an hour, perhaps less.

'What sort of consistency will this piece have, Mr Window Cleaner? Wet plastic? Frog spawn?'

Here, Frank did something so totally out of character that it engendered in my loins a panic more sickening than any I had to that day felt; there was a tightening of the emotional scrotum, as if I were about to be hanged, and I could feel my entrails spilling out of me.

Frank winked. Have you ever seen a blind man wink? It was quite horrifying. His right lid slid over the soiled eye redundant in its socket.

I asked how long Frank's eye would be dressed.

'A couple of days. He should be home in a week. There'll be a gap of between six months and a year before I can do the other eye. Then, if I've done my job properly,' and the ophthalmologist spoke directly to Frank now, 'you'll see the light of day again.'

When Frank asked, 'I hope the donor's eye is fresh. Don't want it addled, do I?' and was told 'It'll be taken from the corpse within twenty-four hours of death,' I wish – how very much I wish – that *I* had seen the light of day.

Within a month of the first graft taking successfully, Frank began to speak of the day he could resume painting. It was something about which he spoke slowly at first, but with the recession of the weeks it intensified, and with the passing of the months the desire to again take brush to canvas or charcoal to paper became unendurable, when he told me that if the second operation were somehow botched he would kill himself. I humoured him: 'How?'

Ten months later the second graft was done, also successfully, and soon afterwards Frank Handley worked for the first time in nearly eight years. Early in the morning he took to his studio, and stayed there all day. To celebrate I prepared a meal of lavish splendour which I planned we should eat on the roof terrace of our house. I had scattered gardenias on the water in the shallow dish of amber and adorned ice with black grapes from which the bloom had yet to be removed. As the sun sank back into itself it promised to be glorious again tomorrow, and I thought of the river glistening in the sunset as a dragon steeped in deep sleep from which it would emerge forever benign for having had its flames drawn; the sun it was that had drawn the flames back into itself, where they rightfully belonged, and had been the stronger for it. The solemn beauty of the river and the grave rays of the retreating sun made me on a sudden want to go downstairs to embrace Frank, as if he and I would then be one, and the stronger for it, but with a ferocity as equally sudden he burst wild and dishevelled upon the terrace. He snatched a decanter from the table and, scattering glass and silver, slopped cognac into a balloon, from which he drank as if it were the sun itself. I was unable to stop him and watched him gulp long and hard, and when he had done he lumbered clumsily into the house, uttering obscenities as he went. 'Another time . . . another time . . .'

He worked every day for eighteen months, up at the crack of dawn and often not taking to bed until after midnight. His studio was territory over which he had cocked a leg and upon which no one dared trespass without getting the rough bark of his anger. His increasing irascibility over those months I attributed to prolonged bouts of work, and I began urging him to let up. 'Be kind to yourself, Frank, give yourself a chance.' He had begun to neglect his personal hygiene, and his eyes, as if celebrating their restoration, were unruly beneath hair neither washed nor combed. It hung like seaweed over the grubby collar of his shirt. There seemed, too, a growing reliance on alcohol, although I rarely saw him with a glass in his hand, and that alarmed me all the more – illicit drinking betokens shame and self-disgust and suggests dependence, I am told. Certainly when we did have moments together his speech was frequently slurred, and when I next felt obliged to caution him his gaze told me I was more than trespassing: it was as if he had caught me going through his wallet and I was made to feel a thief. 'Do you know how long you spent in your studio yesterday, Frank?' His corduroy trousers were baggy and creased and frayed at the turn-ups, the zip had broken and he had tried to fasten it with a safety pin. 'Yesterday?' He ran his hands through his hair, absently, as another will sometimes lick a finger before turning a page in a book, and I saw the dirt engrained beneath, and in the quicks of his nails. The nails were unspeakably long and, not to put too fine a point on it, he looked . . . grotesque.

'Yesterday was Tuesday,' I said, 'and you spent seventeen hours in your studio.'

He fingered his hair with gathering agitation and muttered, 'I didn't work yesterday. What makes you think I worked yesterday?'

He was, I realized, scratching his head: not the mucky strands of lank hair, but his scalp, and I thought he would surely draw blood, and a kind of shudder showed in his face. Fatigue, too. I spoke gently, 'If you weren't working, what were you doing?' He plucked a tiny plug of blood-stained cotton wool from his jowl. Thankfully, he at least still shaved. 'I don't remember working.' I feared his amnesia was yet another step towards alcoholism. He shuffled from the roof terrace and I thought he would trip as he tried to negotiate the spiral treads to our lounge. He descended from sight, and I resolved at all costs to get into his studio without his knowledge. If he were drinking excessively then there I would surely find evidence. When eventually I went down to the lounge, he said, 'I think we should have a party.' He spoke as if shot by little bolts of electricity. 'A *real* party, Michael. A guest list.' You may well imagine my relief, but when I gave him a writing pad and pencil his hand trembled, and I saw the difficulty with which he tried to write. The veins were swollen. He mentioned name upon name. 'Let's call them up now. This minute.'

He threw down the pad and pencil and began dialling a number. His finger hovered over the digits. Clearly he had remembered a number and forgotten it at one and the same time. He put the receiver down and said, 'Michael, Michael,' and a deadening forlornness entered his eyes, 'what's happening to me, Michael?' I retrieved the pad and pencil. 'You've been through a tremendous struggle, Frank, so it's natural there's some kind of, well, psychological reaction, the worse for being delayed,' and 'Michael,' he said, clambering unsteadily to his feet to sit beside me, 'please help me.' When his arm went round my shoulder and he said, 'I'm going mad, I'm sure I'm going mad,' I wanted to embrace him but could not overcome my physical aversion. I had never before turned from Frank, but I was impelled across the lounge because his proximity made *me* feel unwashed. 'Help me, damn you!' I closed the curtains. 'Only if you help yourself.' He pressed his knees together and began kneading them with the heels of his hands. 'How do I do that?' I sat next to him. 'You were going to tell me something—' and he recoiled and said, 'No, I can't.' I adjusted the dimmer switch so that the lounge was bathed evenly in a faint, restful glow. 'Something about *Hyacinth*, Frank.' Agitation drove him across the room and he opened the curtains and closed them and looking slyly over his shoulder said, 'I think I ought to clean myself up, don't you? After all, we're going to have a party, aren't we? Normal society and all that.'

The party was a disaster. Frank spruced himself up to the nines, though, and kept to orange juice the entire evening. The party was a disaster because he spoke to no one until midnight, when he leapt to his feet and said, 'I loathe you all. I loathe you all with a deep and personal and abiding loathing. Of that be constantly assured. Go, all of you.' He spoke with a frightening paranoia, as if he thought he was Christ purging the temple of usurpers.

Frank then made to the bathroom and locked himself away until the small hours. Or so I thought. Unable to bring myself to speak to him, not that he would have had anything to do with me, I went to his studio, determined, if necessary, to pick the lock to get inside. Whatever possessed him somehow had its roots in his studio, I was sure. As I closed my fingers round the white ceramic handles, off which Frank had once seen motes of light bounce like haloes, I sank to my knees. Blood was warm behind my ear. When I came to, the blood had hardened, and Frank sat open-legged and naked on the top tread of the staircase. 'One and one are two, two and two are four, four and four are eight, eight and eight are sixteen, sixteen and sixteen are . . .' and here he paused and struggled and, oblivious of my presence, resumed, 'One and one are two, two and two are four, four and four are eight, eight and eight are sixteen, sixteen and sixteen are . . .' At his feet lay a table lamp hewn from densest ebony and it must have been that he had used below my ear. I dragged myself to my feet and offered to help him to his, but he shrank from me and muttered, 'Sixteen and sixteen are . . .' I knew I should telephone a doctor. It was not the manner in which he sat, nor the simple arithmetic he pathetically pondered, not even the fact that he had viciously attacked me. It was his incontinence; he seemed completely unaware of it. First, though, I would run him a hot bath and lay out clean clothing. When he allowed me to lead him to the bathroom I crossed to the lounge and picked up the telephone. The doctor said he would come as soon as possible. But already it was over. After fifteen minutes I went to the bathroom. Blood pumped out of Frank's jugular, and 'Hyacinth,' he said, 'Hyacinth.'

The least I could do was remove the open, ivory-handled razor from his fist in which the veins were no longer swollen.

All over.
Or so I thought.

The coroner recorded a verdict of suicide while the balance of Frank's mind was disturbed. There was talk of a 'dementing illness', which of course I found distressing to the extreme, but no specific reference to alcohol.

Frank's last testament willed his ashes to me and to this day, even as I write, they repose in a small urn of leaded glass, rather like one of those Victorian fern cases that have only recently been restored to some of their former popularity, and the urn stands on my desk. Frank had been a big man, and bulky, but I could have carried his ashes in my jacket pocket. Is all this morbid? It was some weeks before I could bring myself to unlock the door of his studio, turning those white ceramic handles, and I wished in a moment of spurious self-immolation that those little haloes of light of which Frank had spoken would bounce up for me. Perhaps he really meant angels on pinheads or wings caught athwart gaunt limbs of trees on Peckham Rye. Apart from the artist's usual impedimenta, the studio was empty. Then I saw the walls. All four, from floor to ceiling, were adorned with paintings so bad, so evidently the work of an ungifted amateur, that I thought at last I understood. Each bore what was unmistakably Frank's signature, had been dated in the last two years, and would have caused scorn in even the most indulgent of mothers whose three year old has been let loose in the nursery with its first crayon. Each painting was a horrendous copy of *Hyacinth*.

One sits on my desk next to Frank's ashes. The others I burned so that the spring torrents should reduce them to loam beneath the mud.

'Mr Walters? Mr Michael Walters, the writer?' She was a ragged-looking woman of about fifty. She wore slack clothing and hair was slack about her neck and the skin about her face was slack, too. I thought she might thrust a religious tract into my hand with a zealous smile and the promise of salvation. She was altogether a scrawny sort but bore none of the humourless piety of the pavement evangelist. She switched a huge portfolio, weathered and grubby, from beneath one arm to the other, and the weight of it seemed too much for her. In fact, hers was the bearing of someone for whom everything is intolerable. I felt compelled to ask her in and relieve her of the burden. 'My name's Morton. Mrs Morton. I've come about what I've been reading in the newspapers. About poor Mr Handley.' I looked at the portfolio, leaning unopened against the settee. 'Although I knew Mr Handley well, I'm afraid I'm no judge of painting, Mrs Morton. I take it they're paintings,' and I indicated the portfolio, to the cords of which her fingers then nervously strayed. 'There's something you don't know,' she said, and at once I grew edgy. 'My husband painted. He was a bad painter. He killed himself.' There was no self-pity. 'His last wish was that he should somehow be remembered.' She had untied a second knot. 'Is that why he painted?' She shook her head. 'He won't be remembered for his painting. He was just a copyist.' She unravelled the knots in those strands of the portfolio – and the explanation for much that had pained and baffled me. 'He left his eyes for research. Not both. Just one. The other one was no good, you see.' She laid bare the contents of the portfolio. Each painting was about ten by eight. 'My husband killed himself because he had a devil in him. In his eye. It had done for one and had moved to the other. He didn't actually call it a devil. A ghost, he called it, and it wouldn't stop haunting him. That's why he couldn't paint, and that's why he killed himself. Yes, a ghost.'

She then told me the precise date of her husband's death and said, 'The right eye. The right eye was the good one.'

And the date she gave was the day Frank had his second operation. On his right eye.

This woman said, 'You can keep those paintings, if you like.' To this day I have more than one hundred paintings by the late Mr Morton, whose Christian name I did not even think to ask his widow, and you'll find them in Frank's studio.

But one I keep framed on my desk, between the urn of ashes and the sole survivor of those abominations Frank had done during those last terrible days. Both paintings are identical, each a horrendous copy of *Hyacinth*: black, the deepest black ... as black as earth left newly fallow.

When I woke up this morning and washed and ate and sat down at my desk I saw that something had grown overnight from Frank Handley's ashes: a hyacinth. Its flower is black, the deepest black.

Brian Freemantle

The talisman

Oliver Pryke had always been a superstitious man. Quite unabashed and completely unashamedly so. Indeed, there was something approaching inverted snobbery at the willingness with which he produced the protective talismans for those who expressed either doubt or amusement that someone engaged in an activity as unusual as his should believe in luck inherent in rabbits' feet.

To a strictly limited degree Oliver Pryke sympathized with their surprise, although he was unable to accept their doubt. Perhaps the greatest paradox in his complex character was that he was also a cynic, and as such well aware that few others in his trade believed in anything, not even themselves.

Oliver Pryke – and most others whom he knew – killed people.

Not continuously of course. And in Oliver Pryke's case, no more than he had to. Certainly never with enjoyment. And always in the name of his country, which made it legally if not morally acceptable. But killed, nevertheless. Which, to those in the know, made his mystic paraphernalia appear somewhat out of keeping, even for someone who fitted the classical Geminian pattern of split personality.

For anyone nurtured upon the familiar television or filmic characterization – really, all that is available – it would have been difficult to imagine Oliver Pryke as an intelligence operative and even less as a killer. He was a balding, plump, myopically bespectacled man given to frequent, irritating and unaccountable smiles, like an owl with a pass key to the mouse house dormitory. He wheezed climbing stairs or even slight inclines and saw dazzling black spots before his eyes if ever he looked upwards suddenly, which was rarely, because Oliver Pryke had made it an early rule in his hopefully charmed life never to do anything in haste or without proper consideration.

Upon such a bulged, unshapely figure as Oliver Pryke's it would have been unfair to expect clothes to do anything except provide protection against the cold or indecency, even if the jacket and trousers hadn't been nobbled and gnarled and bumped by the bric-à-brac of his convictions and creased by his disinterest.

The earliest charms upon which he placed any reliance were the wedding rings of both his mother and father, which he wore side by side upon the signet finger of his right hand and which he stroked during moments of stress.

Around his neck, minnows perpetually ensnared in the net of his string vest, hung not just a St Christopher medallion but a cross, a mixture of his mother's Catholicism and his father's Protestant upbringing. He had loved them both and sought their protection from their contented place in the hereafter – which he knew to exist, complete with seasons of the year, frustrations of temporal life and occasional family arguments. Everything as before except death, of course. There couldn't very well be that, could there?

There really was a rabbit's foot, the front left side support of a long dead black and white coney trapped by a New Forest crone who had presented the foot to Pryke the day he had received his appointment letter to the service. He had wandered, conscious of the dangers he would encounter but unable, of course, to confide now in anyone, to the turf-roofed hut near his parent's Bransgore home seeking solace from someone who would understand without the need for explanation.

The two-holed stone was the first amulet gathered in the pursuance of the craft he had practised for nearly twenty years. It was a fossil of undated antiquity upon which the outline of a diminutive bat-like creature little bigger than a bumblebee could clearly be seen. It had come as if by some outside influence into the palm of Pryke's hand as he had lain, arms outstretched and fingers contracting with fear, in a quarry fifty miles from Prague with two dissident Czech scientists and the searchlights of their pursuers flickering harmlessly less than ten yards away. After such convincing proof of that talisman's efficacy, it had seemed sensible precaution to collect others during his missions.

He had actually seen the monkey's paw invested with its voodoo power during the Haitian ceremony in which he'd witnessed a dead man rise from the cemetery grave. Twenty-four hours later he had committed to another burial spot fifteen yards away the cipher clerk from the British embassy in Washington who had chosen Papa Doc's sanctuary to pass over the British contingency plans during President Kennedy's Cuban confrontation to an interested Russian operative named Vladimir Suslov.

To prevent it being accidentally offered as coinage, as well as being a place where it should naturally rest, the buckled, predecimalization half crown piece was always carried in the breast pocket of whatever jacket he wore, the indentation of the East German bullet that would otherwise have killed him that dark December night near the Leipzig trade centre still clearly impressed upon the nickel.

In the right hand jacket pocket, snug in one of those tiny pouches in which High Street jewellers present engagement rings, lay the last acquisition, the Kalashnikov bullet, round and unmarked by any distortion where it had numbingly entered his body on the bridge that bisects Budapest.

Completely careless of clothes and appearance though he was, Pryke devoted unstinting attention to the bits and pieces he felt kept him from evil, carefully taking them each night from the pockets in which they were by custom painstakingly committed and arranging them in the manner of a guard contingent upon the dressing-table top for equally considerate examination and re-assignment about his person the following morning.

Not everyone found Pryke's behaviour bizarre. Lambert certainly didn't. Which was probably why they had become such close friends, despite the ten-year difference of age and the cultural gap of university against grammar school education.

Pryke had always felt a great personal satisfaction that John Lambert had proven himself so good in the service, because there was a vindictiveness in his make-up which made it necessary for him always to be right. Or have the last word, at least. It had been Pryke who had recognized the younger man's potential immediately he had entered the department, and promoted the man against the doubts of Sir Rupert Niblett, the permanent head of the service, and Edwin Farr, his sycophantic deputy. And been right. Probably so. There wasn't a better operative in any station throughout the world and both Niblett and Farr knew it. Why else would they retain Lambert permanently in London if not to have the best man readily at hand to preserve their reputations?

And they'd be bloody glad they had him here for this latest business. They were trying to minimize it, of course, sitting in their clerk-like offices in their clerk-like suits and trying to label it in their clerk-like way, but Pryke recognized it as an act. Dismissing as impossible unless he were a ghost the presence in London of Vladimir Suslov, the KGB's most efficient assassin, was just a child-like attempt to disguise the very nervousness sending them almost every hour into the department lavatory.

Pryke sat in the ground-floor bar of the Royal Garden Hotel, the third vodka untouched before him, staring out into Kensington Gardens for the first sight of Lambert's head-bent, bustling figure. Occasionally his fingers strayed over the signet rings, the only indication of his concern at the forthcoming meeting. There was no reason why Lambert should be surprised by his presence. Or resent another operative. There had never been any jealousy between them, not like there was between almost everyone else in the department. In fact, Lambert owed him a favour it was impossible to repay. And the man was surely sensible enough to realize that he was going to need all the help he could get.

He recognized Lambert from his walk, far away by the pond and long before the man's features were properly visible. Well trained, Pryke had already paid for his drink and hurried from the bar immediately, wanting the meeting to be in the open anonymity of the park. Because Lambert always walked with his eyes cast downwards, as if unsure of the direction he was following, only a few yards separated them when he became aware of someone standing directly in his path and he looked curiously up. Conscious of the other man's control, Pryke thought back with pride at his early championing within the department. From the other man came the calm, unsurprised reaction of a superb professional.

'Suslov?' demanded Lambert, immediately.

'Of course.'

'I had expected undivided control . . . initially, anyway . . .'

'With someone like Suslov it would be dangerous to work alone,' said Pryke. There wasn't any resentment in Lambert's voice, he decided, relieved.

'Except that Niblett and Farr have convinced themselves it isn't Suslov. They say that ...'

Lambert halted, offering his hands in a helpless gesture.

'... that if it's Suslov, it's got to be his ghost,' completed Pryke, aware of the argument. 'I know all about it. Bloody fools.'

'We had positive confirmation of his death,' insisted Lambert. 'The Americans actually possess a picture. We had it wired from Langley yesterday. I saw it with my own eyes. There can't be any doubt.'

Pryke shook his head, irritably.

'For how many other KGB assassins do we get positive confirmation of death, complete with photographs?' he asked.

'All right, I agree,' said Lambert. 'It's rare ...'

'Rare!' stopped Pryke. 'It's unheard of. And you know it. It was a snow job. And everyone let themselves be covered in the avalanche.'

'Suslov failed on a mission,' argued Lambert, patiently. 'From a Czech defector the Americans knew the West German ambassador in Washington was on the KGB death list. So they were able to prepare the perfect ambush, complete with photographic record.'

'Bullshit,' rejected Pryke. 'Why would the KGB want to kill the West German ambassador to Washington?'

'Because Suslov was killed, it was never possible to learn ...' Lambert tried, uncomfortable with the other man's logic, but again Pryke talked over him, exasperated that someone usually so questioning was prepared to accept such an unconvincing set of circumstances.

'The attempted assassination was a phoney, just like the information which the Czech leaked. There *was* a reason for the victim to be an ambassador in Washington. It enabled the death of some poor unknown Russian to be accepted as that of Suslov, so every service in the world would relax and let the bastard have more freedom to achieve what he's undoubtedly in London to do – kill someone.'

'Which is why we're checking it out,' said Lambert, defensively.

'With just one operative!' said Pryke.

'You know damned well that's not true,' said Lambert, letting his irritation show at the unremitting criticism.

'How many?'

'Russian embassy under complete, twenty-four surveillance. Special Branch protection increased on all obvious diplomatic targets. And we're supplementing with our own field men, too.'

'Won't stop Suslov,' said Pryke, positively.

'If it is him,' disputed Lambert. He hesitated, embarrassed again. 'This ghost thing, of course ...' he said, but Pryke anticipated what he was going to say.

'I believe in ghosts,' said Pryke. 'Course I do. And fairies and poltergeists and werewolves and white witches and black witches. I thought Father Christmas existed until I was fifteen. But I'm bloody sure Suslov is Suslov.'

'I suppose you should know,' said Lambert.

'You're damned right I should know. He and I tried to kill each other for years.'

Pryke gestured towards the hotel he had just left and to Millionaire's Row beyond, to the high-walled enclosed embassy at the top from which he was convinced a killer with whom he had been engaged in a personal vendetta for so long was about to move.

'Suslov is there,' he insisted.

'Then we had better confirm it as soon as possible. And then do something about it, hadn't we?' said Lambert.

'Time for a quick one?' said Pryke, quickly, coming back to the hotel.

For the first time Lambert's look was openly questioning. Pryke's decline three years earlier was almost entirely due to alcohol. Niblett and Farr had recognized it as the inevitable collapse of the man's nerve, after such a long career.

'Just one,' said Pryke, trying to keep the plea from his voice.

Lambert fell into step, head bent low again. They made an odd couple, Pryke unkempt and dishevelled, Lambert neatly pressed and tidy, the Homburg hat exactly in place, the folds of his furled umbrella evenly arranged, his shoes buffed to a reflective polish, his discreetly monogrammed briefcase held tightly in his right hand. He lived in a semi-detached house in South London, solicitous over a mother who flourished on ill health and geraniums which did not flourish in the climate of Dulwich. His mother accepted his cover in the Ministry of Pensions, believing him exclusively responsible for recommending budget increases for the elderly. She was very proud.

Halfway up the ramp leading back into the hotel one of the maintenance staff had a ladder up against a window. Pryke snatched out, stopping the stooped Lambert as he was about to pass beneath it.

'Careful,' warned Pryke, guiding the other man around.

'Didn't see it,' apologized Lambert.

'Shouldn't take chances,' cautioned Pryke.

He looked hopefully for the drink he had left half-finished when they entered the bar, then sighed philosophically. He ordered another vodka. Lambert selected orange juice.

'Here's to success,' toasted Pryke.

Lambert drank, without responding.

'Surely the circumstantial evidence against its being Suslov is strong enough?' demanded Pryke.

'Why?' asked Lambert. 'The First Secretary of the Communist Chinese Embassy in Ottawa is killed, a neat efficient job made to look like an accident. The former Taiwanese ambassador to the United Nations is shot dead, apparently the victim of an attempted street mugging during a visit pleading better understanding from the American President in Washington ...'

'... and in both places, the man now acting as a chauffeur up the road was attached to the Soviet legations. And the killings showed Suslov's professionalism.'

'They showed the KGB's professionalism,' qualified Lambert.

'What about the London airport picture?'

'Inconclusive again,' disputed Lambert. 'Okay, so the picture the Special Branch managed to obtain after the Aeroflot arrival *appears* to be a man who closely resembles the only picture apart from the Washington corpse we have of Suslov. And it's so blurred that any positive conclusion is impossible.'

'It's him,' said Pryke, dogmatically.

He glanced hopefully towards the bar, but the waiter was looking elsewhere.

'I suppose we should go,' said Pryke.

'Yes,' said Lambert.

They left the hotel, turning right for the short walk towards Kensington High Street and then into the Row housing most of the foreign embassies in London. It is a wide, quiet highway, conveying the impression more of the countryside than an artery right through the middle of London.

For the first time, Lambert had his head up, gazing around him attentively.

'Our men,' he identified, proudly, indicating a group of apparent council employees pruning the bordering trees. They continued past the Russian embassy without an obvious interest, emerging into Notting Hill Gate. There was a red-and-white striped tent over a gas main in the middle of the road housing a second squad of watchers and Lambert hesitated slightly, checking the positioning of the three cars assigned for mobile surveillance. Satisfied, he entered the one with the best view of the embassy.

'Tell me again about the precautions,' said Pryke, as they settled back into the vehicle.

'The Queen is attending a Mansion House luncheon,' said Lambert. 'Obviously the biggest cover there. The Prime Minister is hosting a reception at Lancaster Gate, so we're covering that in force. The Premier of Australia is at a trade delegation luncheon at their place at the top of the Strand, so that's under observation. And we've also got people at Olympia. There is a Czech gymnastic team there and we thought they might possibly fear a defection and be preparing a deterrent spectacle for their people back home.'

Pryke sat nodding at each of the measures, the atrophied monkey's paw cupped in the palm of his left hand and his right stroking it reflectively.

'Not a lot more you could do, I suppose,' he allowed.

'Thank you,' said Lambert, hoping the other man had detected the sarcasm.'

'That's a bit of luck,' said Pryke, suddenly.

Instinctively Lambert jerked towards the embassy, quiet and unmoving.

'That,' said Pryke, pointing to the front of the car. A black cat had paused walking in front of them to sit and preen itself.

They remained unspeaking for almost an hour before there was any activity and when it came Lambert tensed with excitement.

'A chauffeured car,' he said, tightly.

The official limousine of the Russian ambassador was nosing through the gates, pendant fluttering. The man at the wheel was uniformed, hat low over his eyes, gloved hands visible against the wheel. The ambassador was shielded behind drawn curtains.

'It's him,' breathed Pryke. 'It's Suslov.'

Lambert reached forward for the ignition, but Pryke stretched sideways, stopping him.

'Let the others cover,' he advised.

'... but ...'

'He's driving the ambassador,' pointed out Pryke. 'He's not going to make any move with an accredited diplomat alongside, now is he?'

Lambert frowned at the unarguable logic.

'No,' he admitted, shortly. He spoke briefly into the radio, instructing the other cars, then looked across at Pryke. The older man was still damned good.

'I feel a bit useless, sitting here doing nothing,' complained Lambert.

'Why not positively confirm that it *is* Suslov?' invited Pryke.

Lambert sighed. 'Okay,' he said. 'What have we missed?'

'Glove,' said Pryke.

'For Christ's sake!' erupted Lambert. 'Why has everything got to be a blasted quiz game?'

Pryke smiled at his friend, knowing he was right about Suslov.

'Phone Niblett,' he said. 'Get them to check with Washington whether the body supposed to be that of Suslov had an old bullet wound in the left hand, disfiguring the index finger ...'

Pryke hesitated at the look on Lambert's face.

'... and ensure that the autopsy definitely established that it *was* a proper wound and not just surface plastic surgery, in case a cursory check was ever made.'

'How do you know about the wound?'

'I put it there,' recounted Pryke. 'The nearest I ever got to killing the bastard. Cyprus, 1972.'

Lambert remained unmoving for several moments.

'Well?' encouraged Pryke.

Reluctantly Lambert climbed from the car and walked to the telephone box to make the call to Niblett on the scrambled line. Pryke sat watching his friend's silent conversation through the glass of the kiosk. Lambert returned within minutes, entering the the car without looking at his friend.

'Niblett thought it was a good idea,' he said, at last. 'Something he hadn't thought to ask.'

He swivelled to the back seat for his briefcase and took out a pack of neatly cellophaned sandwiches and a small flask of coffee.

'Ham and tomato,' he invited. 'My mother made them. It's wholemeal bread.'

'Thank you,' accepted Pryke.

'Only enough coffee for one cup each, I'm afraid.'

'I've got a hip flask,' said Pryke. Before Lambert could venture any criticism, he added quickly: 'Have you got the diplomatic events list?'

Lambert went back to the briefcase and extracted the sheet from which the intelligence service and Special Branch mount their daily protection upon diplomats in the capital. Pryke took it, running his finger down, mentally checking off the precautions that Lambert had enumerated.

'Got it!' he said, stabbing at the last entry on the sheet.

Lambert shifted sideways, so he could see over the other man's shoulder.

'Don't be ridiculous,' he said. 'What possible interest could Russia have in a trade delegation from Nationalist China? It's so unimportant that a junior minister almost had to have his arm twisted to receive them.'

'Who died in Ottawa?' said Pryke.

Lambert swallowed, remembering. 'A Communist Chinese diplomat,' he said.

'And who got shot down in Washington?'

Lambert smiled, imagining a fault in the argument.

'A *Nationalist* Chinese ambassador,' he said triumphantly. 'The other side!'

'Which makes a pattern,' declared Pryke. 'Tit for tat. The thing that most worries Russia is the increasing power and world acceptance of Communist China, right?'

'I suppose so,' said Lambert.

'So here in London we have a group of Nationalist Chinese. And the same Russian who was in both places when the other killings took place ...'

'But why on earth would Moscow want to kill people involved in something as low key as a Taiwanese trade delegation? They're nobodies, I tell you.'

'Who says the real victim is in the delegation?'

'Who then?'

'What if the ambassador to London of the People's Republic of China were to be assassinated? And nearby, protesting an innocence that nobody would believe for a moment, was found one of the Chinese attached to a trade delegation of a rival regime?'

'You've got to be kidding!'

'Why?' said Pryke. He thrust the monkey's paw back into his pocket, satisfied.

'It has a neat and tidy look about it,' he said, positively. 'It would take half a day for the newspapers to recall the Canadian and American deaths and project the whole thing into a major diplomatic incident. Britain would be embarrassed and relations with Peking would be damaged. Canada, who linked with Peking long before Nixon's visit, would be in an awkward position. And Washington would be stretched again between both governments.'

He hesitated, the conjuror about to produce the rabbit.

'... and the only people to benefit from the confusion would be Moscow.'

'It's plausible,' conceded Lambert.

Pryke looked pointedly at his watch.

'Niblett should have heard back from Washington by now,' he said.

Lambert returned to the telephone box and again Pryke watched, aware of the strained expression the moment it settled on the younger man's face. Lambert walked more slowly back to the car this time.

'It wasn't a bullet wound,' he confirmed. 'The pathologist had listed it as plastic surgery to cover what could have been a serious burn.'

'So the chauffeur is Vladimir Suslov, not his ghost?'

'It would seem so,' said Lambert.

It was predictable that at last there should be some resentment, accepted Pryke.

'Which means I've been right once,' he said.

'There's no reason why you should be so a second time.'

'Nor why we shouldn't mount precautions in case I am.'

'How?'

'The trade delegation has no surveillance?'

'It wasn't thought necessary.'

'Button them up,' urged Pryke. 'How many are there?'

Lambert shrugged, uncertainly. 'About fifteen I think.'

'Assign a man to each. Make it impossible for any of them to be snatched suddenly.'

'They're due to return tomorrow,' recalled Lambert.

'So if I'm wrong, we've only wasted the time of fifteen men for less than a day.'

'What do you propose we do? I think we should become more actively involved.'

'So do I,' agreed Pryke. 'Everything else has been covered. So we watch the Chinese embassy in Portland Place. That's where Suslov will be.'

Lambert took up the car radio transmitter again, gave his instructions for the Taiwanese party, and then moved off into the traffic in the direction of Marble Arch.

'Know something?' said Pryke, contentedly by his side.

'What?'

'Fifteen was always my lucky number.'

Lambert got a meter with an hour still to expire and parked

facing towards Regent's Park, so that the Chinese embassy was to their left and the overlooking range of five-storey houses clearly visible to their right.

'You could always check to see if there are any publicly known engagements that would involve the Chinese ambassador leaving the embassy,' suggested Pryke.

Completely resigned now to take the lead from the older man, Lambert spoke briefly into the radio, then turned up the volume of the receiver so that Pryke would be able to hear the reply. It took less than five minutes to come. The Chinese had accepted an invitation to a reception being given that night at the Canadian embassy.

'Another link,' said Pryke complacently. He offered the other man a nip from his hip flask.

'Or coincidence,' said Lambert, refusing.

'We'll see,' said Pryke.

Lambert fed the meter more without being detected by the warden, then slumped down into his seat, prepared for a lengthy vigil.

'Pity it's too posh around here for a fish and chip shop,' said Pryke, after an hour.

'What?'

'Fancy some chips,' said Pryke.

'Make the car smell,' protested Lambert. 'Promised I'd take mother to Brighton tomorrow. She wouldn't like the odour of stale fat.'

It had become completely dark, the road quiet under their high-lamped illumination.

Pryke shook the flask to gauge the amount left.

'It's malt,' he said, offering it again in an effort to repair the strain between them.

'We're on a job,' rejected Lambert.

Lambert had left implicit instructions with the other observation teams, warning them what to expect, and it was just before eight o'clock when through the open receiver the watchers outside the Soviet embassy reported that an unusually large number of Russians had left the legation and were being followed past the Albert Hall in the direction of Hyde Park Corner.

'From there, the shortest way to the Carlton House reception for the Taiwanese would be down by Buckingham Palace and then up by St James's Palace,' said Pryke.

Ten minutes later came the confirmation that that had been the route taken by the Russian car. There appeared to be obvious consternation among them, reported the surveillance team, at the protection accorded the Taiwanese.

'Still doubtful?' said Pryke.

Lambert didn't reply, but Pryke sensed movement beside him. He turned, curious at what Lambert was trying to conceal beneath his cupped hand.

'What's that?'

'Rabbit's foot,' said Lambert, shortly.

'It's never let me down,' said Pryke.

'Let's hope it doesn't now.'

'It hasn't,' said Pryke, suddenly urgent.

The car had come slowly from the direction of the park, cruising into one of the many available parking areas directly in front of the now darkened, deserted buildings overlooking the embassy.

'Eight ten,' said Pryke, quietly. 'Ambassador should be moving in about fifteen minutes.'

It was too dark to distinguish anything more than a bulky, muffled shape getting out of the vehicle, but the long canvas case in the man's right hand could easily be made out.

'I want him,' said Pryke, determinedly.

'No,' refused Lambert. 'It's my job.'

'Stay with me,' said Pryke. 'But let me go for him first.'

Before Lambert could reply, Pryke had left the vehicle, letting the door back against the rubber edging but not closing it in case the slight noise alerted the man now hurrying along New Cavendish Street. Pryke moved noiselessly after him, aware of Lambert so close that they almost touched. They paused at the New Cavendish Street junction with Portland Place, using the shadows for complete concealment. Suslov had halted by a side entrance leading into what had been the servants' quarters of the house during its Regency heyday. It was only seconds before he vanished into the darkness.

'He'd have already arranged a key,' whispered Pryke.

They hurried forward again, pressing gently against the now

closed door. The locking bars had been taped back, so there was no impediment to a hurried escape. Pryke led up the completely darkened spiral stairway that climbed through the floors towards the roof, his feet moving experimentally but quite quickly over each step. He had his mouth clamped tightly shut, trying to reduce the sound of his wheezing. The door leading out on to the roof that completely overlooked the Chinese embassy had been taped back, like that at street level far below.

Pryke stood for a moment at the door opening, trying to regain his breath and using its protection while he sought the figure of Suslov. The Russian had wedged himself in the roof corner, so that he would have support for both elbows. Nearer now, Pryke could clearly see the rifle. It was an American-manufactured M-16 and Suslov was bent over it, intent on screwing the infrared nightsight into position. Pryke moved abruptly, surging forward over the twenty yards that separated them, but stopping when he was just feet away. In a controlled, conversational tone he said: 'I've got you, Suslov. I always said I would and now I've got you.'

The shock would have immobilized most other people, but Suslov was a professional. Before Pryke had finished speaking, the Russian had started to turn, rifle scraping off the balustrade and swung at waist level, ready to be fired. But Pryke was a professional, too. He'd moved close enough to intercept the barrel as it came around, bringing up his other hand at the same time so that he cuffed the Russian beneath the chin with the palm, jerking him upwards and completely off balance. They were only inches apart now and Suslov's eyes opened in terror and he grabbed at the rifle, trying to retrieve it. Lambert came alongside, jerking it from the man's grasp and with his other hand free Pryke chopped at Suslov's neck, driving him further backwards over the low protective wall around the roof edge. For a moment they clung together, the Russian straining to regain his balance and fight back. Far below there was a sudden spurt of light as the Chinese embassy door opened and a group of people bustled into the waiting car and moved off towards Oxford Circus unaware of what was happening far above. Suslov was a superbly fit man and might have succeeded in forcing Pryke back by himself. His feet were scrabbling against the roof, gaining purchase, but suddenly Lambert swooped, grabbing the man's ankles and lifting him completely clear. Briefly the Russian was held between them. Realizing what was about to happen he screamed, thrusting even further upwards in an attempt to get away, but they anticipated the movement and used it to their advantage, carrying him on and heaving him over the roof edge. Suslov fell completely silently, the only sound the sickening thud of his body impaling itself on the railings far below.

Pryke and Lambert leaned panting against the balustrade, gazing down into the street. It was difficult to see the body.

'That was a bloody stupid thing to do, warning him,' protested Lambert. 'He might have killed me.'

'Had to do it,' said Pryke. His breathing was still difficult.

'We'd better get down there before the police arrive and bugger it up,' said Lambert.

Pryke picked up the rifle.

'Bet the serial number will prove that it was part of a United States' shipment to Taiwan,' he said. 'That would have made it difficult for the Americans to explain, wouldn't it?'

Lambert halted at the roof door, looking back.

'Okay,' he said. 'It was a brilliant deduction and you were right. All along, you were right.'

'Ghost!' sneered Pryke. 'Jesus Christ, how stupid can you get!'

Pryke didn't re-enter the car from which Lambert summoned people from their department to retrieve Suslov's body. Instead he remained at the driver's door, leaning in.

'That's it then,' he said, when Lambert had finished transmitting.

'Looks like it.'

'Couldn't have done without you up there,' admitted Pryke, vaguely indicating the roof from which they had just descended.

'And without you, we'd have had an international incident on our hands,' said Lambert.

Pryke straightened. 'Enjoy your trip to Brighton,' he said. 'Try English's. The fish is always very good.'

'Mother is allergic to fish,' said Lambert. 'It's her condition. We'll probably take sandwiches and eat them on the beach.'

'Probably the best idea,' said Pryke. 'Goodnight.'

'Goodnight,' said Lambert.

Before accepting the Prime Minister's invitation to head the British intelligence service Sir Rupert Niblett had held ambassadorships in several Asian embassies and made a snobbery of retaining some of the habits he had assimilated. The tea ceremony was one. Today it was Lapsong Souchong, which he brewed perfectly, served in exquisite China cups. Between him and Farr there was a small dish of Garibaldi biscuits and one knife because the deputy had a peculiar liking for butter smeared upon them.

'Amazing business,' said Niblett, a fat, Pickwickian man, hair tufted around a completely bald pate.

'Amazing,' agreed Farr, buttering a biscuit.

'Lambert really did extraordinary well,' said Niblett. 'Quite extraordinary.'

Napkin ready in his left hand, Farr bit delicately into his biscuit.

'Remember how we doubted him at first?' he reminded, careful not to spit crumbs on to the table.

Niblett nodded.

'We were very wrong about him,' he admitted.

'Noticed anything unusual about him lately?' asked Farr, suddenly. He knew Niblett would be critical, but he began buttering another Garibaldi anyway.

'Unusual?'

'Carries a rabbit's foot, always. Says it's for luck.'

'I know,' said Niblett, leaning back reflectively in his chair.

'Pryke's,' he announced.

'Pryke's?' said Farr, looking up disbelievingly, teacup suspended before his face.

'That's the thing I regret most about the whole business,' said Niblett. 'Poor old Pryke. He and Suslov pursued each other for almost ten years. It was just confounded bad luck that Suslov got him with a stray Kalashnikov shot on that bridge joining Buda with Pest. There would have been a marvellous irony had it been Pryke and not Lambert who had actually managed to pull off Suslov's death.'

'Yes,' said Farr, resisting the temptation for a third biscuit. 'There would have been a sort of justice about it.'

Sam Gulliver

Moth

In the beginning – Briley had forgotten exactly how many months ago – they had at least been able to watch the military goings-on. Jet aircraft had roared across the searing sky while distant explosions and dark clumps of smoke marked the direction of Suez itself. But the entertainment had been short-lived; the whole thing was over in less than a week. They had followed the war's progress from the wireless room, but even so it came as a shock when the first Israeli flags appeared on the East bank of the Canal, proving the whole of Sinai to be occupied.

'That'll teach the Gyppos to block off Eilat,' someone had said.

'Stupid buggers.' Briley sucked at his pipe morosely. They had in fact enjoyed being immured by sheerest chance in the middle of someone else's war. The tension, the speculation, the rumour and the BBC World Service news bulletins had excited them all. They had never been in any danger and none of them had thought then that the war would affect their lives. The next month, spent roasting in the heat of an Egyptian midsummer, showed them they were wrong.

'Just a lot of pawns, that's what we are.' It was how everybody described their position, part of the ship's wisdom. The *Platypus* lay at anchor almost at the neck of the Great Bitter Lake. Three hundred yards or so away lay the *Woollongong*, an Australian merchantman similarly becalmed in the doldrums of war. In this region the navigable waters of the Canal were not a simple straight channel; although from the deck of the *Platypus* their hulls remained hidden, the superstructures of various other ships jutted oddly up from the monotonous stony dunes, masts and funnels wobbling in the heat.

Time dragged by. Two and a half thousand miles away in London brokers and diplomats tried to decide what to do about the millions of pounds' worth of shipping and cargo at present bottled up in the Suez Canal. On board those ships, conditions were fast deteriorating. For a while the captains had found work for their crews, carefully rationed occupational therapy. But now the paint stores were empty and the kegs of polish drained. Their ships sparkled and glinted in the desert while the men dozed under awnings. Occasionally vicious fights broke out but a listless torpor soon supervened. Stocks of all but the most basic foods ran out and medical supplies dwindled. Neighbouring captains organized joint parties and competitions but these petered out when the men could no longer bother to row themselves across the glassy water to the next vessel. Their comprehensive private collections of erotica had long since been looted by the Egyptian military who periodically came aboard to discuss the progress of negotiations for repatriating the crews.

Eventually they had gone, escorted to Cairo by the military and flown out at their companies' expense. Not knowing then that their ships were destined to remain in Egypt until the Canal was cleared in 1973 some of the companies ordered a skeleton crew to remain behind to guard their property. Captain Briley's company was not one of those; it insisted that he himself stayed behind, alone, until 'the situation clarified itself'. This it had apparently just done, and now while waiting for his visa he spent most of his days chatting to Purkiss, the skipper of the *Woollongong*, and leafing through the tattered pile of *National Geographical* magazines which the Egyptians had not found salacious enough to steal.

'Jesus, look at that horror,' he said one morning, jabbing a finger at a page of colour photographs.

'Looks like a moth,' said Purkiss, his off-hand tone calculated not to acknowledge what he knew to be Briley's phobia.

'Too damn right it's a moth. But d'you know what's different about this bugger? It can suck blood; it's a vampire moth. They've only just discovered it somewhere in South America. Goes for cattle, monkeys, humans, anything.' Briley, as usual, was wearing only a pair of khaki shorts, grizzled body hair thick over the brown-and-beetroot skin: he had even removed his watch. Despite the heat he felt a chill pass over him like a shadow as he looked at the picture. Purkiss lay back in his canvas chair, amused at seeing this fiftyish Englishman put out over an insect. His amusement was informed by having seen Briley compulsively trying to kill with a teatowel any moth which happened to drift in through the porthole at night while they shared their meal together. He felt blindly for his sunglasses beside the chair and knocked over the jug of water. An icy gush turned Briley's feet into pink promontories, his watch into a metal island.

'Sorry, mate.'

'Do it again,' said Briley good-naturedly. He wiggled his toes luxuriously in the pool and retrieved his watch, shaking the water from it. Not for the first time the Australian noticed how the grey gunmetal back of the watch did not match the rest of the case which was of battered gold.

'No harm done?'

'Take more than a little cold water to hurt this thing,' said Briley, polishing the watch on his shorts.

'Waterproof?'

'I suppose it must be. It's been with me a good thirty years, and apart from losing the back to a crooked jeweller in Rangoon it's never been apart. Bloody marvellous. They don't make them like this any more.'

'Too true.'

Thus the day, like all the others, passed in desultory chatter. The worst of the heat was over when, at about five in the evening, Purkiss spotted a dinghy leaving the Egyptian bank. It was Saleh the egg-man, a seamed old peasant in an off-white *galibeyah* with a wool scarf wrapped about his head. Purkiss had become quite glad to see him. The comings and goings of the local *fellahin*, seemingly unhampered by the military, were nearly the only events to shape the blur of days. Yet he had no idea why Saleh had always behaved so oddly with Briley. Right from the start the Egyptian had treated the Englishman much as a spider treats a fly: part guest of honour and part victim. Now the top of the old man's head appeared beneath the rail and Saleh climbed aboard, one brown tendonous hand clutching a straw-lined basket.

'*Mesa alxeer. Izayyikum?*'

'Wotcha, cock. Not so bad. And how's yourself?' Purkiss

understood not a word of Arabic but in this case hardly needed to.

'Fi bayd kitiir.' Saleh lifted the basket with a grin.

'I can see that,' Briley told him. 'But we've still got about two dozen of your last lot to eat. We'll be growing bloody feathers soon.'

'Kwayyis awi,' the old man urged, raising the straw and revealing large pearly eggs instead of the expected dung-smeared marbles. *'Bayd batt.'*

'He's brought us duck eggs this time,' Briley said.

'Okay Les, we'll try some of those for a change. Where's your screwdriver?'

Paying Saleh was a problem since the ship's supply of Egyptian currency had long since vanished. Now it was a question of barter which like as not involved going round the ship until the egg-man found something he liked. Whole brass fitments had been unscrewed and presented to him. Purkiss and Briley planned to inventory such losses as war damage.

But this evening Saleh seemed distracted and curiously unconcerned with payment. Instead he bent to examine Briley's watch which now lay on a magazine on the deck.

'And you can keep your thieving hands off that,' Briley told him with a kind of jovial roughness.

'Not thief,' Saleh said unexpectly in English. *'Ana msh harami. Abadan.'*

The words of denial came automatically but his gaze was fixed intently on Briley's face, it seemed to Purkiss, with an expression of extraordinary hatred.

When the Egyptian had left, abruptly refusing all payment for the eggs, Purkiss said:

'Odd cobber, that. Strange way he looks at you, had you noticed? As if he'd known you for years. You're sure you couldn't have met before? I mean, you do speak a bit of the lingo, after all.'

Briley reacted to this with startling vehemence.

'I told you, I've never been to Egypt before. How many bloody times do I have to say it? The nearest I ever came to Egypt was in Libya just after the war. That's how I picked up a few words; just kitchen Arabic, that's all. I don't trust that damned Gyppo; there's something about him I don't like. He's got it in for me, Ken, I can feel it. I don't want him aboard again.'

'Fine, Les. But this is *my* ship,' said Purkiss mildly, pointing at the deck. 'That one's yours.' He nodded towards the *Platypus*.

'Of course.' Briley looked up, startled. 'That's right, it is. But if you'll take my advice, keep him off your ship too. Don't you feel it?'

But Purkiss only shook his head gently and thought about the other men he had seen repatriated since early June, made obsessive by the immemorial melancholy of the landscape, by heat, boredom and loneliness. He unlocked his safe and produced a bottle of Suntory whisky, one of the last carefully-hoarded pints from the crate he had bought in Japan. Neither man drank much as a rule: they had lived and worked on board ship in the tropics for too long; but the bottle brought with it an air of normality, even a little festivity, and Briley's apparent panic gradually subsided. As if by magic the local *ma mur* appeared for one of his periodic visits, combining the role of police chief with that of postman. He dropped some letters on the table, their envelopes much savaged by the Cairo censors.

'Whisky no good,' he said in English, his carefully pressed uniform shiny with ironing. The leather flap of his Sam Browne-style holster was held shut by an unravelled paper-clip.

'No good at all,' agreed Purkiss. 'Have some.' He filled a glass.

'Very bad,' said the *ma'mur* genially, as he always did. 'I Muslim. Whisky *haram*.'

'Life is very short,' said Purkiss, 'and most of the best things are *haram*.'

The *ma'mur* looked around him furtively for effect and drained the glass at a gulp. He immediately became rather tipsy. An hour later the bottle was finished and the *ma'mur* had gone through his usual cycle of tearful abuse at the losses inflicted on the Egyptian troops by the Israelis, anger at the mass cowardice of the rest of the Arab world for deserting his country in its hour of need, and a reckless and highly indiscreet denunciation of Nasser for his brinkmanship. At this point there came a faint thump from the side of the ship. Everyone went outside, the *ma'mur* sobering up rapidly and fumbling with his paperclip. There was a tinny clatter and a small metal disc came rolling across the deck to Briley's feet. From the gangway they heard the thud of descending feet and a voice floated up from the dark waters of the Canal. To Briley the words were unintelligible.

'Who the hell was that?' he asked.

'It sounded like our egg-man again.'

'Meen?' asked the *ma'mur*.

'Saleh.'

'Ah, Saleh.'

'What did he throw?' asked Purkiss. In the cabin light they examined the disc. It seemed to be of scuffed gold, the edge bevelled over and threaded. Purkiss experienced that strange feeling of knowing instantly what it was but having to go through the ritual of open wonderment and deciphering the faintly-engraved lettering on one side.

'8261143 Cpl Lesley Briley,' he read. There was a silence. Briley's hand closed over the disc like a kidnapper stifling a victim's scream. 'That's the original back off your watch, Les,' Purkiss said. 'The one that was stolen in Rangoon,' he added unnecessarily. 'How the hell did that old rogue get hold of it?' Still Briley said nothing but gazed down at the back of his own fist. 'None of my business, mate,' added Purkiss. 'None of my business, of course.'

'What was he saying?' Briley broke his silence, raising his eyes to the uncomprehending face of the *ma'mur*. The Egyptian shut his eyes for long seconds as if ransacking his memory for the exact, rare equivalent in this foreign tongue.

'Very bad,' he said at last.

When the *ma'mur* had gone Briley left too, obviously upset, refusing all his friend's offers of a bunk for the night. It was unusually dark, moonless and mostly overcast since the north wind, an autumnal herald of winter, was blowing ragged banks of cloud down from the Mediterranean. By the intermittent starlight Purkiss watched from the rail as the black blob of

Les Briley's dinghy moved away across the Canal and merged with the blacker bulk of the deserted *Platypus*. Then, shaking his head, Purkiss went to his cabin and turned in.

When he reached his own ship Briley found himself drunker than he had thought, the brief moment of wrenching sobriety which Saleh had brought swamped once more by the Suntory. He blundered up the gangway and reeled against the bulkheads and stanchions, finally reaching his cabin. From somewhere in the depths of the ship the hum of a single small generator reminded him of how painful the glare of the light would be, so he undressed in the dark and fell into his bunk. Before sleep dragged him completely under he thought he heard a flapping and rustling from the passageway outside his cabin. But it was not the soft flutter and whir of tiny wings which would set off all his phobic alarms and send him stalking round the hot airless room with a towel held at arm's length, goose-flesh pimpling his thighs. Unconcerned, Captain Briley turned over and fell into a deep sleep.

He awoke with a headache next day and spent the morning nursing it in dark glasses and with all the curtains tightly drawn against the white glare and rising heat outside. It was not until lunchtime that he could bear enough light to shave by, and in the dim orange glow above the mirror saw that a sizeable chunk of hair was missing from the right side of his head.

That evening Purkiss came over, bringing his backgammon set.

'Time for a spot of *towla*,' he said, opening the box and pushing heaps of counters at Briley. 'Your turn to be red, mate.'

They played desultorily, neither referring to the previous night, Purkiss now and then glancing up to read his friend's face. If he noticed the conspicuously missing hair he said nothing. Halfway through the third game both men looked up simultaneously. Standing in the open doorway was Saleh, watching and silent. Briley sprang to his feet.

'Get the hell off my ship, damn you,' he shouted. The peasant made no move. 'I'll throw you off myself, then.' Briley advanced.

From somewhere outside the cabin came the sound of a child's scream of terror, twice repeated, ending in a piteous cry of *'Ya abui! Ya abui!'* All three stood motionless for a moment and then Briley ran for the door, pushing Saleh roughly aside. Purkiss could hear him pounding up the passage, yelling 'Get them off my bloody ship!' He and Saleh followed and found him standing uncertainly on the hatch cover of number three hold, panting and wild. 'Stinking Gyppos,' he said. 'There's kids on this ship somewhere.'

'Binti,' said Saleh softly. His eyes were on Briley.

'What's he on about?' Purkiss asked.

'Says it's his daughter,' muttered the Englishman. 'I expect his whole pox-ridden family's living in a chain locker somewhere. Well, I'll find them.'

But Saleh was pointing to the brightly-lit deck. In the middle, perhaps twenty feet from the nearest rail, was a single pair of clear wet footprints. No others led to or from them. They were very small and very freshly made; as Purkiss watched a runnel of water gathered at one heel and ran towards a nearby rust-pock.

'Binti,' repeated Saleh. Still staring fixedly at Briley he slowly touched a forefinger to the lower lid of his own right eye in a gesture which, despite himself, Purkiss found strangely sinister. Then he turned away and walked off down the companionway.

'Jesus Christ,' said Briley. 'He's off his head, Ken. Did you see that? He put the evil eye on me. What the hell's going on?'

Although moonless it was a night of full starlight and in the cold and ancient glow they watched as Saleh's boat reached the bank and he climbed ashore. It seemed as though he made some indistinct gestures before vanishing over the dunes. A red signal light arched into the sky followed by a distant pop! and the faint sound of shouting and singing.

'Business as usual,' said Purkiss. 'They've lost the war so they're having a party.'

'Malesh,' said Briley with bitter mimicry. 'They've been losing wars since they lost their pharaohs. What's one more?'

They returned to their unfinished game but neither could make a move and they abandoned it. A restlessness overcame them both. Purkiss watched Briley's uneasy gestures as he fidgeted and paced about the cabin, now and then glancing distractedly towards the door. Above the backgammon board a small white moth made an entranced whirligig in the light. Savagely Briley picked up a cloth and slashed the air. The moth vanished; scattered counters rolled across the deck.

'Christ, this bloody place gets to you,' he said. 'Why haven't those incompetent goons arranged our travel permits yet? I've got to get out of here.'

'Yeah, Les,' said the Australian soothingly. 'Sure. So have I. It's enough to give you the screaming habdabs. That officer who came last week said another ten days and then the papers would be through.'

'So?' demanded Briley. 'I can't bloody wait ten days, and that's a fact. I've got to get out of here, Ken. Like tomorrow. I've had this place.' The note Purkiss could not help hearing as fear was replaced by a kind of belligerent resignation. 'Of course he said ten days. He'll go on saying that for months yet. He's got no more idea of what's happening in some office in Cairo than we have. Or rather, he has: bugger all. Just a lot of underpaid illiterates drinking tea and saying "Tomorrow, *bukra*, *bukra*." It's always the bloody *bukra* here, and *bukra* never comes.'

It was still quite early when Purkiss left for the *Woollongong*. Before going he had discreetly tried to sound his friend for a possible explanation of Saleh's behaviour but Briley was locked into an impassioned denunciation of Egypt and the Egyptians which effectively displaced any rational discourse. When he reached the head of the *Woollongong*'s gangway Purkiss found the *ma'mur* waiting for him together with a uniformed man whom he recognized as the officer who had claimed their visas would be through in ten days. Both seemed in high spirits.

'Fi hafla,' said the *ma'mur*, pointing towards the nearest bank of the Canal. *'Kwayyis xalis.'*

'There's a party,' explained the officer. 'A wedding in the village, that's all. The *fellahin* are having a wingding.' Purkiss wondered where he had learned his English. 'We are sorry to come aboard like this without your permission, sir.'

'Don't tell me,' said Purkiss. 'Your Government has annexed all foreign vessels in the Canal.'

'No sir. We are on Australian territory still.' The officer grinned, indicating the deck plates. 'But I have brought good news. Your travel permits to go through the military zone, they will be ready tomorrow.'

'Fine,' said Purkiss. 'No reflection on you, mate, but I'll believe them when I see them. Okay?' He wondered why they had come to tell him this in the middle of a party. From their air of expectant camaraderie it was probable that the *ma'mur* had confided in the officer about the Suntory. Suddenly feeling unaccommodating, Purkiss asked: 'What's up with that bloody man Saleh?'

'Who is Saleh?' asked the officer puzzled. He turned to the *ma'mur* and spoke rapidly in Arabic. 'Ah the *fellah* who brings you eggs, the one who is always asking when the English captain is leaving. He is giving you trouble?'

Purkiss tried to tell him what had happened, but was aware of his failure to make the old peasant sound anything but slightly touched – certainly not menacing. 'He brought his daughter aboard Captain Briley's ship tonight without so much as by-your-leave,' he ended lamely.

The officer conferred some more. This time the *ma'mur* became emphatic and their conversation took several minutes. When it finished the officer said:

'We do not know who he brought on the English ship tonight but it was not his daughter.'

'He said it was.'

'No. There is a story,' the officer went on, his voice serious. 'There is a story in this village which this man knows well—' he indicated the *ma'mur*. 'Years ago, perhaps twenty years when the British were here, there was an English soldier who raped a young girl from the village. Her father was dishonoured and so he had to kill her when he found out.'

'But ...' began Purkiss incredulously. The officer held up a hand.

'I know. But these are primitive people here and their customs are horrible. He drowned her in the Canal right here and then he made a sacred promise to have revenge on the soldier who did it. For these people it is best if the revenge is exactly in the same place as the original crime. But of course by then the soldier had gone. But the *fellahin*, you know, they are very – what is the word? – supernatural, I think. They believe very much in witchcraft. So this man Saleh makes a spirit, an *'afrit*, so the soldier will come back to the village and he will kill him.'

'And Saleh believes that Les *Briley* is the soldier?'

'I know,' said the officer, shaking his head. 'It is mad. But he believes, yes.'

'But Les has never been here before. He told me; the nearest he's ever been to Egypt was Benghazi in Libya.'

'But Saleh believes,' the officer repeated. 'I am worried. It is the trouble with these people' – his gesture included the unseen village behind the dunes and the *ma'mur* at his side – 'they have long memories and nothing to do but think about them.'

'You mean they have endless bloody feuds and grudges,' Purkiss said. 'He's obviously got Les confused with somone else.' All the same, he wished he could rid himself of the mental image of the gold watch-back rolling towards his friend's feet. 'Do you think he's in any danger?' he asked.

'From *'afrit*, spirits, ghosts?' asked the officer seriously. 'Does he believe?'

'Of course not.'

'Then perhaps not,' the officer shrugged. 'But this old man Saleh is probably mad so in the morning he will be locked up. It is better.'

'And the girl on board the ship just now?'

'A trick, obviously.'

'Yeah. Still, I reckon it would be better if he came over and spent the night here.' Purkiss regretted now having left Briley and was about to suggest to the *ma'mur* that for a small glass of Suntory he might like to row over and fetch the English captain when he saw there was something wrong with him. The Egyptian was staring straight ahead at the bulkhead, quivering slightly like a cat that has seen the invisible. At the same time he was aware that the temperature in the cabin had dropped considerably. He shivered inside his thin nylon shirt.

'It's getting cold,' he began, and stopped. From across the water outside there came again the scream of a child followed by the pleading cry of '*Ya abui! Ya abui!*' The officer shot him a glance and strode quickly out on deck. A couple of hundred yards away lay the *Platypus*, one or two yellow lights showing but otherwise a dark hulk. But it was not the ship which took the men's immediate attention. Standing a few feet away at the bow rail stood a motionless robed figure. By the light spilling from the cabin behind them Purkiss could see that in one upraised hand he held a painted object.

'Saleh,' he said. The man gave no sign of having heard. Only his lips moved silently as the starlight cast a sheen of metal over his closed eyelids. Again from the *Platypus* came the terrified wailing scream. 'For Christ's sake,' said Purkiss, 'can't you do something?'

But the young officer seemed reluctant to interfere. He hung back and raised his hands in a gesture of apology.

'You're afraid too,' said Purkiss in disgust. 'For all your military academy sophistication you're just as superstitious as he is.' He waved a hand angrily towards the paralysed *ma'mur*. 'Come on, damn you,' he shouted. 'Tell him to stop this mumbo-jumbo – and let's get to the bottom of this. You and I are going over right now and we're going to find that kid and beat hell out it. The whole thing's just a bloody silly trick.'

At that Saleh swung slowly round, his eyes still closed. He was holding a small box, Purkiss now saw, with little designs and Arabic letters on each of its six sides. His unseeing gaze fixed straight ahead, the old man opened the box and dipped into it. His fingers came out holding a moth by the wings, the plump sac of its abdomen twisting as its legs scrabbled the air for a foothold. Then he put the box on the ground and with the other hand produced from it what looked like a tuft of hair.

'*Allah,*' said the officer under his breath with that devotional fervour which Purkiss had often heard, the two syllables drawn out and separated and ending with a sigh of awe, '*Al-lah.*'

Saleh now began speaking aloud, sometimes seeming to address either the moth or the hair he held, at other times encompassing the starlit wasteland of dunes and scrub which was Sinai.

'What's he saying?' asked Purkiss.

'He says the night has come.' The officer spoke in a whisper, as if frightened of interrupting a devotional ceremony.

'Very observant of him.'

'No, he is making a play with words. I understand. Yes, the night is *leila* and his daughter's name was Leila too ... He says revenge comes always from inside but the power it needs comes from outside.'

'Claptrap.'

'Ssh, sir. It is true. It is the guilty man who punishes himself. It is ...' he struggled for the word.

'Conscience?'

'Yes ... He says it is done by fear itself, what a man is most afraid of. This old man is very strong. He controls the spirit of *xof*, of great fear.'

Saleh stopped talking and held the moth before his face. Very slowly he flattened his fingertips together around the insect's thorax. The abdomen stuck stiffly out, tumescent with the pressure, until with a sudden gush it burst. Yellowish drops sprayed the deck.

On board the nearby *Platypus* Les Briley was standing in a listening attitude outside the wireless room. He had at last run the stowaway to earth. The child's screaming had given way to an odd rustling inside like newspaper pages being rearranged. Briley was shivering with expectancy. The ship had grown very cold, he had noticed, while he was tracking down this elusive young intruder; but it was not the cold which made him tremble as he finally swung the door open and stepped over the high threshold.

'Right, little girl,' he said, '*ya bint*.' For a blank instant he could only gaze at the nightmare inside. The gigantic moth, fully four feet long, was crouched on the table among the radio gear, its heavy fur-covered body dimpling like an underinflated Zeppelin where it overlaid a Morse key. Black compound eyes the size of cricket balls refracted the light from the corridor and rubies sparkled in their depths. The antennae-like papyrus rushed towards him, their filaments trembling in the draught. The last impression Briley took with him as he leaped backwards, slamming the door between himself and the horror, was of a long uncoiled proboscis as straight as a hypodermic needle.

His yells bounced back from the metal walls as he raced for the deck, the hair on his body stiffened into a prickling layer. Once outside he made a dash for the head of the gangway and had already started down when he was brought up short by the sight of his dinghy, oars neatly folded inboard, adrift some ten yards from the ship and moving further away by the second. Blindly he turned and made for the bridge, perhaps out of a desire for the reassuring normality of instruments and command. He reached it panting, slamming the door and dogging it. After a moment's indecision he ran across to the other side and out on to the tiny metal platform welded to the outside of the bridge. He swung the signalling lamp round on its bracket and aimed it at the *Woollongong*, clattering out a message with frenzied jabs of the lever.

Unseen behind him a heavy shape glided out of the night and landed on the edge of the coaming at his elbow. The sudden breeze of cold air made Briley turn, his hand frozen on the lever, locking open the venetian blinds which masked the lens of the lamp. A shaft of white light joined the two ships.

A foetid stench swept over him of decaying cabbages like that which had once filled the shoe-boxes of caterpillars in his childhood. The strength melted out of him, his eyes fixed on its wet and working mouth parts. His hand fell limply to his side. The beam of light went out. The moth reared itself slightly on its hinder legs, proboscis gleaming dully like a length of cane. Then its wings unfurled with a sound of shaken mackintosh, arching up over Briley's head and blotting out the starlight. The spike lunged downwards.

The pain was as sharply engrossing as an orgasm, and as impossible to locate. His hands instinctively outflung to push the insect away encountered only hard chitinous surfaces or cold fur. His fixed vision became clouded over, only the pain remained undimmed. He would have said it was in his chest had he still been able to recall the word but suddenly a whole lifetime's thoughts and vocabulary drained away leaving him with nothing to make but a last inarticulate scream.

It was five minutes before Purkiss and the Egyptian officer reached him, Purkiss sweating with the effort of desperate rowing. The terrible cry of animal pain and loss which had risen from the *Platypus* still echoed in his ears. He pushed the Egyptian to one side and gently pulled the fallen Briley inside the bridge. Staring down at his friend he marvelled at the combination of tortured face and unmarked body. The classic signs, he supposed, of a heart attack.